BRUTAL POSSESSION

He smiled thinly. It was a smile that barely moved his firm lips and never reached his eyes. "So you would fight with me?" he asked, his fingers curling around her wrist.

"You know damn well what's wrong," she said. "It's you. And the way you've been staring at me."

"And should I not do so? Is it not enough that you do not wish me to touch you, now I must not look as well?"

As if he'd been pushed too far, he reached for her, dragging her close against him, his head moving downward, his lips covering hers in a kiss of brutal possession. His hands molded her against the hard length of his body.

At first, she was too shocked to make any response. Then, something seemed to explode between them. His lips were hungry, taking, then offering, persuading. She wanted to reject him, to pull away, but her body refused to respond to her will. Her lips seemed to melt against the seductive warmth of his.

With a cry of triumph, he lifted her into his arms and carried her to the sleeping mat.

"You're mine," he said. "You belong to me."

Apache Sunset

BETTY BROOKS

ZEBRA BOOKS
KENSINGTON PUBLISHING CORP.

ZEBRA BOOKS

are published by

Kensington Publishing Corp.
475 Park Avenue South
New York, NY 10016

First printing: June, 1988

Printed in the United States of America

Dedicated to Nancy

God made us sisters,
Hearts made us friends.

Chapter One

The forest was silent and still in the thickening twilight. The golden light of the evening bled into plum overhead and filtered softly through the pine trees, dappling across the face of the girl who lay so quietly on the snow-covered ground.

The flutter of her long dark lashes against her pale cheeks was at first barely more than a quiver. Then slowly they lifted, revealing large gray eyes. Frowning, she studied the pine trees that rose majestically over her, partially obscuring the palette of the evening sky. Her frown deepened. Somehow, she couldn't remember why, but for some reason she was lying, awkwardly, in the snow.

And she was cold.

She tried to move and vertigo hit her like a whirligig. She drew in a sharp breath, swallowed deeply, and waited for it to pass. When it did, she opened her eyes again and studied the dense trees and shrubbery surrounding her.

Something pushed at her mind. There was something she should remember. Her brow furrowed as she shifted her body, and a sharp pain stabbed through her. She closed her eyes against it.

Finally, it passed. And she became aware of the silence. Everything was still. Not even a stir of wind rustled the trees. Nothing. Not a sound.

She tried to concentrate on the reason she was there. A name teased at her memory for a moment, then made itself known.

Jesse.

The name caused pleasant feelings to flow through her body. And with them, the certainty that she would not be left alone. Jesse had said he would always be there for her. He would come. But he must hurry.

It was so cold.

Again she moved, and, as before, pain streaked through her. Beads of sweat broke out on her face and a red haze danced before her eyes.

With her last bit of awareness, she silently reassured herself. Soon Jesse would come for her. . . .

A drift of pine needles whispered down through the dusty shafts of twilight, feathering across her unconscious face.

The sun hung low over the horizon, splashing the tops of the pines with gold as Swift Arrow urged the

8

black stallion up the narrow path. The day was almost gone, and he needed to find shelter. Already the air had grown colder, making his breath almost visible. He had no wish to stay the night out in the open.

The stallion whinnied, and Swift Arrow tensed, narrowing his ebony eyes as he searched the verdant green forest of Ponderosa pines and spruce.

He had seen no sign of the horse soldiers for two days, but he knew there was a possibility he might run into them. He had to remain alert, prepared for ambush from his enemies. His gaze was wary as he continued to search the dense forest around him.

He found nothing that shouldn't have been there. His gaze fell on a bluejay perched on a spruce limb. Cocking its head at the warrior, the bird scolded shrilly, then flew to another branch. A squirrel darted beneath a piñon pine, scooped up a piñon nut, and shoved it into its mouth.

Swift Arrow smoothed his hand over the stallion's neck, murmuring softly. The animal's ears were perked forward expectantly; something had disturbed him. Still Swift Arrow continued on his way . . . but carefully. He knew better than to discount the stallion's uneasiness.

The horse might have been unsettled by the scent of a bear, or a panther. And if it was the horse soldiers that had disturbed him, they couldn't be very near. Had they been, the jay would have cried a warning, and the squirrel would have hidden.

Swift Arrow had been careful to hide his tracks, and it wasn't the usual practice of the cavalry to come this high into the mountains searching for Indians. They had learned the Apaches had a distinct advantage over them in the mountains. Every rock, every stream was known to the Indians. In the past the cavalry had found it best to fight the Apaches in the desert, to surround them and overpower them with sheer numbers.

But the white eyes did not always use wisdom in their fight to drive the Apaches from their homeland. It was for that reason that Swift Arrow knew he must practice caution.

Suddenly, without warning, the stallion stopped. Instantly alert, the warrior scoured the forest again with his gaze, looking for something, anything out of the ordinary.

There was only silence.

The Apache brave leaned over and ran a soothing hand over the horse's long neck. But the animal tossed his head and blew through his nose.

"What's the matter?" Swift Arrow asked. "Why do you hesitate? I see nothing to cause alarm." He urged the horse up the narrow trail.

Then, at the bottom of a steep incline, he saw what appeared to be a bundle of rags. He dismounted cautiously, tying the stallion to a pine tree.

Warily watching for a trap, Swift Arrow slid down the embankment, coming to a stop at the bottom of the hill near the huddle of fabric.

The hood of a girl's cloak had fallen back, allowing her long, pale hair to fan out around her in the snow.

His dark gaze focused on the blood matting her hair, then moved lower to the darkened bruise that covered the right half of her forehead. It followed the curve of her temple, going all the way down her cheekbone to her jawbone. She appeared to have fallen from the trail above, probably thrown from her mount.

She looked more dead than alive.

Dropping to his knees beside her, Swift Arrow felt for the pulse behind her ear. He let out a sigh of relief when he felt the beat that indicated she still lived. Although the beat was faint, he found it steady.

He ran his hand over her body, checking for broken bones. When he was certain there was no damage done to her limbs, he traced his finger across the curve of her jaw.

She was the most beautiful girl he had ever seen. How could such beauty have come to be in this state? And what reason could she have for coming into these mountains alone?

Softly, he pushed back a silky strand of her hair, which closely resembled the ore the white men were so greedy to possess. The action revealed a gaping wound, glistening with blood above her temple.

His ebony eyes narrowed. The cut looked deep. He drew back as her eyelids fluttered and lifted to reveal dazed eyes.

When she saw him, the corners of her mouth lifted into a smile. His dark gaze sharpened questioningly on her face. He saw no reason for her to smile; surely she must be in pain.

But perhaps she was numbed to it. Or maybe the pain had chased her mind from her body.

"Jesse," she said, her voice barely above a whisper.

She seemed to exert a great effort, lifting her hand to touch his cheek gently. "Is it really you?"

Swift Arrow couldn't understand her, for she spoke in the language of the white eyes. But something about her tugged at his heartstrings.

Quickly damping down the feeling, he studied the girl's delicate features, remaining immobile as her fingers traced the line of his jaw, moving softly down the side of his face before coming to rest against his lips.

Although his face was impassive, his chest constricted tightly, inexplicably, at her caress. But it was only natural, he told himself. He couldn't help sympathizing with a wounded creature, as he would have any creature of the forest.

This woman was a paleface. One of the enemy. Still, he could not find it in his heart to leave her to her fate. If he did, she would surely die. And although that should not have concerned him, somehow, it did.

As it would have were she a wounded deer.

Or a buffalo.

His eyes glinted with a wry humor. Were she a deer or a buffalo, he wouldn't leave her, but he wouldn't take her away alive, either. He would make use of her.

As she was, she'd be little more than a burden to him. Still, he began to consider how to prepare her for the journey that lay ahead. Her skin was deathly cold, and Swift Arrow knew he must get her to a warm place as soon as possible.

She seemed totally unaware of her condition. She

continued to smile dreamily up at him. Suddenly, before Swift Arrow could move, before he could even lift her, the girl circled his neck with one arm and pulled his head closer to her.

He stiffened, but he didn't pull away. Curiously, he allowed her to draw him closer still, until his mouth hovered just above hers.

When their lips met he felt as if lightning streaked through his body. Never had he experienced anything quite like it. Almost reflexively, he wrapped his arms around her, pressing her softness closer against him.

She moaned, and he loosened his grip at once, without breaking their kiss. She was such a fragile thing, so easy to hurt.

Her lips were soft and persuasive as they moved against his, and Swift Arrow's heart beat with the rhythm of ten thousand drums. He had never imagined the white man's way of pressing the lips together could be so thunderously exciting.

As though sensing the tight rein he held on his body, the girl pulled back slightly. Her gray eyes, staring into his, wore a puzzled look.

"Is something the matter, Jesse?" she whispered in a hoarse voice.

Swift Arrow studied the white girl's pale features. He couldn't understand her words, yet he felt something was wrong. The girl was gravely injured; she should be in pain. Yet she lay calmly in the snow, touching her lips to his.

She must be crazed. That had to be the answer. Pain had driven her mind from her body.

The disappointment that streaked through him glittered in his eyes. There could be no other answer. The girl should be in pain. She should *fear* him. And yet, she lay placidly in his arms.

Regret flickered through him with the realization that he must inflict more pain on her. He had no choice; the gash on her head would have to be sewn up.

Her gaze locked with his as he eased her back in the snow, then followed him when he rose. He made his way up the incline to his stallion and removed a water canteen and a buckskin bag, called a parfleche, that contained, among other things, a needle threaded with the sinew from a rabbit.

He returned and knelt beside her. Allowing nothing to show in his expression, he gently cleansed the wound on her forehead, uttering soothing words as he did. It wasn't a clean cut. He had to remove the grit imbedded in the wound. He closed his ears to the sharp cry she gave before she lay still.

Swift Arrow darted a quick look at her pale face. Her lashes lay heavily against her cheeks. He knew she was unconscious and felt it was better that way.

He bent to his work and finished removing the particles from the wound. After sewing up the cut, he applied a healing poultice of ground moss. Then, tearing strips from a soft rag, he wound it around her head to keep the poultice in place.

When Swift Arrow had done all that was possible, he gathered her up, cradling her weight easily in his arms.

Slowly, he made his way back up the incline,

avoiding the fallen logs and debris, carrying the girl's limp body against his strong chest.

The cold wind made a hushing sound through the thick boughs of Ponderosa pines arching over her and sent icy fingers trailing across her face. She shuddered. Where was she? What had happened? If only she could open her eyes.

But she couldn't. They felt incredibly heavy, almost as if her lids were stuck together.

She groaned, and a voice in the distance spoke with words she didn't understand yet having a familiar ring to them. At that moment, her head felt as if a heavy iron band clamped down on it, squeezing it in a vice. She whimpered, and tightened her eyes against the agony pounding through her skull.

A gentle hand touched her face, pushing a lock of hair away, and she gave a relieved sigh.

Jesse would take care of her.

She allowed her mind to rise above her body, to drift up with the pines and float away with the wind.

When she woke again, it was to a gentle swaying. Cautiously, she opened her eyes, peering through narrowed lids. She seemed to be riding on some kind of litter slung between two poles. She tried to move and couldn't. She felt—*she felt paralyzed.*

Fear streaked through her in the moment before she realized she was bound to the litter. She opened her eyes wider . . . turned her head, and a white-hot fire seared through her skull.

15

Squeezing her eyes tight against the pain, she fought the nausea that threatened to overcome her. The litter struck a rock and she flinched, her agony growing.

The black fuzzy haze gathered around her again, and she willed it to come closer, welcoming the darkness that enveloped her, a darkness that was mercifully empty of pain.

Chapter Two

Darkness had fallen and Swift Arrow had nothing to guide him, except the pale light of the moon and the stars that embroidered the sky above. The cold hung around him like a shroud, ruffled now and again by the shivery night wind rustling through the branches of the pine trees. Although he knew the cave existed, he was almost on it before he saw it. He felt a great measure of relief, for he knew the girl must be suffering from the cold.

He carried her into the cave and built a fire nearby. Then he unloaded his supplies and released his horse. The stallion would not stray far and must be allowed to search for grass upon which to graze.

Entering the cavern again, he went to the girl and removed her cape. As he had suspected, her garments were wet clear through. After unfastening the tiny buttons on her blouse, his fingers fumbled at the cords that laced the fragile pink material barely covering her breasts. Lifting her slightly, he stripped both garments from her body before lowering her again. Then he loosened the divided skirt she wore and pulled it down her hips, exposing still another garment. Like the first, this undergarment was made from a silky, fragile material and was adorned with ruffles and lace.

His pulse quickened as he stripped the remaining garments from her body. He tightened his lips and his expression became almost wry. He wished the white woman didn't appear so beautiful to his eyes. It would be much easier to remain immune to her charms if she were a plain woman.

And he must remain immune.

He had learned his lesson a long time ago, a lesson that he wouldn't soon forget. He had loved a woman, and he had lost her to another man. The pain of that love had gone deep. He had no wish to feel such a pain again, and had vowed to keep his heart hidden away from such future dangers. So far, he had managed to keep that vow.

He forced his eyes away from the girl's well-rounded body. Picking up a blanket, he wrapped it around her and laid her gently back onto the pallet of furs. Then he covered her with a soft doeskin hide that would help to seal in her body warmth.

She woke slowly. A dry, musty smell teased at her nostrils. She was in some kind of shelter. Probably a

18

cave. Jesse must have brought her here.

Jesse?

She frowned. Something was wrong. Jesse was dead. Wasn't he? Hadn't her father's men killed him? Or had it been a dream . . . a nightmare?

Yes! It must have been. He couldn't be dead. Jesse had come to her before, had found her where her horse had thrown her, had kissed her. The other, the part where Jesse had died, that must have been the dream.

Jesse was alive, outside the cave somewhere. All she had to do was wait . . . be patient. And he would come back. In another moment. . . .

Again she slept, and this time her sleep was much easier.

When she woke, it was to the feeling of being watched.

Moving cautiously, wary of the pain that could stab through her head at the least movement, she turned her head . . . and saw him.

It was not Jesse.

Although he was sitting on his haunches beside the fire, she could see he was tall, probably at least six feet. The flickering light shone on his chiseled features, giving him a slightly sinister appearance.

His hair was shoulder-length, black as a raven's wing, as Jesse's had been. But, unlike Jesse's, the man's hair was held back by a beaded headband around his forehead. He wore a beaded buckskin shirt, belted in at the waist. His fringed leather pants were tucked into knee-high moccasins. There was a knife at his waist and a small axe hung from a leather thong at the back of his belt.

Her gaze moved upward, to the firm chin, the wide mouth, the straight nose, and she gasped. His expression was tense, his eyes fixed on her.

She swallowed thickly and winced. Her throat hurt, and she felt hot. But she could see how she'd mistaken him for Jesse, especially in her fevered state.

But that was all it had been. A mistake. Jesse was dead. Dead, and nothing would bring him back. The man who had rescued her was an Indian. And though she recognized him for what he was, she felt no fear. She was glad she wasn't alone.

As she watched, the warrior stood, moving out of her line of vision.

"Please," she croaked, afraid he was leaving her, "stay."

But he didn't go.

He knelt beside the fire, picked up a wooden bowl and came to her. Lifting her head, he held the bowl of steaming liquid to her lips. She drank obediently, allowing the warm broth to trickle down her throat. When she could take no more, she turned her head away.

He murmured something, pushing the bowl back to her mouth. Although his words sounded familiar, he wasn't speaking English. Yet she felt she should know it. Perhaps if her mind weren't so fuzzy, if she could just think, remember. . . .

Then it came to her, as though a door to the past had suddenly opened.

When she was six years old, her father had been

20

assigned to an Indian reservation. Unknown to her father, she had become friends with a young girl her age. Since Laughing Water spoke no English, Katherine had learned her language.

The warrior was speaking that language now.

It was the language of the Apache Indians.

"Who are you?" she whispered in his language.

Though he appeared to be startled to hear her words, he recovered quickly, saying, "My name is Swift Arrow."

"You . . . you're Apache, aren't you?" Her words trailed off as her eyelids became strangely heavy. Somehow she seemed to be falling asleep again. He must have given her something in the broth.

His voice came as if from a long distance. "I am Apache," he said gruffly. "I am from the Chiricahua tribe. But you must sleep. When you wake, we will speak together."

Knowing he was right, she allowed her mind to drift away into sleep.

The darkness was thick when she woke, the cavern filled with silence. Although she hurt all over, the worst pain seemed to be coming from the wound on her head. She knew she was lucky not to have any broken bones. Without a doctor's care, such an injury could lead to crooked limbs.

That thought brought a wry smile to her lips. Her father wouldn't be pleased if she wound up with a crooked arm or leg. He could not abide imperfection in anything. Especially his daughter.

Her amusement died as the quiet intruded. Some-

21

how, the lack of sound frightened her. Surely the Apache hadn't left her. Her gaze rested on the creamy white walls of the cave, then slid farther, to the small fire that glowed brightly a few feet away.

The Indian was nowhere in sight.

She panicked.

"Swift Arrow?" she croaked.

"I am here." He rose from the shadows.

"I thought you had gone," she whispered, closing her eyes and willing her panic down.

"You did not wish it?" he asked curiously.

"No." She licked dry, parched lips. "I don't want to be left alone." Her silver eyes held a plea. "Could I have some water?"

He picked up a canteen, came to her, and knelt, lifting her head to hold the vessel to her lips. The cool water had a metallic tang, yet it seemed nothing had ever tasted as sweet.

When she had had enough, Swift Arrow laid the canteen aside and resettled her head on the pallet.

"What are you called?" he asked.

"Katherine."

"From where do you come?"

"Fort Bayard." Her voice was weakening, but she went on. "It's near Silver City."

She shifted her position, then grimaced, closing her eyes against the pain. Then she added, "My father, Major John Carpenter, is commander of Fort Bayard."

A dark expression crossed the warrior's face, and his lips thinned slightly. "Why does your father allow you to ride alone? Does he not know of the dangers that await a lone woman?"

Despite her pain, a small smile played at the corners of her mouth. "I'm afraid I didn't have his permission to go riding."

"You disobeyed him?"

"No. I simply didn't tell him I was going."

Swift Arrow's eyes glinted, but he said nothing.

"My horse," she said. "Were you able to catch her?"

"I saw no horse."

"She must have run away after she threw me. She's usually such a gentle mare. I guess I was lucky you found me."

"You must not let what didn't happen concern you," he said gruffly. "You must think only of getting well." Reaching out a long arm, he picked up a bowl that he had left to warm beside the fire.

"Drink," he commanded, holding it out to her.

"What is it?" She frowned suspiciously at the contents. She remembered what had happened when she had drunk the broth before. "Will it put me to sleep?"

"It is dogwood bark tea. And sleep will be good for you."

She knew he was right. And for some reason she trusted this Apache warrior. Perhaps because he seemed so much like Jesse. Her eyes held his as she drank from the bowl. Then she allowed herself to relax and let the brew lull her to sleep again.

Chapter Three

Katherine's eyelids flickered, then flew open. Her wide gray eyes stared up at the cream-colored limestone ceiling. Something, some sound, had caused her to wake.

The hard bed upon which she lay made her painfully conscious of her scrapes and bruises. And how she came to be in such a state. As always, her pain could be laid at her father's door.

She had slipped from the fort after they'd argued angrily over Jesse's death. And she had had but one thought in her mind; she must put as much distance as possible between herself and the man responsible for Jesse's death. In her distracted state she had exercised no caution and had been thrown from the mare.

She realized she had been very foolish. She could have frozen to death if the Indian had not found her. In her distraught condition, she had forgotten there was such an extreme difference in temperature between the desert land and the mountainous country. Although it was near the end of March and the desert had seen the last of its cold season, the higher elevations were still suffering from winter's chill grip.

Suddenly she became aware of the silence. She turned her head, searching for the Indian.

He was nowhere to be seen.

The fire had been banked, and it glittered with hot coals, giving off only a small amount of heat. Beside it, left drying on a makeshift rack, was every stitch of clothing she had worn.

Katherine felt only mild surprise to learn she was naked beneath the covers. Her clothing was bound to have been soaked. The only sensible thing would have been to remove it. She fingered the soft doeskin that had been spread over the blanket covering her, knowing it must be responsible for keeping her warm.

Against one wall leaned a rifle and the leather bags filled with supplies that had been tossed in a pile. Although she found no sign of Swift Arrow, she felt certain he would return. The warrior would not have left without his weapon and supplies.

She clutched the blanket tighter around her shoulders, and pushed herself into a sitting position. Her gaze found the entrance to the cavern. Although she was in no state to appreciate it, she saw beyond the cavern a winter wonderland. Heavy snow covered the ground and trees. The sun shone down with a blinding intensity, but it gave no warmth to the frigid land.

Her mouth felt dry and fuzzy, and her thirst was almost unbearable. She licked her chapped lips. She must have some water. Her eyes moved around the cavern, falling on the canteen several feet away.

Gathering one of the blankets tightly around her, she rose from the pallet. She felt the cold at the same moment vertigo struck her.

Katherine swayed dizzily as she moved toward the canteen. Her knees felt like mush, and she was hindered by the trailing blanket, but she was determined to reach the water container before her legs buckled beneath her.

She took another wobbling step, and then another. Then she was there, sinking down beside the canteen. She clutched it in both hands and lifted it to her mouth, unmindful of the water that dribbled down her chin.

Suddenly, a shadow darkened the entrance, jerking her head around as Swift Arrow stepped inside, a brown rabbit clenched in one hand. He tossed the rabbit down on the cavern floor and came to her.

"You should not be up."

"I was so thirsty," she said in a slightly hoarse voice. "I had to get up."

"I should have left the canteen near you," he said gruffly. "You should not have had to leave your bed. You must take care to keep warm. Let me help you."

He took her arm, then seeming to realize her weakened condition, scooped her up in his strong arms and carried her to the pallet of furs. After he had tucked the covers around her, he brought over the canteen and lifted her head.

27

"Drink."

She tilted the canteen and allowed the cold water to trickle down her throat. When she had assuaged her thirst, he took the canteen from her and laid it aside.

"The water is close at hand should you need it," he said. "I must prepare the rabbit I have killed."

"I saw it," she said, swallowing hard and averting her eyes from the dead animal.

A glint of amusement appeared in his dark eyes. "You do not like rabbit?"

She gave a weak smile. "It's not that. I'm just—I'm afraid I've never seen a dead one."

His lips twitched. "How can this be possible? Do the white eyes not eat rabbit?"

"Yes," she admitted.

"Then how is it you have never seen a dead one?"

"There's always been someone else to prepare the meals," she replied. For some reason the admission made her feel useless.

He lifted a dark brow. "Who did this?"

"Why . . . why the cooks, of course." At his perplexed look, she explained, "In my world some of us are more fortunate than others. We pay someone else to do our work."

"How do you occupy your time?"

"With needlework . . . and social gatherings . . . and afternoon teas." She could see he thought little of her explanation and she flushed. "I suppose it doesn't sound like much to you." She plucked at the blanket restlessly. "I can't really blame you. At times I found it boring myself."

Amusement glinted in his eyes. "You will have much to learn."

What did he mean? She had led a useless existence in the past, and if her father had his way about it, would continue to do so. Look at me, she chided herself. I'm seventeen years old and as helpless as a babe in the woods. If it were not for Swift Arrow's skills, I would starve to death.

Katherine knew she wasn't stupid. On the contrary, she prided herself on her intelligence. But the responsibility for her own survival had never rested on her own shoulders. Her father, a man of means, had made a career with the cavalry. When Katherine was only a young girl, her mother had died, leaving her to her father's care. As a result, she had been left to her own devices as much as possible. By the time she was seven she could ride like a cavalryman, and handle a rifle with skill, but she had never learned how to master any of the home skills considered so essential to a woman of the West.

When she was barely ten years old, her father had grown tired of her hoydenish ways and had sent her to the East, to her mother's brother and his wife, with instructions that she be trained in the ways of a young lady. Her aunt and uncle had done their best with her. She had been sent to a school where she had acquired a good education. But no one had ever taught her how to cook—or expected her to learn. Like her father, her aunt and uncle had a houseful of servants to do the work. She had returned to her father a polite, refined young lady. But she couldn't cook. She had taken it for

29

granted there would always be someone else to get the food onto the table.

Neither Katherine nor her father had counted on her being stranded in the wilderness. She wondered now what her father had thought when he found her missing.

"How long have I been here?" she asked.

"One day has passed."

Her eyes took on a worried look. "I can't stay here," she said. "I must return to the fort. My father will be searching for me."

"It is too soon," he said abruptly. "We must wait. You are not well enough to travel."

Turning away, Swift Arrow picked up two crotched sticks he had prepared and pushed them into the ground about a foot apart. Then he raked some of the hot glowing embers between them. Working quickly, he picked up the furry carcass and put it on a flat rock nearby. Although Katherine felt squeamish, she forced herself to watch. If ever the need to dress out a rabbit arose in the future, she wanted to be prepared.

Drawing his knife from his belt, Swift Arrow pinched up some of the loose back skin and shoved his blade through it. Then he inserted his fingers and tore the fragile skin apart completely around the animal.

Katherine swallowed hard as he peeled back the lower half like a glove, disjointed the tail and cut off each hind foot. She reminded herself the rabbit was necessary for their survival.

Swift Arrow repeated his actions to remove the top half of the skin, finally severing the head and two forefeet. Her stomach turned over when he pulled the animal open just below the ribs and flipped the entrails out. She looked away.

When she looked back again he was skewering the rabbit on a green hardwood stick. He thrust it momentarily into the blaze to seal in the juices. Then he lay the spit between the two uprights over the hot coals. The rabbit began to sizzle almost immediately.

"While we wait, I must see to your wound," he said.

As he unwound the bandages, she found herself studying his features. He was a handsome man. Was he married? If so, where was his wife? And why was he traveling alone? He seemed to be in no hurry to get to his destination.

He plucked away the poultice and his fingers probed the wound. She flinched at the pain.

"I did not mean to hurt you," he said gently, applying another poultice and wrapping the bandage around her head again.

"How does it look?" she asked.

"The cut is healing."

He fastened the ends of the bandage together and moved back to the fire, adding more wood.

The heat from the flames warmed the cavern, and Katherine pushed all the covers away, except for the blanket next to her skin. She lay quietly watching the flames while the rabbit sizzled and spit over the hot coals. She was indeed lucky that he had found her.

Swift Arrow took the spit from the coals and broke off a large section of the rabbit. He rose and came to her, offering it to her.

"Thank you," she murmured. She bit into the meat, savoring the flavor, and they ate in silence. When they had finished, he made some more herb tea and brought it to her.

"It won't make me sleep, will it?" she asked.

"No," he said. "It is to keep the fever from returning. Drink." He held it against her lips and she reluctantly swallowed the bitter liquid, grimacing with distaste.

Relaxed from the warm food, Katherine found herself sleepy. She closed her eyes, intending only to rest them for a moment . . . and fell asleep.

When she woke again he was still sitting beside the fire. Her head was uncomfortable but did not pain her as much as before, or perhaps she was just becoming used to the pain.

As she watched, Swift Arrow added another stick of wood to the fire. The flickering flames cast shadows across the bronzed planes of his face, making him almost satanic in appearance.

She shrugged away such a fanciful idea, for even though she had heard terrible stories about what the Apaches did to their captives, the warrior had given her no reason to fear him. And she definitely wasn't a captive. He had saved her life. Without his help, Katherine knew she would have died out in the forest.

Katherine's wound began to throb and she pressed her hand against her temple. The movement caught his attention and he turned toward her.

"Does your wound pain you?" he asked gruffly.

"A little," she replied.

He nodded. "It will be best if you try to sleep," he

said. "Would you like me to make you some more tea?"

She grimaced. "Not really," she admitted. "But perhaps you'd better. It did seem to make me sleep."

He nodded and began to prepare the tea.

A few minutes after she had drank it, she felt herself becoming drowsy again. Her lids became heavy and she let herself slip away.

She dozed on and off throughout the day, always seeming to waken to find Swift Arrow's gaze on her. When night fell he banked the fire and lay down on the other side of her. She was amazed at how quickly he seemed to fall asleep.

The two men conversed in low tones for a moment,
horseback.

Chapter Four

Swift Arrow was almost invisible as he silently
crouched on one knee behind the snow-laden bush.
Below him, in the ravine where he'd found the white
girl, two men knelt to inspect the snow-covered
ground. Slightly to his right a man sat on horseback.
He wore the uniform of the horse soldiers.

After only a moment, the two men rose to their feet
and conversed in low tones.

Swift Arrow's eyes glittered, most of his attention
focused on one of the men—he who wore moccasins
with buckskin leggings that pulled above his knees and
a breechcloth wrapped around his waist, the front
hanging down to meet the buckskin of his leggings. His
black hair flowed loosely over the wool shirt that
covered his wide shoulders. His heavy-boned features
were harsh and brutal . . . and familiar.

35

Swift Arrow knew him well. His name was Running Horse, and he was an Apache Indian. He was also a scout for the horse soldiers—a traitor to his own kind.

The two men conversed in low tones for a moment, then they climbed the hill and joined the man on horseback.

"Find anything?" the man asked. His hair was the color of sand, as was his neatly trimmed mustache.

Although he did not understand the language they spoke, Swift Arrow felt sure they were searching for the white girl. And he watched with all the concentration of the hunter he was. Much could be told from the facial expressions of a quarry.

"A few tracks the snow ain't covered yet," said the scout with dark hair covering his face. He wore buckskin that closely resembled the sun-darkened skin of his face. As Swift Arrow watched, he rose to his feet and looked up at the man on the horse. "Enough to know she was here. Nearest I can tell, 'er horse threw 'er. Moccasin tracks all around down there. Reckon the Injuns came along and found 'er."

The lieutenant bit off a curse. "Can you trail them?" he asked.

"Reckon not, lieutenant. Snow's covered the trail."

"Dammit, man. If you can read the tracks down there, you ought to be able to follow them."

The scout's face was expressionless as he pulled a plug of tobacco from a pouch hanging at his waist. He bit off a sizable chaw, then replaced the plug of tobacco.

The young lieutenant's lips tightened. He shifted impatiently in the saddle, waiting for the scout to answer him.

Using his tongue, the buckskin-clad scout worked the chaw of tobacco into his cheek. Only then did he return his attention to the young lieutenant.

"Onliest reason we could read the tracks down there's 'cause the overhanging branches sheltered the ravine from the storm. We know she was carried up the hill, but you can see for yourself they ain't no tracks up here but ours."

The lieutenant's expression darkened. "What the hell are we going to do? We've got to find her. She's out here somewhere. She could be freezing to death."

"Whatever's happening to her, it sure as hell ain't freezin'," the scout assured him.

"Just what do you mean by that?" the other man asked coldly.

"You know what them Injuns do to white women."

"That's enough of that kind of talk."

Swift Arrow's eyes narrowed as he watched the men. It was obvious they were arguing, but about what? His gaze went back to Running Horse . . . and he stiffened. Something about the tense way he held his body, the way he cocked his head, warned Swift Arrow. He flattened himself against the snow just as Running Horse turned his head. The warrior's eyes seemed to see right through the bush to where Swift Arrow lay.

Swift Arrow held his breath, waiting for the alarm to

be given. But, although the scout's gaze never wavered from the bush, he remained silent.

Why? Swift Arrow asked himself. If Running Horse knew he was here, then why didn't he tell the other men? Perhaps he didn't know. But something in the other man's stance suggested he was at least suspicious. Was he only waiting to be certain?

Positioned as he was, Swift Arrow could not leave. He could only wait and see what the other man would do. His gaze left the scout, moved to the other two men. They were still speaking together. He wished he had taken the trouble to learn the language of his enemies. Perhaps, if he got out of this alive, he would have the white girl teach him to speak her language. For now, though, he had to try to find a clue to their words. So, even though he could not understand them, he listened closely to the two men.

As he watched, he could see the play of emotions cross the lieutenant's face. He recognized the man's anger as he listened to the scout's words. Then the hesitation as the other man argued with him, until finally realization that the scout spoke the truth crossed his face and he was forced to agree with him. The lieutenant then turned his attention to the dark gray clouds hanging low in the sky. "That storm's moving in fast," he said, reining his horse around. "You might as well mount up, since we can't do any more right now. We'd better head back to the fort."

Swift Arrow's gaze was puzzled as he watched from his place of concealment. He was certain that Running

Horse knew someone was there. Was the man toying with him? Did he think to take him unawares? Whatever his reason, the other Indian didn't even look back as he mounted his horse and joined the other two men.

Swift Arrow's lips tightened. He wanted to loose his arrows on them, but he knew he had no choice except to allow them to leave. It would be too dangerous to kill them when the rest of the patrol waited at the foot of the mountain. If they realized he was there, then he would surely be a dead man. He knew there was no way he could fight off the whole patrol.

Although he had not understood their conversation, he felt almost sure they were looking for Katherine. And he was determined they would not find her.

He waited until he was certain he could not be seen, then rose and ran swiftly back the way he had come. Although the snow was heavy, it did not slow him down. He breathed evenly as he ran, each breath calculated to bring him greater endurance. As a child he had been taught to run great distances through rough country, carrying a mouthful of water all the way without spitting it out. Now he could cover seventy miles a day on foot on the most forbidding terrain and harsh circumstances.

He had learned, through necessity, that this country could be dangerous for the unwary. He had traveled through it in all kinds of weather, racing afoot as fleetly as the coyote and mountain lion. In his buckskin clothing, he could blend in with his surroundings until he was nearly invisible.

As he was now.

While he ran, he was planning his strategy. He would take the girl and leave. Now . . . while the snow was still falling and would hide their tracks. He felt almost certain the soldiers would return when the weather cleared. And he was going to make sure they found no one when they came. The girl would simply have disappeared.

A rabbit crossed his path, and he dropped to one knee and drew an arrow from his quiver in one smooth stroke. A moment later, the arrow found its mark and the rabbit dropped dead in the snow.

Picking the animal up by its long ears, he resumed his journey.

But fate determined to interfere with his plans. By the time he reached the cavern the storm's fury had increased. Swift Arrow knew without a doubt that it would be dangerous to leave.

Leaning his rifle against the cavern wall, he brushed the snow from his buckskins. His eyes fell on the girl. Her eyes were closed, and she breathed deeply in sleep, her hair tangled about her face, the hair that reminded him of the morning mist hanging low over the mountains. The memory of her pale body, exposed to his eyes as he had stripped her wet garments from her body, still lingered in his memory. Even then, in her unconscious state, he had wanted to stroke the silky skin. He had wanted to cup her full, rounded breasts in his hands, had wanted to caress her silky thighs. It had been all he could do to tear himself away from her. Even now, his breathing became ragged, his manhood rising with the wanting to make her his. He breathed in deeply, forcing his attention elsewhere.

Noticing the fire had burned down, he knelt and added more wood. Then he skinned out the rabbit he had killed. After skewering it on a green stick, he left it to cook over the hot coals.

Although he had carried his rifle along with him, he had used his bow and arrow for the kill. The sound of a shot fired would have alerted the cavalry to their whereabouts. He had not minded using the bow and arrow. For Swift Arrow did not need the white man's weapon to make a kill. He was a great warrior. His skill was surpassed by few. Although he could shoot the feather from an Indian headband at a hundred yards with a rifle, he could do the same with a bow and arrow.

Again and again, his gaze was drawn to the white girl. He had no love for the white man, but he felt a curious attraction for the wounded girl. He attributed it to the fact that he had always been alone, without a woman's influence, after his mother had been killed in a raid by the white men. His father had refused to take another wife, even to help raise his five-year-old son. And so, Swift Arrow had never known the love of brothers and sisters, and that of a mother only briefly. He lived within the tribe, but always alone, with no thought of taking a wife.

Then one day, his eyes had fallen upon Little Turtle,

41

a young woman of his tribe. He approached her father. But too late. The young maiden had already given her heart to another man.

Swift Arrow had hidden his pain well. No one knew to what extent he had been wounded. Then, again, he had found a love, a girl he had captured, a paleface with hair that flamed beneath the morning sun.

And again he'd lost. This time something deep within him died. He would never allow another woman to hurt him. From that day forward he would take what he wanted from women . . . without love.

His eyes glinted. *Yes.* The paleface girl was beautiful, but he had learned well. His heart would never be touched. But there was no reason he could not enjoy her after she recovered.

She shifted, moaning softly. His gaze was unwavering as he studied her. She was too pale. She must have warm food to build her strength, and red meat to build up her blood, to make her well.

Katherine opened her eyes slowly. Her whole body ached; she felt as though she was one large bruise.

She blinked away the mists of confusion. Her gaze traveled around the cave. Memory returned.

She had fallen. And an Apache warrior had found and brought her to safety. She turned her head, her searching gaze sweeping the cave.

"Swift Arrow?" she whispered.

Silence.

Fear raced through her veins, her heart drummed loudly in her ears. She took a deep breath, forcing herself to calm. He had gone, but he was sure to return. He had only stepped outside for a moment. She looked at the entrance expectantly. It remained empty.

Gritting her teeth against the pain, she pushed herself up on her elbows and cocked her head, listening.

"I am here." The voice came from behind her and she turned her head to see him step from the shadows farther back in the cave.

He leaned over to check her head, seeming to be satisfied on finding the bandage still wound tightly around it.

She looked anxiously at him. "How long has it been," she whispered. As his gaze locked on hers her heart fluttered with a panic she could not understand. She licked dry lips. "How long have I been here?" she asked.

"Two days have passed."

"Has there been any sight of a search party?" Even as she spoke, she knew he would not have made himself known to them. She frowned, suddenly realizing how bad her situation really was. How was she to get back to the fort? She didn't think the Indian would risk taking her.

Her lips twisted bitterly. Her father was a hard man and had made enemies of the Apache people. It was for that very reason that she had come to be in this predicament. If he hadn't hounded Jesse, even to the point of framing him for a murder, then Jesse would never have joined Billy Benson's gang of thieves.

Her father had told her they had had no choice when Jesse was killed. He told her the Benson gang had waited in ambush, and it was kill or be killed. But it was peculiar that he had thought it necessary to kill every member of the gang. Katherine suspected it was because he wanted no witnesses to what had really taken place in that outlaw hideout.

Her father wouldn't hesitate to kill the man who had rescued her from certain death. And for no other reason than that Swift Arrow was a renegade Apache Indian who refused to live on the reservation as the white man decreed.

She watched Swift Arrow moving around the fire. Using his knife, he cut off a chunk of roasted rabbit and brought it to her. She tucked the blanket securely beneath her arms and reached for the meat.

"Thank you," she said, biting off a chunk.

Although the meat tasted heavenly, she found she could not swallow. Her throat hurt. She must have caught cold from lying in the snow so long. After only a few bites she quit trying.

"Eat the rest," he said gruffly.

"I can't," she said. "My throat is too sore."

Swift Arrow didn't answer her. Instead, he brewed up some foul-tasting tea and insisted she drink all of it.

"It will help to heal your throat," he said calmly, overriding her protests.

He wouldn't leave her alone until she had finished all of the bitter liquid. Then he left her and began to gather her clothing up.

"You must dress," he said, handing it to her. Then he began to collect his belongings.

"What are you doing?" she asked, squirming into her underclothes beneath the blankets.

"Making ready to travel," he said. "We must leave this place."

"Why? Where are we going?"

He didn't answer.

"Are you taking me back to the fort?"

He seemed not to hear.

She looked outside. The fury of the storm had abated somewhat, but heavy snowflakes were still falling.

"Shouldn't we wait until it stops snowing?" She watched him closely as she slid her arms into the sleeves of her blouse.

"No. We must go now."

He fastened his bundles of supplies on the horse, then doused the fire. Steam billowed upward as the flames sizzled and died.

"We can't go out there," she protested. "We'll freeze to death."

When he didn't answer, her eyes flashed angrily. She didn't like being ignored. She forced herself to a calm that she didn't feel. She owed this man her life. She must remember that the ways of the Apache people were much different than her own.

But, dammit! He could at least answer her.

Her lips tightened as she reached for her riding skirt. She forced herself to relax, deciding to appeal to his common sense.

"Swift Arrow, surely it would make more sense to stay in this cave where we at least have some shelter from the storm. Your stallion is the only mount we have. He can't carry both of us."

"When he can no longer carry two, he will carry only one," he said gruffly. "But we will go."

He left the cavern, and when he returned, leading the stallion behind him, Katherine was struggling with her boots. Swift Arrow knelt to fasten them for her. When he finished, he pulled her to her feet. His grip tightened when she swayed unsteadily.

She shivered in his grasp, as much from his touch as from the cold draft that surrounded her.

Releasing her, Swift Arrow picked up her cape and wrapped it around her shivering form, tying it firmly beneath her chin.

After he'd folded the blankets and tied them behind the other supplies, covering them over with buckskin, he settled Katherine in the saddle and mounted behind her. Then he clasped a hard arm around her middle and pulled her back against him.

She hadn't realized how intimate riding with him was going to be. Her heart picked up its pace and she was certain he'd be able to tell, could feel her pulse with the arm pressed beneath her breast.

As they rode into the damp, whirling darkness, into

the unknown, Katherine knew she should be frightened. Normally she would have been. But wrapped in the cocoon of Swift Arrow's strength, she felt strangely safe.

And yet this man was not just a stranger. He was a savage.

Chapter Five

The snow stopped falling later that night. Then the wind began to blow, and it crept beneath their clothing and chilled their flesh.

Katherine's body shook as the cold penetrated deeply, and Swift Arrow felt certain she would have fallen off the stallion had he not held her tightly against him.

The knowledge that he must find shelter soon weighed heavily on him. He wondered if perhaps he should have waited until morning to travel. But he hadn't dared. He had needed the falling snow to cover their tracks from the enemy. Morning could have been too late.

His gaze moved from side to side. He was searching for a place to shelter and fearing he might have passed one by in the blowing snow.

He felt relief as his eyes found the shallow draw. He knew it was just deep enough to give them shelter from the rising wind.

Swift Arrow reined up the stallion and slid off. Then he lifted Katherine down and set her on her feet. He held her upright when her legs threatened to buckle beneath her. Deprived of his body warmth, Katherine felt her teeth begin to chatter and her body to shake. Pulling the hides from the horse, he allowed her to sit while he erected a crude shelter.

It seemed an eternity passed while she sat in a huddle, watching him stretch a heavy bearskin across a framework of four poles hammered into the frozen ground. He spread another bearskin inside the shelter and motioned her inside. A few minutes later he joined her, dragging their supplies in behind him.

Closing the flap he had arranged at the opening, he reached into one of the pouches and pulled out a cake of pemmican. Although she had never eaten any, she knew it was a nutritious mixture of dried meat, fat, and berries. He offered it to her, but she shook her head, refusing it.

"Eat," he commanded.

"I-I c-can't," she chattered. "I-I'm t-too c-cold. Can't we have a fire?"

"It would be dangerous."

"Why?" she asked.

Something flickered in his eyes before he spoke. "There is much wind. A fire could spread and burn our shelter."

"T-then let me s-sleep."

"First you will eat," he said grimly, holding the pemmican out to her.

Her lips tightened angrily, but she took the patty from him and bit off a piece.

Her teeth were chattering so hard that eating was difficult, but each time she tried to put the food aside, Swift Arrow forced more on her. Finally it was gone. He held out the canteen and she drank from it, her teeth clicking against the metal.

When Swift Arrow pulled her shivering body into his arms, she had no thought of resistance, wanting only his warmth. And she knew it was the only sensible thing to do. Even animals knew enough to huddle together and share their body warmth. They lay down and he pulled the two blankets over them.

Lying next to Swift Arrow, Katherine's thoughts turned to her father. Had he given her up for dead? Would he mourn her passing? She didn't think so. He might feel a momentary regret, but she didn't think he would let it bother him long.

She had never felt close to her father, even as a child. And if he had had any love for her, he was careful not to show it. He was even sparing with his kindnesses. As though showing any would make him less of a man.

Quite unlike Swift Arrow, a man her father would surely call a savage, who had shown her nothing but kindness in the time she had known him. Even now, the warrior's arms circled her, holding her close against him as he shared his body warmth with her. Could she have felt so relaxed in another man's arms? She didn't think so. She had never shared such intimacy with

51

anyone before, not even with Jesse, whom she had loved.

Even now, lying in Swift Arrow's arms, she was totally relaxed. Her eyes were heavy . . . with sleep . . . she'd just close them for a minute . . .

Katherine jerked awake suddenly as a fierce howling penetrated her dreams. She was stiff with tension, her gray eyes wide with fear as she stared up at the hide shelter.

"Do not be frightened," said a male voice close to her ear. "It is only the wind."

Katherine turned her head toward Swift Arrow. His face was only inches from her own.

"Go back to sleep," he said huskily.

The tension drained from her, and she relaxed again. But her sudden movement had caused the blanket to slip on one side, allowing a draft to penetrate her snug cocoon, and she shivered, snuggling closer to the warmth at her back. He reached around her, pulled the blanket tighter, and tucked her closer against his warmth.

Uttering a long sigh, Katherine let her mind drift off again.

Swift Arrow was exasperated. Earlier, despite the fact that he held Katherine in his arms, his weariness had caused him to fall asleep almost as soon as she had. Now that she had woken him up, he found sleep elusive. He could think of nothing except the girl he held in his arms, and the way her body was pressed firmly against his own. His body was responding to her nearness in a way that would be sure to alarm her if she knew.

Even now, she seemed as unaware as a child of what he was feeling. He groaned inwardly as she snuggled closer against him, her rounded bottom fitting nicely in the curve of his hips. Was she doing it on purpose? One look at her blissfully innocent face and he knew she was not. His lips tightened. Did she not know how she affected a man? Perhaps it was different with the white eyes. He did not want to make her afraid of him. He must keep his body under control.

He clenched his teeth. Seeming to feel his tension, she opened her eyes and looked around at him.

"Are you all right?" she asked, her gray eyes wide and innocent. "Is my head too heavy for your arm?"

He swallowed desperately. "No," he grated. "Go back to sleep."

She did.

It seemed to Katherine that she'd only slept a few moments when she was shaken roughly and the blanket was pulled away allowing cold air against her skin. She moaned a soft protest, her hand searching for the cover.

"Wake up," Swift Arrow said brusquely. "You must eat before we continue our journey."

Her lashes fluttered, she stared, bewildered, up at him. He knelt beside her holding out a long strip of jerky.

As the flush of sleep left her face, she looked at the dried venison with distaste. It didn't look the least bit appetizing, though she was hungry.

Pushing her tousled hair from her eyes, she raised herself to a sitting position, then took the jerky from the warrior.

"How long will it take us to reach the fort?" she asked, gnawing on the tough meat. Then, without waiting for his answer, she said, "I'd give anything for a hot cup of coffee."

He handed her the canteen. "This will have to do."

She took it and drank. The water was incredibly cold, but it helped to wash down the tough meat. She smiled her thanks at Swift Arrow.

She knew she was lucky to be alive and had no intention of complaining further about the food. Besides, much to her surprise, the dried venison had assuaged her hunger.

"You didn't say how long it would take to reach the fort," she reminded him.

Something flickered in his eyes. It looked like fear, but surely not. He seemed the most fearless man she'd ever met. For a moment she thought he wasn't going to reply. When he did, his answer was terse. "Two days."

"That long?"

He nodded, chewing his own venison slowly.

"I appreciate the time you're wasting to take me home," she said earnestly. "I'll see that you're rewarded handsomely for your trouble."

"Come," he said. The words had a flinty sound. "It is time to go."

In no time at all their crude shelter had been dismantled and the hides repacked. Then Swift Arrow lifted her to the back of the horse and swung up behind her.

They resumed their journey.

They traveled all day, riding double until the stallion tired, then Swift Arrow dismounted and led the animal for a while. The going was hard, for the snow was deep. They stopped often to allow the stallion rest.

Katherine found herself wondering about Swift Arrow. She was becoming more and more aware of the intimacy of their situation. Still, his matter-of-fact attitude kept her from fearing him.

As the day passed, she began to dread the times he left the stallion and walked. Without his closeness, the wind seemed to chill her doubly.

Late that afternoon the wind died down, and Swift Arrow dismounted, took one of the blankets from its protective buckskin wraps, and tied it behind the saddle, allowing it to drape over the stallion's hindquarters and brush the ground.

She looked curiously at the trailing blanket, frowning. She even opened her mouth to question his actions, but she quickly closed it again.

She was new to the ways of the wilderness. But she didn't wish to call attention to her inexperience. He must have had a good reason for his actions. Perhaps it helped to keep the wind off the horse. But then, she puzzled, the wind wasn't blowing at the moment.

Since the wind had calmed and the sun was shining, she began to feel quite warm and took an interest in her surroundings. The terrain looked unfamiliar to her, but she put it down to the heavy snowfall.

Her gaze dwelt on the man trudging through the snow leading the stallion. What would her father think when they rode into the fort? He would be sure to think the worst, she felt certain. And slowly she began to doubt the wisdom of their return.

Worry darkened her eyes. Her father hated the Apaches. He had sworn he would never rest until he put them all on the reservation. Would the fact that Swift Arrow had saved his daughter's life be enough to guarantee him safe passage?

She was afraid not.

Which meant Swift Arrow would be in danger.

She must not allow him to take her all the way to the fort. Her father could not be trusted. The more she thought of it, the more certain she became that her father would not let the Indian go free. He would only see Swift Arrow as a renegade Apache. And he would take him captive. Or worse.

The thought was enough to make up her mind. Before they reached the fort, Swift Arrow must leave her. She wished there was some way she could express her gratitude. She knew with certainty that she would have died if he had not found her.

Katherine was surprised when they came to a river. Swift Arrow had said it was several days to Fort Bayard, but the only river she could remember crossing in her flight was the Mimbres, which was merely a day's ride from the fort. Perhaps he had misjudged the distance.

"Is this the Mimbres river?" she asked. "I don't remember it being this wide."

He ignored her. She puzzled over it while Swift Arrow untied the trailing blanket and fastened it behind the horse. Then he mounted behind her, urging the stallion into the water.

Although the river was wide, it proved to be shallow and easily forded. When they reached the other side, Swift Arrow didn't dismount. She got the distinct impression he was in a hurry now. But was that really so surprising? The day was fading fast.

Swift Arrow's arm came around her waist, drawing her back against his chest. She leaned into his strength, wondering how soon they would make camp.

She was tired, and her wound had begun to throb. She worried about what would happen when they reached the fort. She must make sure Swift Arrow wasn't seen by the soldiers. In fact, perhaps it would be best if she didn't even mention him at all. She would tell her father she had found her own way home. She sighed wearily. Her father was sure to be furious with her for leaving the fort and injuring herself. She might as well prepare herself for a bitter reunion with him.

She sighed again, resting her throbbing head against her companion. The constant hours in the saddle had taken their toll. As though her pounding head was not enough, her back and shoulders ached, as well. But, despite her discomfort, she uttered no word of complaint. She tried instead to force all thoughts from her mind, to concentrate instead on the peace and quiet of her surroundings.

Somewhere along the way the terrain had changed. The forest had given way to high plateau country, with abrupt, sandstone mesas. Nothing looked familiar to her. Surely they would have come to Cottonwood Pass by now. She voiced the thought.

"That way has been closed by snow," he said.

"Oh."

She frowned, a feeling of uneasiness surfacing. Had there really been that much snow? But then, why would Swift Arrow lie about it? She felt almost certain he would not. Not the man who had saved her from certain death.

For days she had been at his mercy, and yet he had seen to her every comfort. She could trust him with her very life . . . she was certain of it.

When they had reached a box canyon with snow-laden, brush-covered slopes and high canyon walls, Swift Arrow pulled the stallion up and slid from its back.

"Are we stopping here?" she asked him.

A muscle worked in his jaw. For a moment he was still. When he spoke, he sounded almost angry. "There is where we will sleep," he said. At her questioning look, he pointed to the face of the cliff.

Puzzled, Katherine looked up, and she drew in a sharp breath. High up the face of the vertical cliff, about a hundred feet from the mesa top, a single wall of sandstone had been built into a huge recess.

Rooms and towers had been formed, lying quiet and protected in a natural cavern that time and the elements had carved. The empty doorways of some ancient civilization, long abandoned, stood waiting to be filled.

The small windows were shadowed, seeming to stare vacantly across the valley. She caught her breath.

"What is it?" she asked.

"It is the home of the Old Ones," he told her. "My ancestors, the Basket Makers. We can rest there with no fear of predators or of the cold."

"But how will we get up there?"

She was fascinated by the ruins, could hardly believe people had truly once lived there.

"There is a way," he said. Putting his hands on her waist, he helped her from the stallion, untied the leather packs, and handed them to her.

"I—I think I'd rather sleep down here," she said, watching him work at the fastenings of the blankets. "We made out all right last night, didn't we?"

A flush flooded her cheeks as she remembered how she'd kept warm.

A glint appeared in his eyes, as though he could read her thoughts. "If it is your wish to sleep as we did before, then I could build a shelter and—"

"No," she interrupted hastily. "You're right. We'll keep warmer up there." She frowned. "Providing I can make the climb."

"If you think you cannot, then I have no objections to sharing our body warmth again," he said.

She could hear the amusement in his voice, and her heart skipped a beat. Up to now he had been almost stoical in his attitude. She was surprised to learn he had a sense of humor.

"No," she said quickly. "If you can climb it, then so can I." She eyed the cliff uneasily. "At least I hope so," she muttered.

Swift Arrow left her, to disappear into a crevice and then return with a long ladder made from weathered poles. Her doubts grew. He leaned the ladder against the face of the cliff.

Katherine regarded the hand he held out to her uneasily. Then, even more uneasily, the ladder. It was old. Was it strong enough to hold their weight?

Obviously, he thought so. "Come," he said.

She balked.

"It doesn't reach the top," she muttered.

"There is another ladder on the upper level," he reassured her.

She hitched up her skirt, grasped the poles with both hands, placed one booted foot on the first rung of the ladder, and began her climb. With Swift Arrow's help she soon made it to the top. Katherine worried about the delay in her return to the fort. But all she could do was trust him to know what was best, even though the path he was following seemed to be leading her even farther into the unknown.

Chapter Six

Katherine lay on the snow-covered ledge, regaining her breath. But just for a moment. Although there was only a slight breeze, she found it extremely cold.

"Come," Swift Arrow said, gripping her arm and pulling her to her feet. "We will find shelter from the wind behind those rocks."

"Those rocks" proved to be a crumbling adobe wall. And it was obvious from the stack of boulders nearby that some effort had been made to clear the area in the not too distant past. Someone else had apparently used the place for shelter. She found that thought encouraging.

She was amazed by the vast proportions of the ledge upon which the ancient city was built. It had seemed much smaller from the ground.

A tall spruce tree, covered with snow, grew in front

of the dwellings, along with several junipers and piñon pines. And they stood in a courtyard surrounded by the dwellings, some of which were as much as three stories high.

Swift Arrow carried the packs to one of the buildings, which had been made from shaped and mortared sandstone and seemed to be in good condition.

"We will sleep in one of the rooms," he said. "The cold wind cannot reach us there."

Katherine remained where she was. Her whole face glowed as her eyes swept the cavern. It was at least a hundred feet deep and twice that many wide. It was a remarkable city, built high off the valley floor, completely inaccessible to any enemy.

"It's beautiful," she breathed. "And it was brilliant of your ancestors to think of building up here. This place is completely hidden unless you enter the box canyon. And even then, with those ladders drawn up, they would be completely safe."

Swift Arrow seemed to be pleased at her enthusiasm. "I am sure it was for that reason the People of the Rock built their homes here," he said. "We are told by The Old Ones of our tribe that they were a peaceful people and did not like to fight."

"Then they were wise to build here," she said. "For the ladders seem to be the only possible way to reach the ledge."

"Yes," he agreed. "With the ladders pulled up, they could be confident that their families and homes were secure."

A gust of wind caused her to shiver and pull her cape higher around her neck.

"I will leave you here and go back down for our supplies," he said quickly. "The sun will soon be gone, and the stallion must be allowed to roam free."

She looked at him anxiously. "Are you sure he won't run away?"

"No," he assured her. "He has been trained to stay close by. When he is needed, he will not be far."

Hoping he was right about the stallion, she watched him stride to the ledge and disappear over the edge.

Taking the opportunity to explore, Katherine made a quick search of the area. She looked in several of the rooms and found they were all small, about eight by five feet in size.

She speculated that the rooms had probably been used only for sleeping . . . or to keep warm when the weather was exceptionally cold.

The ceilings were low, made of brush and sticks, plastered with mud and held up by wooden beams. A heavy layer of soot covered the walls, suggesting that fires had burned to keep the inhabitants warm.

In one of the rooms she found a large stack of wood and carried an armload back to the courtyard. She looked around for the best place to build a fire and her eyes narrowed on a far corner. There, out of reach of the wind, was a blackened firepit, and beside it were several blackened clay pots that had obviously been used for cooking utensils.

Tossing her firewood aside, Katherine bent and picked up one of the pots, studying the black-on-white geometric design closely. The earthenware vessel still retained some of its beauty, even though it was blackened by countless cooking fires.

"What have you found?" Swift Arrow asked from behind her.

She turned to show him but as she straightened up, a sudden pain stabbed through her skull. The color drained from her face.

Swift Arrow, quick to notice, asked. "Does your head pain you?"

"It did for a moment," she said, making light of the pain. "But it's gone now."

She held the pot up for him to see. "Look at this," she said. "Isn't it beautiful? The people who lived here were obviously skilled craftsmen."

Suddenly, she noticed the saddle he was still holding. "How did you manage to carry that up with the supplies?"

"It was no trouble," he said, still studying her pale features with his sharp eyes.

"You should have let me help." She smiled up at him and he seemed visibly to relax. "You're sure the stallion won't run off?" she asked, replacing the pot on the ground.

"Yes." He laid the saddle near the wall, then untied a rabbit he had fastened to his waist. "He will search for grass nearby."

He knelt and piled up a small stack of kindling. Then he struck a piece of flint off a rock. Sparks flashed. A moment later a small flame appeared, growing larger as he added some more sticks, then bigger pieces of wood.

Soon they were holding their hands out to the heat of the fire.

Swift Arrow sat back on his haunches. His narrowed gaze searched Katherine's pale features. "You are tired," he said gruffly. "And your head still pains you."

Her eyes flickered with surprise. He had known almost as quickly as herself. How was it possible?

"Sit down and rest," he continued. "I will prepare our evening meal."

"I should do that," she murmured. "You must be tired. You walked a great distance today."

His ebony eyes glinted, and his lips twitched. He raised a dark brow and asked. "You wish to clean the rabbit?"

She suppressed a shudder. "Not really," she admitted.

"I did not think so."

She got the definite impression that he was silently laughing at her

"But . . . but I'm willing to try," she offered gamely. "I really haven't contributed much to our survival."

"Do not worry about it," he said gently. "You have not yet recovered from your injury. There will be time enough later."

She flicked a curious glance at him from beneath thick lashes. Time enough later? That was an odd thing for him to say. What could he mean by it? There wasn't much time left at all. Surely they would be reaching the fort sometime tomorrow.

Her mind continued to worry over the words as she sat gazing into the flickering flames. She didn't know how much time had passed until she was roused from her reveries by the mouthwatering aroma of rabbit stew.

She looked at the man who had provided for her every need. "I can never thank you enough for what you've done for me," she said quietly. "I suppose, after tomorrow, we'll never have occasion to meet again. But I want you to know I'll never forget you. I'll always count you as a friend."

For a moment he looked taken aback. When his voice came again, it grated harshly against her ears. "Will you?"

"Yes. I will," she said firmly. Something about his expression caused her to add, "If the truth be known, I'm going to miss you. I've never known anyone like you before."

His jaw tightened. A nameless emotion flashed in his dark eyes. Then, seeming to exert a great effort, he tore his gaze away from her, and his expression hardened.

She frowned. What on earth was wrong with him? Had she done something to upset him? She watched him dish up the stew, then took the bowl he held out to her.

She lifted a chunk of meat to her mouth. It was delicious. She ate every bite, savoring each and every mouthful.

While they ate, darkness had fallen around them. As she laid her bowl aside, Swift Arrow banked the fire. "We must sleep," he said, rising to his feet.

"But it's early yet," she began, in protest. Suddenly, she stopped, remembering they would need to get an early start in the morning. But for some reason, she hated for their time together to end.

Tomorrow—after he saw her safely to the fort—they would be parting. It was doubtful they would ever meet again. Katherine found that thought disturbed her . . . and she wondered why.

She followed Swift Arrow into the room where he had stacked the hides. Katherine watched him spread several of them on the stone floor. Then he covered them over with a blanket.

"Sit down," he said. "I must see to your wound."

She obeyed, and he knelt down beside her. Her pulsebeat accelerated slightly as he unwound her bandage, and she frowned. Why should her senses be so disturbed by his presence?

He grunted with satisfaction. "The wound is healing," he commented.

He wound the bandage around her head again and refastened it. Then he sat down beside her and pulled off one of his moccasins.

Her gray eyes flickered with surprise. "What are you doing?" she asked, her voice slightly husky.

"Taking off my moccasins."

"I can see that. But, why?"

"I do not wish to sleep in them."

Her amusement evaporated, butterflies took wing in her stomach.

"You're not sleeping here!"

He flicked a glance at her. "But I am."

He put the moccasin with its mate and reached for her foot. He began to unlace her boot.

67

"What are you doing?" she asked, frowning down at him.

"Taking your boot off."

She sighed, exasperated. "I can see that," she said.

He tossed the boot aside and unfastened the other one.

"Will you stop that!" she gritted.

He looked up at her.

"If you're sleeping here," she said, "then where do I sleep?"

"With me," he said calmly. His expression was bland as he waited quietly for her reaction to his words.

Chapter Seven

At last Katherine found her voice. "With you?" she repeated stupidly. Then, regaining her senses: "Oh, no, I'm not!"

Before she realized what was happening, Swift Arrow tossed her boot aside, encircled her waist with his long arms, and pulled her down beside him.

She shoved at him, trying to pull free from his grip. "What do you think you're doing?" she snapped. "Turn me loose!" Her efforts to free herself were in vain. His arms were like steel bands surrounding her.

"I can't sleep with you, Swift Arrow," she protested breathlessly.

"Why?" he asked.

His body was stiff with tension.

"Because I don't want to!"

"Nevertheless, you will."

She swallowed hard, staring up at him. A shaft of moonlight shining through a window illuminated her wide gray eyes. Her nerves were stretched to the breaking point as he held her gaze. Although his face was expressionless, she felt as though she had come up against a rock wall.

Uncertainty flickered through her. Why was he doing this? He had done nothing to suggest he would hurt her. Although he refused to release her, for some reason, she still did not fear him. But perhaps she should. After all, he was a member of the dreaded Apache tribe, said to be the most fierce of the Indians. And as such, he lived by different rules than her people.

He seemed to guess the thoughts going through her mind. "I am weary and wish only to sleep. Although we are sheltered, the night air is still cold. And it will be even colder before the dawn. We have already shared a sleeping space and you were not harmed. You have nothing to fear from me."

She stared at him, perplexed. Perhaps he didn't recognize the taboos that decreed a man and woman shouldn't sleep together unless they were married. Should she try to explain it to him? She wasn't sure that would be wise. Nothing in his actions had caused her to suspect him of dishonorable intentions. Was she only putting ideas into his head by objecting to the sleeping arrangements? She couldn't be sure.

"Go to sleep," he said firmly, pulling her head against his chest.

Sighing, she gave in, allowing her body to relax. As he had pointed out, it wasn't the first time they had slept together.

But for some reason, tonight she was very aware of him lying next to her. Her body was reacting in ways she hadn't expected to the feel of his thigh, hard against her own. She trembled with awakening sensations, and his arm tightened, pulling her closer against him.

She felt certain it would be hard to sleep under such conditions, but despite herself, her eyes began to feel heavy. They closed, and soon she was fast asleep.

The next morning, she became aware of a heaviness lying across her upper body. Opening her eyes a crack, she found she was cuddled within the curve of Swift Arrow's neck. His arm was tight across her breasts. Her lashes fluttered, her eyes lifted, and she found herself staring into his ebony eyes.

She drew a deep breath. Bright spots of color appeared on her cheeks. She moistened her lips. "I'm sorry," she apologized. "I didn't mean to crowd you. It must have been the cold."

He didn't answer. His hand lifted, and he smoothed a long silver curl back from her fiery cheeks. His eyes filled with amusement. "You are very beautiful," he murmured in a husky voice. His warm breath disturbed her senses as it fanned across her face.

"Thank you," she said, wriggling away from his embrace.

She sat up, her gaze traveling around the small room. She was looking anywhere, except at him. She felt completely flustered, unable to meet his eyes.

71

She looked toward the open window. The sun had risen, portending fair weather. "It looks like it'll be good weather for traveling," she said.

He sat up, pushing the covers away. "Too much snow," he grunted, pulling on his moccasins. "I will build a fire."

She couldn't suppress the uneasiness she felt as he left the room. She pushed back her disheveled hair and pulled on her boots, lacing them tightly about her ankles.

Too much snow.

Sure. There was a lot of snow, but too much? Too much for what?

Shivering, she stepped from the room and hurried to reach the shelter of the courtyard wall. Swift Arrow had already built a fire and had put a pot filled with water over the flames. When steam began to rise from the heated water he dipped some out into a small container and handed it to her.

While she hurried to wash in the water he had provided, he sprinkled cornmeal into the pot he had returned to the fire. Soon a mouthwatering aroma wafted from the cooking pot.

As they began their breakfast she was surprised to find that dried berries had been added to the mush and it had been sweetened with honey. "This is good," she said, her eyes glowing with pleasure. Although he made no comment, she felt he was pleased.

She cleaned up after they had eaten, then sat beside the fire watching him clean his rifle. As time passed, she became restless. Surely it was time they were leaving. She voiced her thoughts.

"We will not be traveling today."

She felt a sharp stab of apprehension. She didn't quite trust the look in his dark eyes. "I thought we were going to the fort," she said, her voice betraying her uncertainty.

"I have no wish to journey to the fort," he said. His cool answer deprived her of breath. She stared dumbly at him.

He laid the rifle aside and moved toward her. Unconsciously, she flinched away from him, watching with eyes suddenly gone wary.

"Do you mean we'll be waiting until tomorrow?"

His expression darkened. "Are you in such a hurry to leave this place? Do you not like it?"

"It's not a question of whether or not I like it," she said stiffly. "But I must go home. My father will be worried about me." She stood up and moved toward the room they had slept in. "I'll gather our things together," she said.

He reached her in two long strides. "I said we would not be leaving," he growled. There was a grim set to his jaw, a tightening of his lips. "Why should I care how your father feels?" Gripping her shoulders, his fingers dug in until she flinched beneath them. "Your father has no thought for the pain he has caused my people. It is time that he should feel pain, as well."

Although she was puzzled by his words, she was angered by his attitude. And his fingers were hurting her. She would probably be black and blue tomorrow.

"Take your hands off me," she said coldly, trying to pull away from him.

"Do not tell me what to do, Katherine," he said, his grip tightening on her shoulders. "For I am not one of your tame white men. I take orders from no one."

"Exactly what are your plans?" she asked furiously. "Just when are you going to take me home?"

Suddenly fear surged through her. She became aware of the barely restrained fury in his body, and the fact that they were isolated from the rest of the world. Her heartbeat became erratic. Her eyes dilated with fear. Her color ebbed and flowed as she realized she was at his mercy. They were completely alone in the wilderness.

No one knew where she was.

Dear God! There was no one to prevent him from doing whatever he wished with her.

Suddenly the meaning of the trailing blanket became clear. She must have been blind not to have realized what he was doing.

"You covered our tracks," she whispered accusingly. "You didn't want anyone to follow us."

He smiled, a mere stretching of the lips.

"What do you intend to do with me? Are you holding me for ransom?"

Impatience glittered in his eyes. "I want no ransom," he growled. "I saved your life."

"Does that make it yours?" she flung at him.

"Yes."

74

She was astonished by his answer. Whatever she'd expected, it hadn't been that. "My life is my own," she snapped. "I belong to no one."

"You are wrong, Katherine. You belong to me."

"Never!"

His hands tightened on her shoulders and she uttered a hoarse cry of pain. As though impatient with her, he pushed her away. He looked disturbingly tall and potentially dangerous. "Never is a long time," he said. "Do not fight me, Katherine. For you cannot win." With these words, he left the cover of the wall, crossed the courtyard, and disappeared over the ledge.

Swift Arrow was still angry when he reached the valley floor. How could Katherine accuse him of holding her for ransom? He had hoped more time would pass before she became aware that he had no intention of returning her to her father. Even if he did not feel hatred for the man, he would have found it impossible to return her. He had been too long alone. He needed a woman of his own. Although he tried to convince himself that any woman would do, he knew it was not so. He wanted this woman desperately. And he intended to keep her.

Katherine's eyes glittered as she stared at the spot where she'd last seen him. He had just walked off and left her! Did he expect to find her when he returned?

Her chin lifted defiantly. Her eyes blazed with the fire of purpose. He was going to be sadly disappointed. She had no intention of twiddling her thumbs until he came back.

Now was her chance to escape. And escape she would. Then she would find her own way back to the fort.

Katherine moved to the ledge, stopping at the snowline to stare down into the valley far below. A feeling of despair washed over her as she realized the odds of her making the fort alone were very slim.

Snow covered the forest and the plains as far as the eye could see. And she was forced to admit she had no idea in which direction the fort lay.

She rubbed the back of her neck, trying to ease the tense muscles. She refused to give up. Swift Arrow expected her to give in to his demands. He had said her life was his.

Her lips tightened. She had a suspicion that if she did not escape him now, she would get no other chance. She had no fear of descending the ladder alone. It had seemed sturdy enough to hold several people of her weight. But she would need supplies.

Before she could change her mind, she hurried to their sleeping room and pulled a blanket from their bed of furs. Then she took a leather pouch filled with dried meat from the supplies and tossed it into the center of the blanket. After tying the ends of the blanket together, she donned her cape, looped her arm through the bundle, and made her way to the ledge.

Gathering her courage around her like a mantle,

Katherine stepped into the cold snow and moved to the ladder. She gripped the poles with both hands and emptied her mind of everything except the descent. Determinedly, she shoved away all thoughts of Swift Arrow's previous kindnesses.

He was just what her father would have called him: a savage.

Chapter Eight

The instant Katherine stepped on the ladder, she sensed the vast amount of open space beneath her. She felt profoundly affected by that great, dark emptiness that waited below.

The fear was totally irrational, she told herself. It was the same ladder she had gone up with Swift Arrow. But perhaps he was the key. When she had used the ladder before, she had not been alone. Now, her chest felt tight, her throat constricted, and she found it hard to breathe.

Her knuckles whitened as her fear increased. Did the ladder sway in the wind, or had it simply been her imagination?

She hung there for a moment with the wind whipping her cloak around her slender form, tearing the hood from her head. A long lock of pale hair whipped into her eyes, making it difficult to see. But she couldn't let go to remove it. It took all the effort she could summon to resume her descent, and it seemed hours before she reached the last rung of the ladder. A heartfelt sigh of relief escaped her lips as her booted foot came in contact with the snow-covered ground.

Now that she was back on solid ground, her fear evaporated with the wind. She looked around for the stallion. He was nowhere in sight. She spent precious time searching for him, but it was in vain. Swift Arrow must have taken the horse.

Should she forget her plans to leave? She didn't think so. Despite the snow, she felt almost warm with the sun shining high overhead. She could cover a lot of distance before nightfall, and there was a good possibility that she might run into a patrol.

On the other hand, she couldn't know how safe she was or wasn't with Swift Arrow. She still didn't know exactly what he wanted from her. But he had made it clear he wasn't going to take her back to the fort.

No. If she returned home, then it would have to be under her own steam. And it would have to be now, before he took steps to prevent her leaving.

He had told her the fort was only a day's journey away. She could make that distance alone. But what direction should she take?

By her reckoning, they had traveled northwest. Surely she had only to head southeast after she left the box canyon. With a last look at the cliff, she set out on the long journey back to the fort.

A sudden gust of wind pulled a huge scattering of

snow off the ground and whipped it into her eyes. She wiped it away and pulled the cape tighter around her neck. The snow-covered land seemed to stretch out to eternity. It took on an ominous quality, unnoticed before. Weathered formations of rock poked up here and there through blankets of snow and soil. And in the distance, tall pine trees with snow-laden branches reached toward the heavens, seeming to stand as a warning to the wary traveler.

Katherine plodded through the deep snow, sometimes sinking past her knees in a drift. Was it her imagination, or was the temperature falling? Her nose was cold, her breath visible in the cold air. When the cold began to penetrate her body, she stopped long enough to untie her bundle and wrap the blanket around her. Then she continued her journey.

The sun disappeared, and ominous dark gray clouds filled the sky overhead. She felt certain another storm was imminent. She would have to hurry, for she could not find shelter in the canyon. And if she was caught in the open, she would have little chance of survival. She must reach the forest. Surely another hour would see her there. The tall pine trees, although heavily laden with snow, would afford some protection from the storm.

Thoughts of the sheltering ruins filled her mind. Would the fire still be burning? The cliff overhang covering the ruins had kept the storm at bay. And the memory of their journey across the frozen land had dimmed. Suddenly she realized how foolish she had been to leave the safety of the cavern, to venture out into the snow again.

She stopped and turned. Faraway, in the distance, the cliffs seemed to beckon to her.

She remained poised, weighted with indecision. It wasn't too late to go back.

As if to prove her wrong, the storm burst over her. The wind gusted, blowing heavy flakes of snow around her. It howled like a banshee, whipping the cold powder into her face, blinding her.

Faced with what was fast becoming a blizzard, she turned her steps back the way she had come. But before she had gone only a few yards she despaired of ever making it back alone.

Half-frozen, Katherine struggled onward. She could no longer see more than a few feet in front of her. But to give up would mean certain death. All she could see was a nightmare patch of white before her. She lost her footing and fell face downward in a drift. It took all the effort she could muster to get up again. Another few feet and she fell again. This time she lay there, wondering if it would be better if she just gave up.

Swift Arrow urged the stallion on. He must find Katherine. How could she have been so foolish as to leave? He was nearly upon her when the stallion stopped. His heart lurched with fear as he saw her crumpled in the snow. He dismounted and knelt beside her still figure.

He lifted her head and her lashes quivered. "Swift Arrow," she whispered. "You've come."

Lifting her into his arms, he placed her on the stallion's back and climbed up behind her. Then, holding her tightly against him, he made his way back to the cliff dwellings. She was unconscious when they arrived at the base of the cliff. He put her across his shoulders and began to climb. He was breathing heavily from the exertion when he reached the top, but he didn't stop until he had her safely in their sleeping room. Laying her on the bed, he stripped the clothing from her body, then covered her with the blankets.

When she woke up he was bending over her.

"You brought me back," she said.

His dark eyes were turbulent as they held hers. "You were foolish to leave," he grated harshly.

She lowered her eyes, feeling unaccountably hurt. He was angry with her.

"Why do you look away from me?" he asked.

Her eyes lifted, found his, and she caught her breath. There was something in his eyes she didn't understand. It was almost as though he were in pain.

"Where are my clothes?" she asked, becoming aware of her nakedness.

"Hanging near the fire," he said. "They were wet. I'll get them for you if you wish to get up."

"I do."

Without a word he left to get the garments. When he returned with them, he said, "I must go down to the valley and release the stallion. I will not be long."

"Did you leave him tied?"

"No. But he is still loaded with supplies." He did not add that he had been afraid to leave her while she was still unconscious.

A few minutes later she donned her clothes, noticing as she did how ragged they were becoming.

After fastening her boots, she left the room. She knelt beside the fire, which had died down to mere coals, and added kindling, then more wood. The kindling caught fire and the flames sizzled and spit, giving out heat.

Katherine turned, her gaze going beyond the cavern to where heavy snowflakes still fell. It was hard to believe she could be so warm behind the walls of this ancient city. But if Swift Arrow hadn't found her, she would have frozen to death. He had said he would take her back when the storm passed. She wondered why his words hadn't made her happy.

Wondering what was taking Swift Arrow so long, Katherine rose to her feet. Her gaze fell upon the courtyard floor. Her eyes narrowed as she realized there was a pattern to the stones. On closer inspection, she discoverd several circular depressions. Each cleft had a round hole with two weathered poles protruding from it.

Curious, she approached the nearest one, knelt and peered inside the pit. In the dim light she could see a deep, circular recess, six feet deep. And as many in circumference. A stone ledge was constructed a foot from the floor and completely circled the room.

Otherwise, the cavity was empty.

Katherine inspected the next indentation, finding it

identical to the first one, and just as empty.

She rose and studied the pattern of the outer courtyard, finding there were eight of the circular rooms. Her gaze narrowed on the farthest one. A pole ladder lay discarded beside it. And the opening had been sealed with a large, flat rock.

Curious as to why anyone would want to seal it, she knelt beside it and pushed at the rock. It remained steadfast. She pushed harder, putting the strength of her back into it. Stone grated against stone as it moved a few inches. One more try and it yielded, exposing a gaping hole that resembled a yawning mouth. Her nostrils twitched as a dry, musty smell arose from within. She poked her head through and peered inside.

Her eyes registered a flicker of surprise, then sharpened slightly. The room was like the others in appearance. Except for one important difference. This room was not empty. Leather pouches and clay pottery were crowded together on the long bench amid a large stack of hides.

"A storage room," she muttered. "Someone's used it for a storage room." A glint appeared in her eyes. She pushed back a stray lock of hair, tucking it behind one ear. "I don't know what else is down there, but we could use those hides."

She picked up the ladder and slid it down through the entrance. It scraped against the opening, then stopped as it came to rest on the bottom.

Returning to the fire, she selected a likely-looking torch and returned to the sinkhole.

Gripping the ladder firmly, she hitched up her skirt

85

and lowered herself into the darkness below. When she reached the bottom, her fascinated gaze swept the circular room, taking note of the stone pillars that supported the roof.

Eager to examine the leather bags, she unfastened one, and found it filled with pemmican. Another proved to be dried berries, while yet another contained strips of dried meat. When she opened one of the clay pots, it yielded up a large supply of what looked like dried vegetables. Another released the unmistakable odor of wild onions.

Katherine was filled with elation. There was enough food stored in this room to last Swift Arrow and herself for months. Someone had worked hard to set in this store of supplies, and yet, from the looks of the bags, it hadn't been recently.

"Why would anyone leave all this food after working so hard to put it away?" she muttered.

Stepping carefully, wary of what the shadows might contain, she moved to the nearest stack of hides, counting more than a dozen rabbit pelts. Beneath them were the hides of deer, elk, and even a thick bearskin.

She ran the palm of her hand over the top skin. It was smooth and supple. It was no wonder the Indians used the hides for their clothing. The hides would keep the cold winter air at bay.

Her makeshift torch sputtered and flickered, and Katherine knew she must hurry. Her light wouldn't last much longer. She gathered several bags up in her hands and carried them up to the fire.

Swift Arrow still had not returned, and she decided

to prepare a meal for him. She peeled the outer skin off the vegetables she had brought up and soon had them boiling over the fire.

More time passed and Swift Arrow had still not returned. She told herself he couldn't have been gone more than an hour, but still she was anxious. He had said he was going to release the stallion. Surely it wouldn't take him this long.

Had he become lost in the storm? No, she told herself, trying to quell her anxiety, he would be back soon. As though to make matters worse, the wind had risen and an occasional sighing could be heard as it played through the rocks.

What would she do if Swift Arrow didn't return? Granted, she had plenty of food. But she would be completely alone. She had no doubts that she would remain that way throughout the winter if something happened to him.

Feeling restless and apprehensive, she crossed the courtyard, stopping short of the snowline to gaze out over the valley. Only stark whiteness met her eyes. Nothing moved below, except the falling snow.

A gust of wind loosened particles of dust and debris from the face of the cliff. She blinked rapidly against the sudden pain as the grit sprayed against her face. Down in the valley, the lower branches of the trees rustled, scraped, and softly creaked. Nearer to her, the wind howled through the higher branches.

As before, she heard a soft sighing and knew it was the wind blowing in the cavern. But this time, instead of dying down it became a whine, then rose in volume until it reached an eerie screech. The hairs at the back of her neck lifted. And, even knowing what it was, she was still completely unnerved by it.

Why didn't Swift Arrow come?

She returned to the courtyard but couldn't sit still. She began to pace back and forth across the cavern, back and forth, her eyes searching, always searching for a figure that never appeared.

She rubbed the back of her neck. Her nerves were stretched to the breaking point. Swift Arrow had deserted her.

No, her heart denied. *He wouldn't do that. He'll come back for me.*

But what if he did. What did he intend to do with her then?

Certainly no harm, she chided herself. *He saved my life.*

If it was his intention to return, wouldn't he have already done so?

He isn't coming back.

"No," she muttered, angry with herself. "Something must have happened to him."

At the thought, her throat tightened. Even now, he could be lying hurt. *Or dead.*

Hot tears bathed her cheeks. She brushed them away.

Swift Arrow was an Indian. He was used to taking care of himself.

A vision of Swift Arrow lying frozen on the ground filled her mind.

She resumed her pacing, almost wearing grooves in

the cavern floor. If only he would come. Her nerves were stretched tight, her head wound had begun to throb with a steady beat.

A low growl broke the silence . . .

She became aware of eyes watching her.

The hairs at the nape of her neck rose.

She turned . . .

Chapter Nine

The mountain lion crouched on a snow-covered overhang, poised, its muscles bunched.

Katherine froze in her terror, afraid to run, afraid not to.

"Do not move." Swift Arrow's low voice came from behind her.

His admonition was unnecessary. She was certain she couldn't move if she tried.

"Now," Swift Arrow directed, drawing his knife from his belt, "Carefully, get behind me."

Using all the will she could call upon, she eased herself behind him. He was placing himself in danger to protect her. Yet she couldn't help him, couldn't even help herself.

The animal shrieked, a hideous sound that sent prickles of fear down Katherine's spine. The mountain lion had turned its attention away from her, seeming to recognize the warrior as its adversary.

Then the cat sprang, striking Swift Arrow with so much force that the warrior was knocked to the ground. Katherine's scream entwined with the growl of the cat.

She had to do something, had to help Swift Arrow. Frantically she searched for a weapon. The rifle was where Swift Arrow had left it, propped against the courtyard wall. Dashing for it, she snatched it up, cocking the trigger as she brought it up to bear on the cat. Her hands trembled as she aimed. Then she squeezed the trigger.

She barely heard the click as the hammer struck the empty chamber. The gun was empty.

Her frantic gaze was pulled to the Indian again. The cat was on top of Swift Arrow, its neck stretched as it strained to reach his throat. The warrior's muscles were strained too, to the limit, trying to keep the animal's sharp teeth away from him.

"The bullets!" she screamed at Swift Arrow. "Where are the bullets?"

He didn't answer. He rolled over with the animal beneath him. Blood streamed down his arms as he held the cat's teeth away from his neck.

Katherine's frantic eyes searched for something to use as a weapon. As a last resort, she grabbed a stone and rushed to the struggling pair.

She swung the rock at the cat's head, but the blow glanced off the animal's shoulder as the pair rolled over again. She scurried backwards as they rolled toward her. Getting a chance at another blow, she struck at the cat's head with all the strength she possessed. But she might as well have hit the animal with a twig for all the good it did.

Swift Arrow's breath came in short gasps as he wrestled with the animal. She struck out again, hoping to divert the cat's attention from the warrior. The mountain lion turned its head, sending an angry roar her way. She hit out again, striking the animal behind the ear with the stone.

One paw lashed out at her and she jumped back. She was totally absorbed with the animal, completely unaware of Swift Arrow's hand leaving the big cat, reaching for the knife that had fallen to the ground.

The mountain lion returned its attention to Swift Arrow as sun glinted off metal. The warrior's hand lifted, then fell as he plunged his hunting knife into the animal, over and over and over again.

When Swift Arrow's movements finally ceased, the cat was lying motionless atop him. With a grunt, he pushed the dead animal off, rolled over, and lay still, breathing raggedly.

Aghast, Katherine stared down at the dead mountain lion. Beside the lion, Swift Arrow lay, blood streaming down his face, down his arms.

Pushing himself to his feet, he staggered to where Katherine stood, then clutched her by the arms.

"Are you hurt?" he asked.

She swallowed hard, tears welling up and sliding down her face now that the crisis had passed.

"I—I was going to ask you that," she said, her voice

ragged with emotion.

"I am fine."

Through a veil of tears she saw the numerous cuts and scratches on his face and arms and shook her head back and forth.

"No," she choked. "You're not. He nearly killed you." She began to tremble violently.

"But he did not." He pushed a pale lock of tousled hair away from her face, tucking it behind her ear.

She buried her face in her hands. "He almost did!" she burst out. "And I couldn't do anything—nothing to help you at all."

Suddenly everything coalesced, became too much to hold inside. Her face convulsed, and huge, racking sobs came from deep within her body. She couldn't have stopped them if her life had depended on it.

Pulling her hands away from her face, he folded her gently into his arms, holding her close against him. "Ssshhh," he said gruffly. "Don't cry."

But she couldn't stop. The tears had been dammed up too long. They had to be released. She cried from relief that Swift Arrow's life had been spared, and she cried for Jesse who had lost his life so young. She cried for her dead mother and the father who'd never loved her. And last of all she cried for herself.

With the sensitive fingers of one hand, Swift Arrow stroked the back of her head, holding her tightly until her trembling stopped and she grew quiet. Slowly, she became aware of his heart thudding loudly in her ear as it beat in rhythm with her own.

94

Although her tears continued to fall silently, her arms seemed to move of their own accord around his neck, her fingers twining through his dark hair. The softness of her breasts pressed against his masculine chest. She was barely aware that she was wetting his shirt with her tears.

"Why do you weep?" he asked, his breath fanning her cheek.

Despite her efforts at control, the tears spilled over faster, sliding hotly down her face. "Because you could have been killed," she cried.

"But I wasn't," he consoled. "Instead, the cat is dead." He tilted her chin, forcing her to meet his eyes. Lifting his hand, he wiped a tear away with one large finger. "Cease your crying," he said. "It is over. We will think about it no more."

"I should have been able to help you," she said. "I tried to shoot him, but the gun was empty. And I didn't know what else to do. I'm completely useless to you."

"No. Don't say such a thing. It is not true." He traced the line of her jaw with a finger while he studied her pale face closely. "You have many things to learn, but I will teach them to you," he said, stroking her hair gently.

Although she wanted nothing more than to stay in his arms, she drew away from him, studying his scratched face closely. "Let me see to your wounds," she said. "If they aren't treated, infection could set in."

He pulled off his shirt and sat down on the courtyard wall. She examined the claw marks, none of which proved deep, except for one slash that had ripped through his buckskin shirt and gouged its way into his shoulder. She cleansed and applied a healing poultice to the wound. All the time, she was inwardly berating herself for not having been able to help him when he needed it.

As she finished, he caught her trembling hands in his. "Sit down," he said. "Let me look at the cut on your head."

"It's nearly healed," she said. "I hardly know it's there anymore."

"Let me see," he insisted.

She took his place on the rock wall and his fingers gently separated her hair to expose the wound to his gaze.

"You have gentle hands," she said.

His movements stilled, and she looked up into his dark eyes. Tension sparked, alive, dangerous, breathtaking. The long, piercing look that passed between them was devastating in its intensity. Her body trembled in response to the desire he wore so blatantly.

The moment stretched, timeless, endless. As if to shatter it, she tremulously dampened her dry lips with the tip of her tongue. It didn't help; it seemed only to magnify the moment.

Swift Arrow lifted her to her feet and clasped her close against his naked chest. She breathed in his scent, a mixture of leather and pine. Then she gave a quivery sigh and pushed gently against him.

"I've probably ruined the meal," she said. "I'm afraid

you're going to have a lot to teach me."

"I don't mind," he said. He tilted her chin with one hand, forcing her to meet his eyes. "I think there are many things that you could teach me."

"Like what," she whispered, her eyes moving to his mouth.

"Like the white man's way of touching the lips together," he said. "I find it very appealing."

He lowered his head. His mouth was only a few inches away from hers. Her breath quickened, her heartbeat increased its rhythm, beating in time with his.

What was happening to her? she wondered.

As his lips came nearer, she turned her head, feeling his mouth brush the sensitive area below her ear. A shiver chased up and down her spine, goosebumps broke out on her arms.

His arms tightened around her, and his breath was warm against her skin. She closed her eyes and shuddered.

"Look at me," he whispered.

Taking her chin in one hand, he tilted her face to his. Her lashes fluttered gently against her cheeks, then her eyes opened to the slumbrous passion in his. Her brain sent up warning signals that her muscles refused to acknowledge.

She must stop this before it got out of hand. She opened her mouth to speak just as his lips closed over hers. His lips were firm in a testing, questioning, kiss. Her mouth moved beneath his and his arms tightened around her, his lips becoming hard, demanding.

Katherine moaned, wanting more from him. The tip of her tongue snaked out, tracing the edges of his inner mouth, sending ripples of shock waves through her body. She felt his reaction immediately.

Swift Arrow's breathing was harsh as he lifted his head and stared down at her with glittering eyes. His body had hardened against her, and her cheeks reddened as she felt him throbbing against her lower belly.

"I-I'd better—" she began but was quickly interrupted.

"Touch me," he commanded, taking her hand and pressing it against his warm chest.

Her hand trembled as he guided it over his hard chest, letting her feel the ripple of muscle under the rough skin. When his hand went beneath her blouse, smoothing over the soft skin of her waist, finding the swell of her breast, she tried to pull away.

"No," she protested.

"Do you not wish me to touch you?"

"N-no," she said, lowering her eyes from the blaze that was his.

"Liar," he said softly.

His palm closed over her breast, kneading it gently. Her nipples tautened. She squeezed her eyes shut tight, unwilling for him to see the blaze of her desire for him.

"Open your eyes," he murmured. "Look at me."

Bravely, she held his gaze, held it until he swung her up into his arms. Then he carried her into the sleeping room and laid her down on the bed of furs.

He worked at the buttons on her blouse, his fingers fumbling in their impatience. She stirred restlessly, wanting to feel his body close against hers.

Suddenly a piercing scream rent the air and she froze, her eyes widening with fear.

Chapter Ten

Placing a hand over her mouth, he rose from the pallet. He looked out on the courtyard and turned back to her.

"It is as I suspected," he said. "The she-cat has discovered her mate."

"There were two of them?"

"Yes. But do not worry. She knows her mate is dead and will not venture here."

He returned to the pallet and took her into his arms again. Her body was stiff, unresponsive. His gaze held a question as he began to stroke her breast.

She bolted out of his arms. "Don't," she pleaded, scooting across the bed, away from him.

"Why?"

"Because I don't want it."

"Don't lie to me," he said sternly.

The extreme confidence in his voice proved to be his undoing. When he reached for her again, she slapped his hand away.

"I said, don't!" she snapped at him, fighting down a strange trapped feeling.

She had to get away from him. She must . . . before something irrevocable happened.

"Do not try my patience," he said. His eyes were deep, piercing, by far his most intimidating feature. Added to his raw strength, they spelled danger to Katherine. His arm snaked out, he grabbed her wrist in a fist of steel, pulling her close to him.

"Don't do this," she whispered. "If—if you do . . . then I'll always hate you for it."

He stared grimly at her. Something undefinable flickered in his eyes. Then he released her wrist and left the room.

She stared after him. Her emotions were churning with a mixture of relief and disappointment.

Dear God, she groaned inwardly. Why did he have to be so handsome, so . . . appealing. She had never felt this way about a man before. Not Jesse. No one. Why had this happened to her? Why had she gone all these years . . . and then almost given herself to an Apache warrior?

Pushing her hair out of her face, she rearranged her clothing and left the pallet. She wasn't about to cower in bed as though she had done something wrong.

She found him in the courtyard, dishing up food. He looked up when she joined him. She blushed as his eyes dwelt on her slender form before moving up to her face.

"Swift Arrow," she said, seating herself on the courtyard wall. "I'll give you anything you want, if you'll take me home."

"If I took you back to your father, I would be giving away what I want."

"Why?"

"Because I want you."

She felt helpless. "I'll pay you," she said. "I'll pay you any amount of money you ask."

"I do not want money."

"Then what do you want?"

His eyes were dark as they held hers. "You. Because you belong to me."

"No!" she denied.

"Be quiet!" he said harshly. "We will discuss it no more. I will not take you back to your father. Your place is with me." He held the bowl up to her. "Sit and eat."

Her lips thinned. Although she wanted to refuse the food, she was hungry. She flashed him a furious look, but took the bowl from him.

They ate in silence, and then she cleaned the dishes.

She stayed by the fire long after the need was over, long after dark, unwilling to go to the bed. Finally, Swift Arrow came to her and pulled her to her feet.

"Come to bed," he ordered. "You have no need to fear me."

"I wish to sleep alone," she said.

"No," he said grimly. "Your place is with me."

She tried to pull away. "Why do you keep saying that?"

103

"It does no good to argue," he said. "The end will be the same. We will sleep together."

Katherine found herself being pulled into the sleeping room. As he had done the previous night, he took his moccasins off, then unlaced her boots and laid them aside. She tried to resist, but he pulled her down onto the pallet and into his arms. Then he covered them both with the blanket.

"Go to sleep," he said.

She lay stiffly beside him. After awhile, she fell into a deep sleep.

The next morning Swift Arrow woke her with a cup of steaming beverage. Sulkily, she lifted the brew to her lips.

"It's tea," she said then, smiling in spite of herself. "Real English tea."

She closed her eyes, breathing in the aroma, then took another sip. "You're full of surprises," she said.

"You will learn to know me well," he told her gruffly.

"Swift Arrow . . ." she began, her hands clenching on the cup. "You don't really mean to keep me here, do you?"

His eyes darkened ominously and he stalked away from her.

"If we discuss this logically," she said. "I'm sure—" She broke off when she discovered she was talking to an empty room.

The air between them was filled with tension as they ate their morning meal. Swift Arrow didn't leave the dwelling that day at all, and as the sun marched across the sky, Katherine's temper worsened.

He sat on the courtyard wall regarding her in a way that made her skin prickle. Tendrils of antipathy curled through her stomach. He was looking at her the way a man looked at a woman he desired.

She wanted to forget what had happened the night before, but how could she when every look he directed at her was a reminder. She had practically fallen into his arms. Her only excuse was that she had been so shaken after the mountain lion attacked. And so certain that he had barely escaped death. Today she was in full possession of her senses.

Flicking a glance at him, she found his gaze still on her. Her lips tightened and she moved across the courtyard to stare down into the valley. Even then she could feel his eyes on her.

Finally, she could take it no more. She turned on him, trembling with fury . . . and something else she couldn't put a name to.

"All right," she snapped, her throat tight with anger. "If we're going to fight, then let's get it over with."

He smiled thinly. It was a smile that barely moved his firm lips and never reached his eyes. He stood up and moved toward her. "So you would fight with me?" he asked, his fingers curling around her wrist.

"Well, it's a damn sight better than what's going on right now!" She jerked away from him.

"And what is that?" he purred.

"You know damn well what's wrong," she said. "It's you. And the way you've been staring at me."

"And should I not do so? Is it not enough that you do not wish me to touch you, now I must not look as well?"

As if he'd been pushed too far, he reached for her, dragging her close against him, his head moving downward, his lips covering hers in a kiss of brutal possession. His hands molded her against the hard length of his body. At first, she was too shocked to make any response. Then, something seemed to explode between them. His lips were hungry, taking, then offering, persuading. She wanted to reject him, to pull away, but her body refused to respond to her will. Her lips seemed to melt against the seductive warmth of his.

She could feel the hard contours of his hips through her clothing, feel the heat that flooded through her from the touch of him. She groaned, pressing her body closer to his. All thought of denial had left her.

"Katherine," he groaned, lifting his head to stare into her flushed face.

His hands moved down to her hips, binding her tight against him. He thrust against her, making her instantly aware of his arousal.

When his lips found hers again, her tongue sought the inner moistness of his mouth, her hands shifted downward, crept beneath his shirt and caressed his bare skin. With a cry of triumph, he lifted her into his arms and carried her to the sleeping mat.

"You're mine," he claimed. "You belong to me."

She offered no protest as he fumbled with her clothing. She was just as busy trying to remove his.

And then she was naked against his naked chest, her

body warm beneath his. He squeezed her breast lightly, and a sense of shock flowed through her.

He kissed her again; she trembled against him, completely lost to everything except his lovemaking. His tongue dueled with hers, and white-hot flashes of desire seared through her. She cried out her need, arching involuntarily against him.

Groaning, Swift Arrow clutched her tightly to him. His manhood throbbed against her thigh as he held her body motionless, while he tried to control his breathing.

She whimpered deep within her throat, longing for something nameless. Her nipples were taut peaks beneath his fingers, her lips soft and yielding under his, her skin sensitized to his slightest touch.

With his hands, he roamed her body, moving from her firm breasts to her stomach, then down her hips. She felt the whispering brush of his fingertips on her inner thigh and stiffened. Slowly, he worked closer to the heat of her, ever nearer, stroking here, touching there, bringing to her feelings she had never dreamed possible.

Then, with his finger, he thrust into her most secret place . . .

"Oh, my God," she moaned, and he stilled her groan with his kiss, swallowed her guttural desire.

When his body covered hers, she was ready for him. His entry was but a moment's pain, bringing a surprised gasp from her. Then he moved deep within her body, building flames of passion she knew would never be quenched. Higher and higher they blazed together, fed by the fire he had fanned, leading her along unexplored passages. He thrust deeper and faster, building the flames into an all-consuming desire. She was hardly aware of what she was doing as her body lifted, met each thrust of his until they catapulted through eternity together.

Just when she was sure she could no longer bear such pleasure, ripples of the most exquisite ecstasy of all shuddered through Katherine, echoed by Swift Arrow's own climax.

Within those all too brief moments, Swift Arrow had thrust her into a star-kissed heaven, and together they had walked among the clouds.

Chapter Eleven

Bright sunlight streamed through the window, dappling the floor with its rays. Katherine opened her eyes, feeling slightly disoriented. A gust of warm air stirred the hair around her temples, and she frowned.

Warm air? With snow outside?

Turning, she bit back a gasp as she saw Swift Arrow, his mouth pursed to blow another breath against her hair. His face was so close that she could see the passion in his dark eyes. Desire coursed through her like a bolt of lightning. She pulled back slowly, her eyes still caught with his.

"I find I am becoming attached to the white man's way of touching the lips together," he said.

His smile, slow and sensual, seemed to fill her vision. His head lowered to allow his mouth to capture hers. Her breath felt restricted, and she tingled from head to toe, but she fought against the desire to pull him closer. She had to stop this. She had to break the spell he was weaving around her. She tried to remain passive beneath his touch, but her body betrayed her. Her nipples hardened against his naked chest.

Naked? *Dear God! They were completely naked!* Had she lost every sense of decency she had ever possessed? She'd allowed him to make love to her.

Not just allowed, she reminded herself. She had welcomed it wholeheartedly.

Remembering the passion they had shared the night before, she was filled with self-loathing. How could she have behaved in such a manner? For that brief period of time she had completely forgotten Jesse. Jesse, whom she had felt she would love forever. No matter that he was dead. She had vowed to mourn him always.

Her lips twisted bitterly. She hadn't counted on her body betraying her. Disgust swept through her as she remembered how passionately she had responded to Swift Arrow last night.

So much for loyalty.

Swift Arrow felt the difference in Katherine almost immediately. Her body had stiffened as his lips covered hers. And she did not respond to his caress. He might as well have been holding a hunk of clay in his arms for all the satisfaction he found in the kiss. It seemed he must have her cooperation in order to enjoy the white man's kiss.

Pulling back, he studied her with questioning eyes.

110

What he saw in hers caused him to flinch inwardly. There was no mistaking the loathing in the gray depths. He had seen the same look many times before when the white eyes had looked at him. Then, he had not cared. He found it was different now.

It wounded him deeply to have Katherine give him such a look. But he would not have her know this. His dark eyes hardened, and he released her.

"I see you are of a different mind this morning," he said, forcing a calm he did not feel. "It does not matter. I am in no hurry. We will wait for the night."

"No," she said, her voice sounding slightly strangled. "Last night was a mistake I don't intend to repeat. It should never have happened. It must not . . . ever again."

"Don't be foolish," he grated harshly. "We cannot live here together without it happening again. The time of the long cold is not yet over. I need a woman to warm my bed. Since we are alone, you must be that woman."

Her eyes sparked with sudden anger. "Don't you care how I feel?"

"No," he lied. "Your feelings do not matter. Your cooperation would please me, but it is not necessary. Although . . ." His eyes glinted. ". . . a woman has a duty to please her man."

"You're not my man!"

"Perhaps not," he said, hurt by her words. "But you are my woman. And I will take you whenever it is my wish."

She uttered a strangled sound, which he ignored.

111

Pushing back the covers, he rose from the bed of furs.

She quickly averted her eyes from his nakedness. Hot color flooded her cheeks as she studied the pattern of the stone ceiling overhead. But even so, she could not banish the memory of his perfectly proportioned body.

She felt his gaze on her, but refused to look at him.

"I will build a fire," he said. "Then you can prepare the morning meal."

The rustle of clothing told her he was dressing, but she remained silent, her body tense . . . waiting for his next move.

She heard his footsteps receding. Then there was silence.

Turning her head, Katherine discovered the room was empty. She pushed back the covers and hurried into her clothing. She wouldn't put it past Swift Arrow to come back in.

You are my woman, and I will take you whenever it is my wish.

His words had wounded her beyond belief. He didn't care a whit about her feelings. He would take what he wanted from her, with or without her cooperation.

Her lips tightened as his words filled her mind, over and over again. She was his woman. But he wasn't her man. What kind of distinction was that? It certainly left a lot to be desired from the woman's point of view. It bound her to the man, while leaving him free to do as he pleased. She had heard that some Indians had several wives.

She found that idea didn't set well with her.

She reached for her boot.

For some reason, she couldn't bear the thought of Swift Arrow holding another woman as he had held her, making love to her in the same way. . . .

She yanked the boot on, laced and tied it, then reached for the other one.

The thought of Swift Arrow sharing such intimacy with another woman stabbed at her. But why should it? After all, wasn't Jesse her world? He had meant everything to her.

You never felt this way about Jesse.

No, she admitted. She hadn't felt the same way about Jesse. What she had shared last night with Swift Arrow was something she would never find with another man. *Why couldn't he have felt the same way?* But he didn't. To him, she was just another woman.

She fastened her boot and rose to her feet, making her way to the inner courtyard. The fire was blazing, but Swift Arrow was nowhere in sight. Steam rose from a blackened pot that hung over the fire. Upon finding that the pot contained water, she inserted her little finger. The water was already warm. Dipping a small amount in a bowl, she splashed water on her face and hands.

A soft cloth was thrust into her hands and she turned to find Swift Arrow standing beside her, his dark eyes probing as he studied her. She dried her face, wondering if he would mention the scene inside their sleeping room. She was relieved when he held his silence.

"You'll have to show me how to prepare the meal," she said.

He nodded, and she listened closely as he explained the correct proportions of cornmeal and water to make the mush they ate in the morning. He suggested she add dried berries and honey to give it more flavor and nourishment when they were available. Since they had a plentiful supply of both, she added them.

While they ate their meal, she broached a subject that had been bothering her. "You said we might be here the rest of the winter."

"It is possible."

"Would you teach me to use your weapons?" she asked.

She was surprised when he agreed.

"It has been in my mind to do so," he said. "You must learn to care for yourself."

She didn't know he was concerned about her safety should anything happen to him. The episode with the mountain lion had made him very aware of her vulnerability.

"There's one other thing," she muttered, sparing a quick glance at her soiled and tattered garments and making a grimace of distaste. "I can't keep wearing this riding habit. It's filthy. On top of that, it's so tattered I'm afraid it'll fall apart any moment." She flicked a glance at him from beneath thick lashes. "Would you show me how to make a dress out of animal skins?"

His dark eyes were thoughtful as they met hers. "I

should have thought of it myself. I will skin the mountain lion, but it will take time to cure the skins, and deerskin would be better for a dress. I will hunt today. If I am lucky perhaps I will find a buck."

Astonishment flickered through her. He didn't know about the storage room yet. She had forgotten to tell him. "There's no need," she said, giving him a quick smile. "We have hides already."

His expression was puzzled. "The only hides we have are those we use for our bed. We cannot use them to make a dress."

"We don't need to," she said, her expression animated. "The mountain lion drove everything else out of my mind. Yesterday, while you were gone, I found a whole treasure trove of supplies."

"You found them?"

"Yes," she said eagerly. Grabbing his hand, she tugged at him. "Come on," she urged. "I'll show you. One of those rooms in the courtyard floor is full of supplies." She pointed to it. "Over there."

He followed her. "In one of the *kivas?*" he asked. Then, in answer to her obvious puzzlement, he explained. "It is what the rooms are called."

"Then, yes. I found them there." In her enthusiasm, she'd completely forgotten her anger. "Come with me and see."

He hung back. "The *kiva* is a ceremonial room, Katherine, a holy place."

"It's all right," she urged. "Whoever put the supplies there must have intended them to be used." She paused. "But we'll need a light."

115

Still reluctant, Swift Arrow picked up a thick green stick and began winding the drying cloth around it.

"Don't burn that," she cried. "It's all we have to dry with."

His lips quirked, but he allowed the cloth to be taken from him. Then he tossed the green stick down and picked up a dead one. It would burn for a while. Thrusting the stick into the fire, he waited until the end caught. Finally, holding it aloft, he followed her to the *kiva* where she waited impatiently.

He went first. When he'd disappeared into the hole, she followed. At the bottom, he held the flame above his head, studying the stacks of furs and bags filled with supplies.

"Lone Wolf must have left them," he muttered.

"Who?"

"A friend," he explained. "He took a paleface for a wife. She did not wish to stay with him at first. He brought her here."

"He held her prisoner?"

"Yes. It was necessary." He moved toward the leather bags. "I wonder if the supplies are still good."

She stared at him.

It was necessary.

What about the girl? Didn't he care that she was held prisoner?

Of course not, she answered herself. *She was only a woman. And a paleface at that. Her wishes meant less than nothing to him.*

Katherine seethed with indignation, which slowly turned to bitterness.

Unaware of her feelings, Swift Arrow opened one of the bags, reached in and felt the contents. "Was this room sealed?" he asked.

"There was a big stone over the opening. I moved it when I came in."

"That is the reason the supplies have kept. You have done well," he told her. "There is enough here to see us through the winter. And plenty of skins to make all the dresses you want."

The fire had burned down until it had almost reached his fingers. He shook it out, and they were left in the murky light of the *kiva*.

Swift Arrow made no move to leave. Instead, he crossed the floor to stand beside her. Her senses were alive to his presence. She could smell the warm maleness of him, became acutely conscious of his breathing, knew the exact moment when his heartbeat quickened to beat in time with her own.

She caught her breath, willing her heart to be still. Why did she react in such a way to him? He had no thought for her wishes. He thought only of his own gratification.

Be fair. He was gentle in his lovemaking.

No, she argued. *He thought only of himself. By making me feel pleasure, his is increased tenfold.*

If only he didn't affect her senses in such a manner. She released a shaky breath, and it sounded loud in the silence of the *kiva*.

He reached out and pulled her close, cupping her chin with one hand, lifting her face, forcing her to meet his turbulent dark eyes.

117

"Katherine," he whispered. "I could lay you down right here and make love to you."

"No matter how I feel about it?"

His gaze was puzzled. His hand fell away from her. "What do you mean?"

"Exactly what I said. You don't care how I feel."

"Do you deny that I made you feel pleasure?"

"A gentleman would not speak in such a way."

"That is a word for the white eyes. It does not apply to the Apache."

"No," she said harshly. "You make up your own rules as you go along."

"Is that what you think?"

"It's true."

"You could never fall in love with an Apache," he said grimly.

"No," she agreed. "I could never love anyone. I already love another man."

He became still. "Who is this man?"

"His name was Jesse."

His face was expressionless as he turned away. He had not noticed she had used the past tense. He had only heard her lay claim to loving another man.

He moved to the skins and gathered up several of the hides. She was puzzled that he showed no reaction to her words. Instead, he only motioned her to precede him up the ladder. When they reached the top he carried the skins into the inner courtyard and knelt to examine them. He looked at her no more than was necessary as he measured and cut the soft skins into the pattern he wanted. He felt her eyes on him often but paid no attention. He didn't want to continue the conversation they had been having. He wanted to hear no more of the man she loved.

He had made up his mind. The woman was his and she would remain that way. The unknown Jesse would remain in her past. In time, perhaps she would come to love him. It would take patience and understanding, but he would supply plenty of that.

Chapter Twelve

In the days that followed, Katherine showed an eagerness to learn that completely astonished Swift Arrow. While she acquired the knowledge of how to scrape, salt and stretch the hides out to dry, then rub them with brains and oil to make them pliable, she taught him the language of her people. He proved to be an apt pupil. As she did. And while he taught her the ways of his people, he also told her the stories that had been handed down from son to son. When he had finished, he spoke bitterly of the white eyes who had slaughtered the buffalo, the mainstay of the Indians' way of life, and left the meat to rot on the plains. As he spoke, she felt his pain when he told her of the white man's treatment of the Indians, and his bitter anger that had been born of the many betrayals and broken promises of the white man.

121

While he talked, Swift Arrow worked beside her, helping in whatever chore she was bent on. If she didn't need his help, he practiced with his weapons, always intent on perfecting his skills. She watched him hit his mark time after time, never once missing his target. She was fascinated by his skill and determined she would be as good . . . or nearly.

They set aside a time of day to practice with the bow and arrows. At first, she found the weapon very awkward to use. But before long, she became used to it and came closer and closer to her target each time she let an arrow fly. Once Swift Arrow realized her potential, she found him a relentless teacher. He set her seemingly impossible goals. And she improved swiftly, perhaps only by constant repetition. But as the days passed, she became adept with the bow and arrow.

He evinced no surprise when she asked him to take her hunting with him. Although her request seemed to please him, he said nothing to indicate his feelings. In fact, he even seemed to discourage her.

"Hunting is left to the men of my tribe," he said.

"Everything worth doing seems to be left for the man," she grumbled. "You taught me to use the bow and arrow. I see no reason why I shouldn't be able to hunt."

"Sometimes we must travel a great distance to find game. It takes great strength and endurance. More than a woman possesses."

"I'm strong. I can keep up with you."

His lips quirked. "Then you may come," he said grandiosely.

"I can?" she asked, her eyes widening in surprise. "You'll really take me?"

"Didn't I just say so?" he asked, his voice filled with amusement.

"Well, yes," she admitted. "But I didn't expect you to agree."

He gave a long-suffering sigh. "I have learned it is best to keep my woman happy. We will go together at daybreak."

His woman. Despite herself, she felt a thrill at his words. It wasn't the first time he had used them. She wondered what they really meant. Since she had mentioned Jesse and the love she had felt for him, Swift Arrow had not tried to make love to her. She had begun to wonder if he no longer desired her. From the way he looked at her, she didn't think that was it. But then, why had he made no advance toward her? Why did he only gather her into his arms, then fall asleep at night?

She found no answer to her questions.

Morning came early. Sunlight streamed through the window as Katherine donned the shapeless doeskin dress she had made, leaving her legs free to maneuver. She wore knee-high moccasins that Swift Arrow had made, and, at his suggestion, plaited her hair in one long braid that hung down her back.

After they had eaten, she put on her cape, gathered up her bow and quiver of arrows, and with Swift Arrow bringing up the rear, descended the ladder to the valley floor.

A *chinook*—a warm, dry wind—had blown in the night before. It had started the snow melting, and the animals had come out of hiding to forage for food. It wasn't very long before they came across rabbit tracks. They changed course, and she found the tracks easy to follow in the slush and wet soil. The tracks disappeared as the ground turned to rock.

"Where did they go?" she asked.

"We must circle the rocky area and search all the ground around it. If we are lucky, we will pick up the trail again. You search that way," he said, pointing to the west. "I'll take this direction."

She felt elated when she discovered the tracks a few minutes later. They were clearly imprinted in the soil around one particularly large rock. Swift Arrow joined her and they followed the tracks until they ended near a bush.

Reaching out a long arm, Swift Arrow stopped her. "The rabbit is beneath the bush," he said. "You remain here while I flush him out."

Katherine could hardly contain her excitement. She was actually going to be allowed to kill their supper. Stringing an arrow in her bow, she waited while Swift Arrow moved around the bush.

Although she was expecting it, she was still startled when the rabbit jumped from its hiding place. Then, to her consternation, it stared at her, its nose quivering with fear.

"Shoot it," Swift Arrow called.

She aimed the arrow and let it fly. The rabbit fell, its legs kicking reflexively.

"You have learned well," Swift Arrow said, coming to stand beside her. "Soon there will be no need for me to hunt. And I will grow fat and lazy."

Katherine gave a weak laugh. Her gaze was on the furry carcass sprawled on the ground. Its body was covered with blood where the arrow had pierced its body. She swallowed hard as she knelt and picked it up, reminding herself of the rabbit stew she would make for supper.

Moments later Swift Arrow sent an arrow winging toward another rabbit.

"Now we have two," he said, bending to pick up the furry carcass. "That is enough for two meals. We can go home."

Although she had had enough of killing, she wondered aloud if they shouldn't shoot as many as they could to avoid hunting as often.

"No," he said. "We have enough dried meat already. And it is the way of the Apache to kill only what we need. Unlike the white man, who kills for pleasure," he added bitterly.

She was unable to dispute his words, so she followed silently behind him. She could understand his bitterness. And she could find no excuse for the things her people had done to his.

She was glad when he didn't pursue the subject. And that night, snuggled warm in their bed, he told her how proud he was of her achievements.

"You don't think I'm useless anymore," she teased, unable to hide her pleasure at his praise.

"Did I say you were?"

"You thought it."

"You weren't completely useless," he admitted. "You had a few hidden talents."

"Such as?"

"Such as . . . kissing. I have always liked your way of pleasing a man."

Her heart began to flutter wildly. "Have you?" she asked in a husky voice.

"Shall I show you?"

Before she could answer, his mouth claimed hers in a kiss of such intensity, it literally took her breath away. She was hardly aware of his fingers on the fastening of her dress, of his fingers pushing the soft doeskin aside to allow his lips access to the sensitive skin at the nape of her neck.

She gasped as his lips moved down, over the silken peaks of her breasts. Her eyes were laced with passion as his mouth closed over one of her tautened nipples.

Unable to lie passive beneath his touch, she threaded her fingers through his dark hair, holding him closer against her. He had the ability to arouse her body, to set her aflame with passion as no other man had ever done. The feeling she had had for Jesse had never been like this. She had thought she loved him, but she realized now that her love had been that of a sister. She admitted to herself that nothing would ever be able to compare with this overpowering love she felt for Swift Arrow.

Yes. She finally admitted it. She loved him. Totally. Desperately. And she needed him. Her body quaked with excitement as he suckled at her breast. Her hands slid beneath his shirt, smoothing across his bare skin. She needed to feel his flesh against her flesh. The wanting had become more than she could stand.

She pushed him away and he looked at her with puzzled eyes. Her fingers began to work desperately at the lacings on his shirt.

Understanding glittered in his eyes, and he helped her remove the offending garment. A moment later he was naked beside her. Then he pulled her dress over her head. Before he could come to her again, her mouth was on his body, tracing wet kisses across his chest. Her lips opened, closing over one taut, flat male nipple.

He stiffened with shock, then his large frame began to tremble as she worked at the nipple, at the same time running her soft hands across his body caressingly. Her hand moved between them, closing over his manhood, and he groaned loudly, his masculinity throbbing with unbridled passion.

She thrilled to the knowledge of the feeling she was stirring to life in his strong body. She had never realized a woman could stir such emotions in a man. It was a heady feeling.

When his fingers penetrated her moistness, she felt

an intense pleasure shoot through her. Trembling with desire, her tongue circled his nipple wetly.

He drew in a sharp breath. Then he bent and nipped the tender skin beneath her ear. While he worried the sensitive flesh, he gently massaged her throbbing, aching, inner core. Each move he made was designed to tease and torment her into submission.

Raising his head, he stared into her blazing eyes. She knew he was aware he could do as he wished with her, for her eyes issued the invitation.

When he claimed her lips, he started a raging fire burning deep inside her. Her arms slid around his neck, drawing him closer, ever closer to her. Her body craved the blending of their bodies. A fever raged in her blood. She knew the only way to quench the fire was to feel the oneness with him that she had felt before.

Never releasing her mouth, he slid her legs apart and thrust forward with urgency. As he entered her warm, throbbing body, she cried out her pleasure. It was muffled beneath his lips.

He began to move, slowly at first, then with a burning urgency that she felt deep within her own body. She seemed to be guided by some primitive instinct as she thrust her hips up to meet his.

They began to climb the mountain. Higher and higher they went, faster and faster, until, finally, they were soaring on the wings of eagles, bursting into flames as they reached their completion together.

They lay in the aftermath of their love, his arm about her waist, clasping her tight against his sweat-dampened skin.

Her heart swelled with love for him. Had there ever been such a man as he? She knew in that instant that no matter what happened in the future, she would always love this man.

Always. Forever.

But this, she swore to herself was a different kind of forever than that she'd pledged to Jesse.

Chapter Thirteen

When Katherine woke, she was immediately conscious of a sense of well-being. She felt warm and comfortable against Swift Arrow's body, and she arched sensuously. She turned her head and found his dark gaze on her.

There was a stillness about him, a watching, as though he wasn't sure how she was going to react.

"Good morning," she whispered, raising her hand to trace the outline of his lips. "Do I get a kiss this morning?"

His body relaxed and he lowered his mouth to claim hers in a kiss of such infinite sweetness it brought a lump to her throat.

When he broke the kiss and lifted his head, she sighed deeply and snuggled closer against him.

He laughed softly above her head. "Do you intend to

sleep away the morning?" he teased.

"Actually, I had other things in mind to do with it," she replied, curving a hand across his hip.

She felt his reaction almost immediately. His body tightened against hers, but instead of gathering her against him, Swift Arrow pushed the cover away and exposed their naked flesh to the cold morning air.

"What are you doing?" she protested, reaching for the covers.

He kissed the end of her nose. "Getting up," he said.

"Why?"

"We have much to do this morning," he said, reaching for their clothing and tossing her dress at her.

"What's so urgent?"

"I must go hunting," he said.

"We can do it later," she suggested huskily.

He had one foot in his breeches already. He paused and flicked a quick look at her. His gaze darkened as it rested on her flushed face. Then, he sighed and slid his leg into his pants. "No," he said. "Now is the time. The sun is shining and the animals will be out of hiding. It will make the hunt easier." He pulled the breeches up and fastened them. "Make haste," he said.

"Slavedriver," she muttered, pulling the dress over her head. "We already have more time than we need."

"Are you complaining?"

"Me? Complain?" She deliberately widened her eyes. "Little good it would do me." Although she had started out teasing, resentment crept into her voice. "You don't really care about my wishes. You always do what you want." She supposed it was one of the differences in

132

their way of life. And one that she would have to accept if they were to find happiness together.

He had been pulling on his moccasins, but at her words his body tensed and he turned to look at her. "Do you still wish to return to your father?" he asked.

"Do you need to ask?"

"No." His voice held a tinge of bitterness. "I know your wishes." He tugged on the last moccasin and turned to look down at her through narrowed eyes. "I have not changed my mind," he said. "I won't take you back."

Katherine's movements stilled. She stared at him in confusion. He held her gaze with glittering eyes, then with a harsh exclamation, turned to leave.

"Swift Arrow?" she called.

But there was no one to hear. The room was empty.

I won't take you back.

Was it possible he still believed she wanted to return to her father? Obviously he did, she answered herself. She reached for her moccasins, determined to let him know he was wrong as soon as possible.

Swift Arrow berated himself as he watched the flames lick at the wood. Why had he been such a fool as to mention her father? Until then she had been warm, pliable. It took only one word about her father to remind her. Would she never put him from her mind?

Perhaps he was fooling himself that she would come to accept her fate. She had told him many times that she wished to return to the fort. Was he being selfish in keeping her against her will?

Perhaps. But he would not let her go; he *could* not. She had become too important to him. If she were to leave, his life would hold nothing but emptiness. Until he found Katherine, he had not realized how alone he was. He had not intended to let her become the focal point of his life, but, somehow, it had happened. Life without her would be bleak, empty.

No. He would not let her go.

Instead, he would keep her. And he would use patience. In time, she must come to accept him as her fate.

A rustling sounded in the stack of supplies near the courtyard wall. His eyes narrowed, fell on one of the parfleches just as it moved.

Something was foraging in the pack for food.

Rising swiftly, Swift Arrow moved on silent feet toward the leather bag. As though the thing inside had sensed his presence, the bag stilled. He reached out a long arm and pulled the opening apart.

A sharp snout appeared from the bag, followed by a bushy, silver-gray head with two small beady black eyes looking out from a black mask.

It was a raccoon. More than likely it had climbed from the spruce tree to the ledge. Its fur would make a nice warm cap for Katherine, Swift Arrow decided. He drew his knife from its sheath.

"No!" Katherine cried sharply, at his elbow. "Don't kill it."

He looked around at her. "Why?" he asked. "Its coat would keep your head warm."

"I wouldn't wear a cap made from its fur." She shuddered. "And look at it, Swift Arrow. It doesn't seem to be frightened at all." She reached out a hand, palm up, toward the creature. "Hello, there," she crooned. "What've you been up to?"

"Eating our food," Swift Arrow answered drily, indicating the half-eaten pemmican in one of the creature's tiny paws.

"Surely you don't begrudge him that little thing," she said. "We've plenty to spare."

He shrugged. "It seems you have been given back your life," he told the animal. "I hope you are properly grateful."

The raccoon cocked his head and studied each of them. It seemed in no hurry to leave.

Emboldened, Katherine moved her hand nearer to the creature. Swift Arrow caught and held it in his own. "If you feel the raccoon must be touched, then I will do it," he said. "The animal will not find my finger so easy to bite off."

He reached out cautiously. When the animal paid no attention, Swift Arrow picked it up. The pemmican fell to the ground and the raccoon's eyes followed it, but it offered no objection and seemed to be totally unafraid of the two humans confronting it.

Katherine could keep her distance no longer. She put the palm of her hand on the raccoon's furry head and stroked it lightly. The animal made a light chattering noise . . . almost like a purr.

"Look, Swift Arrow," she said. "It's not going to bite me. Please let me hold it."

"Be careful," he said, handing the raccoon to her.

She held the animal close against her. "Let's give it a name," she said. "Let's call it Blackie."

One dark brow lifted. "You would give a name to this creature?" Swift Arrow asked.

"Certainly," she said. "It's going to live here with us. And we can't keep saying *it* all the time. Not if it's going to be a pet."

"The raccoon is a creature of the wild, Katherine," he reasoned. "You cannot make a pet of it. If we are not going to make use of the animal's fur, then it must be allowed to go free."

"I won't restrict its freedom," she pouted. "But surely I can feed it when it comes around." She tilted the animal's head up and looked at it. "Can't I, Blackie?" she asked the raccoon.

The raccoon's eyes glittered up at her, and it moved restlessly, its claws scraping against her doeskin dress.

"Put it down, Katherine," Swift Arrow said. "Or else it will claw you."

Stooping over, she lowered the animal to the ground and watched as it snatched up the half-eaten pemmican patty and scampered up on the courtyard wall. Its gaze fixed on Katherine and Swift Arrow, the raccoon ate, taking tiny bites until the food was gone. The coon washed its hands with its wet, pink tongue when it was finished.

"Isn't it sweet, Swift Arrow?"

"I do not know what you mean by this word," he said with a frown.

"Uh . . ." Katherine thought for a moment. She had never been asked to define sweet and for a moment couldn't think of how to do so. "It means . . . clever and . . ." She stopped, and flicked a quick glance at him. "It's hard to explain," she said.

At times like these, she felt very aware of the differences in their cultures. "It's like when a baby takes his first step. . . ." She stopped, frowned. "No," she said. "I guess it's not like that at all."

"Never mind," he said. "I can see you have a fondness for the animal. I will accept that." He smiled at her. "I will even share our food with it . . ." his voice grew husky, ". . . for you."

"You will?" She felt almost breathless, as though she had been running.

"Yes. I will." His glittering gaze held hers as he lifted a lock of her silky hair, letting it slide slowly through his fingers. "Katherine," he whispered huskily. "You are very beautiful."

"Swift Arrow," she murmured. "About before . . ." She stopped, unsure how to continue. "I—I don't want you to think . . . I don't want to return to my father."

"You don't?"

"No." She held his gaze steadily. "I want nothing more than to stay with you."

His eyes glittered down at her. "Do you mean it?" he asked throatily.

"Yes. I do."

He pulled her tight against him. "Is it too much to hope that you care for me?"

137

Her cheeks flushed with confusion. Did she have to be the one to declare herself first? She cleared her throat. "We-ell . . ."

"Katherine?"

"Well—yes," she admitted shyly. "I guess I really do."

"Then I am pleased."

To her absolute astonishment, he released her abruptly, and turned away. "I will get some fresh water while you cook our meal."

Snatching up the water container, he left the courtyard and strode across to where the ledge made a curve.

Although she knew he had found a source of water, she had never been there, for the cliff overhang narrowed at the curve, and several feet of snow had accumulated. Katherine knew it was unreasonable, but she had a fear of the snow pulling loose from the cliff and herself plunging to the canyon floor with it.

Swift Arrow felt Katherine's gaze on him. He knew he had confused her and he was well aware that she was ready to return to their bed with him. But he was confused himself. Somehow, he couldn't say the words she wanted to hear. He still wasn't sure of his feelings for her. He knew he wanted her, felt he must keep her with him.

But was it love?

Even if it was, wouldn't telling her give her too much

power over him?

She had told him she cared for him, that she no longer wished to return to her father. But that was in the flush of her burgeoning womanhood. Once the newness of their lovemaking had dimmed, would she still choose to stay with him? Especially if she were presented with the opportunity to leave? He didn't know. And until he did, his feelings for her would remain undeclared.

When he reached the spring, he dipped the water container in and filled it to the brim, then he returned to their campsite.

Katherine looked up from the pot she was stirring. "Blackie's decided to make himself at home," she said.

The raccoon had built a nest on the bags of supplies and was reaching into the parfleche for another pemmican patty.

"Stay out of that," Swift Arrow commanded, swatting the animal's paw.

As the creature looked up at him, Swift Arrow closed the bag and fastened it up.

"That raccoon will have to be watched to see it doesn't ruin our supplies," he said with a frown. "If it proves to be any trouble, I will throw it to the wolves."

"You wouldn't!"

"Yes. I would," he said. "These animals are pests, Katherine. They can be trained, but it takes much persistence."

"Let it stay," she said. "I'll make it mind." She turned to Blackie and picked him up. "The wolves would eat it."

"Yes. It is the time of the cold and food is hard to find. That is the way of nature."

"Then I must keep it," she said. "It will have to stay with us."

"Only if we can train it," Swift Arrow said grimly.

"Do you hear that, Blackie?" She looked into the animal's black eyes. "You've got to mind or you'll be food for the wolves."

Pulling its head away from her, the raccoon pressed its cold nose against her neck. She stroked her hand across its back. She could almost have sworn the animal understood her and was depending on her for its protection. And she was determined not to let it down.

"How old do you think it is?" she asked.

He shrugged. "I do not know. But it is not yet fully grown. When it is, it will look for a mate."

"A mate?" She looked startled. She hadn't thought of that. "Is it a male or female?" she asked.

He took the raccoon from her, turned it over, then grinned. "I should have known," he said, putting the raccoon on the ground.

"What?" she asked.

"He is a male."

"Why should you have known."

His dark eyes sparkled. "He seems to enjoy being held by you. As any male would."

Despite her efforts, a flush reddened her cheeks. She turned back to her cooking pot. "Stop teasing me and wash up," she ordered. "The meal is ready to be dished up."

Although his look spoke volumes, he turned away to do her bidding. She couldn't help feeling a slight disappointment. She knew it wouldn't have taken much effort on his part to persuade her to leave the meal until later. With a wistful sigh, she picked up the bowls and began to ladle out food.

Chapter Fourteen

The afternoon sun was warm against her skin as Katherine sat on the courtyard wall putting the finishing touches on the beaded buckskin shirt she was making Swift Arrow. He had supplied her with needle, thread, and a bag of colored beads, then left her to do the rest while he made himself scarce.

Her sewing was constantly interrupted by Blackie, who kept stealing her beads. She was glad the raccoon had found his way to them, for she found him to be a constant source of amusement.

She had no idea how long Swift Arrow had been gone when his voice intruded on her concentration.

"Put down your sewing, Katherine, and come with me to the spring."

Looking up from her work, she found Swift Arrow standing beside her.

"I wondered where you'd disappeared to," she said, poking the threaded needle through the soft leather one more time before laying the needlework aside on the courtyard wall.

Reaching down his long arm, Swift Arrow grasped her wrist and pulled her to her feet. "Come with me," he repeated. "You have yet to see the spring. And it is a beautiful place."

She flicked a frowning glance toward the narrowed ledge. It had not changed one smidgen. The snow was still several feet deep and looked the same as before. Dangerous.

"I think I'd rather wait a while yet," she hedged. "Until the snow has melted away."

"There is no danger."

Reluctantly, she allowed him to lead her across the ledge. She hesitated when they reached the point where the cliff curved.

Swift Arrow mounted the pile of frozen snow, then paused, looking back and over his shoulders. When he saw she hadn't moved, he stopped.

"Why do you hesitate?" he asked. "There is nothing to fear."

She flicked an uncertain glance toward the bottom of the canyon far below them. Her stomach lurched. She shook her head at him, unable to speak. If the snow pulled loose she would fall to the canyon floor. She was certain of it.

She licked lips that had suddenly gone dry. A fall from such a distance would mean certain death. She tried to calm her fears, unwilling to appear cowardly to him.

He stood waiting, his dark eyes never leaving her. He represented all the strength, all the security that existed in her life. Because of him she was alive now. He wouldn't take her where it wasn't safe to go.

Gathering her courage around her, she stepped onto the frozen snow.

Each step she took seemed an eternity. Katherine was almost afraid to breathe for fear it would cause the snow to melt. As she rounded the bend the overhang above them widened, providing a protective roof. There was hardly any snow left on the path, making it much easier to traverse.

She followed Swift Arrow along the tan limestone cliffs to the head of the box canyon. As they drew closer to the closed end of the canyon, the scrubby oak trees growing beside the trail gave way to tall, sturdy trees of both pine and oak. She remarked on this to Swift Arrow.

"There is a plentiful supply of water," he said.

"A plentiful supply?" She stared at him, confused. "I thought there was just a spring."

"It is much more than a spring," he said. "Look." He stopped and pointed ahead.

She looked, blinked in amazement, then looked again. Beyond the trees, almost hidden from view, a thin sheet of water fell from the cliff, splashing gently onto the protruding ledge below. As they drew nearer, she could see an open cavern behind the waterfall. In the cavern was a pool of water.

"It's unbelievable," Katherine whispered in awe.

145

"Why hasn't it frozen over?"

"It must be very cold before the running water will freeze. When it does, there is still water bubbling up from beneath the earth into the spring. The run-off has formed a natural pool."

She moved closer, enchanted with the waterfall and the pool beneath the cliff. "I would love a bath," she said wistfully.

"Then have one," he suggested.

"But it's too cold."

"How much is too cold?"

She smiled up at him. Trust him to ask a question like that. How did you define *too cold*?

She didn't try. Instead she said, "I don't dare have a bath. The water must be like ice."

"Perhaps. But we will not let that trouble us. Wait here for me."

Puzzled, she sat down on a rock beside the pool and watched him stride back up the path toward the cliff dwellings.

When he had disappeared from view, she returned her attention to the pool. Her reflection showed her hair to be disheveled and dirty. But she wasn't surprised. It had been a week or more since she had washed it. Dismissing the dirty hair she watched fish swim lazily past her reflection.

Fish?

It took her a moment to comprehend what had caused her to pause. Then elation filled her as she realized they could eat fresh fish.

And . . . perhaps even frog's legs. She frowned. She

didn't see any frogs. Shouldn't there be?

At that moment Swift Arrow returned carrying a blanket. She asked him about the frogs.

"The frogs are sleeping."

"Sleeping?" Her expression was puzzled. "What do you mean?"

"They are having a long sleep. It is always so when the snow comes."

When the snow comes.

Sudden comprehension dawned. "Are they hibernating?" He obviously didn't understand. "Like the bears?" she asked.

He nodded.

"I didn't know anything else hibernated besides the bears."

He laughed. "All cold-blooded creatures hibernate," he told her. "Frogs are such a one. Like the lizard, they cannot take the cold."

"Where do they go?"

"They dig into the earth around the pools of water. Also they hide under rocks."

With the question answered, her eyes went to the blanket he was still holding. "What are you going to do with that?" she asked.

"Like a child, you are full of questions," he teased. Tossing the blanket down, he turned to her. "Stand up," he said. "And remove your clothing."

She gasped. Her color fluctuated madly. When she didn't move, his fingers came out to unfasten her dress.

"What are you doing?" she cried, as his knuckles brushed her breasts.

147

"Surely you do not wish to take a bath with your clothing on."

"No. But I—"

"Then let me remove them."

She didn't know what he meant to do. But a bath would feel heavenly. While she was still considering his words, his fingers were busy with the leather fastenings on her dress. The cold wind hit her as he pulled it over her head and tossed it aside.

She shivered.

"We must hurry," he said, his fingers fumbling with her undergarments. "You cannot be long in the wind. You will get a chill."

Blushing, she removed the rest of her clothing, turning away from him when she added her chemise and pantalettes to the other garments.

When she turned, she found him naked. Her gray eyes widened in shock. She drew in a sharp breath. Did he intend to make love to her in the snow? She found the idea oddly pleasing.

Swift Arrow wrapped his arms around her and pulled her against his body. Then he stepped beneath the spray of water.

Katherine gasped as the shock of the icy water hit her. "It-it's c-cold," she chattered, struggling in his arms.

"Keep still," he commanded, holding her tighter against him.

Immediately the warmth of his body began to penetrate and she stopped struggling against him. Her front side was getting remarkably warm, and she could feel his manhood rising against her stomach, doing strange things to her body.

He lifted his hand and began to rub his fist in her hair.

"What are you doing?"

"Washing your hair."

"With your fist? I don't think that's enough. We need some soap."

He grinned. "We have no need of such things. The root of the yucca plant will cleanse your hair just as easily."

"The root of the yucca plant? Is that what you're using?"

He nodded, his hand never pausing in its scrubbing. Finally, he released her to use both hands in her hair. Immediately she felt the cold water between their bodies and wrapped her arms around him to pull his warmth closer to her again. She heard him suck in his breath but ignored it.

When he had rinsed her hair he rubbed the yucca root across her skin, stoking the fire that had begun to burn deep within her body. Then, using one hand to rinse the suds from her body, he cupped the other one around her chin and lifted her face to his.

Her thick lashes lifted, and her silver-gray eyes met his dark, turbulent gaze. She couldn't move; she couldn't even breathe as she stared, mesmerized, at him.

When he lifted her into his arms she rested her head in the curve of his neck. A few minutes later he laid her on the blanket and joined her, his flesh against her flesh, his breath soft against her face.

She stared up at him with an unnamed longing shining for him to see. He stared at her with a feverish need in his gaze that she knew must be reflected in hers. She felt an urgent need to touch him, to know every inch of his body.

Giving in to the urge, her hands began to roam, touching, caressing him all over. She stroked the ridged muscles of his stomach, then moved her fingers over the hard length of his thigh.

He sucked in his breath sharply, and his body began to tremble. Unable to resist, she slid her fingers around the throbbing heat of his maleness, and he groaned deep in his throat.

"Don't," he gasped. "You must not touch me so."

"Why?" she asked softly.

"Because I will not be able to last," he ground out. "I will not be able to make it good for you."

Withdrawing her hand from his body, he began to caress her. His hand found its way between them and his fingers began to stroke her lightly. She sucked in her breath as ripples of sheer pleasure streaked through her. She pressed closer to him, yielding her softness up to him. The sweet possession of his touch spread through her like liquid sunshine.

His mouth closed on hers, and the roughness of his tongue found the inner sweetness of her mouth. As he continued his stroking, her hips rubbed urgently against his. She was desperate to have him assuage her aching need.

"Hurry," she whispered hoarsely. "I can't wait any

longer. Please, Swift Arrow, take me now."

He needed no further urging. She felt the full, hot length of him as his body penetrated hers. He filled her completely with his strength. And then he began to move. Slowly, at first. Moving lightly, keeping her wanting more, feeling just a moment away from satisfaction.

She clutched his hips tightly, urging him onward, lifting her hips to meet his thrusts, forcing him deeper and deeper into her body, faster and faster as they moved in time with the beat of their hearts.

Suddenly, he went wild. He grabbed her buttocks with both hands, holding her tightly as his thrusts became almost frantic, sending her soaring high upon the wings of an eagle.

As Katherine felt the gathering intensity, rippling sensations spread through her body like wildfire, spreading out in thundering waves until they burst from her in a shuddering pleasure that found voice in a high keening sound. At the same moment Swift Arrow uttered a cry of triumph, then collapsed on her and lay still, his arms holding her tightly against him.

Katherine lifted her head and kissed him gently. She felt her heart would burst with the love she felt for this man. And although he had never told her he loved her, surely it wasn't possible that he could feel anything else, not after the ecstasy they had just shared together.

Chapter Fifteen

The warm winds had blown in and the snow had begun to melt in the mountains. Blackie had become restless and often strayed from the camp to forage for food on the canyon floor below.

Katherine watched Swift Arrow as he sat on a rock and bent over his whittling. The carved figure of a duck was slowly taking shape beneath his knife.

She was well pleased with the way he had progressed with his English lessons. She had expected it to take much longer than it had. She looked at his bowed head, resisting the urge to coax him back to their bed. Like Blackie, she had become restless. She didn't know what to attribute it to, but for some reason, she kept remembering what Swift Arrow had said about his friend who had left the supplies in the *kiva*.

"What happened to the girl your friend brought

here?" she asked, keeping her voice casual.

"Nothing."

"Did she return to her family?"

"No. She is with Lone Wolf, her husband. As she should be."

He seemed to be totally unconcerned at the fate of the white girl. Did you expect otherwise? she asked herself. He's never pretended to have any love for your people. Or you.

A lump formed in her throat. Had the girl come to love her captor, as she herself had?

For some reason, the question tormented her. Unable to stop herself, she asked Swift Arrow, "Did she ever come to love him?"

"I do not know."

Or care?

"How long has it been?" she asked. At his questioning look, she added. "Since your friend was here."

"Seven summers."

"Seven summ . . ." Her eyes grew round with horror. "That's seven years," she burst out.

"Yes. That is the white man's way of counting." He looked at her curiously. "Why?"

She swallowed around the lump in her throat. "Did she ever try to escape from him?"

"Many times. But it made no difference. Lone Wolf always found her. He would never let her go. She belongs to him."

As I belong to you? But the question remained unasked.

Her breathing felt constricted as she stared at him.

154

How long would he keep her with him? Years? Or would it be only a matter of months before he tired of her? She didn't really know that much about him. She paled as a thought occurred to her.

Perhaps he even had a wife!

God, no!

She quickly dismissed the thought. If he had a wife, he would not have been traveling alone. *Would he?*

She flicked a quick glance at him, but he seemed not to notice. His face was expressionless as he continued to whittle on the wood.

She tried to make her voice sound casual. "Where were you going when you found me?"

"To the mountains," he said, slicing another curl of wood from his carving and blowing the shavings away.

"But where?"

"Just the mountains." He flicked a glance at her. "Why?"

"No reason. Just curious."

He resumed his whittling.

"Have you never thought of taking a wife?" The words popped out of her mouth before she could call them back. Spots of color appeared on her cheeks.

He raised his head and she recognized the humor that glinted in his eyes. "Did I say I have no wife?"

Pain stabbed through her, and her cheeks lost their color. "Do you?" she asked faintly.

"You are full of questions." He threw an oblique look at her. "And you take much for granted."

"You don't exactly act married," she muttered.

He didn't answer. Instead, he gave her a slow smile,

one that succeeded only in irritating her.

Her soft mouth set stubbornly, and she held his gaze. "Are you?" she persisted.

He raised an eyebrow. "No." A deep chuckle escaped him and spread into a wide grin.

A wave of anger washed over her. Damn him! He was laughing at her.

"I fail to see what amuses you," she said coldly, thrusting her chin out at a defiant angle.

"Is it not better to be amused then to grow angry at your demands?"

"I'm not making demands! The only thing I've ever asked of you was to take me home."

"You are home," he said in a hard voice. "It is best you forget you ever had a father. You will never return to him."

Never? Her eyes glittered. There was something in the tone of his voice that she hadn't heard before. She couldn't quite put her finger on it. But when he spoke of her father . . .

"What have you got against my father?"

He put the knife down and left her. She watched him walk to the edge of the cliff and stare down into the valley below. Her heart filled with dread. She should leave it alone. But somehow, she couldn't.

She followed him. "What have you got against him?" she asked again.

He turned to look at her. "He killed my mother."

The words fell like stones between them. Her body grew still. Leave it alone, her heart cried. You don't want to know. But her mind refused to listen.

"How?" she whispered.

"What does it matter how he did it?"

"But how did he know her? Why would he kill her?"

"She was Apache. For your father that was enough. The raid he led killed my mother and my sister and ten others of our tribe."

"But he only led the raid. Surely he didn't kill them himself."

"It does not matter that his was not the finger on the trigger. He killed them. Then he herded those who were not dead back to the reservation. If my father had not come for me, I too might be like Running Horse, an Apache too weak to live the life of our ancestors."

"Is that the reason you've kept me with you?" she asked, her voice strained.

His eyes were watchful as he answered her. "Yes."

"I see."

Katherine felt as though she had been kicked in the stomach. She averted her eyes quickly, unwilling for him to see the pain he had inflicted.

Turning away, she picked up the water jug. "We need water," she said. "I will fetch it." She hurried away before he had time to say more.

A deep sadness filled Katherine's being as she left the cliff dwellings and made for the spring. The water had only been an excuse to escape from Swift Arrow. She didn't want him to see how deeply his words had wounded her.

She had been living a dream, a dream that had suddenly turned into a nightmare. She had fallen in love with a man who didn't love her. A man who had only kept her with him to punish her father.

She had thought he loved her, but she had been mistaken. She had thought she'd found happiness. Again she was mistaken. Would she never learn?

A bitter laugh escaped her lips. Swift Arrow didn't know that his efforts to hurt her father had been in vain. Her father didn't care about her; he cared for nothing except his career.

A squirrel ran down a tree and into her path. She automatically stepped around it, paying it little heed. Her mind was in turmoil. What could she do? She was in love with a man who didn't care a thing for her.

She knew he desired her. But desire without love was empty, she told herself. Tears welled up and spilled down her cheeks. She wiped them away with the backs of her hands.

Swift Arrow didn't love her, and the day would come when he would grow tired of her. When that happened, what would become of her?

Exactly what did an Apache warrior do with an unwanted possession?

He sold it.

Oh, God! Was that what her future held? Would he really sell her? No, her heart cried. Swift Arrow wouldn't do a thing like that. Despite what he said, he had to care a little for her.

Didn't he?

She blinked rapidly, clearing the moisture from her eyes. Dipping the water container in the spring, she filled it with water. Then she made her way back to the camp.

It was empty.

Where could he have gone?

She set the water container down on the wall and picked up the wood carving he had discarded. The duck's wings were spread in flight. Swift Arrow had nearly finished the carving. It was a beautiful piece of work.

She ran her fingers lovingly over the smooth lines, then put it back down.

Knowing she would feel better staying busy, she picked up the hide from which she had decided to make a new pair of moccasins. Spreading it out on the rock floor, she laid the pieces of an old pair on it. Then, using the knife Swift Arrow had given her, she began to cut out the new moccasins.

Although she tried to push thoughts of their conversation from her mind, she didn't have much luck. His words kept surfacing, over and over again.

Your father killed my mother.

Her father had a lot to account for. Perhaps it was only right that she try to pay his debts.

The hour was late when Swift Arrow returned. She had begun to wonder if he would come back at all. But of course she should have known he would. After all, he saw her as a way to punish her father.

He took one look at her mutinous face, then tossed the doe he was carrying across his shoulders onto the ground.

"Dress it out," he commanded.

Her eyes widened. He had always dressed his kills out himself. Why had he suddenly decided to have her do it?

He's showing you who's the master.

Dawning realization brought fury surging forth.

"Do it yourself," she snapped.

His dark eyes glittered. "I will not stand for a disobedient woman, Katherine. You will dress out the doe."

She stood before him, her hands on her hips. "And what will you do if I refuse?" she taunted. "Will you sell me? Trade me off the same as you would any other unwanted possession?"

His lips tightened. "Perhaps it would serve me better to do just that," he said grimly. "A disobedient woman is something I do not need."

Her face drained of color and she stood stunned. He had admitted it! He was thinking about discarding her like so much unwanted garbage.

He stared at her pale face and something flickered in his dark eyes. He reached out a hand toward her, then stopped, letting it drop to his side.

"I am going to the spring," he growled. "When I return, I expect you to have that doe cleaned."

The hardest thing he ever had to do was to walk away from her. She looked stricken. He knew that his harsh words had hurt her. Especially after hearing how he felt about her father.

He wanted to take her in his arms and tell her he didn't mean it, but he knew she must learn who was in control. He had allowed Katherine her way too often already. Perhaps that was the reason she was not content to stay with him.

His father was a wise man and he had told his son never to allow a woman to think she was in control. Such a relationship could never be happy. Swift Arrow had seen the truth of his father's words many times in his village. And he did not intend for such a thing to happen to them.

He rounded the ledge and made his way to the spring at the head of the box canyon. Discarding his clothing, he stepped beneath the waterfall and let the spray cool his heated body.

Perhaps they should leave this place and travel to his village. He had no doubt that Katherine could benefit from being among the women of his tribe. An Apache woman's role in life differed greatly from that of the women with the pale skin.

Just the thought of leaving the city of his ancestors where he had found so much happiness filled him with regret. He had thought Katherine was happy, too, but perhaps he had been wrong.

Sighing, Swift Arrow left the cooling spray and donned his buckskin breeches. He shouldn't have been so harsh with her. He would return to the cliff dwellings and help her with the deer. He didn't like it when there was discord between them.

Regret flickered in his eyes. She was probably crying her eyes out while she struggled to clean the deer. With his mind made up, he returned to the cliff dwellings.

As he rounded the bend, his gaze fell on the deer lying in the courtyard where he had left it. Otherwise,

161

the courtyard was empty.

Where was Katherine?

Why was she not working to clean the doe?

His heart gave a leap of fear. Had something happened to her? Had she perhaps cut herself while attempting to clean the animal as he had ordered?

"Katherine," he called, striding swiftly across the courtyard to the room where they slept.

Silence.

"Katherine!"

He ducked his head and entered the room.

His pulse went wild. She lay face down on the bed of furs, her hair tousled as though she had thrown herself there.

Was she injured . . . or crying?

"Katherine?" he said hesitantly.

When she didn't move, he touched her shoulder. She spun away from him quickly.

"Don't touch me!"

"What happened?" he asked harshly. "Did you hur—"

"Not a damn thing happened!" she snapped, her eyes flashing with temper. "And nothing's going to happen either. I'm not your slave. And I'm not going to clean that . . . that *damn* deer. If you want it done, then do it yourself!"

Swift Arrow's surprise quickly gave way to fury. He didn't see the hurt behind her anger. He only saw the front she had thrown up to cover it. And he didn't like it one bit.

Grabbing her arm with fingers of steel, he yanked her

162

to her feet and dragged her out into the courtyard. He didn't stop until he was beside the deer.

"Clean the deer," he ordered savagely.

"I won't do it," she said stubbornly. "And you can't make me."

"Yes I can," he said grimly. "And you won't like how I do it." His fingers dug into her shoulders as he shook her roughly. "You are not dealing with a white man who has no way of controlling his woman. I am an Apache warrior, and I will not stand for disobedience."

She stared up into his glittering eyes and fear spread through her. She struggled against his grip. "Let me go," she cried. "Turn me loose."

"No. Not until you learn to obey me."

She swallowed around a lump in her throat. And suddenly the fight drained out of her. Her lips quivered. Her shoulders slumped with defeat. "All right," she said. When he released her, she sank to her knees beside the deer and picked the knife up off the floor.

He had won, but for some reason it gave him no satisfaction. With an oath, he left her there and disappeared over the ledge.

Chapter Sixteen

A deep sadness filled Katherine's heart as she watched Swift Arrow go. He was so angry with her. And for a moment she had really been frightened. She tended to forget he wasn't from her world. Perhaps she shouldn't have defied him.

It wasn't that she really minded cleaning the deer. She would gladly have done anything he asked of her. But there lay her problem. He hadn't *asked* her to do anything.

He had *ordered*. And coming on top of what she had learned about her father . . . and Swift Arrow's reasons for keeping her, it had been more than she could take. Her hurt had erupted, taking the form of anger.

She shouldn't have yelled.

She would apologize when he returned. She would make him understand how much she loved him and how deeply he had hurt her. She would . . .

Her chin lifted, and her eyes began to glitter. She dropped the knife and it clattered against the stone floor of the courtyard.

Why should she apologize to him? She had done nothing to apologize for. Besides, she was only a possession. And possessions couldn't apologize.

For a while they had been happy, but it seemed that time had come to an end. If only she had been able to make him love her. To him she was no different than his horse, or his rifle. He used them while they gave pleasure. When they didn't, he got rid of them.

She wasn't a horse, dammit! She had a brain. And she would use it. Her gray eyes narrowed, becoming hard. She stood up, her nails digging into the palms of her hands as she paced the cavern. She strode to the ledge and stared down into the valley far below.

Swift Arrow had completely disappeared from sight. Her heart lay heavy in her breast as she wondered what to do. She lifted her anguished eyes to the heavens. Why did she always have to love those she couldn't have?

As she turned away from the ledge, a movement in the distance caught her attention and she narrowed her gaze, straining her eyes.

Cavalry!

She was certain of it, even though she could barely make out the column of soldiers.

There lay her escape. She would not have to find her way to the fort—only to the soldiers who searched for her.

A deep sadness settled over her at the thought of never seeing Swift Arrow again. But she knew she had no choice. It was time for her to go. She must return to her own people.

She looked down at her buckskin dress. The cavalry must not know about Swift Arrow. She would tell them she had survived on her own.

Without giving herself time to change her mind, she found her riding habit and quickly put it on. Then she gathered up a few supplies . . . a blanket, a canteen of water, a leather pouch of dried jerky . . . and her bow and quiver of arrows. No. She couldn't take the bow and arrows. There was no way her father would believe she had made it herself. She settled instead for Swift Arrow's extra knife.

Her mind dwelt for a moment on the raccoon. What would Blackie do when he returned to find her gone? Would he stay with Swift Arrow and keep him company? She hoped so.

With one last look at the place where she had found love . . . and lost it, she left the ruins of the ancient civilization and eased herself over the ledge.

When she reached the valley below, she began her journey at an angle, hoping to cut the troopers off before night.

The snow was almost gone, and tufts of green grass were breaking through the soil in spots. In other places she found herself floundering through mud, making the going rough. It took Katherine two hours of hard travel to reach the forest. And she knew several miles still separated her from the cavalry.

167

Katherine blocked all thought from her mind. She had no time to spare on regrets. She had only one thought in mind. To reach the cavalry before they outdistanced her.

She did not give up until night began to fall. By then she had become hopelessly lost.

She came to a stream of water and knelt to drink. Cupping her hands, she dipped up a handful of water and splashed her face. Then she slumped down with her back against the trunk of a Ponderosa pine and wrapped her arms around her legs. Her heart felt battered and bruised. She would never see Swift Arrow again. Tears of grief blinded her and she lay her head on her knees. After a while, her sobbing turned into an occasional hiccup. Minutes later she was fast asleep.

Sometime in the night, she woke up. A terrible loneliness filled her being as she looked up at the star-studded night. With a heavy sigh, she pulled the blanket over her, stretched out on the grass, and closed her eyes. She slept the sleep of exhaustion.

She didn't see the deer that stepped out of the brush and lowered its head to drink. Or the squirrel that scampered down a tree. She didn't hear the owl hoot or the answer it received farther in the forest. She remained asleep, impervious to the sounds that filled the night.

Swift Arrow frowned as he threw the rabbit down in the courtyard. Except for Blackie, who was asleep on the courtyard wall, the dwellings were empty.

168

"Katherine?" he called, an uneasy feeling flooding over him.

The raccoon lifted his head and looked up at him, but nothing broke the silence.

A sense of urgency swept over Swift Arrow. His long strides carried him swiftly to the spring.

It was empty, as well.

Where had Katherine gone? The memory of his harsh words surfaced. Had she run away from him?

He felt as though an arrow had pierced his heart. The pain stabbed through him, leaving a great open ache behind it. How could she have left him? He had returned with an apology on his lips. And she was not there to receive it.

He was a fool.

The woman had enchanted him. For a little while the world had been a different place. Life had taken on meaning with her by his side. But she was fickle. She had deserted him. The way to a woman's heart was not to be patient and loving. He had been too weak. He should have commanded her. Ordered her to obey. A woman did not want a weak man she could sway. She wanted a strong man who took what he wanted.

So be it!

She could not have gone far.

He would find her.

And she would no longer find him biddable.

He would be the man she wanted. And she would eventually give him her heart.

He would not lose her. *He would not!*

Even though she was a paleface, she meant too much

to him. He knew life without her would be unbearable.

When she woke the sun was bursting over the treetops, covering them with gold.

Uttering a groan, Katherine moved to the water and washed her face. It refreshed her slightly.

She refilled her water canteen, ate a piece of dried venison, and resumed her journey.

Keeping her eyes on the sun, Katherine traveled southeast, knowing it was in that direction that she would eventually find the river. And from there, she could surely find her way back to the fort.

Katherine walked until she was too tired to travel farther before she stopped to rest. She allowed herself only a few moments to catch her breath before she resumed her journey.

Her heart was heavy as she put more and more distance between Swift Arrow and herself. What had he thought when he found her gone? Did he care?

As she had expected, she found the river. She heard it long before she saw it. But she still wasn't prepared for what she found.

Katherine's eyes widened in dismay as she stared at the river. When they had crossed it before, it had been shallow. But the melting snow at the higher elevations had caused it to rise. Now it was swollen and out of its banks. There was no way she could cross it.

Perhaps she should turn back.

Fool! You're just looking for an excuse. Would you return to a man who will only cast you aside when he's had his fill?

No! She had more pride than that!

Hitching her supplies higher on her shoulders, she turned her steps down the river. She had no choice except to travel that way until she found a place to cross. She traveled all morning. Then, to her dismay, the canyon narrowed, and the river plunged over a ledge to a foaming pool fifteen feet below.

She stopped, her anxious eyes searching for an answer . . . a way down.

Evergreen bushes made impenetrable thickets in spots. The only possible way would be the sparse growth of junipers clinging to the hillside. Her eyes narrowed. Perhaps she could get down by clinging to the trees for support.

It was certainly worth a try. The only alternative would be to retrace her steps. And that was unthinkable.

Without giving herself time to think, she started down the rugged hillside, slipping and sliding from one tree to another. She dug her heels into the ground as hard as she could, sliding a foot or more at a time.

Slipping, sliding, going farther down, down, clinging to one tree, then lowering herself to another. She stayed as close to the river as she could manage, looking for a place to cross. She had nearly reached the bottom when she came to a flat spot and stopped to rest on a flat rock that hung out over the water.

She had no more than sat down when she felt the rock shift, and then she was falling . . . falling . . .

She plunged into the icy water and her arms moved

swiftly as she fought her way to the surface. Her head reached the surface, and she coughed the muddy water out of her lungs, breathing in fresh air. Then she was caught by the current, rolled over, and pulled swiftly downstream.

Her arms worked frantically as she tried to stay on top. She saw a log heading toward her and reached out for it. Her fingers slid off, and she used every ounce of her nearly spent strength to propel herself toward the log. It struck the side of her head as she grabbed it, abrading her forehead, and then the churning water was carrying both the log and Katherine swiftly downstream.

She shivered in the cold as she was swept downriver. The journey through the debris-filled river became a never-ending nightmare. Katherine had no time for thought. She found it took all the effort she could summon to hang on to the log.

Although she was too exhausted to try to reach shore, Katherine clung stubbornly to the log. She had no hope for rescue. She was alone in the wilderness, but still, she refused to give up.

Time passed. She didn't know how long she'd been in the icy water, clinging to the log. She only knew that she couldn't hold on much longer. If help didn't come soon, it would be too late. The angry water foamed and rolled around her, trying to pry the log out of her chilled fingers. Blood streamed down her face from her forehead where the log had struck her.

She felt almost separated in mind from the girl who clung tenaciously, fighting for her life. It was as though she were only a casual observer, essentially uninvolved.

She watched as the girl lost her grip; watched as she was sucked under, the cold water swallowing her, enveloping her.

Katherine acknowledged the panic as her own body was twisted about, arms and feet working frantically, reaching for the surface where she grasped a single breath before she went under again. She could feel the panic, and yet, a strange sort of peace was washing over her.

Let go, she told the struggling girl. *Forget it. Just give in and it will soon be over.*

But even as the thought was born, Swift Arrow's face appeared before her and another sort of panic set in, surging through her mind, demanding recognition. She couldn't give in! She had to turn back. She had to see him again.

Kicking furiously, she clawed at the heavy walls of water above her. Her lungs were in agony, burning for air, but still she fought. Then she was free, breaking the surface as a solid wooden object crashed against her head. It was another log. Reaching out, she grabbed it and held on. She tried to keep her hold as the angry water fought to pull her free from it.

Chapter Seventeen

Katherine's fingers were numb with cold. She knew she couldn't hold on much longer. She shouted Swift Arrow's name, and thought she heard an answering shout. Her eyes searched frantically as her fingers slipped, then dug into the log. She thought her mind must be going when she saw a man on the riverbank.

Her gray eyes widened. Had he moved? He must be real. He couldn't be a figment of her imagination, could he?

Raising an arm, she waved desperately at him. It proved to be a mistake, for she lost her grip on the log and went under again.

Katherine thrashed wildly in the churning water, unaware that she was no longer alone until something caught in her hair, giving it a sharp tug. Another sharp tug and her head broke surface. She coughed and water spurted from her mouth.

Blinking the water from her eyes, she became aware of the blue skies overhead, and she felt the arm that circled her middle. The man on the riverbank had come to save her. But the current was working against him, trying to force them apart.

Whoever he was, he had a strong grip. And he was pulling her toward the nearest bank. It was a nightmare struggle, a struggle that she was sure he was going to lose.

"Leave me," she gasped. "S-save yourself."

His only answer was to tighten his grip and continue to fight through the raging river.

Although Katherine wanted to help, her arms were leaden, useless. She knew she should feel fear, but she was beyond that, too exhausted to feel anything.

Suddenly, she felt firm ground beneath her feet. Using it for leverage, she endeavored to help the man who was doing his best to save her from a watery grave.

They lurched together, struggling to gain another few feet, to escape from the strong current that still tried to capture them. A few minutes later she lay gasping for breath in the shallows of the river.

She lay still for a moment, too weak to move. Then, afraid she would lapse into unconsciousness, she clawed with both hands at the roots of a tree and sank down into a clump of grass and weeds.

For a brief time Katherine lay in a stupor. Then, slowly, she became aware of another presence and realized her rescuer was close at hand. His breath was coming in strangled gasps.

She turned her head and saw an old man with faded gray eyes staring at her from under beetled white brows. His face had the texture of old leather—what she could see of it, for he sported a walrus mustache and a full white beard.

"I'm . . . a-gettin too . . . old fer such . . . as thet," he said between strangled gasps. His buckskin-covered chest heaved with the exertion of his breathing. "You all right, youngun?" he asked.

"Yes," she whispered unsteadily. "What . . . about you?"

He managed a weak grin. "I'm too . . . dad-blamed . . . ornery to die."

She pushed herself weakly to her elbows, then struggled to her knees. "Thank . . . you," she said. "If you hadn't come along and . . ." Breaking off, she drew a shuddery breath. ". . . and pulled me out when you did, I'm sure I would have drowned."

He wiped a weary hand over his drenched face. "You . . . did look to be a-headin' in thet . . . direction," he said. His shrewd gaze held hers. "How'd . . . you come to be in . . . such a fix?"

"I was traveling downriver when I fell in," she said. "I was certain my life had come to an end."

"It pert near did, girlie," he said gruffly. "How'd you come to be on your own?"

"I . . . uh . . ." Katherine blushed. She had never been good at lying, but she had no intention of mentioning Swift Arrow's name. Her mind quickly settled on the simplest explanation. "I went riding and

177

lost my way," she said. "My name is Katherine Carpenter. I live at Fort Bayard with my father."

He eyed her shrewdly. "So you're the major's daughter thet's been lost," he growled. He seemed finally to have got his wind back. "You been gone quite a while. Everybody figgered you fer dead. What's more, yore goin' in the wrong direction to find the fort." He got to his feet. "My packs're back up the river aways," he said gruffly. "Had to get shed of 'em mighty quick when I went in after you." He reached a hand to his waist, then swore softly.

"What's wrong?" she asked, wondering if he had injured himself.

He gave a loud sigh. "I lost my plug of tobacco," he growled. "Got another'n with my pack." He squinted up the river. "Wonder how far downriver the current washed us?" He turned to her, his gaze searching. "You able to travel?"

She nodded, although she wasn't really certain. Her clothing was wet, but it was all she had. It would eventually dry on her.

"Reckon if yore a-wantin' to get to the fort, we'd best be movin' on," he said.

"You didn't tell me your name," she reminded him.

"Folks call me Buck," he said. "Last name's Winters."

"Do you have a horse?" she asked hopefully.

"Nope," he said. "He broke a leg a few miles back. Had to shoot 'im." He scowled at her, his expression fierce. "Sure hated to do it, too. He was the best damn

178

horse I ever had."

"That's too bad," she murmured.

Shading her eyes, she looked around, noticing for the first time that the canyon walls had opened up into a wide valley with trees and prickly pears. To the east lay desert country.

Katherine knew the land now. It was all familiar to her, for she had ridden here many times with Jesse. The fort lay to the east of them. She knew it couldn't be more than a dozen more miles or so ahead.

Perhaps she and the old man could even reach it before nightfall. If they didn't, at least she could take comfort in the fact that she was no longer alone.

They made their way back up the river until they found the old man's gear. He pulled on a pair of worn moccasins and settled a coonskin cap on his head. Then he picked up one of the packs and shrugged it on his back. Wordlessly, she bent to pick up the other one.

Together, they began the long journey to the fort.

The sun felt hot as it beat down on her head. And the desert appeared to go on endlessly. Katherine had plenty of time to think and wished she hadn't.

Had she been foolish to leave Swift Arrow? She was beginning to think she had. She was surprised by the intensity with which she missed him. She could have been lying in his arms this very minute, instead of trying to find her way back to a father who cared nothing for her.

Yes, she admitted to herself. She had been a fool

to leave.

Katherine was so busy with her thoughts that she didn't hear the distant thunder of hooves on the hard ground until the old man put a hand on her arm.

He cocked his head, listening. "Horses comin'," he commented. "Ridin' hard. Reckon they ain't no use in tryin' to hide. Wouldn't do no good noways. Ain't nary a thin' to hide behind."

"It's probably the cavalry," she said. "I saw a scouting party early yesterday morning."

Although she should have viewed her rescue as a triumph, for some reason it was a hollow victory, and she was filled with a disconcerting sense of disappointment.

"You saw 'em?" he asked. "How'd you come to do a thin' like thet, an' them not see you?"

"I—" She broke off. She couldn't tell him she had been at the cliff dwellings. No one must know of that place. If anyone found out and became curious enough to investigate, they might find Swift Arrow. "I was too far away from them," she murmured.

"Somethin' 'bout them horses don't look quite right," he growled.

She raised a slender hand to shade her eyes from the glare and frowned. Although she didn't know what he found wrong with the horses, she knew that something was definitely wrong.

"Dammit all!" he growled. "It's Injuns."

She heard the concern in his voice but had no time to comment, for a moment later they were surrounded

180

by at least a dozen Indians. Her heart beat fast with fear when she saw the bright paint streaking their faces.

"Don't let on yore a-feared," Buck growled. "It'll only make things worse."

At that moment one of the warriors leapt from his horse and grabbed her by the hair. Pain streaked through her scalp. His face was savage as he loomed over her, raising his arm back that held his knife. She waited helplessly for the blow to fall.

When it didn't, she struck out at him. It was a mistake. Fury flared in the Indian's eyes. He threw her down and followed her to the ground. She fought desperately against his weight, vaguely aware of Buck cursing loudly behind her.

Sparing a quick glance toward the old man, she saw that he was busy fighting off two braves. She could expect no help from that direction.

Kicking out with her feet, she struck the savage above her in the area of his groin, connecting with something soft. He yelped loudly and fell back.

Immediately, she rolled over and sprang to her feet. Wasting no time, she sprinted away from him, running as fast as her feet would carry her.

Behind her, she heard a roar of rage. Tossing a quick look back, she saw her attacker had taken up the chase. And from the sound of it, the howling horde was following him.

For a moment, the thudding of her heart covered the sound of thundering hooves. When she heard it, she knew all was lost. The Indian was chasing her on his horse. Although she knew she couldn't win, she refused to give up. She had to keep trying.

Her breathing was labored, her chest hurt with the effort to draw air into her tortured lungs. With a whoop of victory, the Indian gave a leap and tackled her. She hit the ground with a heavy thud that knocked the air from her lungs.

She lay stunned, unable to draw a single breath. A dark haze gathered around her, threatening to envelop her, and she fought against the blackness.

A harsh voice spoke. The weight of the warrior lifted from her. Katherine's chest began to rise and fall as she sucked in loud, agonized breaths of life-giving air. Slowly, she became aware that silence had fallen on the group.

Afraid of what she would find, she opened her eyes. And they widened in disbelief. For the warrior who stood beside her was Swift Arrow. His knife was drawn, his stance threatening. It was a moment before she realized it wasn't herself who was being threatened.

"The woman is mine," Swift Arrow growled in the Apache language.

"If she is yours, why was she with the old mountain man?" her captor asked.

"She ran away from me," Swift Arrow said.

The other man looked as though he would argue the matter. But another look at Swift Arrow's fierce expression changed his mind.

Katherine felt a momentary elation, which quickly fled as Swift Arrow sheathed his knife and reached for her. He gripped her roughly and hauled her to her feet. His eyes were blazing with fury, and something else . . . something she couldn't as yet put a name to.

Her legs trembled as he looped the end of a rope around her neck. "What are you doing?" she asked.

"Making sure you don't escape me again," he growled.

She reached for the rope, intending to remove it, but something in his eyes warned he had about reached his breaking point, and she let her arms fall limply to her sides.

She made no move to resist as he dragged her roughly to the small group of women who seemed to materialize out of nowhere and stood silently watching. "Stay with the women," he snarled.

"Hold on one damn minute," growled a voice that was becoming familiar to her.

Swift Arrow and Katherine both turned to face the old mountain man, who struggled against the two men holding him by the arms. A thin trickle of blood flowed down his face from a cut above one eye, making his expression appear even more fierce. His glittering eyes held the warrior's.

"So we meet again," Swift Arrow said grimly.

"Seems so," the old man said. "And I shore didn't expect our next meetin' would be like this. Let the girl go."

A glint appeared in Swift Arrow's eyes. He looked pointedly at the old man's imprisoned arms. "You do not appear to be in a position to make demands," he said in a cold voice. "And it is not my wish to free her." His gaze sharpened. "What is your interest in her?"

"I'm takin' 'er home," Buck said.

Swift Arrow's eyes narrowed. Something like hope flared deep within the ebony depths. "Did you steal her away from me?"

"Steal her away?" Buck's expression was puzzled. "Away from where?"

Swift Arrow's expression became bleak, but he didn't answer the old man.

Buck's shrewd gaze moved from the warrior to Katherine, his shaggy brows lowered, pulling into a deep frown. "You know this Injun, youngun?"

She flickered an angry glance at Swift Arrow. "Yes," she muttered. "I know him."

"It 'pears to me he thinks he owns you. He got any reason fer thinkin' thetaway?"

Before she could reply, Swift Arrow interrupted. "Silence. You will speak no more." He looked at the warriors who held Buck. "The old one cannot be trusted," he growled. "Bind his arms."

"No!" Katherine cried. "Leave him alone. He only wanted to help me!"

Swift Arrow ignored her. "Listen to me," she said. "He didn't do anything."

She might as well have been talking to the wind, for all the good it did. The two warriors bound the old man's arms in front of him, then vaulted onto their mounts.

Swift Arrow mounted his stallion and took his place among the other mounted warriors.

Accepting her defeat, Katherine joined the old man and the women who followed the warriors on foot.

The small band of Indians traveled the rest of the day. Several times Katherine stumbled and fell. The rope would have strangled her if Swift Arrow hadn't noticed immediately. He always did. But he only stopped the horse until she regained her feet. Then he moved on again.

At first she had been numbed by his attitude, but as the day passed, she began to grow angry.

How dare he treat her in such a way?

Her eyes flared with anger, glittering brightly as she stared at his back. Although her anger smoldered just below the surface, she forced herself to remain silent.

Katherine was determined she would wait until the chance came—as it would—and then she would show the warrior he couldn't treat her in such a way.

Buck stumbled. His strength had already been drained by the river. Now the trip was taking its toll on him.

"Are you all right?" she asked.

"I'll make it," he growled. "Cain't fer the likes o' me figger out what's got 'im so riled up." He looked at her. "You got any idea?"

Her lips tightened. "Yes. I have an idea."

"He said you ran away from him."

"I did." Her answer was abrupt.

"Guess you don't wanta talk about it."

185

Before she could answer, Swift Arrow turned and glared at them. Katherine refused to be intimidated. She glared right back. She had a feeling he didn't want her talking to the old man. Suddenly, perversely, she decided that was exactly what she would do.

Swift Arrow could hold her prisoner, but if he wanted to silence her, then he would have to use a gag.

Defiantly, she turned to Buck. "He refused to take me back to the fort," she said. "So I ran away."

Swift Arrow pulled his mount up. He spoke in low tones to the warrior nearest him. The man vaulted off his horse and moved toward them. Grasping the old man's upper arm roughly, he pulled him away from Katherine.

"Leave him alone!" she cried. She turned to look at Swift Arrow. "Release him. It's me you're angry with."

Swift Arrow paid her no attention. Instead, he began a low conversation with one of his comrades.

For the rest of the day Katherine found herself walking alone. She had plenty of time to regret her deliberate defiance.

As the day wore on, Swift Arrow's anger abated somewhat. Enough for him to regret his harsh treatment of Katherine and the old man. He almost relented and had them freed, but then he would remember how she had deliberately defied him.

He could not accept such an attitude from his woman. If he did, he would appear weak before his people. He knew he couldn't let that happen.

He cast a quick glance behind him. Katherine's chin was tilted defiantly, and her steps were firm. She was a strong woman, and he would not like to break her spirit. But she must learn to obey him. It was the Apache way. And it was a good way. It would take her time, but she would learn. And in time she would come to understand.

At least, he hoped she would.

Chapter Eighteen

The sun had dropped below the horizon by the time they stopped. Katherine gave a weary sigh, sinking to the ground beside Buck. All day she had choked on the dust stirred up by the horses. She was hot, her temples throbbed, her throat was parched, and every muscle in her body screamed out in protest.

"You okay, youngun?" the old man asked, using his bound hands to wipe the perspiration from his brow.

"Yes," she said, casting an uneasy glance toward Swift Arrow. "I'm all right."

"Don't think he'll bother us," Buck said, intercepting her look. "I reckon he was just bent on showin' who was boss. How'd you come to tangle up with him anyways?"

She looked at him. "I'm sorry, Buck. I didn't tell you everything. I was injured in the fall from my mount.

189

Swift Arrow found me. He took care of me."

"I reckon thet ain't all he done," the old man said shrewdly.

She blushed. But before she could answer, she sensed another presence standing above her. She knew without looking up that it was Swift Arrow.

"There is no time to rest," he said gruffly. "There is food to be prepared."

"Then make it yourself," she muttered, all too conscious of the rope he had placed around her neck. "I'm too tired to move."

"Get up," he commanded. "Would you have the other women think you are weak?"

"Let them think what they want!" she snapped, lifting her eyes to glare at him. "I don't care."

But even as she said the words, she struggled to her feet. She lifted her eyes to his, saw something flicker in his dark gaze as she swayed unsteadily.

"I don't know what's eatin' you, son," the mountain man growled. "But if it's what I'm a-thinkin', you ain't gonna fix it thet away."

Swift Arrow threw him a contemptuous look. "Stay out of it," he said coldly.

"Cain't rightly do thet," Buck growled. "Here I was thinkin' you an' me was friends. Guess I was wrong, seein' as how you got me trussed up like a turkey."

"Enough!" Swift Arrow said. He looked at Katherine. "Go to the women!"

Tightening her lips, she locked her knees in place, and reaching up to the rope that still encircled her neck, she loosened the loop and lifted it off, then threw it

190

away from her. Her gray eyes sparked as she silently dared him to put it on her again.

To her surprise, he ignored the action.

"Release the old one," he muttered to a warrior standing nearby.

She watched him join the other men who were making a rope corral for the horses, wondering why he had given orders to free Buck. They obviously knew each other, but he was angry with the old man's interference.

Sighing wearily, she moved to where the women were preparing the meal.

A young woman with copper-colored skin and dark braids that hung down to her waist looked up as she approached. She appeared to be about the same age as Katherine.

"What can I do to help?" Katherine asked the girl.

Surprised flickered in the girl's eyes. She threw a quick look at Swift Arrow before she answered. "It is good you speak our language," she said. "Not many white eyes do. I am going to gather firewood. What does your man wish you to do?"

Katherine didn't even bother trying to deny that Swift Arrow was her man. "He told me to help the women."

The girl smiled shyly. "Then come with me," she said. "I am a woman. And I could use some help."

Several women had already left the others and were searching for firewood. Katherine and the Indian girl joined them.

"I am called Bright Feathers," said the girl. "What is

your name?"

"Katherine."

"That is pretty," the young woman said, stooping to pick up a few sticks that lay in their path.

As Katherine began to search for wood, she found it was very scarce. The two young women had to travel quite a distance from the camp to gather enough wood. When they finally had all they could carry, they turned and began to retrace their steps.

Suddenly, an uneasy feeling settled upon Katherine. She felt as though someone was watching her. Turning her head, she found the source of her unease. An Indian brave with a short, squat frame was watching her.

Bright Feathers's expression grew troubled as she noticed the man. "Crying Wolf finds you good to look upon," she said. "Swift Arrow will not be pleased."

The squatty Indian moved nearer, blocking their view of the camp. His flat black gaze never left her face. "Go, Bright Feathers," he growled. "I would speak alone with the paleface woman."

"No," the young woman muttered. "I will stay. She does not wish me to leave."

Crying Wolf threw her a dirty look, then spoke to Katherine. "I wish to know if Swift Arrow spoke the truth," he growled. "Are you his woman?"

"Do you dare to call an Apache warrior a liar?" Bright Feathers asked in a voice filled with shock.

Crying Wolf ignored her words. His gaze was insolent as it left Katherine's face and dwelt on the swell of her breasts. She recognized the lust in his black eyes as they moved down her body before returning to her face again.

"Answer me, white girl."

"What do you want here, Crying Wolf?" a harsh voice growled.

Katherine knew it was Swift Arrow, even before he took her hand in an iron grip and pulled her to him.

"The woman is mine," he snapped. "You will not approach her again."

Crying Wolf's narrowed gaze challenged the other man, then he shrugged his shoulders as if to say it didn't really matter and walked away from them.

"Keep your eyes away from Crying Wolf," Swift Arrow growled. He stood over her, breathing roughly, his eyes dark with anger, and something she didn't recognize. His fingers tightened around her wrist, bruising a little, but she uttered no protest.

Suddenly, as though completely disgusted, he flung her hand away from him. Without a word, he turned and strode away.

She stared at him, resentment burning deep within her body.

"He is only looking after you," Bright Feathers consoled. "Crying Wolf is a cruel man. His last wife died from the beatings he gave her."

Katherine watched Swift Arrow rejoin the men. Was Bright Feathers right? Was he only being protective of her? That thought kept her quiet as they joined the women around the fire.

It was late before the men were fed. And only then did the women sit down to eat. Katherine brought Buck's food with hers and they both ate hungrily.

When he had finished, the old man reached for his pouch of tobacco and bit off a large chunk. "You got a likin' fer thet Apache warrior?" he growled.

She flicked a surprised look at him from under her fringe of thick lashes. "Why should you think that?" she asked evasively.

"I'd have to be stupid not to see somethin's betwixt the two of you. Now I ain't never claimed to be the smartest man aroun', but I sure ain't stupid neither."

"Swift Arrow helped me when I needed it," she said quietly.

"Ain't surprised," he commented. "He's got a habit of doin' just thet."

"Helping people?"

"Yep."

"So it wasn't just me," she said slowly.

"Nope. He's helped plenty a folks. Even me."

She worried the old man's words over in her mind. "How long have you known him?" she asked.

"Been nigh on to a year now," he said. He spat a long stream of tobacco at the ground. "Him an' his friends come on me an' my friends kinda sudden-like. Fact of the matter is, they dropped right outta the trees on top of us. When the smoke cleared away we was all trussed up like a bunch of hogs a-headed fer slaughter." He shook his shaggy head. "Fer a while there, I thought we was all goners."

"What happened?"

"We managed to convince 'em we had business at their village. Good thin', too. Else we'd a-met our maker right then an' there, 'cause them Injuns was mighty mad thet day."

"Did you really have business there?"

"Yep," he grunted. "We surely did."

Deciding he wasn't going to elaborate, and wanting to learn more about Swift Arrow, she spoke.

"You said that was the first time you saw him. When was the last?"

"Now thet's another story altogether," he said. "We was buddied up to help save Miss Heather from Cantrell, and after it was all over, then—"

"Heather?" Katherine said quickly. "You don't mean Heather O'Day, do you?"

His faded gray eyes narrowed. "Thet was her name afore she married up with Shaw. Do you know Miss Heather?"

"Yes," she replied. "I know Heather. She was a good friend to me."

Although she knew he was curious, Katherine fell silent. Her mind had flown back in time to the day when Heather had helped her to free Jesse from the jail in Silver City. She sighed with regret. Heather had been a good friend, but Katherine felt certain she would never see her again.

She became aware they were no longer alone, and looked up to find Bright Feathers standing next to her.

"It is time to make the bed for your man," the Indian woman said.

Katherine thanked the other girl, then moved to where Swift Arrow waited beside the supplies. She felt a need to clear the air between them, but one look at his hard expression was enough to dissuade her.

195

She ignored him and stooped to take the thick bearskin off the top of his supplies. Something moved in her peripheral vision. Her gray eyes opened wider. It was one of the leather bags. As she watched, it quivered, then grew still. Her heart skipped a beat, then picked up speed. Something was in the bag. Something alive. Could it be . . .

"Blackie?" she whispered huskily.

She was only vaguely aware of the old man approaching. Her eyes glittered with tears as they lifted to meet Swift Arrow's. "Did you . . . you didn't . . ." Her gaze dropped again to the quivering bundle. A black nose poked out of the opening. Then two beady black eyes appeared.

"Blackie!" she cried. "It *is* you!"

Her eyes were shining as she reached for the raccoon. He came willingly into her arms, scrabbling wildly with his hind legs as he hurried to climb up to her shoulder.

A smile broke out on her face, and she was unaware of the old man stopping to stare at her. Then, without a word, he turned and retraced his steps to the campfire, leaving the warrior and the girl alone.

Katherine's eyes misted over and a lump formed in her throat. "I thought I'd never see him again," she whispered huskily.

When Swift Arrow remained silent, she put Blackie down and picked up the bearskin, carrying it a little distance from the camp. She felt surprised when Swift Arrow didn't follow her. Instead, he joined Buck beside the fire. The two men began to speak in low voices.

After spreading the rug on the ground, she went for

more skins. This time, she carried two in her arms. Tossing one of the pelts down, she spread the other on the bearskin. With Blackie scampering along at her feet, she finished preparing the bed for Swift Arrow.

She was conscious all the while of Swift Arrow's gaze returning to her again and again as she worked.

After she had made his bed, she used the remaining skins to prepare another a few feet away from the first. She knew the exact moment when he saw what she was doing.

A moment later he was beside her. "What are you doing?" he growled.

"Making my bed."

"Your place is with me."

Although she wished for nothing more than to be with him, his cold tone brought out the perverse side in her. "And if I do not wish it?"

"It does not matter," he grated. "You are my woman. And you will sleep where I sleep."

She stared into his eyes. Part of her wanted to give in, and the other part wanted to defy him. She realized he had the upper hand and decided she would offer no resistance. But he would find no pleasure in her company.

Without a word, she moved to the bed she had prepared. After removing her boots, she lay down on the bed of furs. The raccoon, needing no encouragement, curled up at her feet. The bed rustled as Swift Arrow joined her.

She felt tense, expecting him to reach out to her at any moment. She was all ready with her rebuke. For she was determined he would find her cold and unresponsive. But to her surprise, he lay still, making no move toward her at all.

Time passed. Her body grew stiff as she waited for him to make a move. Hoping he wouldn't. And yet . . . hoping he would.

Her jaw ached from clenching her teeth. Her fingernails cut into her palms. But still she waited.

She tried to force everything from her mind, except the full moon that rode high overhead. After a while the tension began to drain away. Her body relaxed. Her eyelids grew heavy . . . heavy . . .

"Why did you leave?"

The words were harsh as they came out of the darkness, jerking her awake.

She blinked rapidly, trying to bring reality into focus.

Why did she leave?

She took a deep breath and turned her head toward him. "I had no choice," she said.

"Explain that to me."

She sensed something in him, something vulnerable. She wanted to reach out and touch him, but she stayed her hand. She thought of a way to answer his question. Should she tell him she could not bear it because he did not love her? Or should she explain to him how used she had felt when she discovered he had only kept her to spite her father? No. She couldn't say that. For then he would know how much she cared.

"You know I must return to my father," she said. "He must think I'm dead."

His broad chest rose and fell. "It is better that he should think so," he muttered. His eyes glittered as he studied her. Finally, he gave a long sigh. "Go to sleep," he said, turning away from her.

For a long time she lay awake. But finally, her tense body relaxed. Exhaustion overtook her and she fell into a deep sleep.

When she woke it was daybreak and she was alone.

She rose, helped the women to prepare the meal, then packed their belongings together and made ready for another day's journey. She wondered where they were going, wondered also if perhaps Bright Feathers would tell her.

She had no chance to find out.

The warriors began to mount their horses. She waited for Swift Arrow to bring the rope. She was all set to fight with him about it, for she did not intend to wear it around her neck like one of the livestock.

To her utter astonishment, Swift Arrow seemed not to even notice her as he mounted the stallion. Katherine uttered a sigh of relief.

The band of Indians moved out across the plains, and Katherine and Buck fell in line with the women who followed them. The raccoon scampered along at her feet.

They traveled in a northeasterly direction, moving toward the distant mountains. She wondered again where they were going.

The day proved much like the one before. They traveled without stopping until darkness began to fall. Then they stopped and ate and prepared for the night.

Swift Arrow found a shallow ravine and ordered her to prepare their bed there. She did as he directed. As she removed her boots and placed them neatly at the foot of the bearskin pallet, she threw an uneasy glance at him from beneath lowered lashes.

She was worried about why he wanted to move from the sight of the others.

She had a right to be worried.

He removed his clothing and reached out a long arm. His fingers were like steel as they closed around her wrist.

"No," she protested.

"Do not tell me no," he growled, pulling her hard against his chest.

"I don't want this."

"Don't lie to me."

"I'm not lying." Tears started in her eyes. "I don't want you to touch me while you're angry."

"Do I not have reason for my anger?"

"I suppose you think you do."

"You do not?"

"No."

He was silent for a moment. Then, "You ran away from me."

"You had no right to force me to stay."

"I had every right. You are mine."

"Like your horse?"

"Yes."

Fury surged through her. "All right!" she snapped. "If that's the way you want it, then, all right!"

She ripped open her blouse, unmindful of the

200

buttons that flew off and fell to the ground. Pulling the blouse off, she tossed it aside and unfastened her riding skirt. It went the way of the blouse.

She stood in her pantelettes and chemise, her bosom heaving, her gray eyes glittering. Then, deliberately, she unfastened the chemise, allowing the perfect mounds of her breasts to spill out. She smiled with savage satisfaction as she saw his astounded gaze become riveted on her.

Then, with the perfect ease of a strip teaser, she peeled the pantelettes down and kicked them aside, standing in the moonlight in all her feminine perfection.

She saw his eyes move down to the curly blond hair between her thighs. His Adam's apple bobbed up and down as he swallowed hard.

When his eyes lifted to hers, she saw the glitter of passion in his ebony gaze before he tore his eyes away and left her alone in the moonlight.

Katherine curled up in a tight ball of misery on the bed of furs. She hated Swift Arrow. He had treated her cruelly. Why then, did she long so desperately for his return?

Chapter Nineteen

When Katherine woke the next morning she was still alone. She looked at the empty space beside her, wondering if Swift Arrow had returned to their bed. Pushing back the covers, she reached for her clothing. Blackie, who was curled up beside her, opened his eyes and looked up at her.

She grimaced with distaste at her torn blouse. She had completed its ruin in her sudden burst of anger last night. Now what would she wear?

The raccoon stood up and arched its back, drawing her attention to the garment he had been lying on. It was one of the dresses she had made at the cliff dwellings.

"Now how did that get here?" she muttered.

She knew Swift Arrow must have left it.

Donning the garment, she rolled the hides together

and went to join the women already preparing the morning meal. Bright Feathers looked up as she approached, her gaze dwelling on the dark circles beneath Katherine's eyes, but she made no comment.

Katherine looked for Swift Arrow and Buck. Neither one of them were in camp.

When the two men had not appeared by the time the meal was ready, Katherine could hold her silence no longer. It had become imperative for her to find out where they were. She waited until she caught Bright Feathers alone, then she spoke.

"Have you seen Swift Arrow and Buck this morning?"

"No. Laughing Turtle told me they rode out with Crying Wolf and her husband, Hollow Log, while it was still dark. She said they are going to ride behind to make sure the horse soldiers do not follow and surprise us."

Katherine breathed a little easier. At least Swift Arrow hadn't deserted her. She was glad that Crying Wolf had gone as well. She didn't feel comfortable around him. The Indian always seemed to be following her with his eyes.

She felt no surprise to hear a rear guard would be following the small band of Indians. It wouldn't do for the cavalry to surprise them. The mounted warriors would probably escape, but the women who were forced to walk would be captured.

Since the warriors had left their supplies behind, the other horses would have to carry a double load. Katherine helped pack the supplies and redistribute them. Every available spot was used and the excess packs given to the women. Then they resumed their journey.

"Where are we going?" Katherine asked, shifting her pack a little higher on her shoulders.

"To the village of Chief Tall Feathers," said Bright Feathers, trudging along beside her.

"Chief Tall Feathers?" The name had a familiar ring. "Will it be safe there?"

"It is not safe anywhere," the woman replied. "But when the horse soldiers discover us missing from the reservation, they will expect us to go to the land of the dark-skinned ones."

"Mexico?"

"Yes. That is the place." Her expression held a glint of humor. "The white eyes will search the desert, thinking we are headed for the Sierra Madre mountains. But they will search in vain, for we will not be there."

"How can you be certain that's where they'll look?"

Bright Feathers shrugged. "The only thing one can be certain of is death."

Katherine watched the young woman stoop to dig a root from the soil with a pointed stick. "Are you married?" she asked curiously.

Bright Feathers smiled at her. "No. But I have been spoken for."

She indicated a man who rode slightly ahead of them. Katherine had noticed him before. He was slightly taller than the rest. He had a muscular build, and his features in profile looked almost handsome.

205

"Do you love him?" Katherine asked.

"Yes," the other girl said. "He is good to look upon. But what is more important, he is a strong warrior. He will protect me and provide well for our future. And . . ." her eyes twinkled, ". . . he will give me many fine sons."

Katherine studied the other girl, wondering how she could possibly want children, living as she did.

"Wouldn't it be a hardship to have children? You travel around so much."

"It is not the travel that is hard," Bright Feathers said, a touch of bitterness to her voice. "Often there is not enough food for our people. It is the children and the old ones who die first." The girl's gaze seemed to turn inward. "It was not always so," she went on. "Once this was a land of plenty. The great buffalo covered the land, stretching out as far as the eye could see. Then the white eyes came. It wasn't enough for them to steal our land and imprison our people, they killed the buffalo as well."

"I'm sorry," Katherine said, a feeling of shame washing over her. "I know your people have suffered severely. You must hate me."

"Have you done this thing?"

"No. Not personally. But my people did."

"I think you would have stopped it, if you could."

"Yes," Katherine said gravely. "I would have."

At that moment, the warrior who was to marry Bright Feathers turned around to look at them. He caught the Indian girl's eyes and she smiled at him. Remembering the girl's talk of children, Katherine asked her why there were no children traveling with the band.

"We knew we must travel fast," Bright Feathers said. "They were left behind because they could not keep up with us. The old ones who could not travel will look after them. With the rest of us gone, there will be more food for them."

"Surely there is enough food for everyone," Katherine said. "That was part of the agreement between our government and your people."

"The white eyes broke their promises. You have never been on a reservation, have you?"

"I was there as a child."

"Perhaps you were too young to realize the situation. Our people are half-starved. There is not enough food to go around. The reservation agent expects our people to cultivate the land and grow our own food. But that is not the Apache way. And the land we are given is useless. There is no water. Nothing will grow there. It has become all we can do to survive."

Katherine remained silent for a moment, unable to reply. She could hear the bitterness in the other girl's voice and could not blame her for her feelings. She had known things were bad for the Indians, but had not known to what degree.

She decided to change the subject.

"Do you like children?" she asked.

"Yes," replied Bright Feathers. "And you?"

"Yes," Katherine said. She wondered what a child of Swift Arrow's would look like. Would his son have his dark hair and eyes? And if they had a girl, would she be blond? Katherine realized suddenly that she'd had very little dealings with children. Especially since joining her father at the fort. Children weren't exactly encouraged there. In fact, when she came to think of it, there were very few married men.

"I think I'd like to have a baby one day," she said softly.

"Perhaps you will have many," Bright Feathers said, her eyes on her betrothed. "As I intend to."

Katherine caught the direction of her gaze.

"Why do the men ride?" she asked. "And the women walk behind?"

The girl's eyebrows lifted. "Is it not so in your world? The warriors must ride ahead in case we have need of their protection. We are safer behind them."

It was sound reasoning. Katherine couldn't argue with it. That day she learned more about the Indians. And she learned the names of all the travelers. There were Sleeping Hawk and his wife, Many Tongues, who was overly fond of talking. There was Laughing Turtle, and her husband, Hollow Log. And Running Elk, and his wife, Two Moons. And Jumping Bullfrog, and Grassy Waters. And Sitting Wolf and Eagle Claw. The women were friendly enough and seemed eager to have someone else to talk with. The day passed more swiftly than the one before.

It was late when Swift Arrow and the others returned. As they dismounted, two other warriors rode out to take their place.

Swift Arrow didn't look at her as he sat down with the other men beside the fire. Dishing up his food in a bowl, she handed it to him, then rejoined the other women who were cleaning the cooking utensils.

He is still angry.

The thought caused her pain. She threw a quick look at him, but his expressionless face gave her no indication of his feelings.

Katherine had had plenty of time to regret her actions of the night before. She had come to realize that it would have served her better to forget the past and be grateful for their time together.

When the meal had been cleared away, she prepared their bed. She had just finished when Swift Arrow appeared out of the darkness. He remained silent as he lay down beside her, not even removing his moccasins.

The silence stretched out between them, and she became unnerved. Hot tears burned beneath the backs of her tightly closed eyelids.

"Are you angry with me?" Despite her best efforts at control, her voice had a quavery sound.

He turned his head, staring down into her face. His probing gaze narrowed on the dark circles under her eyes. Heaving a tired sigh, he slid his long arm beneath her and pulled her close against him. "No," he said. "Not angry."

"You didn't say good-bye this morning."

His eyes were intent as they studied her. "Did you wish it?"

"Yes," she admitted. When he didn't answer, she said. "Do you think the cavalry could be following us?"

"It is possible."

She lay in the circle of his arms thinking about his

209

words. What would she do if the cavalry found them? And more to the point, what would happen to Swift Arrow and the other Apaches?

They would be sent back to the reservation.

A lump formed in Katherine's throat. The Apaches would not go easily. There would be a fight. Some could die. Perhaps Swift Arrow would be one. And she could not stand that. What would she do without him?

Her expression was agonized as she looked at him. "Would it not be best if we traveled faster? Perhaps we shouldn't be resting so often." But even as she spoke the words, she knew the answer.

"Our warriors are conditioned from childhood to go long periods without rest. But not the women. Without rest, they would soon drop in their tracks. We know this from experience."

His hand splayed out on her back, moving in a circular motion. "What would you do, little paleface, if the horse soldiers caught us? Would you run to them and help them kill my people?"

"No," she said sharply. "How could you ask me such a question? Surely you know I don't want you dead?"

"Do you want me?" His voice was husky.

"I-I—" She swallowed convulsively. She was unable to say the words. How could she admit her feelings when he only wanted her to use against her father.

"Why did you leave me?" he asked.

"How could I stay when I found out why you wanted me?"

He frowned down at her. "What do you mean?"

"You wanted to keep me so you could punish my

father," she said bitterly. "Surely you didn't expect me to stay after I found out."

He was silent for a moment. "And how did you come by this information?"

"You told me."

"I told you?" A shadow crossed his face. "You are mistaken, Katherine. I said no such thing to you."

"Maybe not in so many words. But you didn't have to. I already knew."

He cupped her face gently, forcing her to look at him. "Listen to me," he said. "You are wrong in what you think. I kept you because I wanted you." His gaze darkened. "Do you know how I felt when I returned home and found you gone?"

She shook her head, waiting for him to continue.

"I felt as though I had lost a part of me." His dark brows drew together. "I must admit I never expected to feel in such a way about a woman. I am not happy with it, but there is nothing I can do."

"Are you saying you love me?"

"No," he said gravely. "I do not think I know the meaning of the word. But make no mistake, Katherine. I want you."

He doesn't love me, but he wants me, she thought. *Will I be able to settle for that?*

Swift Arrow's lips moved slowly across her face. Then he spoke again. "I felt as though a knife had made a wound in my belly when I found you gone." His lips touched her eyelids, as soft as a butterfly's wings. "And when I could not find you, the knife twisted and twisted, wounding me so severely that I could not eat or

211

sleep." His lips found hers and tasted gently. Then he continued. "Do not think it is your father that makes me want you, little one. As long as this feeling remains, you must never leave me."

As long as this feeling remains.

How long would that be? How long before he grew tired of her, asked her to leave?

The knife twisted and twisted, wounding me so severely that I could not eat or sleep.

Her lips curled into a smile. If he didn't love her, maybe what he felt was near enough.

"Is it possible you return my feelings, Katherine? Do you want me, little one?"

"Yes," she groaned. "I want you desperately."

She pressed warm kisses against his neck and he groaned low in his throat.

"Now is not the time," he said huskily. "We are too near the others. I think you would not want them to hear."

"Of course not," she said, blushing. She hid her face against his chest, reveling in the maleness of his body, his strength, his protection. Her body began to relax against his, and she fell into a deep sleep.

Chapter Twenty

It had been three days since Katherine had joined the Apaches, and they had finally reached the foothills of the mountains. The day was clear, a little past noon. Only a suggestion of clouds filled the sky.

The warriors decided they must rest the weary horses and replenish their supplies before traveling any farther. They made camp on open ground with only a scattering of trees nearby.

"Do you need any help?"

Katherine turned to see Bright Feathers standing behind her. "Have you finished your wickiup already?" she asked.

"Yes," the other girl said. "And I am ready to help with yours."

Katherine grimaced, arching her aching back. "You wouldn't think it would be so tiring working with such materials." She indicated the pile of brush and sticks and the clay pots filled with mud. "When I watched you, it seemed easy enough."

Bright Feathers bent and picked up a handful of mud. Then she pushed it into a hole. "It will take time. This is only your first wickiup."

"The thing that bothers me most," Katherine said, wiping the sweat from her brow with the back of her hand, "is that it's not permanent. Swift Arrow said we'd only be here a few days before we continue our journey to Chief Tall Feathers's village."

"That is so," Bright Feathers replied. "But we have already come a great distance. And it is still a long way to the village in the mountains. The horses are tired. And so are my people. The wickiups will give us shelter while the horses forage for food."

As always, Bright Feathers's reasoning was sound. The girls worked together in silence for a while. Katherine listened to the hum of voices around the wickiups. Everyone seemed to be glad of the chance to rest for a few days. For herself, she would have felt better had they traveled farther into the mountains.

Across the clearing she saw Buck and waved at him. He lifted a hand to her, and pulled the ever present plug of tobacco from his pouch.

"He is much man, that one."

"Yes, he is," Katherine agreed. "Did you know him before?"

"No," the girl said. "But I have heard of him."

Katherine's gaze was curious. "Tell me what you've heard," she said.

"He is a mountain man . . . a trapper. It is said that my people stole the girl he loved many years ago. That is the way we know of him. For many years he searched for her among our villages."

"Did he find her?"

"He was told that she died."

"He was told?" Katherine looked at the other girl. "It wasn't true?"

"No. But it was the only way to stop his search."

"Does he still believe she's dead?"

"No. He knows the truth."

"How did he find out?" Katherine asked softly.

"He found her at Chief Tall Feathers's village."

"When?"

"Last summer."

"How sad. And for him to believe her dead. How long were they separated?"

"White Dove was a young girl. Many winters have come and gone."

Many winters? How many? Buck was an old man. But at least he had finally found her. "Will they let her go now?" she asked.

Bright Feathers spared a quick glance for her. "She does not wish to leave. She is the mother of Chief Tall Feathers."

"His mother? But—that means she must have been with them . . . years."

"Yes. She was," the Indian woman said. "Chief Tall Feathers is not a young man." She slanted a quick glance at Katherine. "Does the thought of living with my people for the rest of your life disturb you?"

"No," Katherine said softly. "I want only Swift Arrow. I will live wherever he is."

"I think you would do better to return to your world," Bright Feathers said sadly. "The time of the Apaches has almost gone. We will lose our fight with the white man."

"There's nothing there for me," Katherine said. "I won't go back. Not as long as he will let me stay."

"I would feel the same. A woman will do much to be with the man she chooses."

"When will you be getting married?" Katherine asked.

"Soon," the other girl said. She smiled. "Very soon, I hope."

"That's a mighty handsome wickiup you've got there," Buck said, coming up beside them. "You're learnin' fast, youngun."

Katherine smiled at him. "Thank you."

"I've a mind to be on my way," he said gruffly. "You still figgerin' on tryin' to get back to the fort?"

She shook her head. "No," she said. "I've changed my mind." She looked at him. "But I think you already knew that."

He nodded. "Figgered as much. You gonna be all right with them Injuns? They ain't like yore own folks."

"I know that," she said. "And I'm glad of it. I wouldn't want them any different. But I'll hate to see you leave, Buck." She looked at him curiously. "Will Swift Arrow let you go?"

"Yep. Me 'n him done talked 'bout it. I swore I wouldn't tell nobody you was with 'em, an' he took my

216

word fer it." He looked at her from beneath beetled brows. "I took it to be what you was a-wantin'."

"Yes," she said softly. "It is." She grinned up at him. "But suppose I had wanted to leave. What would you have done then? I mean," she teased. "You gave your word and all."

"Guess I'd'a just had to break my word," he said gruffly. "'Cause it's a certain fact, thet i'n you was a-wantin' to leave, then I'd see you went."

"Then perhaps it's best I decided to stay," she said quietly. "Because I don't think Swift Arrow would have let me leave."

"Reckon not," Buck growled. "It's fer sure one of us would of died."

She shuddered slightly. She didn't even like to think about it. She smiled and laid a hand on his arm. "I'm going to miss you," she said. "Are you sure you won't come with us?"

"Yep. I'm sure. But you can do somethin' fer me."

"Anything," she said earnestly. "After all, I owe you my life."

"You don't owe me a thin', girl. But I'd take it kindly if'n you was to tell the medicine woman at Chief Tall Feathers's village thet if she ever needs me, I'll be a-waitin'."

"I'll do that," she said, looking at him curiously. "What's her name?"

"Her name's Rachel. But in thet village, she's called White Dove."

Surprise widened her eyes. White Dove was the girl he had loved. So she had become the medicine woman.

"I'll tell her," she promised.

"Much obliged," he said gruffly, spitting a wad of tobacco at the ground. His head turned to study the trees. "Reckon them hunters is a-headin' back this way," he said. "Wondered where they'd got off to."

She turned to follow his gaze. Her eyes lit up as Swift Arrow came into view. Across his shoulders was a doe. His head turned, his searching gaze sweeping the wickiups, settling on her.

She watched him toss the doe to the ground near the central fire pit and come toward her.

"Reckon I'll leave you now," Buck said. "Swift Arrow won't be thankin' me fer hangin' around his woman."

Swift Arrow's woman.

She liked the sound of that.

"The old man will be leaving soon," Swift Arrow commented as he joined her.

"I know," she said, turning to look at him. "He just told me."

"You will miss him." It was more a statement than a question.

"Yes. He saved my life."

"For that, I am grateful," he said.

"Are you?" she asked, feeling a trifle breathless.

"Do you doubt my words?"

"No. You've never lied to me."

"And I never will."

She swayed toward him, then, conscious of the other people milling about, she straightened. "Did you have a good hunt?" she asked.

"Yes. But I could almost wish it were not so."

"Why?"

"Because now there will be much celebration. It will be late before we can go to our wickiup." His voice was husky, his eyes saying things he couldn't verbalize.

"Not too late, I hope."

"It is never too late," he said. His eyes were filled with regret as he took a step away from her. "So many hours to be got through. How will I ever survive?"

A bright flush stained her cheeks. She wanted nothing more than to go into the wickiup with him at that moment, but they were not alone. It would not be seemly for them to disappear in broad daylight.

"Since I must wait, and you have work to do, I will join the other men." His voice dropped to a husky whisper and he bent closer to her, stirring the hair at her ears with his breath. "But the waiting will be very difficult for me. I have been long without your sweet kisses, little paleface."

With a heart full of love, she watched him move away. Then she joined the other women, who were preparing the meat the warriors had brought in.

Late that night Katherine and Swift Arrow entered the wickiup. The moment they were inside he turned and gathered her into his arms. When his mouth found hers, they shared a kiss of such longing it brought tears to her eyes.

His fingers were gentle as he removed her garments. Then she lay on the pallet and waited for him to join her. He stood above her, his ebony eyes glittering with desire as he held her gaze.

219

She lay watching him, waiting.

The corner of his mouth lifted into a smile as he slowly unfastened his buckskin shirt. He pulled it over his head and tossed it aside. A shaft of moonlight shining through the smokehole in the top of the wickiup gilded the brown hollow of his throat and his broad chest that was sculpted with muscle, free of hair.

She clasped her fingers together as they tingled with the need to touch his smooth, coppery skin, his flat, male nipples that resembled copper coins. Her chest felt constricted, and she drew a deep, shuddery breath as his hands went to the fastenings of his buckskin trousers.

His gaze held hers, warm with promise as he slid the trousers down his hips. Her lips parted softly and her breasts rose and fell with her quickened breathing as he bared his naked flesh to her gaze.

Color burned high in her cheeks, and she grasped at the edges of her composure. He was taking pleasure in making her anticipate their union. Her nerves fluttered with agitation, expressing itself in the erratic beating of a pulse at the base of her throat.

A soft, knowing laugh escaped his lips as his breeches fell down around his ankles. He kicked them aside and stood naked before her. She felt like a mule had kicked her in the stomach. Her abdomen contracted sharply. There was a tightening in her loins. He was beautiful, an Adonis. And he belonged to her.

Her throat was dry, she licked her lips. "Swift Arrow," she groaned.

He came to her, leaning over her and pulling her into

220

his arms. His lips found the pulse at the base of her neck, and then he was clutching her tightly against him. A fierce joy stabbed through her and she scattered kisses across his face, his neck, his shoulder. Then he was parting her thighs, and coming to her. His entry was swift, and a small cry left her as he slid deep inside. She embraced him tightly as he began to move within her, slowly at first and then faster and faster until they were plunging in an ecstasy of desire, a pulsating and sensual frenzy that took them to a place beyond reckoning. They climbed together as he thrust strong and steady with the rhythm of a heartbeat. Their bodies gleamed with perspiration as the tension built . . . and built . . . and built. . . .

Swift Arrow drove into her harder and deeper, throbbing inside her, his fingers clutching her hips tightly as though he would take her inside himself. His movements fueled the fire that was almost consuming her.

Finally, unable to stand the intense pleasure he was creating, her body grew rigid. She arched upward in an explosion of volcanic proportions. Then, with one last thrust, he collapsed on top of her, leaving her shuddering with ecstasy beneath him.

Chapter Twenty-One

Katherine woke to the sound of a shot. Then, a piercing war cry rent the night, chilling her blood. After that all hell seemed to break loose. The night was filled with gunfire, bullets whistling through the air and the sound of screams.

At the first sound Swift Arrow had leapt to his feet and run to the entranceway. Katherine, moving almost as fast, was right behind him. The sight that met her eyes filled her with fear. For in the ghostly light of the moon she saw cavalrymen firing rifles and using bayonets on the Apaches, who had been taken by surprise.

Swift Arrow spared one quick look at her. Her silver-blond hair looked almost white in the moon's pale light.

"Cover your hair," he growled. "And stay inside

the wickiup."

Without another word he stepped outside and began firing at the advancing militia.

Before she could react, a dark figure appeared, raised his gun, and aimed it at Swift Arrow.

"Get down," he said, shoving her aside and leaping toward the man. His long, sinewy arm reached out, knocking aside the rifle barrel just before it went off.

Katherine barely had time to recognize the man's blue and gold uniform before the two were locked in a fierce battle.

Swift Arrow's rifle was useless at such close range. He drew his knife from his belt, slicing a long cut across the other man's arm. The man yelped in pain, dropping the rifle with a clatter. The trooper grabbed his own knife, making a lunge for the warrior. Swift Arrow leapt agilely away, streaking out with his knife, drawing another yelp from his opponent.

All around her, Katherine could hear the screams of the women amid the shots and shouts, the war cries and the thudding of flesh against flesh. Unable to watch the fight any longer, she looked away . . . and her eyes widened in horror at the devastation surrounding her.

The clearing was strewn with fallen bodies, and Katherine shrank back from the horror around her. Men and women alike had fallen beneath the attackers' guns. The noise beat at her ears, the sight sickened her. She saw Many Tongues running from a soldier, her terrified screams blending with the others. As Katherine watched, the soldier raised a rifle to his shoulder, aimed it, and a blaze of flame spouted from the barrel.

ACCEPT YOUR FREE GIFT
AND EXPERIENCE MORE OF
THE PASSION AND ADVENTURE
YOU LIKE IN A
HISTORICAL ROMANCE

Zebra Romances are the finest novels of their kind and are writ-ten with the adult woman in mind. All of our books are written by authors who really know how to weave tales of romantic adventure in the historical settings you love.

Because our readers tell us these books sell out very fast in the stores, Zebra has made arrange-ments for you to receive at home the four newest titles published each month. You'll never miss a title and home delivery is so convenient. With your first shipment we'll even send you a FREE Zebra Historical Romance as our gift just for trying our home sub-scription service. No obligation.

BIG SAVINGS
AND FREE HOME DELIVERY

Each month, the Zebra Home Subscription Service will send you the four newest titles as soon as they are published. (We ship these books to our subscribers even before we send them to the stores.) You may preview them *Free for 10 days.* If you like them as much as we think you will, you'll pay just $3.50 each and *save $1.80 each month off the cover price.* AND you'll *also get FREE HOME DELIVERY.* There is never a charge for shipping, handling or postage and there is no minimum you must buy. If you decide not to keep any shipment, simply return it within 10 days, no questions asked, and owe nothing.

The woman fell to the ground and lay still.

Katherine's throat constricted. In just a few moments her world had turned into a nightmare. She looked back at the two men locked in combat near her. With a quick swipe, Swift Arrow dispatched his opponent, slicing open his throat.

Swift Arrow turned to her. "Quickly. The white eyes must not see you," he said. "You must hide."

He had barely a glance to spare for the destruction surrounding them before his attention was caught by another man who had taken the place of the first. As he had done before, Swift Arrow knocked the rifle aside, but his opponent retained his grip on the gun, deftly turning it around and bringing it down like a club. Swift Arrow jerked aside. The gun missed his head, but landed with a heavy thud on his shoulder, knocking him to the ground.

Katherine panicked as the other man followed him down, clubbing at his head. He was going to kill Swift Arrow!

Oh, God! He was going to die!

She made a dive for the rifle, aimed it, and fired. The bullet hit the man squarely in the forehead. He flipped backwards and sprawled on the ground. He twitched for a moment, then lay still.

Swift Arrow regained his feet and grabbed her arm. "Come," he said. "We must flee."

They ran for the horses, but a soldier saw them and raised his rifle.

"Look out," she screamed.

But it was too late. The man had fired.

Swift Arrow's body flinched as the bullet struck. His eyes were agonized as they met Katherine's. A red circle blossomed on Swift Arrow's chest, and he staggered. Then his legs collapsed beneath him and he fell to the ground.

Tears flooded her cheeks as Katherine knelt beside him. She was completely unaware that the noise had stopped. And as unaware of the shadowy figure who stopped beside her. Of the astonishment filling the eyes that came to rest on her silvery hair.

"Katherine?"

As the voice penetrated her consciousness, she looked up . . . into the face of Lieutenant Hawood.

"Help him, Cal," she pleaded brokenly. "Please don't let him die."

Something flickered across Calvin Hawood's face. He seemed taken aback at her words. His gaze moved from Katherine to the fallen warrior, then back to her again.

"Please, Cal," she whispered. "You've got to help him."

Lieutenant Hawood turned away abruptly. He stopped a man who was passing nearby. "Sergeant, get Dr. Walsh," he ordered.

Katherine bent over Swift Arrow's inert form. *Don't let him die,* she prayed silently. *Please don't let him die.*

"Take it easy, youngun," said a gruff voice. "Everthin's gonna be fine now. The cavalry's done found us."

She looked up at the old mountain man. "Why did this have to happen?" she cried, swiping at the tears that continued to flow down her cheeks.

Taking her arm in an iron grip, Buck pulled her up and into his arms. His voice was low when he spoke. "Don't say nuthin'," he growled. "It won't serve no purpose fer 'em to know the way the wind blows. And it would be worth thet boy's life if they were to find out."

Her eyes were wide, uncomprehending, as she looked at him. As his words penetrated, she flinched. Her eyes darted to Swift Arrow, then back to meet Buck's shrewd gaze. A silent message passed between them.

"You wanted me, lieutenant?" A voice intruded in the silence that surrounded them.

Katherine looked at the man who had joined them. He threw a curious glance at her, and as the moonlight fell on the silvery strands of her hair, his eyes widened slightly.

"Hell!" he exclaimed. "I didn't know they had captives." His eyes fell on Swift Arrow, and he prodded the fallen man with the toe of his boot.

"See to the Indian," Lieutenant Hawood said. "I'm afraid he's badly wounded."

"So are a lot of 'em," the man growled. "Not to mention a few of our own men."

"Nevertheless, see to this one first," the lieutenant commanded. Reaching out, he took Katherine's arm. "Come with me, Kathy," he said gently.

"No," she protested. "Not until I know—"

"Go with 'im, youngun," Buck growled commandingly. "I'll take care of things here." His voice held a warning, as did his eyes.

"Katherine," Lieutenant Hawood said softly. "You're

227

beside yourself. Come away from all this. You'll feel better."

She wanted to refuse them both. She wanted to stay with the man she loved. But, for the first time, she became aware of the attention they were attracting from the other men. Some of the looks thrown her way were puzzled. If these men ever found out what had happened between her and Swift Arrow, she felt sure they wouldn't hesitate to kill him. She must take care they never learned what he meant to her. Already, her worry over him was causing speculation. She must give them a reason for her concern.

She drew a shaky breath and raised her chin a degree higher. "Doctor, I would appreciate it if you would see this man is well taken care of," she said calmly. "He saved my life. Without his help I would certainly be dead. I could not, in all conscience, do less for him."

Lieutenant Calvin Hawood's expression showed relief at her explanation. He smiled down at her. "Of course, you're right, Kathy. We'll certainly do everything in our power to help him."

Katherine drew a breath of relief and allowed herself to be led away.

Her brain was working furiously, concocting a story that would satisfy her father. There was no way she could allow them to find out she had been with Swift Arrow for nearly a month.

As she had anticipated, the lieutenant pressed her for details.

She chose her words with care. "You know I was upset when I left the fort." Sadness washed across her

228

face. "I had just learned of Jesse's death. And my father's . . ." She broke off. She couldn't bring herself to tell him about her suspicions regarding her father's part in Jesse's death. "I rode into the mountains. Something frightened the mare and she threw me." She planned on sticking to the truth as much as possible. "I sustained a blow on the head, and Buck found me."

"The old man?"

"Yes."

He frowned. "Why didn't he bring you back to the fort?"

"The blow I received was bad. I was unconscious when he found me. He took me to a cave where he was staying and cared for me. By the time I was able to tell him who I was, a blizzard had struck. There was no way we could leave the shelter of the cave."

"You were snowed in all this time?"

She could see he was doubtful, and searched her mind for something that would convince him.

"You might as well tell him about my bunged-up leg, younggun," Buck growled beside her. She looked up, startled. "Ain't no good tryin' to pertect me." He spat a long stream of tobacco on the ground and glared at the young lieutenant. "What'cha askin' all these questions fer anyway? Cain't'cha see this little lady's near to faintin'?" His eyes sent a signal to Katherine. "How you holdin' up, youngun'?"

She put a trembling hand to her brow. "I—I feel weak," she said.

"Course you do," the old man said. He glared at the other man. "An' you ain't helpin' matters none with all

229

these questions. Body'd think you don't trust 'er, or some such thing."

Lieutenant Hawood looked uncomfortable. "I'm sorry, Kathy," he apologized. "I'm afraid I wasn't thinking."

"Buck." She looked at the old-timer with anxious gray eyes. "How is . . ."

"Ain't no call fer you to worry none," Buck assured her quickly. "What's done is done. Many Tongues is dead. So's 'er husband. But worryin' about it's gonna do no good. Thet Injun who helped us is bein' took care of. I've had worse'n what he's got an' kept right on a-whistlin'." His fingers gripped her arm, but his eyes held the other man's. "Now you leave this'n alone an' give the order to travel if'n yore gonna. Cain't see no sense in stayin' here. Cain't never tell who's gonna ride up and surprise us."

"You're right," the other man said. "If we start right now, we should make the fort by dark."

He turned away from them and joined a group of troopers who were watching the prisoners.

Katherine looked at the old man. "Why did you want him to leave now?" she asked. "Our only chance is to escape from them."

"Nope," he growled. "Swift Arrow wouldn't stand a snowball's chance in hell of pulling through if he has to run."

Her face drained of color. "Is he going to die?" she whispered.

"Not if we can get 'im to a place where he can be took care of," he said gruffly. "The fort's the only place he

230

won't have to run from."

"But my father will kill him!"

"He ain't gonna know nuthin'," he said grimly. "Not if we keep our mouths shut. Them other Injuns sure as hell ain't gonna talk. What'd you tell thet young lieutenant?"

She told him what she'd said. He told her to stick to the story and say that he'd broken his leg and couldn't travel. Then, when they could travel, they had been swept away in the river while trying to cross. Then Swift Arrow had come along and pulled them out. That would give them a good reason to be traveling with the Apaches.

"Do you think they'll believe it?" she asked.

"They cain't prove nuthin' else," he said.

They stopped speaking as the lieutenant rejoined them. They told their story to him and he listened thoughtfully, asking a question occasionally, which Buck answered to his satisfaction.

She felt sure they were believed.

"I'm sorry some of them were killed," the lieutenant said. "Especially since they helped you. But our orders are to bring in any renegade band we find off the reservation. It could have been a lot worse. We were damned lucky we had Running Horse."

"Running Horse?"

"Yes. He's our Apache guide. These Apaches are elusive bastards. We'd never have been able to get anywhere near them if it hadn't been for his being one of them and knowing their ways."

"An Apache led you here? He helped you kill his

231

own people?"

"He's not the first one that's a turncoat, Kathy. And the army's quick to make use of him and his kind. Without men like him we wouldn't stand a chance against the Apaches."

How could a man turn traitor against his own people? She looked at the man in question, saw his dark eyes watching her. She felt a tremor of fear chase up and down her spine, for he seemed to see right through her.

The Indians were rounded up, and Katherine's eyes swept over them. She counted only six. Half their number had been killed. Her eyes flickered with pain, for Bright Feathers was among the missing. All that was left of the small band was Laughing Turtle, Grassy Waters, and her husband, Creeping Bullfrog. She saw Running Elk, and Bright Feathers's betrothed, Eagle Claw . . . and Crying Wolf.

Katherine's heart lay heavy in her chest as she felt Eagle Claw's pain at the loss of the woman he loved.

A chittering sound from the bushes caught her attention. She could just make out a gray furry head with a black mask.

Blackie!

She moved toward the bushes and he came running out to her on all fours. She picked him up and buried her face in his fur. "Thank goodness you're all right," she murmured.

The sun was just bursting over the horizon when the lieutenant came to tell her they were ready to begin the long trek back to the fort. He looked at the raccoon in her arms.

"Where'd you find him?" he asked.

"He's been with me for a long time," she said. "He's coming with me."

He nodded.

Katherine felt the eyes of the small group of Apaches on her as she was put astride a horse. She held the raccoon close against her, taking a meager comfort from his warmth. She felt ashamed that she was being treated better than the others. But she didn't allow her feelings to show. Swift Arrow's life could depend on her acting ability. No one must guess how much he meant to her.

She sat up straight on the horse, her head held high.

She intended to take full advantage of the lieutenant's sympathies for her plight. For it allowed her to receive better treatment for Swift Arrow. It was at her insistence that he was placed on a litter and dragged behind one of the horses.

The trip back to the fort was necessarily slow because of the Apache captives on foot. They were herded like animals toward the center of the column. Swift Arrow was the only one left alive who had been wounded badly enough to require a litter.

Lieutenant Hawood came riding up beside her. His hat was pulled low over his forehead, hiding his eyes from her gaze. "Your father will be glad to see you," he said. "We all thought you were dead."

"And so I would have been if not for Swift Arrow . . . and Buck," she added quickly. "I hope my father takes into account the way they helped us when he's dealing with the Apaches. These people have come to be my friends."

"You know better than I do how your father feels about Indians," he said. "I'm afraid there's very little that can change that."

"Cal . . ." she hesitated. "Would you do everything you can to see they're treated right?"

"You don't even have to ask," he said. "Of course, I will."

She eyed him steadily. "I don't think it's going to make any difference to my father that the Apaches saved my—our lives. I want you to promise me you'll not let him harm them in any way."

"When your father sets his mind to something, there's very little I can do," he said. "I know he's your father, but . . ."

"You also know what he did to Jesse."

"Yes. I know," he admitted. "And I'm sorry. If I'd been here, then possibly I'd have been able to prevent it, but . . ."

"I know. He had you transferred."

"Yes. And he could do it again."

She looked back at the travois that carried Swift Arrow. He was lying so still. Her heart lurched. He couldn't die. What would she do without him? "Cal," she said. "If Father gets you transferred again, then perhaps you could tell someone what's happening out here. Someone in higher authority. . . ."

"What would I tell them?" he asked gently. "Exactly what crime has your father committed?"

"He was instrumental in Jesse's death," she said

234

fiercely. "It was his orders that killed him and the rest of those men."

"They were outlaws, Kathy," he said gruffly. "Most people would think the West was better off without them."

"Jesse wasn't an outlaw."

"He joined them."

She was silent for a moment. "There are some people who wouldn't agree with the way my father deals with the Apaches," she said.

Blackie sensed her agitation and stirred restlessly in her arms. He looked up at her with his beady black eyes.

"I'll admit there are a few who care," he said. "But there are even more who don't. They sit back in their easy chairs and talk about controlling the Indians. And make no mistake, they don't care how it's done. All they want is for the Apache raids to stop. They don't give a damn how it's accomplished."

"It's not right," she muttered. "Maybe if you went to the newspapers and told them what's going on. . . ."

"It would take too long to do your friend any good," he said, his gaze intent on her. "You're not fooling me at all, Kathy. I know you too well. That Indian means something special to you. But for God's sake, don't let anyone else see. If your father had any suspicion at all, he'd have the man killed immediately."

Shock ran through her. She had thought she was hiding her feelings about Swift Arrow so well. Had she really been so transparent? "I'm not sure I know what you mean," she prevaricated.

"Yes. You do. At the moment, the other men haven't the faintest idea. But I'm afraid they've guessed there's more to the picture than meets the eye. You'll have to hide your feelings better, if you want to keep them in the dark."

If she wanted to? God! She must. Swift Arrow's life depended on her. Her heart was despairing as she looked back at him . . . lying so motionless on the litter. If he died, how could she go on?

Chapter Twenty-Two

A lone buzzard circled in the sky above, seeming to be an ominous sign of the future to Katherine's troubled mind. Before them the fort lay sprawled out in the desert.

Tension stiffened Katherine's spine, and her heart filled with dread as they approached the garrison.

She could feel the taste of fear in her mouth, not for herself, but for the man she loved, and she swallowed hard.

Turning in the saddle, she looked back at the litter that carried Swift Arrow. What was waiting for him behind those gates? Imprisonment? Or perhaps even death?

She swallowed again, lifting her eyes to the mountains they had left behind in the Gila river country. They rose, tall and majestic, toward the heavens. She had known happiness in those mountains. Was her future to hold only despair?

As the distance to the fort slowly narrowed, the lieutenant sent a rider ahead to alert the guards to the patrol's return, and to inform Major Carpenter that his daughter had been found. As they drew nearer, she could see the gates stood partially open.

At a shouted command from Lieutenant Hawood, the gates were opened wider, allowing the column of soldiers and their captives to enter the compound.

As they went through the gates Katherine was aware of all the eyes on her. A work detail had paused to gawk. A heavy-set woman stood in the doorway of the laundry and watched them pass. Three women and a soldier stood together on the porch of the Sutler's store. Katherine recognized the women as officers' wives. When she met their eyes, all three looked away as if they had been caught doing something shameful.

After turning command of the column and the captured Indians over to the sergeant, the lieutenant rode with Katherine to the adobe building that was the major's office. He dismounted and turned to help her.

She handed the raccoon down and Lieutenant Hawood put him on the ground.

As the lieutenant swung her down, she leaned toward him. "Cal," she said, keeping her voice low. "Promise me you'll see he's taken care of."

He nodded, having no need to ask who she meant. "I'll do what I can, Kathy," he assured her.

A tall man dressed in a blue gold-braided uniform stepped out onto the veranda. With his polished boots

238

and the saber swinging at his side, he was a picture of military perfection. For a timeless moment, Katherine stared at him.

His gray eyes held hers, becoming cold as they dwelt on her doeskin dress. No detail of her appearance escaped his attention. Not the long pale braid hanging down her back, nor the sun-browned skin that had been so pale when she'd left the fort.

Her nerves were strained as tension held her in its grip. The moment seemed locked in time. Suddenly, to her astonishment, his eyes softened. His arms came out, surrounding her and pulling her close against him.

"I thought you were dead," he said harshly. "I thought I was completely alone in the world."

She closed her eyes and allowed herself to relax against him. Tears welled, unbidden, to her eyes. Could it be possible that her father really loved her? She'd never known him to show such feeling before. Never known he was even capable of it.

He pulled back slightly, cupping her face in his hands. His restless gaze studied her, taking note of the changes time had wrought. Heaving a long sigh, he smoothed damp tendrils of hair back from her face.

"Come with me," he said. "Let's get you cleaned up." He threw a quick look at the band of captives across the compound. "I'll see those devils pay for what they did to you. I swear it, Kathy. If it's the last thing I do, I'll make them pay."

The color drained from her face. "No!" she cried. "Please don't. You've got it all wrong. They haven't harmed me. They saved my life."

239

She could see he didn't believe her, so she quickly told him the story she and Buck had concocted between them. She made a point of not mentioning Swift Arrow's name at all.

"Are you sure you're not just trying to protect them?" he asked, his gaze probing her face for the truth. "You always did have a soft heart for what you considered the underdog."

"I swear to you, Father," she said earnestly. "I was shown the utmost consideration."

"They must have known who you were and thought to curry favor with me by taking care of you," he muttered. "Well, no matter why they did it, at least I have you back again." His voice hardened. His gray eyes became cold. "And it's the last time you'll ever leave this fort alone, young woman."

Her heart sank. He had put a guard on her once before . . . when he had learned she had been seeing Jesse. If he did it again, she would never be able to find a moment alone with Swift Arrow.

She lowered her eyes submissively, hiding her feelings from him. She had to make him believe all the fight had left her. Perhaps then her movements wouldn't be hampered by a guard.

"What will you do with them?" she asked softly.

"Lock them up until I can send them back to the reservation," he said.

"Father . . ." She made her voice hesitantly pleading. ". . . since the Apaches were so good to me, couldn't they be set free? They wouldn't hurt anyone. They could . . ."

240

"No!" His expression became cold, his eyes wintry. "It's unthinkable for you even to suggest such a thing to me. You're a major's daughter. You should know better than that."

"How could you expect me to show them less kindness than they showed me?" she asked. "I couldn't live with myself if I didn't do everything in my power to help them."

"That's enough," he said sternly. "Go on to the house. We'll finish this discussion later. Right now, the lieutenant's waiting to make his report."

So much for his show of concern, she thought bitterly. *It didn't last very long.*

She knew she would get nowhere by pleading with him. He wasn't a man who reversed a decision easily. She would just have to find another way to help the Apaches, and Swift Arrow.

Katherine bent to pick up Blackie. The raccoon came willingly into her arms. Without another word, she turned to go.

"Kathy!"

The one word was a command. She stopped abruptly, waiting.

"What are you doing with that raccoon?"

She clutched Blackie tighter against her breast. The animal growled at her in protest. Katherine loosened her grip and turned to face her father. "He's mine," she said defiantly.

"Well, he can't stay in the house. Give him to one of the men."

"No. He stays with me." She turned and left before

he could say anything else.

Her troubled gaze swept the small knot of captives across the compound, but she couldn't see the man she was searching for.

She wanted desperately to see Swift Arrow, to make sure he was still living and everything possible was being done for him, but she couldn't make her wishes known. It would only worsen his plight if her father discovered their relationship.

She continued across the parade ground until she reached the row of adobe houses that housed the officers who were assigned to the fort. She was conscious of curtains being discreetly pulled back from windows, and she smiled with grim amusement.

Katherine looked neither to the right or left as she headed for the third house on Officers' Row. Grasping the doorknob with one hand, she entered and let her gaze travel around the familiar surroundings.

Nothing had changed.

The house she had shared with her father since coming to Fort Bayard was considerably larger and better furnished than the rest of the quarters. A handwoven black, fuschia, and gray rug covered the highly polished hardwood floor. A gray velvet sofa and two chairs of fuschia silk picked up the colors of the rug. A painting of Brittany, Katherine's mother, hung over the mantel, and brightly colored Mexican pottery was on display in a mahogany cabinet. Overall, the effect was one of grace and beauty.

She put Blackie down and he scurried behind an overstuffed chair, obviously nervous at his surroundings. She moved toward her bedroom, but before she reached it, a figure stepped from the kitchen door.

"Miss Katherine?" The voice was barely a whisper.

She turned quickly to see a large woman with coffee-colored skin staring incredulously at her.

A genuine smile spread across her face. "Minnie!" she exclaimed. Tears welled in her eyes, spilled over, and slid hotly down her cheeks.

The woman held out her arms to the girl and Katherine ran into them and found herself held tight against a large, heaving bosom.

"Is you all right, honey chile?" Minnie asked. "Is you really here . . . an' alive?"

"Yes," Katherine choked. "I'm really here, and I'm certainly alive."

"But you done been gone for more'n a month, honey chile," the woman said. "We wuz plumb sure dem 'Paches done had you."

Katherine pulled out of the woman's embrace and wiped the tears away with the back of her hand. This woman might understand her feelings. But she had to be sure before she spoke them. She couldn't take a chance with Swift Arrow's life. Perhaps if she handled things carefully, Minnie might even be her way of keeping in contact with Swift Arrow.

"The Apaches did have me," she said quietly. "But not in the way you think. My horse threw me and I was gravely wounded. I lay in the snow until I was found." She explained how she had been carried to safety and cared for. And how her wound had been stitched up. She told of how they had been snowed in, unable to go

243

anywhere. But in her explanation, she avoided all mention of Swift Arrow's name, making sure she told the story she and Buck had agreed upon. She kept her eyes averted from the woman when she had to resort to lies, but her voice never wavered. She knew she could not allow the slightest hesitation to show in it. The woman knew her too well. And she couldn't be sure she wouldn't betray her to her father.

"Sounds like you was mighty lucky runnin' into dem good Indians." Minnie shook her grizzled head. "Yore daddy ain't gonna be too happy 'bout no 'Paches savin' yore life, honey chile."

"I know," Katherine said, gazing into Minnie's dark, sympathetic eyes. "He's keeping them prisoner. He said he's going to send them back to the reservation, Minnie."

"Well, don't worry yore head no more 'bout dat now." Minnie's dark gaze traveled over the girl's doeskin dress, her disheveled hair. "What you needs right now is a hot bath. Don't dem 'Paches believe in baths?"

"Of course, they do," Katherine said, a little more sharply than she'd intended. "I'm afraid there was barely enough water out in the desert to drink, let alone take a bath in."

"Well, we's gonna take care of dat dis very minute," the woman said. "Now you git on in yore room an' take dem hides off'n yore back, an' I'll start de water heatin'."

Giving the girl a gentle shove toward her bedroom, the woman bustled back into the kitchen.

244

As Katherine opened the door to her bedroom, Blackie scurried out from behind the chair and followed her inside.

She found this room, too, as she had left it. A large four-poster bed covered with a flower-garden quilt dominated the room. Against one wall stood an elaborately carved armoire, and against the opposite one sat a dressing table with a stool in front of it. The braided rug on the floor had been made by her own hands when she had joined her father two years ago. As had the gaily colored curtains on the window. A cloth-draped steamer trunk served as a bench beneath the window.

Someone shouted outside and Katherine's heart leapt with panic. What was happening? The voice had sounded angry. Was the anger directed at Swift Arrow? She ran to the window and pulled the curtains back.

Chapter Twenty-Three

Katherine didn't have to search for the problem. The Indians were being herded together toward the stables. And although Katherine could see very little sign of resistance on the part of the Apaches, the soldiers were using their rifle butts as clubs to force the Indians into a large building that had been used to store weapons until a more durable building had been built.

Her eyes flashed angrily. There was no excuse for the treatment the Apaches were receiving. She meant to confront her father about it.

"Patrol comin' in," the sentry shouted. "Open the gates."

Katherine watched as the gates opened and dust boiled beneath the cantering hooves of cavalry horses as another troop of cavalry rode into the fort.

She knew her father would be occupied with reports

from both patrols for a while. She might as well clean up before she saw him. Perhaps after she had discarded her Indian clothing he might be a little more receptive to her pleas on the Indians' behalf.

Sighing, she moved back from the window and removed her dress and soiled underwear. By the time Minnie brought the first bucket of water into the bedroom, she was clothed in a dressing gown, and her soiled garments were folded neatly on a chair.

"Umm . . . mmmm," Minnie muttered, casting a disparaging look at the clothing. "Yore daddy musta been fit to be tied when he saw you in dem animal skins. He musta—" She broke off with a shriek.

Katherine stiffened. "What's the matter?"

"Dey's a wild animal in dis room!" Minnie cried. "Go git de shotgun, honey chile, while ole Minnie fights de creature off."

Katherine laughed as she followed the black woman's gaze. She saw a fuzzy gray head and two black eyes peeking out from beneath the bed where Minnie's shrieks had sent the frightened raccoon.

"It's only Blackie," she said.

"He sure am black, all right."

"He won't hurt anything, Minnie. He's as frightened as you are."

"Ole Minnie ain't a-feared of no possum," the woman declared stoutly.

"Blackie's not a possum," Katherine corrected. "He's a raccoon. I've made a pet of him."

"Umm mmmm," Minnie said. "Yore daddy ain't

248

gonna like havin' nothin' like dat aroun' dis here house."

Katherine's lips tightened. "I don't care," she said. "Blackie stays with me."

Keeping a wary eye out for the raccoon, Minnie gathered up Katherine's soiled clothing and left the room, mumbling under her breath about Apaches and wild animals and a Miss Kathy who had become tetched in the head by her ordeal.

A few minutes later, Katherine lay soaking in a tub of hot water. As she washed herself, her brain whirled with activity. She had to find a way to help Swift Arrow. But at the moment she didn't know how. Soon she rose from the tub, determined to send Minnie to find Buck and ask him to come see her. She could stand the suspense no longer. Surely he could find out how Swift Arrow was doing.

After she had dressed, she crossed to her bedroom window. From the small garden outside came the sweetly fragrant scent of honeysuckle. Her gaze went to the building where the captives were confined. It looked innocent enough, appearing the same as usual. There was no indication that it was being used as a jail. Was Swift Arrow there with the others?

Worry wrinkled her brow as she went in search of Minnie. She found the woman in the kitchen.

"Minnie, I've got an errand for you to run," she said.

The woman looked at her shrewdly. "What does you want ole Minnie to do?" she asked.

"I want you to find Buck . . . the old mountain man

249

who was with me. Tell him I want to see him."

"Cain't it wait till tomorrow?"

"No. I must see him now. And hurry, before my father comes home."

"Yore daddy prob'ly ain't comin' home fore suppertime," the woman muttered. "Makes no nevermind dat his onliest chile's done come back from de dead. No sirree. He gonna stay at his job like always."

"You're wasting time, Minnie," Katherine said. "Hurry up and find Buck for me. I'd go myself, but Father will expect me to stay here."

"You can say dat again," Minnie grumbled, untying her apron. "He ain't gonna let you step foot out'n dis house for a long time to come. Not after what you done been through."

Katherine watched impatiently as Minnie left the house. Then she began to pace across the parlor. She moved from the window to the hallway, then to the window and back again.

It seemed an eternity before Minnie came back into the room, but actually only fifteen minutes had passed.

"Did you find him?"

Minnie nodded. "He say he's comin'," she said, then went back to the kitchen to resume her work.

It was another ten minutes before the old man knocked at the door.

"Thank God you've come," Katherine said, pulling him into the house and closing the door behind him.

"What's happened, youngun?" Buck growled.

"You tell me," she said bitterly. "What have they done with him?" She didn't dare use Swift Arrow's

250

name in case someone was listening. But it wasn't necessary. The old-timer knew who she was talking about.

"They's somethin' funny goin' on," he said. "They didn't put 'im with the others."

Katherine's face paled. "Where did they take him?" she asked.

"They got 'im in thet old shack thet used to store tools. The walls is mighty thick." He gave a short laugh. "Reckon they figgered it'd take thet to hold 'im when he comes to 'is senses. Could be they're right."

"I don't like it," she muttered. "Why did they separate him from the others?"

"Could be 'cause he's hurt," Buck commented. "They might figger to take care of 'im better."

"My father wouldn't take his welfare into consideration," Katherine said. "Do you think he's suspicious?"

"I ain't sure," he said. "Don't see any reason fer 'im to be."

"I've got to find out."

"If you ain't mighty careful what you say, you could do the boy harm," Buck said. "Why don't you leave it be? I'll keep my ears open. See if'n I can find out what's a-goin' on."

Katherine barely heard him. Her mind was in a turmoil as she tried to figure out what was happening. "Why did they put him in that place?" she muttered. "There's no windows there." A thought suddenly occurred to her. "Is he locked in?"

"Course," Buck said gruffly. "An' under guard. Yore pa ain't takin' no chances, youngun."

"Why should they put an injured man under guard after he's been locked up?"

"'Pears they suspect somethin' ain't quite right."

"But how could they?"

"How far can you trust thet young lieutenant?"

"Cal wouldn't say anything to hurt me."

"Maybe he's a-thinkin' he's doin' what's best."

"No. He wouldn't do that," she said. "He's the only one who understands my reasons for leaving the fort. There's no love lost between my father and Cal. I'd trust him with my life."

"And the Injun's?"

Her eyes flickered with uncertainty. Could she trust Cal not to betray her feelings? It was true he didn't like her father. But he was a soldier. His orders were to bring the Indians in. Could it be possible he had taken it on himself to keep her separated from Swift Arrow? She honestly didn't know.

"I don't know whether I can trust him where Swift Arrow's concerned or not," she admitted. "I think I can . . . but I just don't know."

He nodded.

She laid a hand on his arm. "Could you find out how he is, Buck?"

"I figgered thet was what you was a-wantin'," he growled. "So I stopped to see 'bout 'im. Thet jackass they got guardin' the door warn't gonna let me in. But thet young lieutenant happened by."

"So you did get to see him?"

"Yep. An' all I can say 'bout it is, he's still alive."

"It's so dirty in there," she said fiercely. "And dark.

He could easily get an infection. Can't you get him moved to the dispensary?"

"How? By tellin' yore pa how you feel about him?"

"Oh, God!" she muttered. "No. My father would see him dead if he knew."

"Reckon so." He reached out a gnarled hand and patted her shoulder awkwardly. "Don't worry, young-un," he said gruffly. "I'll keep an eye out fer 'im. The doctor's done took out the bullet. I'll check on 'im ever day."

"And you'll bring word to me?"

"Yep. I'll bring word."

"Thank you," she whispered. "Thank you so much."

The door opened abruptly, startling them both. Her father entered and stopped short.

"What're you doing here?" he asked Buck coldly.

"Came callin' on the youngun," Buck replied stiffly. "Wanted to see how she was farin'." His gaze returned to Katherine. "Reckon I'll mosey on down to the Sutler's store and get a bite to eat," he said. "I'll pay my respects tomorrow, if'n you got no objections."

"Please do," she murmured politely. She nodded graciously and watched him leave. Then she braced herself, and turned to face her father.

"Damned trapper," her father said. "I expect he'll want some kind of reward for helping you." He turned back to his daughter. "I suppose you know your reputation has been irreparably damaged," he said, eyeing her grimly. "I had such high hopes for you, girl. But now, we'll be lucky if we can find a man who'd marry you."

"My God!" she exclaimed. "Is that all you can think about? My reputation?"

"The loss of one's reputation is no small matter, Kathy. Yours had already suffered a lot of damage from that business with the Mexican kid."

Although she knew he was right, she could have cared less. Inwardly she railed against the conventions that allowed a man to do as he wished while condemning a woman for the same thing. But public disapproval had never weighed heavily upon her.

"I don't think it would be wise for us to speak of Jesse," she said, her gray eyes flashing.

"Isn't that what is at the bottom of this whole thing?" he asked. "It was because of him that you snuck out of this fort. Against my express orders, I might add, and managed to get yourself thrown from your horse. If it hadn't been for that, you wouldn't have had to be rescued by that trapper, and the Apaches would never have had a chance to get their hands on you."

"You're turning things around," she said coldly. "I left here because I found out my father cold-bloodedly took the life of the only friend I ever had."

"Friend!" he spat. "Is that what you called it? It was my impression that you intended to marry the bastard!"

Her face went ash white. She stared at him with horror. "Is that why you killed him?" she whispered.

"Stop saying I killed him," he commanded. "It wasn't me who shot him."

"Yes. You did. Perhaps you didn't actually pull the trigger, but it was your orders that did it."

"That's enough. I don't wish to continue this conversation. I have some work to do in my office. I only returned to bid you goodnight."

Turning on his heel, he left the house, slamming the door behind him.

Katherine went to her room and undressed. Then she crawled into bed, listening to the sounds of the night.

Out on the parade ground, the bugler played taps. She listened to the familiar strains: the long, sad notes that rose, sending a lonely call out in the night, reaching higher, until they faded into a final sigh.

Although the sound had finished, its silent echo lingered a moment before its memory faded away.

She gave a long sigh and forced her body to relax. She needed to rest. She knew she was weary in both mind and body. And she needed all her wits about her for what she had planned for this night.

Chapter Twenty-Four

The moon hung in the ebony sky, a pale globe surrounded by glittering stars. A warm breeze lifted a lock of Katherine's silvery hair, blowing it across her face. She pushed it away impatiently, intent on keeping to the shadows as she made her way across the parade ground.

The buildings were dark, except for the Sutler's store, which seemed never to close.

High upon the guardwalk, she could see a sentry. The guard stood with his back to her, his attention directed outside of the fort.

Her wary gaze swept the compound, lingering momentarily on the lanterns that were hung at twenty-foot intervals to disperse the darkness within the walls before moving on to probe the shadowy corners. Finding nothing to alarm her, she slipped through the darkness and made her way toward the distant building where Swift Arrow was confined.

Footsteps crunched on gravel, and she melted into the shadows. Her heart drummed loudly in her ears as she waited, but no other sound penetrated the stillness.

The footsteps had stopped.

Had she been seen?

Was the someone she had heard waiting for her to leave the shadows before an alarm was raised?

"How's it going, Bill?" a loud male voice asked from somewhere close by.

"All's quiet," called a man from somewhere above.

Katherine's heart gave a startled leap, then settled back down as she realized the second man must be the sentry on the wall.

The man on the ground laughed. "Don't let any Injuns inside."

"They're already in," joked the sentry.

"Who's guardin' 'em?" the man on the ground asked.

"Charlie Shanks."

"Then they ain't goin' nowheres."

The sentry remained silent.

"What about thet Injun in the shack over there? I thought the major put a guard on him."

"He did," answered the sentry. "But he was pulled off. Reckon they decided he wasn't up to doin' much harm."

There was a moment of silence before the man on the ground spoke again. "See you in the mornin'."

The guard grunted.

Katherine waited until the footsteps had subsided,

then inched her way along the wall farthest from the sentry, keeping a wary eye on him as she went. Some sixth sense warned her he was going to turn a moment before he did. She made a headlong dive for cover.

Dirt and pebbles bit into her hands as she hit the ground at the side of the building. She lay still for a moment, then cautiously peered around the corner.

A match flared, showing the guard's face in profile for an instant. He was unfamiliar to her, his features appearing almost sinister in the red light of the flame before it was fanned out.

Suddenly, without warning, he turned his head toward her. She started, her booted foot knocking against the wall, sounding loud in the silence.

"Who's there?" he called.

Thrum . . . thrum . . . thrum. . . . Her heart pounded furiously inside her tense body. She waited for the shout that would mean she had been discovered.

It didn't come.

"Musta been my imagination," the sentry muttered.

A moment later she heard the sound of his boots moving along the guardwalk . . . away from her.

She turned her attention to Swift Arrow's prison.

She was at the side of the building, and the door was at the front. Proceeding cautiously, she edged around the building to the door. Then her heart sank. The door was fastened with a padlock.

She heard a scuffling noise inside the shack, then there was only silence from within. She put her lips against the door to muffle the sound.

"Swift Arrow," she called softly.

Silence.

"Swift Arrow!"

She heard a groan. It came from inside the building.
Oh, God! He needs help.

"Swift Arrow? Can you hear me?" Tears welled into her eyes, spilled over, slid hotly down her cheeks. "Please," she begged. "Answer me."

A door slammed at the sutler's store. Heavy footsteps sounded again on the boardwalk.

They're coming this way!

Hugging the wall, Katherine dashed around the corner. Her heart pounded with fear as she waited. The door banged again.

"Hey, Colby. Wait up. I'm leavin', too," a male voice shouted.

"Hurry up, then. I ain't got all night."

"What's the hurry?"

"I been out on patrol fer three days. I shoulda been in bed hours ago."

"You know something? I think you must be gettin' old."

Katherine realized the voices were getting closer all the time. She stepped backward, intent on seeking concealment behind the shed, knowing she would be discovered when the two men drew closer, if she didn't.

Suddenly, without warning, a hand came out of the darkness and clamped over her mouth. An arm circled her waist, dragging her behind the shed.

She struggled, kicking, grunting behind the pressure of the hand. Fighting, she was able to turn enough to recognize Running Horse, the turncoat Apache who scouted for the army.

Her fear was so strong that she was not aware the two men had passed her by until Running Horse spoke softly. "I mean you no harm," he muttered. "But you must not be seen here. Only harm can come from it." He released her. "Swift Arrow is being cared for. You must bide your time until he is well. Then perhaps he can be helped."

She edged away from him. "Why should I listen to you?" she asked, keeping her voice low. "It's your fault he's in that shape. You led the troopers to us."

"That is my job," he said. "But I did not know Swift Arrow would be there."

"You think that makes it all right? It doesn't. Have you no loyalty at all to your people?"

"There are things you do not understand about me and my people."

"What things?"

He fell silent for a moment, then he said. "This is not the time . . . or the place to talk. You must go now. Soon others will come, and they must never suspect you are his woman."

"You aren't going to tell them?"

"I cannot help Swift Arrow, but neither will I bring harm to him. Never to him."

Before she could question him further, the sutler's door banged again, and Running Horse gave her a little push.

"Go now," he said. "Quickly."

He left her then, moving around the corner.

"What're you doin' out so late, Injun?" came a

261

drunken male voice.

She couldn't hear his reply, but she wasted no time in making a dash for the nearest building. Circling behind it, she waited until the compound was quiet again, then worked her way back toward her father's house. She breathed a sigh of relief as she let herself in. Too soon, she found.

"Where've you been?"

Katherine started.

Steady, she warned herself. *He must not suspect.*

She turned to face her father. He was wearing a wool bathrobe, and in his hand he carried a glass filled with water.

"I've been outside," she said, forcing a calm into her voice that she didn't feel.

"I can see that, Kathy. What I want to know is, why?"

"I needed a breath of fresh air."

His eyes narrowed suspiciously. "I know you, Kathy. You've been up to something you know I wouldn't approve of. Have you been with those Apaches?"

"No," she said quickly. "Of course not. Why should you suppose I have?"

"You looked guilty as hell when you came in here just now."

"Your imagination is working overtime," she said coldly. "I have no reason to feel guilty over taking a walk."

She could see he wasn't convinced. But at the moment she was too upset over her thwarted plans to see Swift Arrow to really care. She stepped past him and opened the door to her room.

"Wait a minute," he said.

She turned.

"Stay away from them."

She raised her eyebrows. "Who?"

"You know damn well who," he snapped. "I'm talking about those Apaches. You've got it in your head they saved your life. And you think you owe them for it. But they're nothing but a bunch of savages. I don't want to see you anywhere near them."

"Or what?" she asked defiantly.

"Or I'll make them sorry," he said softly.

Fury surged through her, overshadowing her good sense. She opened her mouth to tell him she'd see them anytime she pleased. Then, remembering suddenly the power he held at the fort, enough to make good his threat, she clamped her lips together, swallowed her words, and left him alone.

Stepping into her room, she resisted the urge to slam the door behind her, knowing it would only worsen the situation. Her body was trembling as she threw herself on the bed fully clothed.

She knew it had already begun. Her father intended to take up where he'd left off, watching every move she made to make sure it was the right one. She was treated little better than a prisoner herself.

It was a long time before she fell asleep.

* * *

263

The next morning Katherine was weeding the flower bed when Buck joined her. She told him what had occurred the night before.

His expression was concerned as he studied her pale face. "You sure yore pa thought it was the Apaches you wanted to see . . . and not Swift Arrow?"

"He seemed convinced of it."

"Then try to keep 'im thet-a-way," he said. "An' don't do nothin' else to make 'im suspicious of that boy. He's gotta have time to get well."

"I know," she said. "But I was so worried, and still—"

She broke off as the sentry on duty sounded the alarm.

"Riders comin'!" he shouted.

"How many of 'em?" called the sergeant.

"Two. And they're ridin' hard."

"Injuns?"

"Nope. Looks like one of 'em's a woman."

"Be back directly, youngun," Buck growled. "I'm a-gonna see what this is all about."

She watched him cross the compound to the gate. By the time he had reached it the riders had come through. The horses were lathered, as though they had been ridden hard for a long distance.

Katherine, anxious to discover what had happened, hurried to join them. A small crowd had gathered by the time she reached them, one of whom was her father. He threw a dark look at her but remained silent.

Everyone's attention was focused on the man, who

was telling how the stagecoach had been held up by bandits.

"Was there anyone else on the stage?" Major Carpenter asked the man.

"Nope," the man said. "Jist me an' the lady there. But them gents got away with all the valuables we was carryin'."

Katherine watched him a moment longer before turning her attention to the woman. She wore her iron-gray hair coiled at the nape of her neck, and atop her head perched a black hat with a drooping feather. A bit of ivory lace relieved the stark blackness of the traveling dress she wore. Although her weariness showed in the lines of strain on her face, when her gaze met Katherine's, her chin lifted slightly.

Buck moved restlessly beside Katherine. Moving to the side of the woman's mount, he reached up to her, circling his gnarled hands around her waist and lifting her to the ground.

"Much obliged," she said, holding his gaze steadily. "I wasn't too sure my legs would hold me up."

"You all right, ma'am?" he asked gruffly.

She laughed. "Reckon I'll live," she said. "I'm no weak ninny, but we've rode a mighty long piece today." A shadow crossed her face. "How far is it to Silver City?"

"Too far to ride today." Buck's faded gaze moved to Katherine. "She needs a place to spend the night, youngun," he said.

"Of course," Katherine said quickly. "You're welcome to stay with us. Please come with me."

The woman nodded and made to follow Katherine. Suddenly, she put a hand across her eyes and swayed. She straightened immediately. But it was too late. Buck had recognized her weakness. He wrapped an arm around her waist. "Lean on me," he growled.

To Katherine's surprise, the woman allowed Buck to help her.

Katherine ran ahead of them to her house. By the time they arrived, she had the door open. Buck helped the woman up the two steps, then into the house. He waited until she was seated in an easy chair before he spoke again.

"Don't worry, ma'am," he said. "I'll tell your man where he can find you."

The woman looked startled, then comprehension dawned. "He's not my man," she said quickly. "He's the driver of the stage. I'm sorry I didn't introduce myself. My name is Sara Cole."

Buck took the hand she held out. He seemed to be studying it. It was a moment before he spoke. "Are you travelin' alone, Miz Cole?"

"Yes. I'm a widow. I was going to visit my sister in Silver City." She looked at him curiously. "You didn't tell me your name," she reminded him.

Katherine was astonished to see Buck's face flush. "People call me Buck," he mumbled. "Name's John Winters, though. And I'd be mighty proud if'n you called me John."

Katherine stifled a chuckle. She could hardly believe it, but the old rascal was attracted to the widow. Her eyes glinted with humor. Could it be possible that Buck had found a woman he wanted after all these years? She sincerely hoped so. He had spent too many years mourning a lost love.

Her thoughts turned to Swift Arrow. Was she destined to suffer the same fate as Buck? Had her love for him been doomed from the beginning?

Chapter Twenty-Five

Swift Arrow wavered in and out of consciousness for nearly a week. He called often for Katherine in his delirium, but luckily, the doctor and the guard were the only ones who heard him, and neither one of them understood his language.

When his fever finally passed, he found himself lying on a pallet of straw in a windowless room that had a dry, musty smell. The only light that penetrated its shadowy confines came from the cracks between the thick boards that made up the shack.

His gaze traveled around his prison. Several burlap bags lay discarded a few feet away. Farther to the right, four empty crates stood against one wall. As his gaze circled the room, it fell on the three kegs near the door. One of them had been turned over, and horseshoe nails spilled across the dirt floor.

He saw nothing that could help him to escape from his dark cell.

His thoughts turned to Katherine. Was she all right? But why shouldn't she be? he answered himself. After all, was she not back among her people?

Had her father discovered what had happened between them? Swift Arrow thought not. Otherwise, he wouldn't have been left alone so long. He felt sure he would already be dead if her father knew he had held her captive . . . and the rest of what happened.

If the white eyes didn't already know what they had shared between them, they must never learn. Katherine would not tell them. For a white woman who had been with an Indian was considered defiled. No decent man of her race would look upon her with favor.

For that very reason, he felt an urge to tell them, even though it would mean his death. For at least it would insure that no other man would ever hold her slender body as he had. He dismissed the thought. She was too lovely to remain alone.

Footsteps sounded outside the door. Wood grated on wood as the latch was lifted . . . and the door opened. Bright sunlight filled the room, and he squinted against it. He had been in the darkness so long the bright rays hurt his eyes.

A horse soldier with a rifle pointed squarely in the middle of Swift Arrow's chest was the first one to enter. Behind him was the lieutenant. A man the Indian didn't recognize brought up the rear.

"Lower that rifle, corporal," the lieutenant growled. "That man's too weak to cause any trouble."

"You can't never tell about these red-devils, lieutenant," muttered the corporal, lowering the rifle reluctantly. "They got a habit of springin' back to life just when you're certain they're dead. Man could get his hair lifted trustin' 'em too much."

"Does he speak English?" the lieutenant asked. Then, as if suddenly aware the prisoner had a tongue in his head, he looked directly at him. "Do you savvy English?"

Swift Arrow remained silent, his face expressionless as he met the other man's probing gaze.

"Don't think he does," the unidentified man said, stepping forward. "When he was raving he was usin' the Apache language. Funny thing happened. He kept calling Miss Katherine's name."

The lieutenant frowned. "I didn't know you could speak Apache."

"I can't. But I sure as hell know how it sounds. And a name's a name. No matter what language you're speaking." He moved toward the bed, then stopped. "You better keep that rifle trained on him, corporal, while I check his wound. I don't trust him any more than you do."

The man's words identified him as the doctor, and Swift Arrow felt some measure of relief. At least they weren't going to let him die from an infected wound. He was acutely aware of the rifle trained on him as the doctor unfastened the bandage on his chest, pulled it aside, and inspected the wound.

"Looks like it's healing okay," he muttered. He covered the wound again and fastened the bandage. "I

271

don't know why we're worrying about it. If we'd just let him lay, it'd been one less Injun to worry about."

"Your orders are to take care of the injured, captain," the lieutenant reminded him. "They didn't specify any particular type of wounded . . . or race."

"You don't need to tell me what my orders are," the doctor said. "I know just as well as you."

"Yes, sir," Lieutenant Hawood said. "If you're finished, I'll have some food brought to your patient."

"You'll have food brought to the prisoner," the captain corrected softly.

"Wasn't that what I said, sir?" the lieutenant asked politely.

"No, lieutenant. It wasn't."

The captain walked to the door, and with another glance at the injured man, left the room.

"What was that all about?" the corporal asked.

"The captain tends to let race make a difference to his treatment of his patients," Lieutenant Hawood said. "I'm afraid he's forgotten his Hippocratic Oath."

"What's that?"

"A part of it is a doctor's promise to render aid to any man who needs his help."

"Well, can't say as I blame him. A redskin ain't exactly a man."

The lieutenant looked at the corporal. "You're a fool, corporal," he growled. "And on top of that, you're wasting time. See that this man gets some food."

"Yes, *sir,*" the corporal said smartly. He waited until the lieutenant had left the room before backing out himself, his eyes never leaving the wounded man on the bed.

Swift Arrow heard the sound of the wooden bar being replaced before the footsteps receded. He lay there a while, thinking about the conversation between the men. For some reason the lieutenant didn't seem to have the same hatred of Apaches that the others did.

He wondered why.

His gaze traveled around his prison again. A small band of light speared across the floor of the shack, coming from a crack between two boards. He struggled to a sitting position, then pushed himself to his feet. Stumbling across the dirt floor to the wall, he pressed his face against the boards.

Across the parade ground, directly in his line of vision, stood Katherine with the young lieutenant. Fury surged from deep within him, blazing in his ebony eyes.

He should have known. She had pretended to love him, and yet, the moment he was out of the way, she had eyes for another man. As he watched, Katherine laid a hand on the other man's arm. Swift Arrow's fists clenched tightly, wishing he had her slender white throat in his hands.

Loneliness and despair welled up from deep within him. How could Katherine have been so false? She had completely fooled him. With her soft words and skin, she had beguiled him. All the time she had been waiting for the white eyes to find her, to bring her back to her former pampered life.

He had been a fool!

His knees were weak, his strength almost spent.

Returning to his pallet, he sank down on it. He stared up into the darkness, his mind searching for a way out.

He must leave this dark, musty prison.

He longed to feel the sun against his face, to strip naked and bathe in the clear, cold waters of the mountain streams. The white eyes wanted to take this from him, but surely the Great Spirit would not allow it. HE who lived in the trees of the forest, in the hawk and the deer. HE would show him what to do.

His eyes glittered in the darkness. And Katherine would not free herself of him so easily. As long as there was breath in his body, he would keep her. The only way she could be free would be to kill him.

He would make certain of that.

The days passed, and Swift Arrow forced himself to practice a patience that he did not feel. He must wait until he grew stronger. And then, one day soon, the white eyes would make a mistake . . . and he would be ready.

Although he longed to throw the food he was brought into the face of the white eyes who carried it, he restrained himself, realizing he must eat to get well. It would have been futile for him to try anything anyway, since the man who brought the food was always accompanied by an armed guard.

His visitors were few in the days that followed. Except for the man who brought the food, there was only the doctor, and the young lieutenant, who always accompanied him. It wasn't long before Swift Arrow discovered from their conversation that the doctor would not have come unless prodded by the lieutenant.

274

One night, after he had eaten, he was lying on his pallet trying to force his body to relax when voices at the door caused him to tense.

Why have they come so late? he wondered. It was not their usual practice to come after the evening meal. The door opened and a man was shoved inside, then another. An armed guard stood in the entrance. He grinned at Swift Arrow.

"Brought you some company," he taunted. Holding the weapon at ready, he backed away and slammed the door shut, enclosing Swift Arrow and the others in darkness.

A loud groan caught Swift Arrow's attention. It was followed by a voice speaking the Apache language.

"Are you hurt badly, Running Elk?" Swift Arrow recognized Eagle Claw's voice.

"No. It is only a knife wound," Running Elk said.

"What has happened?" Swift Arrow asked, trying to see through the darkness to the two men.

"We tried to escape—to get help. The white eyes captured us." Running Elk's voice was puzzled.

"Our enemies seemed to know of our plans," said Eagle Claw bitterly.

"Perhaps you were overheard," Swift Arrow said.

"No," said Running Elk. "Only our people knew of our plan. We took care the enemy could not hear."

"Could someone have betrayed you?"

"None of our people would have betrayed us to the hated blue-coats," said Eagle Claw.

"And yet you say they expected you," Swift Arrow murmured.

"It is puzzling," said Running Elk.

"Yes," agreed Swift Arrow. "It is puzzling."

There was silence in the room. Swift Arrow wanted to ask them for news of Katherine, but was afraid of the answer. Perhaps, he told himself, it was better to be ignorant of her affairs.

"We must get out of here," Eagle Claw said. "The white eyes must be punished for what they did to our people."

"How many of our people are left?" Swift Arrow asked.

"Only Laughing Turtle, Crying Wolf, Creeping Bullfrog and his wife . . . and the two of us."

So Bright Feathers had been among the ones to die. Swift Arrow could only hope that her death had been quick. He agreed with the others that the white men should be punished. But he told them they would have to wait for the right opportunity.

But the opportunity never came, for the next day the men were taken from the room.

Swift Arrow didn't know what fate was planned for them, but their removal renewed his determination to escape his captors.

Chapter Twenty-Six

Katherine sat in the parlor with a book of poems in her lap. Despite the bright sunshine that filled the room, she felt depressed. She tried to concentrate on the prose, but her mind continued to wander.

Several days had passed since Sara Cole had left for Silver City. She had been accompanied by the stagecoach driver, and Buck, who was determined to see the widow safe at her sister's home before leaving her.

Katherine's lips twitched. She had barely restrained herself from teasing the old man when he returned. He was obviously quite taken with the widow.

Sighing, Katherine shifted in the chair. The movement caused the book to fall to the floor. It lay there, unheeded.

What was the matter with her? Why was she sitting

there doing nothing? She should be expending all her thoughts on getting Swift Arrow free. There should be something she could do . . . something she hadn't yet thought of.

A movement near her foot caused her to look down. Blackie had the book in his hands and was ripping at the pages.

"Naughty, naughty," she chided, reaching for the book of poems.

The raccoon clutched the book tighter and jumped back out of her reach. His eyes watched her reaction closely. She could nearly have sworn he was laughing at her.

"Give me that book," she said. "If Father finds out you've got it, you'll be skinned alive. You know he only tolerates you as it is."

The animal growled teasingly at her, scampering farther away, then making a leap for the mahogany cabinet. He skittered behind it, dragging the book with him.

"Blackie!" she cried, getting down on all fours. She supported herself on one elbow while she reached out with the other arm, stretching it to its full length, reaching behind the heavy piece of furniture. "Give me that book!" she demanded.

The raccoon made a hissing noise. As her hand swept near him, he gave a half-growl and moved a little farther back until he was just beyond her reach. Then he sat up on his hind legs and scolded her loudly.

She glanced uneasily at the doorway. She had to get the book back before her father came in for dinner.

Although the raccoon had adapted to civilized life rapidly, she and her father had nearly come to blows several times over the animal's mischief. Seeming to realize his daughter was on the verge of a nervous collapse, the major had finally given in to the raccoon's presence in his household. But she knew it wouldn't take much to make him change his mind.

A knock at the door saw her scrambling to her feet. Although she knew it couldn't be her father—he would never knock at his own door—she flushed uneasily.

Smoothing her skirt down, she opened the door. Buck stood on the threshold, his hand raised as he prepared to knock again.

"Buck," she cried. "Come on in." A flicker of fear crossed her eyes and constricted her chest. She reached out and pulled him inside. "Has something happened?"

"Plenty," he said grimly. As her face paled he hastened to reassure her. "But not what yore a-thinkin'. Last time I checked, Swift Arrow was holdin' 'is own."

"When was that?" she asked.

"It's been a few days," he admitted. "He still had the fever and didn't know me last time I looked. But I'm purty sure he's a-gettin' well. Cain't think of no other reason fer them keepin' me away from 'im."

"What do you mean?" she asked faintly.

"What I said. Them guards got orders I ain't to see 'im. 'Spect they ain't sure how far they can trust me."

Fear closed her throat. Why should they mistrust Buck? Perhaps they wouldn't let him see Swift Arrow because he was dead.

Oh, God! No!

He laid a gnarled hand on her shoulder, squeezing it lightly. "Thet boy's mighty tough, youngun," he said gruffly. "He's a-gonna be fine."

"How can you know that?"

"I had me a talk with thet young lieutenant."

"Cal?"

"Yep. Lieutenant Hawood. The one what brought us here in the first place."

"He's seen Swift Arrow?"

"Sees 'im nearly ever day. Leastways, thets what he says. I been talkin' to thet young lieutenant. An' I don't think he's a-gonna say nuthin' thet'd do you hurt."

She nodded. "That's what I thought."

She noticed for the first time that he was carrying his rifle and his tobacco pouch looked to be full. "You said something had happened. What is it, Buck?"

"Thet's what I come to see you about," he growled. "Fact is, I come to say good-bye."

"Good-bye!" Her gray eyes widened. "Buck, please," she cried. "You can't leave yet. You've got to help me get Swift Arrow out of here."

"Cain't take 'im anyplace till he's able to travel, youngun. I aim to be back by the time thet happens. Right now, somethin's come up thet needs my attention."

"What is it?"

"Words out thet Geronimo's turned himself in."

"Isn't he always doing that?"

"Yep. But this time he says it's fer good. Says he's tired of runnin' an' he ain't gonna fight no more."

"Why does that concern you?"

He remained silent for a moment. Then he reached for his plug of tobacco and bit off a sizable chaw. When he had it firmly lodged in his jaw, he spoke.

"Heard some folks talkin'. They said the major's found out where Chief Tall Feathers's village is. Way I figger it, it was them damn 'Pache scouts of his'n what found it. They rode in 'bout an hour ago."

"What are you going to do?"

"I gotta help 'em, youngun," he said gruffly. "They ain't no way I'm a-gonna let 'em hurt Rachel. An' thet's where she's at."

"Do you think they would harm her?" As soon as she asked the question, she knew it was stupid. Many Tongues and Bright Feathers had done nothing . . . but they were still just as dead.

"They's ways to hurt a body thet don't have no way of showin'," he said. His faded eyes were hard. "She'd take it mighty hard if'n somethin' happened to thet man of hers. Or her son. I mean to see it don't happen."

"Buck . . ." She hesitated. "You're only one man. What can you do?"

"If'n I leave right now, I can warn 'em," he said. "So's when the cavalry gets there, they'll be long gone." He held her gaze. "I ain't a-wantin' to leave you in yore trouble, youngun. But the way I see it, yore man's not in any danger right now. Rachel an' her kin is."

She knew he was right. But that didn't make it any easier to see him go. "I understand," she said. "You go on, Buck. Don't worry about us here. Just go and warn your Rachel and the others."

He nodded his grizzled head. "Knew you'd take it

this-a-way, lass. You got a lotta gumption in you. I knowed it as soon as I pulled you outta thet river. Now you ain't gonna come to no harm here. Try not to worry 'bout thet man of yore'n. He's goin' to be right as rain a-fore you even know it."

Tears misted her eyes. She swallowed around the lump in her throat. "I hope so," she said. "Now you'd better hurry and warn your friends."

When he turned to go, she laid a hand on his arm. "Buck," she said. "Where will they go?"

"Don't know yet." His faded gray eyes were clouded with worry. "If'n I did, reckon as how I wouldn't say. Fewer thet knows where they're a-goin', the better off they'll be."

"Yes," she said. "Of course, you're right. Is there any way I can help?"

"Reckon not. Just take care of yoreself and try not to worry. I'll be back as soon as I can. Maybe yore man'll be well by then. An' we'll get our heads together and figger out what to do." He stopped near the door. "One other thing," he said gruffly.

"Yes?"

"Would you get word to Sary thet I had to leave? Tell 'er I'll see 'er when I get back."

"Sary?"

"The widder Cole," he mumbled. "I kinda told 'er I'd come callin' tomorrow."

"I'll send word to her," Katherine said.

He nodded and left.

Katherine's heart was heavy as she watched the mountain man mount his horse and ride toward the gate.

Her shoulders slumped with despair as she turned back into the room. What could she do now? She had depended on Buck to help her free Swift Arrow . . . and now he was gone.

He'll be back, she reminded herself.

Katherine leaned back in the chair, forcing herself to relax. Buck had said Swift Arrow was getting well. If he didn't come back within a few days, then she would take steps to free him herself.

You'll need help. You can't get near him alone.

I'll worry about that when the time comes.

She felt something tug at the hem of her skirt and looked down to find Blackie trying to climb into the chair. Leaning over, she picked him up and cuddled him close against her.

"We'll get him loose," she muttered to him. "And we'll find a way out of here." Putting her hands beneath the coon's head, she looked into his black eyes. "That's a promise, Blackie," she said grimly. And as she spoke, Katherine knew it was the truth. She would gain Swift Arrow's release, even if she had to do it alone.

It was late afternoon and Katherine had been helping Minnie in the kitchen when the knock sounded on the door. Knowing it couldn't be Buck and too low in spirits to want to speak to anyone else, Katherine remained where she was.

Minnie cast a worried look toward the girl and went to answer the door. Katherine heard the murmur of

283

voices in the parlor. A few minutes later she heard the door closing and Minnie's heavy footsteps returning to the kitchen.

"Minnie," she said, turning to face the door. "What do you want done with these turn—"

She broke off, her eyes widening with surprise at the sight of the blond girl standing behind the house-keeper.

"Heather?" she whispered. "Is it really you?"

"Yes," the other girl laughed. "It's really me."

She held out her arms. Tears flooded Katherine's eyes, spilling over as she flung herself at the other girl and embraced her.

Katherine drew back and knuckled away the tears. "What are you doing here, Heather?"

"I heard in Silver City you'd been found," Heather replied. "I'm afraid I made Robert's life miserable until he consented to bring me to see you." She studied Katherine's pale face. "Has it been hard, Kathy? We heard rumors that the Indians had kidnapped you."

"No," Katherine said fiercely. "They didn't. Swi— they found me injured and took care of me. Now, Father's got them locked up and—and—" She broke off, unable to say more.

"And you want to help them. Is that right?"

"Yes." Katherine glanced uneasily at Minnie. Although the woman was busy peeling turnips, Katherine knew her ears were tuned to the two girls' conversation. "Come with me to my room," she urged. "We won't disturb Minnie there."

"You ain't botherin' me none, chile," the old woman said. "But you don' want old Minnie listenin' to what you gotta say." She grinned at them to show she didn't mind. "You young folks run along. Ol' Minnie's got work to be done."

Heather followed Katherine out of the room. As soon as the bedroom door closed behind them, Katherine turned to her friend.

"Heather," she said. "I'm glad you've come. I was feeling so low. You couldn't possibly know how much I needed to see a friend. Someone who won't condemn me."

"Is that what people are doing?" Heather asked with a frown. "Condemning you?"

Katherine laughed. "I'm not really sure. I don't see anyone to know what they feel. I think I'm being ostracized. But that's not really important."

"Not important?" Heather's blue eyes flashed indignantly. "Of course, it's important. Anyway, who's doing such a thing to you?"

"All the women on the fort," Katherine said wryly. "Would you believe Minnie's the only one I've talked to since I've been back? But as I said, it's not important."

"If that's not worrying you," Heather said, "then what is?" Before Katherine could reply, she continued. I had a feeling something was wrong the minute I entered this fort. Now tell me what's the matter."

"Father's got the Indians locked up."

Heather nodded. "I heard that in town. But I'm not sure that we can help."

Katherine bowed her head. What had she expected? Of course Heather couldn't help. Just because the girl had helped break Jesse out of jail, even risked her life to do it, didn't mean there was any way she could help now.

"Kathy."

Katherine lifted her head and met the other girl's gaze.

"There's more that you're not telling me," Heather said.

"One of them was wounded," Katherine said reluctantly. "Swift Arrow was the one who—"

"Swift Arrow?" Heather said sharply. "He was the one who helped you?"

Katherine's eyes widened. She had forgotten Heather knew Swift Arrow. Buck had said the warrior had helped Robert find and free her from the men who had kidnapped her. Could Robert Shaw be persuaded to help Swift Arrow? She wouldn't know unless she gave it a try.

Quickly, she explained the situation to Heather, leaving nothing out, for she felt the girl would understand her feelings for the Indian.

"And now your father's got him under guard?" Heather asked.

Katherine nodded. "I'm so afraid for him," she said. "Do you think your husband will help him?"

"I'm sure Robert will try," Heather replied. "He knows Swift Arrow saved my life."

"Yours, too?"

Heather nodded. "Mine, too," she said. "I'll talk to Robert. I'm sure he'll try to help."

As Heather made to leave the room, Katherine followed her. "I'm coming with you," she said.

"I don't think that's a good idea," Heather said. "You were right to keep Swift Arrow's part from your father. If he knows you're making an issue out of it, Swift Arrow may not live until Robert can arrange his release."

The color drained from Katherine's face. "I know you're right," she said. "That's what's been worrying me."

"Try not to worry anymore," Heather said. "I'll talk to Robert and we'll see what can be done."

After Heather left, Katherine moved to the window. Her gaze found the building where Swift Arrow was confined . . . and stopped there.

In her imagination, she entered the building, walking through the walls as though they were nothing. He was lying on a soft bed, covered by a patchwork quilt. He turned his head and saw her. A smile spread across his face, and he held out his arms to her.

Before she had time to run into his arms, the front door opened and jolted her back into reality.

"Robert's gone to see him," Heather said.

Katherine stared at her in confusion. Time had passed without her being aware of it.

"Does that mean Father's agreed to release him?" Katherine asked huskily.

"No," Heather said. "I'm afraid not. But he did allow

Robert to see him," she said encouragingly. "And Robert won't stop there. He'll do something. Don't worry about it. He'll figure out a way to help Swift Arrow, even if he has to go to Washington to do it."

"Washington? But that could take months."

"I know," Heather admitted. "But at least your father will know other people are interested in Swift Arrow's fate. He won't be so quick to have him killed."

"Other people knowing didn't help Jesse," Katherine said bitterly. "He's still dead."

Heather put a comforting hand on Katherine's shoulder. "Don't think about it," she said. "Wait until Robert comes. Then we'll talk."

When Robert Shaw knocked at the door, both girls gave a start. Katherine quickly opened it and let him in.

"Hello, Katherine," he said. "It's good to see you're safe."

"How is Swift Arrow?" she asked quickly.

"He didn't look too bad," Robert said. "Of course, he's not very happy at being confined. But then, that's only to be expected."

"Can you help him?"

He frowned. "The major's feelings are beyond reason. He refused to release Swift Arrow, even after I told him I would hire him to work on my ranch. He said the warrior was a renegade, and as such, belonged on a reservation."

Heather's shoulders slumped with defeat. "I guess that's it, then," she said.

"No," Robert said. "That's not the end. I'll go to Washington and see what I can do to get his release."

"It'll be too late by then," Katherine said. "But thank you for trying."

"Don't give up," he said. "I'll think of something."

Although Katherine nodded, she knew it was hopeless. There could be no help from that direction. She would have to help Swift Arrow alone. As she had always known she would.

Chapter Twenty-Seven

Her concern for Swift Arrow was becoming almost more than Katherine could bear. And her enforced idleness didn't help any. It left her with entirely too much time on her hands, time to think about the past . . . and Swift Arrow.

For some reason the fort seemed much smaller than it had before she'd left. After more than a month out in the fresh air, feeling the wind on her face, she longed for the mountains again. To feel the warm sun beating down on her. But most of all, she longed for her Apache lover.

She crossed to the window and stared out at the shed where she knew Swift Arrow was being held prisoner. Although Robert had told her the warrior was recovering, she was still worried about him. She had been at the fort for a week now. And Swift Arrow must be wondering what had happened to her, and why she hadn't tried to help him.

She must see him.

Perhaps if she were just to stroll by the building, she would be able to offer him encouragement.

It's too dangerous, said a little voice in her mind. *Your father has spies. You can't take a chance they'll see you hanging around Swift Arrow's prison. If he ever finds out . . .*

She shuddered to think what would happen.

"I won't go to the shack," she muttered. "I'll go to one of the Apaches on the work detail. Perhaps one of them can tell me something."

"What is you whisperin' about?" said a voice behind her.

She whirled around, heaving a sigh of relief as she recognized Minnie. "You scared me," she said, her voice sounding angry. "You always move so quiet, no one knows you're around."

The woman had obviously come from the kitchen, for she was wiping her large hands on her apron. Her dark eyes probed the girl's. "Onliest time it seems to bother a body is when dey got somethin' to hide. What you plannin' on, chile?"

If only she could tell her. Could enlist her help. But she knew she couldn't ask the housekeeper for help. If she were seen near the prisoner, it would be reported to the major. And Minnie's bulk would be hard to miss.

No. It would be much better if she handled it herself.

"I'm not planning a thing, Minnie," she said. "I just thought I would walk down and visit with my Indian

292

friends. Father's assigned some of the women to a work detail."

"You ain't goin' do no such thin'!" Minnie snapped, putting her hands on her ample hips. "Yore daddy done tole me you gotta stay away from dem folks down dere."

"I don't care what he says. The Indians saved my life." She looked away from the woman's probing gaze. "Are you spying for my father now, Minnie?"

"Don't you talk to me like dat, missy." The woman jabbed her finger at Katherine. "You know ol' Minnie ain't no spy. But I knows you, chile. I done raised you up. Dey's somethin' goin' on you don't want folks to know. An' I know dem Injuns ain't like other folks is. Dey gonna be thinkin' 'bout you up here all dis time in dis here house . . . and dem, down dere. And dey ain't gonna like it none. No. You stay away from dem folks."

"Would you abandon them if you'd been the one they saved?" Katherine asked quietly.

"Don't matter none what I'd do," the big woman said. "Don't matter a-tall." She shook her grizzled head back and forth as she returned to the kitchen, muttering beneath her breath about Indians scalping decent white folks at the least excuse.

Katherine reached for the doorknob and opened the door. Then she stepped outside and left the house. She forced herself to walk slowly as she made her way down the compound. As she neared a block of buildings, a figure stepped from an alleyway and joined her. She looked up to see Lieutenant Hawood.

"Where are you going?" he asked, falling into step

293

beside her.

"I'm going to see my Apache friends," she said defiantly.

"You can't do that," he said, keeping his voice low. "You're not fooling me, Katherine. It's not the captives you're concerned about. Take my word he's being taken care of."

Her steps didn't falter as she continued across the compound. "I have to talk to the Apaches," she insisted.

"Why?"

"Because they are my friends. I want them to know I have nothing to do with the way they're being treated."

"If you go near them, you'll accomplish nothing. It may even get Swift Arrow killed."

That stopped her in her tracks. "What do you mean by that?" she hissed. "Why should my seeing the others endanger his life?"

"Your father gave orders that you were to be kept away from them, whatever it took."

"Are you saying you'd tell my father?"

"Of course not," he growled. "But I wouldn't have to. One of those Apaches is a traitor. He's been informing on the others, currying favor from the army."

"Informing on the others?"

"Yes. There was an escape attempt last night. He sent word to the major he had to see him. We stopped the attempt cold."

Her face whitened. "Who is it," she whispered.

"His name is Crying Wolf."

She should have known. "What did they do with the

Apaches who tried to escape?"

"They'll be moved as soon as possible."

Her silver eyes were hard, her lips tightened into a thin line. "The others have to be told about Crying Wolf," she said grimly.

"Stay away from them, Katherine," he warned. "Crying Wolf told your father other things as well." Her eyes widened with apprehension. "The major didn't believe him. But if you go down there, make any attempt whatever to see him . . . then, who knows?"

He was right. Her eyes filled with tears. "What am I going to do?"

"If you want him to stay alive, then keep away from him," he growled. Without another word he walked away from her.

Defeated for the moment, she retraced her steps to the house, unaware of her father watching her from his office window.

She thought long and hard about what Lieutenant Hawood had told her. She must get word to the Apaches of the traitor in their midst. And she must see Swift Arrow.

That night, after everyone was asleep, she crept silently across the bedroom to the window. Grasping the edge, she pushed it up. It grated alarmingly.

Holding her breath, she waited. There was no sound. No one had heard. Lifting her skirts, she crawled through the window and dropped to the ground.

The moon gave off a pale light as she hurried across the parade ground, darting down an alleyway and shrinking into the shadows as she heard the sound of footsteps approaching.

She waited until the footsteps had passed before leaving the sheltering darkness and moving swiftly toward the bleak building that housed the injured warrior. She breathed a sigh of relief as she neared the building without discovery.

She reached for the wooden latch and stopped as a hand covered hers.

She turned. To face . . . her father.

He stared down at her, his eyes thunderous.

Gripping her arm, he pulled her away from the shed. Unwilling to have Swift Arrow hear, she remained silent as he dragged her toward the house. For she knew it would only alarm him. And he would be unable to help her.

They entered their house. Her father closed the door and turned to her.

"All right," he growled. "You've got some explaining to do. I want to know exactly what's between you and that Indian."

"I don't know what you're talking about," she prevaricated.

"You're lying, Kathy. I know you were in a wickiup . . . alone with him when you were found. You even killed one of my men to help him."

"Who told you a thing like that?"

"It wasn't Lieutenant Hawood. And he'll have to answer for that. One of the men who thought it might be important came forward."

Although he didn't mention Crying Wolf, she knew the Apache had to be his informer.

He stared grimly down at her. "My own daughter," he said. "Killing one of her own kind to save a murdering redskin."

"He saved my life," she said. "I couldn't see his taken."

"No!" he grated harshly. "Instead, you'd rather see a decent man dead. Where's your loyalty girl?"

"That *decent* man was trying to kill Swift Arrow," she said. "I told you I wouldn't be alive if it wasn't for him. Don't you care about that at all?"

"I care about one of my men losing his life by my own daughter's hand," he said grimly. "And I care that she left my house to meet a redskin on the sly."

"Stop calling him that," she said. "His skin's no more red than yours or mine."

"That's not the point," he said. "The man's a savage. What were you bent on tonight, anyway?" He gripped her arm savagely, his fingers biting into her skin. "Answer me, Kathy. Why were you trying to see him?"

"Because he's been in that stinking hole for more than a week," she said. "He hasn't been taken care of properly. How could you do that to him? His wound could become infected in that dirty shed."

"I don't believe that's all there is to it," he said grimly. "I know there's more than you're telling." His expression was furious. "Is there something between you and that man? Did he bed you, girl?"

His question shocked her. How had he arrived at such a conclusion? She had thought she had been so careful. At least he wasn't certain of his facts. Although he was definitely suspicious. That meant Crying Wolf hadn't told him everything. For that, she should be grateful.

Her continued silence only served to enrage him further. He grabbed her by the shoulders and shook her until her teeth rattled. "I said answer me, damn you! What do you feel for that savage?"

Something long held back erupted inside of Katherine. Her eyes flashed silver fire as she met her father's gaze.

"I love him!" she said fiercely. "And there's nothing you can do about it."

Suddenly aware of what she had said, she covered her mouth with her hand. But it was too late. The damage had already been done. Her father dropped her as though she were a live coal.

"I'll kill him," he raged. "I'll have the bastard strung up and skinned alive."

"No!" she shouted, rushing toward the door. She stood with her back pressed to it, her eyes glaring up at her father. "You touch one hair on his head and I'll leave this house and you'll never see me again."

"You don't know what you're saying."

"I know exactly what I'm saying! You killed Jesse! But I won't let you touch Swift Arrow. I mean it. You hurt him and I'm gone. And I won't stop there, Father. I'll go back East to Uncle Bill and Aunt Louise. I'll tell him every dirty, underhanded thing you've ever done."

Her father's face drained of all its color. "Bill wouldn't believe you," he said. But she could hear the uncertainty in his voice.

"He'd believe me, all right," she said. "And he'd go

298

straight to Congress with it." Her voice was strong, sure, as she loosed the final arrow. "You'd lose your commission, Father. I wouldn't rest until I saw to it. And you know it could happen." Her eyes narrowed on his, and she moved aside. "Now, go do your damnedest. And see what happens."

He looked at her, shock in his expression. "You'd threaten your own father?"

"It's not a threat," she said. "It's a promise. If you harm one hair on his head, then I'll carry it out."

John Carpenter had got where he was by being able to manipulate people. His expression became grievous, hurt. "Kathy, I'm no longer a young man. You're all I have left since your mother passed on, and . . ."

"Stop it!" she snapped. "I won't fall for that trick. I'll fight you tooth and nail for Swift Arrow's life."

"And if I promise to leave him alone?"

"No. Not just leave him alone. You're going to turn him loose."

"Turn him loose! You've got to be out of your mind. I could never do that."

"You *will* do it."

"Supposing I agreed. You'd promise to stay with me? To keep your mouth shut?"

"Yes. But I want to see him one more time."

"No. That's out of the question."

"It's a condition. I intend to see him."

"Very well. Then I'll arrange it. But you're not to see him until just before he leaves. And no one must know. I'll throw a party and issue invitations to the townspeople and the troopers. I'll make sure the guard is taken away from the corral. It'll have to be an escape."

"No. They'll try to shoot him."

His lips thinned. "There's no other way," he said grimly. "My orders are to bring the Apaches in. Not turn them loose. It will have to be an escape."

"All right. But you make damn sure the guard is taken off the gate as well," she said.

"That'll leave the fort unprotected."

"An hour isn't going to hurt," she said. "And it's the only way I can be sure you haven't double-crossed me."

Something flickered in his eyes.

She laughed harshly. "I can see it occurred to you. But you'd better forget it. I won't stand for him being shot while attempting to escape. And you'd better not let it happen."

"I'll give the guard permission to attend the party for an hour. That's the best I can do."

"What about the other prisoners?"

He glared at her. "They stay."

She started to protest, but he stopped her.

"One prisoner could escape without damaging my reputation," he said. "But not the whole bunch. Now either take it or leave it."

She had no choice. She must take Swift Arrow's life and be grateful for it. She turned to her bedroom, reaching for the doorknob.

"And Kathy . . ."

She stopped.

"I'll expect no more problems from you. After the Indian's gone, I'll expect you to be a dutiful daughter."

"Of course," she said wryly. "And I'm sure I'll have a guard to make sure I remain that way."

"I see we understand each other," he said.

"Yes," she muttered. "We certainly do."

"You never used to be like this," he said. "It's that damn savage's influence. The sooner he's left my fort, the better I'll like it."

Chapter Twenty-Eight

It seemed the major was bent on making the dance the social event of the season. Invitations were sent out to Silver City and the surrounding ranches. A five-piece band had been selected from the enlisted men, and the officers' mess had been decorated by the women at the fort.

Katherine had chosen her gown with care. She wanted to look her best for her last meeting with Swift Arrow. Her heart beat fast with the anticipation of seeing him again, and yet, it ached with the thought of his leaving the fort, for she knew it was likely that they would never meet again.

She took special care with her toilette as she prepared for the party. Minnie was summoned to fasten the tiny buttons running up the back of the gown. It was made of silk, in a color that exactly matched her eyes and enhanced her sun-kissed complexion.

The style of the gown was very plain, with tiny cap sleeves. It fit snugly around the waist, drawing attention to her slender figure. The skirt flowed softly out around the hips and fell in a silvery mist to the floor. Her shoes were of a matching silver satin, completing her ensemble. She had arranged her pale hair in loose curls high on top of her head, fastening them in place with two ivory combs. The only jewelry she wore was an ivory pendant that had belonged to her grandmother. It hung by a silver chain around her neck.

Slipping on her silver-colored elbow-length gloves, she studied her reflection in the mirror.

"My, my. Ain't you a beauty," said Minnie, beside her.

Katherine gave her a smile, then left the room to join her father in the parlor. He had been sitting on the settee, looking at some papers. He laid them aside and rose to his feet to greet her.

"I still don't see why you feel it so necessary for me to attend the party," she said coldly.

"We've been all through this," he said. "It would look peculiar if you didn't attend. Especially, since all our friends have been invited."

"Was an invitation sent to the Shaw ranch?"

"Yes. But it seems as though they decided to take a trip." He looked at her. "I hear they went to Washington."

Washington. Her heartbeat picked up speed. Apparently Robert Shaw hadn't forgotten Swift Arrow. She wondered for a moment if she should delay the escape, then, just as quickly, dismissed the thought. It could be months before the rancher was able to accomplish anything. And even then, the results couldn't be guaranteed to be favorable. No. It was better this way.

Providing her father held to his end of the bargain. She would have to settle for one last meeting with Swift Arrow.

She looked suspiciously at her father. "You aren't going to try to prevent me from seeing Swift Arrow, are you?"

"I made a bargain with you, and I shall keep it," he said, his gaze holding hers. "As you will keep yours," he reminded her stiffly.

"I have no intention of breaking my word," she replied.

"Then we understand each other," he said. As though some problem had been satisfactorily settled, he took her hand in his and smiled. "You are looking especially lovely tonight, Kathy. You remind me so much of Brittany."

For some reason, mention of her mother hurt. She felt sure her mother would have understood her feelings for Swift Arrow. But her mother wasn't here. She had died. Now there was only her father. And he had never even tried to understand.

She pulled her hand away from his and deliberately ignored the arm he held out to her.

"Still upset with me?"

She didn't answer him. Raising her skirt with one

hand, she swept out of the room and stepped out into the night.

Her gaze went instantly to the bleak building that held Swift Arrow prisoner. She longed to go to him, but knew she must remain patient for another hour. That would allow everyone to be at the party. Then she could slip quietly out for one last meeting with her love.

You'll never see him again, her heart cried.

She swallowed around the lump in her throat, knowing it was far better never to see him again, and yet know he still lived. If he stayed, she knew her father would never rest until Swift Arrow was dead.

She tried to put thoughts of their plight from her mind and act as natural as possible when they arrived at the party. There was an atmosphere of gaiety in the officers' mess where the party was being held. As they crossed the parade ground, Katherine could hear the sound of laughter and the humming of voices, mixed in with the sound of instruments being tuned.

They crossed the threshold to the officers' mess, which was an unusually large room for the time, especially since there was only a handful of officers assigned to the fort. The room was crowded. It seemed everyone who had received invitations had come. The room, which had been decorated with plants and flowers had a festive air about it. As they entered, a hush fell over the crowd.

Several heads turned to stare at them.

Katherine had kept to herself since returning to the fort. Now, she flinched inwardly from the look in the eyes of the nearest woman. Mrs. Hershell had always been so friendly, but at the moment, she was giving a good impression of having just encountered something that she found particularly undesirable.

Lifting her chin a fraction of an inch higher, Katherine's gray eyes met the other woman's with a faintly challenging look.

Instantly, she felt her father's hand tighten on her arm. His fingers dug in painfully as he pulled her toward the woman with grim determination.

"Good evening, Mrs. Hershell," he said, his body as stiff as his voice.

Spots of color appeared high on the woman's cheeks. "Good evening, Major Carpenter," she murmured, gathering her skirts around her as Katherine drew nearer.

Katherine spared a quick glance for her father. His face had a grim expression. It was obvious he wasn't happy about the way his daughter was being received. He continued to glare at the woman until she spoke again.

"Good evening, Kathy."

Major Carpenter's grip relaxed slightly on her arm. And as they made their way through the crowd, she found Mrs. Hershell's attitude reflected by most of the other women there. They seemed to feel she had become soiled while living with the Indians. The men, she found, were little better. They tended to go in the other direction, being just a little *too* jovial, a little *too* familiar.

Katherine even felt at times that she detected a leer in several of the men's eyes. But only when her father wasn't looking. There was no way any of the men under his command would offer an insult to his daughter in his presence.

The band struck up the first waltz, and Katherine felt relieved when Lieutenant Hawood joined them and asked her to dance.

"Relax," he whispered, taking her into his arms, and swinging her out onto the floor that had been cleared for dancing. "They don't really matter, do they?"

"It wasn't my overactive imagination, then?" she asked, looking up at him with wide gray eyes.

"No, I'm sorry to say, it isn't." His expression was pained as he held her gaze. "Don't think everyone is that way, Kathy," he said. "There are some who don't blame you for what happened."

"What did happen?" she asked, studying him curiously. She had wondered all along just how much he did know.

"I think I'm the only one who knows you're in love with Swift Arrow," he said, keeping his voice low so they wouldn't be overheard. "But your father has been suspicious ever since he talked to that Indian, Crying Wolf."

"I know," she said bitterly. "Swift Arrow should have killed him when he had the chance. Crying Wolf doesn't deserve to live."

He nodded. "If the Indians ever find out he's an informer, I'm sure they'll take steps to get rid of him. But they may not find out. Your father rewards the traitors well for their information, and he does his best to protect them."

"Why?"

"We both know it's not because he feels any compassion for them."

"No," she said. "My father doesn't know the meaning of the word. But he can never tell when he'll need their help again."

"Exactly," he said grimly.

While they talked, the music had ended and Lieutenant Hawood led her back to where her father stood talking with two men. All three turned to look at Katherine as she joined them.

The younger of the three was a dark-haired man with a neatly trimmed beard of the same color. He eyed her with bold brown eyes. "May I have the pleasure of the next dance, Miss Carpenter," he asked with a smile.

"I'm afraid I've had enough dancing for the moment, Captain Loren," she replied.

"Nonsense," said her father. "You two young people go right ahead and enjoy yourself."

Before she could object further, Katherine found herself swept out onto the dance floor once again. She made an effort to hide her annoyance, but Captain Loren's hold was just a shade too familiar to suit her.

"You're holding me too tightly," she said firmly, her gaze lifting to meet his.

"Don't tell me you don't like it," he said, his lips curling slightly at the corners.

"I don't," she said coldly. He was far too bold to suit her. He needed taking down a peg. When he didn't loosen his hold, she said. "And I don't like your attitude. Either you loosen your hold on me," she

309

gritted, "or I cause a scene in front of everyone."

His eyes darkened with anger, but her threat had worked, for he immediately loosened his grip around her waist. "I'd've thought them redskins had taught you a thing or two about men," he said recklessly.

"Would you care to explain yourself?" she said icily.

"Don't play the innocent with me, Miss Carpenter. Everyone in this fort knows what you've been up to. Did you tell your pa how many of them bedded you? Or did you lose count?"

Wild color splotched her cheeks as fury surged within her. She had never liked this man, but this was the first time he had ever insulted her. She stopped in the middle of the dance floor. "How dare you," she hissed furiously. "You don't know a thing about what happened. You—"

"Come away, Kathy," said a low voice beside her. "You're attracting attention. I'll deal with him later."

She turned to face Lieutenant Hawood. She didn't care if she was attracting attention, and she was just about to tell him so, when suddenly she remembered what she had to do later. She didn't need people watching her when she was ready to slip out and release Swift Arrow.

Summoning up a smile, she placed a hand on his shoulder. "Dance with me, Cal," she said invitingly.

"That's my girl," he said, taking her into his arms and swinging her out into the whirling crowd. When the waltz finished, he didn't take her back to her father, but waited until the band started up again. He kept her out on the dance floor for another fifteen minutes. All the time the crowd was growing.

Finally, she decided that everyone was in attendance, except for the guard on the gate.

It was time to make her move.

Excusing herself, she left the party and crossed the parade ground, intent on the shed where Swift Arrow was a prisoner. She was unaware of the silhouette of a man who had left the party just behind her.

He followed slowly, keeping always to the shadows, pausing when she paused, stopping when she stopped, but never for a moment losing track of her.

Katherine continued on her way, her every thought concentrated on the man she was going to see, and what she would tell him when she got there. She knew it would have to be as little as possible, because they would not have long together. Not nearly enough time to say their last good-byes. Not nearly enough to keep her heart from crying while she watched him ride away from her.

God!

How would she be able to stand it? How could she be expected to go through life without the man she loved? To grow old and gray, still doing her father's bidding and still longing for the man she could never have?

Chapter Twenty-Nine

Moonlight filtered through the cracks between the boards as Swift Arrow lay on the straw pallet. His body tensed as he heard a slight sound at the door. Someone was out there. Beyond the door. But why had they come in the dead of night? Did it have anything to do with the other two captives being moved earlier in the day? Perhaps the major had wanted to insure that there would be no witnesses around to testify to what was taking place.

He heard the sound of the latch being lifted and pulled back. The door grated as it swung open. A dark silhouette outlined by the moon, appeared in the entrance, stopped a moment, seeming to be searching the darkened recesses of the room.

But Swift Arrow could not be seen. The instant the door had opened, he had moved. Silent as the wind he

313

had reached the dark corner beyond the door . . . and he was waiting.

His long arm snaked out, finding the throat of the intruder, coiling around, tightening, shutting off the life-giving air. His other arm circled lower, imprisoning his captive's arms, squeezing relentlessly so the intruder would be forced to drop any weapons he might be carrying.

As soon as he felt the unmistakable softness of a feminine form beneath his forearm, he loosened his strangling grip around the throat and wheeled the woman around to face the pale light of the moon streaming through the doorway.

The soft light illuminated a small, slender form in a silver satin gown that showed to perfection her high full breasts, tiny waist, and graceful neck.

He would have recognized her anywhere. Even with her soft silver-blond hair arranged high on her head instead of in one long braid down her back. Her wide gray eyes held a half-startled, half-scared expression as they stared up into his.

"Katherine," he grated harshly. "What are you doing here?"

It took her a moment to gather her wits about her, and another to force any sound from her throat. It had been so long since she had seen him.

Katherine wanted to throw herself into his arms, smother him with kisses. But most of all, she wanted to leave this place with him. To ride to some distant land where there was no distinction between the white man and the Indian. A place where they would be allowed to

314

live in freedom.

But it was useless. There was no such place.

She should be happy her love was alive.

"I asked you what you were doing here."

"I was worried about you," she said softly. "Are you all right?"

"My wound has nearly healed," he said. "But I have no taste for being shut up in this dark room." He glanced at the door. "How many soldiers wait for me to step through the door?"

"What do you mean?"

"Where is the man who guards me?"

"There is no guard. He's been taken off for a little while."

"Why?"

She bit her lip. "To allow me to have some time alone with you without anyone knowing." She stared into his face, willing him to trust her. "I've come to let you go."

Instantly his eyes grew wary. "Does your father know of this?"

"Of course." Now she glanced over his shoulder, into the night.

"Why do you not look at me?" he asked. There was steel laced through Swift Arrow's words. "Is it possible you are hiding something?"

She shook her head with unnecessary vehemence. "I'm not hiding anything," she denied, turning away from him.

"You lie," he grated harshly. "There is something you do not wish me to know. Even now, the white eyes could be outside waiting. Are their rifles pointed at the entrance? When I reach out to take the freedom you offer, will the blue-coats kill me?"

"No," she whispered, her expression anguished. "How could you believe such a thing? I would never be party to such treachery."

She blinked back the tears that sprang to her eyes. It was crazy to drag it out. Although it was tearing her apart, she knew she had to be strong. She must watch him ride away from her. No matter how it hurt. But there was a need to hurry.

"You're wasting what little time there is," she said. "I could only convince my father to allow you an hour. You have to hurry."

For a long moment he held her gaze. Then, as if finally accepting all she offered, he said. "Then we must go quickly." He moved her toward the door, his fingers hard on her upper arm.

She swallowed around a lump in her throat. "I can't go with you," she said in a faint whisper, barely audible even to her own ears.

He stopped abruptly. "What did you say?"

"I can't go with you." Now her words were separate and emphatic, but nonetheless painful.

For an instant there was silence in the room. Then he spoke in a voice containing anger and some other element she couldn't identify.

"I will not leave without you, Katherine."

She grabbed his arm, her eyes pleading for his understanding. "You must, Swift Arrow."

"Why?" he demanded fiercely. "Give me a reason."

"I promised my father I would stay."

"You had no right to make such a promise," he snarled.

His head lowered until it was only inches away from hers. He stared at her as though he had never seen her before. "You are my woman," he growled. "You belong to me." His dark eyes caught fire, and his voice became bitter. "You have taken everything I have to give. Is it as I suspected? Are you now throwing it away for the things your father can give you?"

She pushed a lock of blond hair back from her forehead, turning away from his harsh face. "I do not wish to remain here," she said heavily. "But it must be. It is part of the bargain for your release."

He grasped her chin roughly, forcing her to look up at him. "You had no right to make such a bargain," he said.

"Do you think I wanted to?" she cried. "Don't you know it's tearing the heart out of me to see you go? I love you, dammit! I'll never love anyone else! But I'd see you gone from me rather than dead. At least I would know you still lived!"

His gaze was probing as he stared down into her face. Finally, he spoke. "Do you think your father will keep his bargain?"

"Yes. He wants me with him." She let the words sink in before adding, "He has arranged for the troopers to attend a party he's giving. The sound of music will cover your escape. There is only one guard at the gate, and none at the stables." Her eyes beseeched him. "You must hurry. You can be miles away before the others know you're gone."

"I will take with me one last kiss, Katherine," he said roughly.

Wanting it as much as he, she raised herself to meet his lips. The kiss was bittersweet, flavored by her tears. When he lifted his head, she stared up at him through tear-blurred eyes.

"What of my people?" he asked huskily when the kiss was ended. "Did your father agree to release them as well?"

"I could only bargain for you."

"Then your bargain is no good. Surely you knew I would not leave without them."

"But Father wouldn't agree to it."

"If there are no guards, he will not know until it is too late." His eyes were penetrating. "We will take the horses we need, so everyone can ride. The others we will drive away so we cannot be followed quickly."

That was not part of her bargain, either, but she could see the sense to it. "All right," she whispered. What else could she do? She couldn't deny him the right to free his people.

"I will need your help."

She nodded. "I'll do anything you say."

"Hold it right there."

Katherine stopped short, staring at the figure who filled the doorway. It was Captain Loren, and he was pointing a pistol toward them. The man's eyes were filled with hate as they fell on her.

"Bitch!" he snarled. "You thought you were too good for me, but you couldn't wait to get to this redskin

318

lover of yours. Well, it ain't gonna do you a bit of good. As soon as I get rid of him, I mean to have you."

"You're crazy!" she cried. "If you touch me, my father will kill you."

"Not when I make it look like the redskin did it. He'll probably see I get a promotion for preventing the redskin's escape. Especially after he killed his daughter."

"You'll never get away with it," she said.

He laughed. "Too bad you won't be alive to see how well I can pull it off. I—"

He broke off as Swift Arrow lunged for him. The warrior's balled-up fist caught the side of Loren's head. With his other hand Swift Arrow wrenched the gun from the stunned man.

Captain Loren recovered quickly, and with an oath, struck Swift Arrow a savage blow on the jaw. Swift Arrow landed on the ground with a bone-jarring jolt. But he bounded up again and swung at the other man.

Katherine stood frozen as the two did battle. She heard the dull thud of flesh striking flesh as the two men continued to struggle. Blood streamed from both men's noses, and Captain Loren's lip was cut and bleeding. He delivered a hard blow that landed on Swift Arrow's chest, and the Indian staggered beneath the blow.

Katherine's heart leapt with fear as blood appeared on his bandages. His wound had been reopened. While she stared in horror, he struck the other man a lucky blow that downed him.

Captain Loren shook his head groggily, pushed himself to his elbows, then fell back to the floor, unconscious.

"We must tie him up," Swift Arrow said, breathing heavily. "I'd kill him, but the sound of a shot would bring the others."

"You're hurt," she said.

"It is nothing. We must hurry. There is a piece of rope in the corner."

She picked up the rope and handed it to him. He tied the other man quickly, then tore a strip from the blanket and gagged him.

He stepped from the building where he had been kept imprisoned for the past week, and she followed closely behind him. His narrowed eyes swept the compound.

Katherine could hear the sound of music and laughter coming from the officers' mess, but otherwise, the fort was silent.

His gaze scanned the ramp that ran the length of the stockade wall. A lone sentry paced the wall. They waited until the sentry was the farthest he could get from them, then left the cover of the building.

Katherine was conscious of the moonlight as they hurried across the compound. It shone brightly down, illuminating the cleared area with its pale light. If the guard turned around he would be sure to see them. Then the alarm would be given and all would be lost.

Luck was with them and the sentry remained unaware of their presence. Katherine heaved a sigh of relief when they reached the shadowy buildings where

320

the Apaches were being held.

As Katherine reached for the bar across the door, Swift Arrow gripped her arm with fingers of steel and pulled her into the shadows again. Before she could open her mouth to speak, she saw him.

A lone guard, standing sentry over the building where the Apaches were confined. Putting a finger to her lips, Swift Arrow waited until the guard's back was to them, then he left the shadows and struck him a hard blow on the head. The guard dropped silently to the ground.

Using a length of rope hanging on the side of the building, Swift Arrow tied the soldier up. Then he lifted the bar on the door and they entered the large room.

Eagle Claw was the first to see them. He raised his hand in welcome, and the rest of the Apaches were quickly wakened.

Katherine had forgotten about Crying Wolf. Until she saw him sidling toward the door.

"Swift Arrow," she cried. "Stop him. Crying Wolf is a traitor. He told my father about the escape plans."

The Apaches followed her gaze and found the truth in Crying Wolf's desperate need to escape. One of the warriors made a swift leap, stopping the traitor in his flight. Moonlight filtered through the door, gleaming on a knife as it arced, descended, and found its mark.

Crying Wolf fell and lay still.

The sentry on the wall was quickly dispatched, and the Apaches made their way to the stables. The pungent smell of hay filled her nostrils as Katherine

321

entered the building with the others. The time had arrived when they would part. How could she bear it?

Swift Arrow's stallion whinnied a greeting as he recognized the warrior. It didn't take long for all the Apaches to select the horses they would ride.

Then Katherine stood beside Swift Arrow, certain of the pain of his loss, but feeling a sudden urgency for him to be gone.

"You must hurry," she said.

"Ride with me to the gate," he said. "I want to hold you in my arms once more."

She knew she should refuse, knew she was only postponing the inevitable, but she didn't care.

Wordlessly, she allowed him to help her on the horse in front of him. She leaned against him, into his strength, savoring, one last time, the feel of his body against hers. It would have to last her a lifetime.

They reached the gate and slowed. Katherine thought her heart would surely break when Swift Arrow was gone. At best, her life would stretch out endlessly, with nothing to look forward to.

She braced herself. Although the parting would be nearly more than she could bear, she had no choice. She had given her word.

With a sigh, she stiffened, prepared to be swung down to the ground. When he made no move to help her, she turned her head and looked up at him for one last time.

"You are a fool, Katherine," he said huskily. "How could you believe I would ever let you go?"

"I promised him," she whispered, tracing the line of

322

his jaw. "I have no choice but to stay, in exchange for your life."

She was vaguely aware of the small band of Apaches filing through the gate, driving the rest of the horses before them. But her attention remained fixed on Swift Arrow, this man she loved so desperately.

He smiled, but the smile was without humor, a mere baring of the teeth. His eyes were thunderous as they held hers.

"I made no such promise," he said. "And I refuse to be bound by yours. You are mine, and you will remain with me." Kneeing the horse, he urged him forward, through the gate and out into the night.

Chapter Thirty

Dawn crept like a gray mist through the pine trees as Katherine and the small band of Apaches moved deeper into the foothills. She drew a deep breath of pure mountain air.

They had traveled hard all night, driving the extra horses before them to make pursuit by the soldiers impossible. The army would be forced to wait for additional mounts from Silver City.

She could only imagine her father's rage when he discovered that she had not only helped the rest of the Apaches escape, had not merely taken all the horses, but had gone herself. She shuddered to think what would happen if he ever caught them. Major Carpenter had been made to look a fool before his men. He wouldn't forget that when they met again.

Katherine had switched over to a mount of her own a

few miles out of Fort Bayard. And now she looked at Swift Arrow, who rode ahead of her. He was pale and drawn, and she felt certain his wound was still bleeding. She knew the wound should be tended and was grateful when he pulled up his mount and said they would take time to eat and rest the weary horses.

His movements were awkward when he dismounted, and Katherine was so worried about him that she hardly noticed her aching muscles as she slid from her own horse.

Eagle Claw and Running Elk were sent out to hunt and Creeping Bullfrog was set to watch the horses. Grassy Waters and Laughing Turtle began immediately to gather wood for a fire.

"Sit down," Katherine told Swift Arrow. "Let me see your wound."

He sighed wearily and sank down with his back to a tree. "Your dress has been torn," he said.

Surprised at his words, she looked down at the gray satin dress that had been so elegant last night. Somehow, it had become ripped. She couldn't think how it had happened, but neither did she care.

"It doesn't matter," she said, kneeling down beside him.

She unfastened his shirt and pulled the bandage aside. Worry knit her brow as she saw the amount of blood covering the area. "You've lost a lot of blood," she whispered.

"Yes. I know."

She flicked a quick look at him. "I've got to get some

water to cleanse this," she said.

A shadow fell on them, and Katherine looked up to see Laughing Turtle standing beside her. The Indian woman held a dampened cloth out to Katherine that had obviously been torn from her own garment.

Thanking the woman softly, Katherine cleansed the wound and found it puffy and swollen. She turned anxious eyes to Laughing Turtle.

"I will make him a poultice," Laughing Turtle said. "It will help to stop the bleeding."

When the woman had gone to search near the stream for herbs, Katherine turned back to Swift Arrow. "It's my fault this happened," she said bitterly. "I should have been more careful. After all you taught me, I should have realized Captain Loren was following me."

"Why was he following you?" Swift Arrow asked, his eyes probing hers.

"I—I had resisted him at the dance. I suppose he meant to catch me alone and—" She couldn't go on, but she didn't need to say more.

His face darkened with anger. "I should have killed him."

Laughing Turtle returned. "Put this on his wound and bind it," she directed.

"Thank you," Katherine murmured, taking the damp green poultice from the woman. She barely looked at it as she applied it to Swift Arrow's wound.

Lifting the hem of her gray dress, she tore a wide strip from her petticoat. She ripped a large square from

327

the strip and placed it on top of the poultice, then she used the rest to bind it in place. When she had finished she sat back on her heels.

With a grunt of satisfaction, Laughing Turtle joined the others. The two warriors had returned with several rabbits; Grassy Waters had already cleaned one and reached for another.

"I suppose I should go and help them," Katherine said.

"No," said Swift Arrow, reaching for her hand. "Stay with me."

The women really didn't seem to need her help. So she sat down beside him, and he pulled her against his good shoulder.

She tilted her head to find him staring down at her with inscrutable eyes.

She waited for him to speak. The silence stretched out between them. She moved uneasily. Finally, she could stand it no longer.

"Are you angry with me?" she asked.

"Should I be?"

"You seem so. Why?"

"Perhaps because I had to force you to come with me. Perhaps I wished you to come on your own."

She studied her fingernails. "I explained that to you. I promised my father."

"A promise that has been forced is worthless. It was forced, was it not?"

"How could you doubt it?"

His fingers tightened around her upper arm. He

seemed to be in the grip of some strong emotion, barely restrained.

"I love you," she assured him gently. "I thought you knew that. I wanted so badly to come to see you, but I didn't dare."

"Why?"

"Buck said it would be best if my father knew nothing of our feelings. And I'm sure he was right. When Father found out, he threatened to kill you." Her voice became bitter. "I had no doubt he would have done it, too." Her expression became troubled. "Swift Arrow," she said hesitantly, "I should have stayed there. We will never know a minute of peace. He'll never let me go. He'll follow us. He'll search every inch of these hills until he finds us. There is no place we can go to escape him."

"Then I will be forced to kill him," Swift Arrow said calmly. "For I will not be separated from you."

"Don't say that," she begged. "He's my father."

"Do you care more for him than for me?"

"No!" she denied vehemently. "My love for him died a long time ago. But even when I loved him, it was nothing beside what I feel for you. It would tear my heart out to live apart from you."

"As it would mine." His gaze was intense. "But I believe you are right about him following us. And if he did not, someone else would. I have thought long while I was imprisoned. The Apache people have lost their war with the white eyes. Our numbers are too small for us to continue our fight. For every soldier that falls, another takes his place." He closed his eyes. When he opened them again, she could see the pain in them. "I fear the time of the Apache is done. The white eyes will never be satisfied until we are all on their reservations."

"But there must be a way."

"A new way, perhaps." His eyes flared. "But as the Great Spirit is my witness, I swear it will never be the way of the white eyes. Somewhere there is a place where we can live in peace. *There must be.*"

"And we will find it," she soothed. "Look." She tried to infuse a little enthusiasm into her voice. "The rabbits are done."

Katherine took the meat Little Turtle had brought to them and thanked the woman. Swift Arrow had little appetite and ate sparingly. Although she was anxious about him, Katherine was hungry. She bit eagerly into the meat. When she had finished, she lay down beside Swift Arrow for a few hours' rest.

Swift Arrow's body relaxed as he slipped into sleep. Finally, he felt himself growing weightless. So weightless, in fact, that he could feel himself drifting. He knew surprise when he felt himself lifting . . . higher . . . until he was actually separating from his body. He looked at Katherine, nestled in the arms of his empty body, and tried to call out to her.

No sound came from him.

The wind rose, rustling the leaves on the ground,

330

whistling through the branches of the pine trees. He was moving, floating, drifting on the wind ... away from Katherine ... away from the other Indians.

Why did no one see what was happening? Why didn't Running Elk, who stood guard, realize his friend's body was nothing but an empty shell?

Swift Arrow found himself moving faster, lifting higher on the wind until he was sailing high among the clouds. Down below he could see the forest and streams rushing by.

He sailed still higher, over mountaintops that gave way to prairies, then to valleys and great rivers, and then to forests and mountaintops again.

Was this a dream? Or perhaps it was a vision. What did it mean? Where was he going? And what was taking him there? He knew he had come a great distance since he had left his body and Katherine.

He began to move slower. An eagle cricled a mountain that rose in the distance. The mountain was higher than any he had ever seen before.

As he neared the topmost peak he saw before him a figure, standing with arms upraised. A man, an Indian.

Suddenly, the eagle dived, straight as an arrow, until Swift Arrow was certain the bird meant to attack the man who stood below.

To Swift Arrow's astonishment, the eagle swerved at the last moment and lifted in flight again. It circled once more, then fell gently to perch on the arm of the man.

331

Eager to see what man could command an eagle, Swift Arrow drifted lower until the man came into clearer sight.

Katherine sighed. Her pillow moved beneath her and she opened her eyes. As memory returned, she turned her head and looked up at Swift Arrow.

He gazed down at her.

"I didn't mean to fall asleep on you," she apologized. "Did I wake you?"

"No."

He seemed to be puzzled about something.

"What's wrong?"

"I had a dream," he said, a frown creasing his brow. "I believe it was a sign, yet I do not understand it."

"What did you dream?"

"I saw a man standing on the peak of a great high mountain. An eagle circled in the sky high above his head. The man held out his arm and the eagle came down to rest on it."

She placed a palm on his forehead. "You have a fever," she said. "That's what caused your dream. We need some of the bark you used when I was sick."

"No. The dream is a sign. I'm sure the Great Spirit is leading me."

She wondered if he could be right. "Did you recognize the man?" she asked.

"Yes," he said. "It was Sitting Bull, medicine man of the Sioux tribe."

"But what could Sitting Bull have to do with us?"

"I don't know. But I must find out. I am sure the dream has given me the answer, if I can but find it."

"Where was the mountain?"

"I did not recognize the place," Swift Arrow said. "I am sure I have never seen it, for it seemed to be a great distance from here. I think we are meant to go there, Katherine. In such a place, perhaps we could find the peace we seek."

"If only it were so," she said.

"I am sure of it." He thought for a moment, then spoke. "It does not make sense to me. Sitting Bull is on the reservation. He has given up his fight and lives the way of the white man."

"Swift Arrow," she said hesitantly, "there are no reservations in the mountains."

"No," he agreed. "But Sitting Bull was not on a reservation in the dream."

He became silent, puzzling over the dream.

"We must decide where we are going," she said softly.

"I know," he said. "We will go to Chief Tall Feathers's village."

"We can't," Katherine said.

He looked at her.

"Buck went to warn Chief Tall Feathers. My father knows where they are. He plans on sending men to bring them in." Suddenly her eyes glinted with humor. "Of course, it'll be a while now before he can do it. We took all his horses."

"It will not take him long to get more," Swift Arrow said. "But by the time he gets there, they will have gone."

He remained silent for a moment, then he sighed. "We must go back to the land of the dark-skinned people," he said.

"To Mexico?"

"Yes. To the Sierra Madres." He looked at her. "It will be hard," he said. "There is not much game. We will have many hardships to endure."

"I don't care," she said softly. "We'll be together."

"We must find food to carry on our journey. It will take many days to cross the desert to the mountains."

"What about the cliff dwellings?" she asked. "There's food there."

For a moment he was silent. Then, "Yes," he said. "The soldiers do not know of it."

He attempted to rise, then faltered. Beads of sweat broke out on his head. He fell back weakly, a dark stain seeping through his bandages.

"Oh, my God!" she cried. "Your wound is bleeding again."

Again he struggled to stand. "It is nothing," he said. "You must not be concerned."

She pushed him back to a seated position. "It's much more than nothing. Let me look at it."

Carefully, she unwound the bandages, paling at the amount of blood he had lost. Scrambling to her feet, she called to Laughing Turtle for help.

334

"Swift Arrow is bleeding again," she said. "We've got to find some way to stop it."

While Laughing Turtle searched for herbs to stop the bleeding, Katherine tore another strip off her petticoat, wet it in the stream, then washed Swift Arrow's wound. She could see little change in it. It was puffy and swollen but seemed no worse than before, nor did it seem better.

Katherine was vaguely aware that someone had come to stand beside her. She looked up to see Eagle Claw. His gaze met hers, then moved to his friend. "The wound is bad," he said.

"It is nothing," Swift Arrow replied.

A moment later Laughing Turtle brought a handful of something that resembled cobwebs. When Katherine questioned the woman, she found that was exactly what it was.

"It will cause the blood to clot," the woman said, applying the webs to the wound. Then she applied more of the green poultice and helped Katherine to bind the wound again.

"He cannot travel much longer," Laughing Turtle told Katherine. "You must find a safe place for him to stay until the wound has healed."

Katherine intercepted the look that passed between Swift Arrow and Eagle Claw.

"We must leave you," Eagle Claw said. "You will not be able to keep up. If we do not leave now, the blue-coats will find us."

"You can't be serious," Katherine said. "Surely you

335

wouldn't abandon him just because he's wounded. Had it not been for Swift Arrow, you'd still be held prisoner at the fort."

"Katherine!" Swift Arrow's voice was sharp. "Be still. It is the way of my people. Those who cannot keep up must be abandoned for the good of the tribe."

"There'd be no tribe if not for you."

"Do not talk of what you do not understand. This is the way it must be."

"But what about the cliff dwellings?" She looked anxiously at him. "Couldn't you make it that far?"

"I will make it. But the others will not go there."

"Why not?"

"They believe it to be haunted by the spirits of our departed ancestors."

"That's nonsense. Tell them we've been there and nothing happened to us."

"It will do no good. Let them go, and do not blame them. It is our way."

"It's still stupid," she muttered. She turned to Laughing Turtle. "At least give me some of your medicine for him."

Silently, the old woman took some of the contents from her medicine bag and handed it to Katherine.

"Grind it well with a stone to make a paste," Laughing Turtle said. "And apply it many times each day. If the fever comes upon him, give him tea made from the bark of the dogwood tree."

The warriors helped Swift Arrow to mount his horse, then watched as he and Katherine left. Her back was stiff with resentment as they rode away. Although she feared for their future, she refused to allow the others to see her feelings.

When she finally looked back, the Apaches were already breaking camp and preparing to resume their journey.

Turning around again, Katherine faced forward. She didn't know what the future held for them, but at least they would face it together.

tested for the edification, the witheld to those who
have . . . see his calling.

when an family, in fact . . . as the American way
scene, thinking, living and . . . family get together
. . .

forms an alliance . . . between two local . . .
you quite know who has families . . . to decide which
find them in old San Francisco.

Chapter Thirty-One

By the time they reached the cliff dwellings, Swift Arrow was in a weakened state. Katherine suspected it was from all the blood he had lost. The fever had taken its toll, as well, and as they pulled up at the base of the cliff, he slid from the stallion, unconscious.

"Swift Arrow!" Katherine cried, her heart contracting with fear.

She slid from her mount and knelt beside him. Picking up his wrist, she let out a relieved breath. Although his pulse was weak, it beat steadily beneath her thumb. Her next step was to get him up the cliff where she could be sure of safety.

She stared up at the face of the almost vertical cliff, feeling utterly helpless, knowing it would be impossible for her to get him up to the cliff dwellings while he was unconscious. And yet, how could she not make the attempt?

Major Carpenter and his men would be scouring every inch of these mountains in their efforts to find them. The cliff dwellings would be their only chance to escape detection.

A distant howling of wolves presented another danger to them, and she shivered with fear. If the wolves picked up their human scent and came after them, could she fight them off alone?

She didn't think so.

She must get him up to the city of his ancestors.

She didn't know how she would accomplish it, for it seemed an impossible task from where she stood.

Her lips tightened with determination. If her father found them, he would kill Swift Arrow. And she refused to let that happen.

She *would* get him up the cliff, no matter what it involved. She would find a way to accomplish the seemingly impossible.

She studied the situation. He was too heavy to carry up the ladder. Her brows creased with worry, her gaze searching for some way out of her predicament. Her searching gaze fell upon the spruce tree high above her that grew in front of the stone and mortar structures.

Suddenly an idea came to her. There was a lariat on the saddle. Perhaps she could use the tree for leverage and pull him up with a rope.

She turned the idea over in her mind, discarded it as impossible, then returned to it again. Why wouldn't it work? At least it was worth a try, for no other idea had presented itself to her.

Yes, she decided. If she tied a rope beneath his arms, then she . . .

No. Swift Arrow's chest wound could be made worse if the rope slipped. It could hurt him badly. She searched for another answer, knowing there must be a way. There *had* to be.

Her gaze fell on the blanket tied behind the saddle. An idea began to take form in her mind. But would it work? She didn't know. But anything was worth a try.

She would tie the blanket around him. It would offer some protection, however scant, from the sparse shrubbery that managed to survive on the rocky cliff.

Moving to the stallion, she removed the blanket and rope and returned to the injured man. She spread the blanket out next to him and managed to roll him onto it. Then she gathered the ends together and tied them tightly.

When she had finished, she tied one end of the rope to the blanket. Then she removed the long ladder from its hiding place, leaned it against the face of the cliff, picked up the loose end of the rope, and began her climb.

When she reached the top of the ladder, she placed the second ladder against the cliff and soon found herself in the courtyard of the ancient city. Using the spruce tree for leverage, she pulled on the rope.

Nothing happened.

Anxiety stabbed through her. She had to make it work. She simply *had* to.

Leaning away from the rope, she gripped it until her knuckles were white and strained hard against the weight. Katherine put everything she had into the effort . . . and was rewarded when the rope moved slowly around the tree.

Granted, it was only a few inches, but, nevertheless, it *had* moved.

She rested only a few moments, then pulled hard again. Sweat broke out on her forehead with the exertion. As before, the rope moved a few inches . . . then stopped.

It was going to work. She knew it was.

Exultantly, she dug her heels in more firmly, took a deep breath . . . pulled tighter . . . and fell over backward as the rope suddenly went slack.

Horror-stricken, not even aware of her scraped elbows or the bruises she had sustained in the fall, she stared at the rope dangling limply in her hands.

Fearing that she had unwittingly injured Swift Arrow even more, she scrambled to her feet and peered over the ledge. The blanket-wrapped figure lay unmoving on the ground far below.

She quickly descended the ladders, afraid of what she would find when she reached the ground. Untying the ends of the blanket, she ran her hands over the injured man's limbs, heaving a sigh of relief when everything seemed to be intact.

She brushed a lock of dark hair from his face and stared helplessly at him. "God!" she muttered. "What am I going to do?"

Suddenly his eyelids flickered. He opened his eyes and stared up at her. "Why do you weep?" he asked faintly. Lifting a finger, he brushed it across her face, wiping away the tears she hadn't even been aware of.

"I don't know how to get you up the cliff," she said helplessly.

"And for this you weep?" he asked.

She nodded, feeling no need to add that the tears were concern for his safety.

"Then dry your eyes," he said, struggling to his elbows. "I will get myself up the cliff."

"Are you sure you can make it?" she asked anxiously.

"I must," he said, attempting a smile. "Otherwise, I fear you will drown me with your tears."

"I'm sorry to be such a baby," she muttered.

"No. Do not apologize. Just help me to my feet."

She gave him her hand, and between them, he managed to stand up. He leaned heavily on her as they made their way to the ladder.

"You'd better go first," she said. "I'll have to pull the ladder up behind us."

He nodded and gripped the pole ladder with both hands. She could see the effort he had to exert to climb. Sweat beaded his forehead as he struggled upward, and he was only able to go a few feet before stopping to gather his strength together again.

It seemed an eternity before they reached the top. Then he lay on the courtyard on his back, unmoving. It was a few moments later when she realized he had lapsed into unconsciousness again.

Unwilling to leave him so close to the edge, she went into the room they had used for a bedroom. As she had expected, she found a blanket there. She used it to pull him closer to the inner courtyard wall.

When Katherine had decided he was far enough from the ledge, she unfastened his shirt and checked his wound. She found fresh blood on the bandage.

She cleansed the wound and applied another poultice. Then she made a tea from the bark of the dogwood tree to help keep down the fever.

Kneeling beside him, she trickled some of the tea into his mouth. She was relieved to see his throat move as he swallowed the tea.

Katherine made several trips into the *kiva* that stored the supplies, bringing up armloads of hides and containers of dried vegetables and meat. Using the dried foods, she made a nourishing broth, and managed to get Swift Arrow to swallow some of it, as well.

Then, feeling she had done all she could do for him, she rolled him onto the bed of hides, being careful of his wound, and lay down next to him. Then she pulled the blanket up, covering them both.

During the night he woke up shivering. She could feel the heat emanating from his body and knew he had developed a fever. Fearfully, she checked his bandage and discovered the wound looked worse.

"Dear God," she whispered. "Please, don't let me lose him."

He opened his eyes. "What is wrong?" he asked.

"The . . . your wound is . . . seeping," she said, her voice husky with pain and fear for him. "Please . . . I don't know what to do."

He lifted a hand and touched her face. "Do not worry," he said. "I will tell you."

"All right."

"You must build a fire," he said.

The words had hardly left his lips before she was moving to do his bidding. She added kindling to the hot coals, and as the flames flared hotly she added larger pieces of wood, until the fire was blazing. Only then did she return to him.

"It's done," she said.

His eyes had been closed. At her words he looked at her. "Now you must cut away the bad flesh, Katherine," he said.

"Cut away?" Her heart began to race madly. She tried to control her panic. "I—are you sure about this?" she muttered.

He gripped her hand weakly. "Yes," he said. "I'm sure of it." He seemed to sense her uncertainty, and he squeezed her hand. "You must do it, Katherine. For there is no one else."

She closed her eyes. He was right. She would have to find the strength to do what was necessary. She drew a shaky breath.

"Tell me exactly what to do."

"In the *kiva* where the food is stored, you will find a knife. Get it and put the blade in the fire. Wait until it is hot. Then you must cut away the bad flesh with it." His gaze held hers. "You must not falter, little one. After you have finished, wipe the knife clean and put the blade in the fire again. Then lay it flat against the

345

wound to seal the flesh." He closed his eyes weakly. "Do not fear. You will find the strength to do it."

"Yes," she said, swallowing around the lump in her throat. "I know I will. It's just that . . . I know it's going to hurt. And I can't bear to cause you more pain."

"I have no fear of pain, my love," he said calmly. "Many times I have felt its bite, but it has never conquered me. Nor will it ever."

She could believe that. And yet, she had never been the one to cause him the pain. Her gaze fell on the seeping wound. She knew she had no choice. There was no one else to help him. No one but her.

Rising, she added more wood to build up the fire. Then she went to the *kiva* and found the knife hidden behind the bags of food. She returned to Swift Arrow and inserted the blade in the flames—as he had bidden. Then she tore some more strips off her petticoat to use for fresh bandages.

"The knife should be ready," he said.

She picked it up and knelt beside him. Her hands were trembling and she tried to will them to be steady. The flesh seemed to resist the first pressure of the blade.

Gritting her teeth, she pushed harder, and the flesh parted beneath the blade. She threw a quick look at him but, he hadn't even flinched.

Katherine bit down hard on her lower lip, drawing blood as she cut into the wound. She forced her mind to forget him as she worked on the flesh, occasionally swabbing the pus and blood that flowed from the wound. Suddenly, his body relaxed. She glanced up at

346

his face and saw he was unconscious.

Remembering what he had said, she inserted the blade into the fire again. A moment later, she removed it and moved back to him. Laying the blade flat against the wound, she flinched at the smell of burning flesh. When she had finished, she applied another poultice, then ripped some more strips off her sadly depleted petticoat to bind the wound again.

After banking the fire, she returned to the pallet and lay down with him again.

All the next day his fever raged. Katherine never left him for a moment, intent on tending to his needs. When his temperature seemed to shoot incredibly high, she stripped his body of clothing and bathed it over and over again with water she carried from the spring.

Although she grew weary from the effort and strain, she kept it up until the fever had abated somewhat. Then she lay down beside him to rest.

The second day his temperature fluctuated. Just when she thought he was free of the fever, his temperature would rise again. She began to worry, as their supply of dogwood bark was fast being depleted. If he didn't start getting well soon, she would have to go in search of some more. And although she knew where to find more of the precious bark, she would have to leave him to do so. And she was afraid to go away and leave him alone.

He must get well soon. Dear God! He must.

Her prayers were in vain, for Swift Arrow's fever stayed with him. He seemed to be getting weaker and

weaker as time passed. And his periods of consciousness were getting fewer all the time.

During one of his wakeful moments he studied the
circles beneath her eyes.

"So much burden to put on the shoulders of one so
young," he said softly. "You are making yourself ill."

Unbidden tears welled up in her eyes, overflowing
and slipping wetly down her pale cheeks. She took one
of his hands in both her own. "I'm so afraid you won't
get well," she admitted.

"Do not worry so," he said. "My body will heal itself.
It will just take time."

"But you've been so ill. I can't seem to keep your
fever down."

"You have no need to be concerned," he said. "The
dogwood bark tea will eventually rid me of the fever."

She didn't tell him she had already used the last of
the bark. She couldn't find the words. He must not be
made to worry. He had to use all his strength to get
well.

"We must get you out of the chill night air," she said.
"Do you think you could help me get you into the
sleeping room?"

He nodded.

With her help he managed to make it across the
courtyard to the small room where she had made his
bed. She could see what an effort it had been for him to
make the move. Beads of sweat covered his forehead,
and his skin felt clammy to the touch.

After she had him settled on the pallet of hides, she
fed him the last of the tea she had brewed. Her eyes

never left him as she waited until he fell asleep again.

Katherine sat beside the fire way into the night, knowing she should rest, and yet her worry over Swift Arrow was so great that she knew she couldn't.

Finally, she lay down beside him, afraid of what tomorrow would bring, but knowing whatever it was, she would more than likely have to face it alone.

Chapter Thirty-Two

An eagle cast a circling shadow high above the canyon floor. Katherine spared it only a glance as she stared down into the valley. She was too worried about Swift Arrow to take in the beauty of the wilderness.

Although she knew she would have to leave him and gather more of the bark from the dogwood tree, she wanted to put it off as long as she could.

He had drifted in and out of consciousness during the night, and she was afraid his condition had worsened. Sighing heavily, she crossed the courtyard and entered the room where he lay. Her eyes were clouded with worry as she knelt and placed her palm against his forehead.

His temperature had escalated again.

As though becoming aware of her presence, he stirred, his eyelids flickered, and lifted. He stared up at

351

her with his dark eyes.

"You look . . . tired," he muttered weakly. "Have you . . . had no rest at all?"

"I can't rest until you're better," she choked. Taking his hand, she lifted it to her face, her eyes never leaving his. "You must get better," she said fiercely. "You can't leave me. You have to keep fighting."

Before she had even finished speaking his eyes had closed again. She wasn't sure if he was asleep or unconscious.

Feeling the need of contact, she ran her hand caressingly over his face. She swallowed heavily as fear closed her throat. Was his temperature even higher now than a few minutes ago. She couldn't be sure. But she was afraid it was. She could wait no longer.

She had to go after the bark from the dogwood tree.

She wasted no time after the decision was made. She only took time to change into one of the doeskin dresses she had made on her previous stay, knowing the garment would allow her more freedom of movement.

Leaning over, she placed a soft kiss on his forehead. "I'll be back soon, my love," she whispered.

He stirred uneasily as though aware of her words, but he didn't wake up.

With one last look at him, Katherine left the room and gathered up the knife and his bow and arrow. She left the rifle, aware that the sound of a shot would give away their presence.

She paused at the base of the cliff to get her bearings. Swift Arrow had showed her the tree when he had taken her hunting. It was located in an area that was heavy with brush. She could make it faster without the stallion. If she hurried, she could be there and back in three hours.

Katherine sprinted down the trail, jumping fallen logs and other obstacles. She intended to travel as fast as she could where she could, for the brush would slow her down.

She was breathing hard by the time she reached the brush. Then she pushed and shoved her way through, uncaring of the scratches she received in her haste. Soon the brush gave way to dense forest. She was getting closer.

Now she began to go slower. She must not pass the tree by. Precious time could be lost if she did. Time that she could not afford.

Although she had only been there once, the area was familiar. She was sure the tree lay just a little farther to the north. Beyond that big rock. As she rounded the rock, relief spread through her.

The tree was large, standing nearly twenty feet tall. It was covered with delicate pink flowers.

Drawing the knife, she cut into the bark and peeled it back. Then, slicing off large pieces, she stuffed it in the parfleche attached by a thong to her waist. When she had filled the bag, she closed it and turned to retrace her steps.

She raced fleetly through the forest, her blood singing in her veins. Her mind was busy with plans as she ran, pushing aside the foliage automatically.

She would have to chop the bark and boil it well to make the tea for Swift Arrow. Then, while she waited for his recovery, she could—

Her thoughts broke off suddenly as she pushed aside some heavy foliage and found herself confronted by two men. In her haste to reach Swift Arrow, she had become careless.

Her heart pounded loudly in her ears as she stared up at the two strangers. Their clothing was stained and dirty, and they were both unkempt. They both seemed just as surprised as Katherine.

But they recovered quicker.

The one nearest her pushed back his broad-brimmed hat and approached her with a leer. He was built like an ox, with wide, powerful-looking shoulders and a thick torso set on short, squat legs. He had small dark eyes, set close together. They peered out at her from above a tangled web of beard.

"Well, I'll be damned," he swore softly. "Just lookee what's done fell in our laps, Clyde."

"I'm a-lookin', Jeb," the other man replied. "She looks like a squaw to me. Even with that light-colored hair."

"More'n likely she's some Injun buck's woman. That right, honey?" the first man questioned.

She remained silent, her body tense, her hand coming to rest on the knife swinging from its sheath at her waist.

Clyde grinned widely at the action. "You think she's maybe warnin' us off?" he asked his companion.

Jeb laughed harshly. "Could be. But I ain't gonna let a little bitty thing like that stop me."

"Don't reckon as how I will neither," Clyde said,

reaching out for her.

Although her heart beat rapidly with fear, she allowed none of it to show. Instead, she leapt back out of his reach, dragging the knife from its sheath and holding it threateningly in front of her.

"Stay away from me," she hissed.

"Wal now," Clyde said. "She can talk, cain't she. I wasn't rightly sure before."

"Danged right, she can," said Jeb.

"But she ain't actin' very friendly-like," growled Clyde. "Maybe you better get around behind her."

She watched Jeb start to circle behind her, and she moved quickly, forestalling him.

All the time Clyde had been advancing steadily on her. His eyes carefully scrutinized her every movement as she backed cautiously away.

As he came closer, the rancid smell of body sweat caused her nostrils to twitch. She made a stabbing movement as he reached for her. He yelped and jumped back.

He looked at the flecks of blood appearing on his hand from the small cut she had inflicted. As she watched, his mouth spread into a leering smile, showing stained, rotten teeth.

His gaze flicked beyond her shoulder and she whirled, stabbing out at the man who had come up behind her. The knife sliced a long gash in his arm and he yowled out with pain.

Turning quickly, she slashed out at Clyde, who had thought to catch her unawares. She struck the side of his face with the tip of the blade. With a muttered curse of anger and pain, he jumped back out of reach.

"Dammit, Clyde," Jeb growled. "Grab her!"

"Grab her yourself," the other man snarled. "I ain't fixin' to get myself cut up."

She was breathing heavily now, her heart thundering loudly in her chest. Her eyes darted back and forth, trying to keep both men in sight.

"You ain't gonna let a girl get away with bestin' you," Jeb growled.

"Shut up an' let me see you handle her."

She watched them warily. They both seemed to be wishing they'd never started this. Perhaps they could be persuaded to go away and leave her alone.

"Dammit, Clyde," Jeb said. "We ain't got time to be foolin' around here. If you want her, take her."

Her eyes were on Clyde, who seemed to be the instigator of the whole thing. She was watching him and didn't anticipate the other man's sudden rush for her until it was too late.

Rough hands clamped her arms tightly to her sides. Her wrist was seized and squeezed tightly until she was forced to drop the knife. She struggled fiercely against him, but found herself forced to the ground.

"I'll get the horses while you have your way with her," said Clyde. He laughed harshly. "But it ain't gonna take me long, so be quick about it."

Then he left.

The man pulled at her skirt, yanking it above her knees with one rough hand while he held her down with the other.

She struggled against his strength, kicking out with her legs. He raised back his hand and slapped her hard across the face. The blow made her senses reel.

He struggled with his fly, trying to get it unbuttoned with one hand while he held her down with the other. As he accomplished his task and leaned over her, trying to force himself on her, her hands scrabbled desperately in the dirt, searching for something to use as a weapon. Her fingers encountered something hard—a chunk of wood. She gripped it hard and brought it down with all her strength on the top of his head.

He grunted and fell away from her.

She scrabbled quickly to her knees, her frantic gaze searching for the knife. She found it among the leaves. The man was shaking his head groggily. He blinked, then opened his eyes. They were enraged.

Katherine made a leap for the knife as he lunged at her, pinning her beneath his weight. Her fingers gripped the knife hard. Then, with all the strength she possessed, she brought it up and then plunged downward.

The blade made hardly a sound as it sank into his back. His eyes widened in surprise. His mouth worked silently.

She hadn't killed him!

She could feel the sticky, warm, gush of blood pumping up around her fingers as she tried to pull the knife free. Her stomach roiled, nausea welled up, spreading through her as the blade left his body.

It took all the courage she could muster to bring the

knife down again. His eyes glazed over and he fell across her.

Shuddering from the horror of being attacked in such a way—and from being forced to take a man's life—she used every ounce of strength she possessed to push the man's weight from her.

She stared down at the man she had killed, hardly able to believe what had happened. Her gaze left the fallen man, fell on her bloody hands.

Oh, God! It was his blood. She had to get it off.

Katherine had completely forgotten the other man, until he pushed aside the dense foliage and stopped short, staring down at the man who lay dead on the ground.

"Goddamn!" he said in an awed voice. Then his gaze fell on her. "You done kilt Jeb," he said in an aggrieved tone. "What'd you have to go and do a thing like that for?" His eyes were puzzled. "We warn't going to hurt you none."

He wasn't going to hurt her?

She stared at him, feeling completely confused. "You—he—he was bent on rape," she said. Uncertainty filled her eyes. "Wasn't he?"

"Course he was," he growled. "But what of it? It ain't like we was bent on a-killin' you nor nothin' like that."

She stared at him in amazement. The man really didn't see any harm in raping her. When he moved toward her, she scrambled quickly to her feet and held the knife out before her.

"Stay away," she warned. "I'll kill you if you touch me."

He drew his gun from its holster. "You ain't gonna do nothin'," he growled. "'Cause I'm gonna shoot that knife right out'n yore hand afore I come any closer. Then, I'm gonna finish what Jeb started. And when I'm done with you, well, I guess if'n yore still alive, then I reckon I'll just have to put you out of yore misery."

He meant to rape her and then kill her. And if he did, then what would become of Swift Arrow? She had to stop him.

He grinned, his eyes on hers as he slowly raised the gun, taunting her. Her eyes remained fixed on his as she wondered if she could still hit her mark as Swift Arrow had taught her. She knew her very life and his depended on it.

She watched Clyde's eyes, saw the minute he decided to make his move and let the knife fly. It struck him high on the left chest. His gun fired, sending a loud explosion ringing over the canyon. Then he fell to the ground and lay twitching on a carpet of pine needles.

Sickened, she turned away and swallowed thickly. After several minutes had passed, she looked at him. He lay still, obviously dead.

She moved to him, bent, and drew the knife from his chest. Emptying her mind of all thought, she faced north and began her journey back to the ancient city . . . and Swift Arrow.

For some reason, Katherine's vision was blurred. She stumbled over an unseen log and went sprawling among the pine needles. Picking herself up, she resumed her journey, unaware of her torn clothing, her disheveled hair and scratched face and arms.

She could hear no sound except the steady thrum . . . thrum . . . thrum . . . of her heart beating loudly in her ears. Golden rays of sun tipped the branches of the pine trees, but she was unaware of the beauty before her.

A scuffling sound stopped her. She snapped her head around. A movement to the right caught her attention. Her gaze searched the forest, became still. Was that a human arm disappearing behind a tree?

"Who's there?" she cried, her searching gaze sweeping the verdant green forest.

Silence.

Branches snapped off to the side, sending fear crackling up her spine. Her pulse raced as she drew her knife from her waist. Then she turned.

He stepped out from behind the tree. The bloodstain on his shirt combined with his savage expression froze her on the spot.

"I thought you were dead," she gasped, her eyes going to the gun he was holding.

"You mighta did Jeb in," he taunted, his eyes dark with hate. "But it'll take more'n a chit like you to kill the likes of me."

His steps were heavy as he moved toward her, crushing the pine needles beneath his feet.

"Stay where you are," she warned, following his movements with her knife.

He grinned. "You done tried thet once," he taunted. "It ain't gonna work a second time. This time, I got you cold."

Katherine knew she had little chance of avoiding his bullet. She was sure it was faster than her knife. And her hand was trembling so badly she was sure to miss him. But she knew she couldn't just stand there and do nothing. The nearest tree was too far to offer cover. But she wouldn't go down without a fight. As his gun leveled on her, she threw the knife and flung herself sideways.

Chapter Thirty-Three

The sound of a shot split the silence, echoing across the valley, and waking Swift Arrow. His fever-glazed eyes opened, studying the ceiling overhead. He knew something had woken him, and he forced his mind to concentrate on the way it had sounded.

He listened closely, heard the wind sighing through the ruins. Could that have been what he heard? *No,* he answered himself, it had been loud. Like the crack of thunder. Was it going to rain?

His gaze went to the window. The sun was shining brightly beyond the room.

The sound hadn't been thunder.

Suddenly he became aware of the silence. The only sound was the wind blowing softly through the cavern.

Alarmed, he pushed himself to his elbows. "Kath-

363

erine," he called.

There was no answer.

Struggling to a sitting position, he waited until his dizziness passed, then rose unsteadily to his feet. He found that in his weakened condition he could only remain erect by supporting himself against the wall. Moving slowly, he went in search of Katherine.

His gaze swept the empty courtyard and fear clutched at him. Where was she?

Moving unsteadily, he neared the ledge. His gaze searched the narrow valley below. But he could see no sign of movement.

He tried to still his fears.

Perhaps she had gone to the spring after some water.

Yes, he told himself. *She's only gone to the spring.*

All he had to do was be patient, and soon she would return.

Weakness assailed him. He felt himself growing dizzy again and sank down on the courtyard wall. Clasping his head in his hands, he waited until the world had righted itself before he stood up again.

He had only been fooling himself. For he knew, deep in his heart, that something was wrong. Everything felt wrong. Katherine was nowhere to be seen. She hadn't just gone to the spring. Somehow, the sound he had heard was connected with her disappearance.

And it had sounded like a shot.

He was certain of it. He had to find her. She might be in danger, might need his help. But what could he do? He was almost too weak to stand.

Calling on an inner reserve of strength, he moved on shaky legs, making his way toward the spring, hoping he was wrong, praying that he would find her there.

His spirits plummeted when he reached the spring and found it empty. He sank weakly down on a rock, waiting until strength returned to his shaky legs before attempting the journey back to the cliff dwellings.

Thoughts filled his head as he made his way back up the trail. Had someone discovered their hideaway and taken Katherine against her will? If so, then why hadn't he been killed to prevent him following her captors?

The answer eluded him, but he fully intended to find out.

Swift Arrow cursed his weakness over and over again. Whoever had taken Katherine must have left tracks. He must find and follow them before she was harmed. He must . . .

But the effort proved too much for his spent strength. His head whirled dizzily and everything went black as he fell to the ground unconscious.

A shuddering sob released the pent-up air from her lungs as Katherine stared at the body of the man she had just killed. He lay on his side, his face turned toward her. His mouth hung slackly open and fresh blood dribbled from one corner. His eyes stared grotesquely, looking somewhat obscene with the blade of her knife wedged firmly between them.

She swallowed heavily, closing her eyes for a

moment and pressing her hands against her pounding temples.

Get control of yourself. Think! The shot could have been heard. It could bring someone snooping around. If anyone finds the bodies, they might find your tracks. Then the cliff dwellings would no longer be safe.

Getting to her feet, she grabbed Clyde beneath the armpits. She alternately pushed and pulled, until she had him wedged firmly beneath a bush. Then she covered him with brush and leaves and retraced her steps to where she had left Jeb. She dragged dead branches and covered him the same way she had done Clyde. Then, using a pine branch to sweep away her tracks, she made her way back to the cliff dwellings.

She found Swift Arrow lying on the trail leading to the spring. She sank down beside him and examined his wound, giving a heartfelt prayer of thanks when she discovered it had not started bleeding again.

Rising to her feet, she built up the fire and put water on to heat. Then she chopped the dogwood bark into small pieces and added it to the water. She didn't let it boil long before she poured up a bowl and trickled some of the liquid down his throat.

He coughed, sputtered, then opened his eyes. As awareness flooded over him, he grasped her wrist, staring up at her.

"I . . . thought you were . . . gone," he said weakly. "Was it . . . only a dream?"

Instead of answering his question, she lifted his head, and held the cup to his lips again. "Drink some of this," she said.

He sipped slowly at the brew until it was all gone.
Then she lowered his head.

"Could you walk if I help you?" she asked.

"Yes."

With her help he managed to stand on his feet. Then
they made their way to the sleeping room. His gaze
was puzzled as he lay down on the pallet of hides.

"I do not remember leaving the bed," he said.

She held her silence and watched his eyes close
heavily. When he was breathing deeply again, she left
the room and crossed the courtyard to the outer ledge.
Her searching gaze swept the valley, but she could see
nothing amiss.

Nevertheless, to be safe, she pulled both ladders up
the cliff. After laying them down on the outer
courtyard, she went back into the sleeping room and
lay down next to Swift Arrow.

A moment later, exhaustion took its toll and she fell
asleep.

When Katherine woke, darkness had descended. She
looked up to find Swift Arrow watching her. He looked
unutterably weary, but his fever had abated.

"You look tired," he said gently. "I fear I have been a
heavy burden to you."

She felt such relief to hear him sounding normal
again that she burst out in tears. An agonized
expression crossed his face and he gathered her close

against him.

"I did not mean to make you cry," he said.

"Y-you d-didn't," she sobbed. "I-it's just that I'm so happy you're finally getting well." She wiped her eyes with the back of her hand. "I was so afraid. I thought— I thought—"

"What did you think?" he asked gently, wiping away tears that were still rolling down her pale cheeks.

"I thought you were going to d-die," she admitted.

"And leave my little love?" he whispered, his lips trailing soft kisses across her cheeks. Although his gaze was intense when he lifted his head, his voice was teasing. "You will not rid yourself of me so easily," he said.

"I never want to be free," she told him. "Never. If you were to die, then I'd follow you. Because life without you would hold no meaning."

"It is the same for me," he said, his lips closing over hers.

As always, she felt a thrill running through her body as he deepened the kiss. But her mind warned her to keep control of her emotions. The sickness had left him in a weakened state. As much as she wanted him to make love to her, she knew she couldn't allow it.

Gently, she pushed him away.

He lifted puzzled eyes to study her.

"Why do you resist?" he asked.

"You have to regain your strength," she said. "We must wait."

He gave a long-suffering sigh and lay back down. His

eyes held a glint of humor as they met hers. "If you are not going to allow me to make love to you, then I insist you feed me."

She smiled. "So now you're making demands of me," she mocked. "That's a sure sign you're getting well."

"Is it?" His gaze swept her wan face. "My illness has nearly spent your strength," he said. Suddenly, his gaze narrowed, focusing on a darkening spot on her jaw.

"What have you done to your face?" he asked, pushing himself to his elbows.

"My face?" She reached up, touched her jaw, and winced with pain.

His brows had drawn together in a frown. "Your face is bruised," he said. "How did it happen?"

Although she knew instantly the bruise must have come from the blow Jeb had delivered, she searched her mind for an answer that would appease him.

His dark gaze had left her face, moved lower, then stopped. He lifted his eyes to her. They were expressionless. "Your dress is torn," he said grimly. "What has happened?"

Aghast, she stared down at her dress. He was right. It was ripped at the neck. Why hadn't she noticed before? But the answer was clear. She had been utterly exhausted. Weary of mind and body, her thought processes had had more than they could take and had almost completely shut down on her. She had been like a wounded animal seeking shelter from danger when she returned to the cliff dwellings, wanting nothing more than to hide from its enemies and tend

369

its wounds.

Knowing she had no choice, she lowered her eyes and began to relate to him what had happened. When she had finished, she threw a quick glance at him . . . and wished she hadn't. For a fleeting moment she saw something hard and intense and almost frightening in his face. His jaw was grim, and his eyes were blazing with fury. His hands were clenched tightly, his knuckles showing white.

"What did you do with the bodies?" he asked in a harsh voice.

"I covered them with brush and swept away my tracks like you showed me," she said, alarmed by the intensity of his gaze.

"The brush will not keep the animals from the bodies," he said. "They must be buried. I would not care what the scavengers did to them, but we must not leave the bones for the blue-coats to find."

Her eyes filled with tears. She wanted to protest that she had done the best that she could, but no words came from her lips. As though aware of what she was feeling, he reached for her, pulling her against his tense body.

"No one could have done more," he said gently. His voice became agonized. "I swore I would protect you, and yet I let this happen."

"No!" she protested sharply. "It wasn't your fault. You were sick."

"They could have killed you."

"But they didn't. I'm safe and here with you."

He cupped her chin in one hand and looked at her.

370

"After we eat we must go and bury the bodies. If anyone else discovers the bones they might decide to look farther. This place would no longer be safe."

"I know," she said. "But I'll go back alone. You aren't strong enough to go."

"I will not let you leave this place without me," he said. "We will go together."

Chapter Thirty-Four

Although Katherine tried her best to dissuade him, Swift Arrow remained adamant about going with her, saying they would ride the stallion as far as possible. When she realized further argument was futile, she ceased to resist. She admitted to herself she had dreaded returning to the dead men on her own.

At the bottom of the cliff, Swift Arrow gave a shrill whistle. An answering whistle sounded in the distance, and the black stallion appeared a moment later. She shuddered inwardly when they reached the place where she had left Clyde. But outwardly she gave no sign of the feelings of terror the place still held for her.

As Swift Arrow had expected, the animals had been at the body. The remains were scattered around the clearing. Katherine knew Swift Arrow hadn't regained enough strength to bury the bodies alone, so she swallowed her nausea and closed her mind against what she was doing. She tried not to see the bloody mess left by the animals, tried to see it only as parts to be found as she helped Swift Arrow cover the remains with dirt and rocks.

When they had repeated the process with Jeb's body, she allowed herself a sigh of relief. Her gaze moved often to Swift Arrow, knowing the work had taken much out of him. She feared he would have a relapse if he wasn't careful.

The trip back to the cliff dwellings was completed in record time. Then they scrubbed themselves up and removed their soiled clothing. After they lay down on the pallet in their sleeping room, Swift Arrow gathered her closely into his arms. Then, with a weary sigh, he closed his eyes and was instantly asleep.

It wasn't as easy for Katherine to sleep. Memories of the burial flitted through her mind. Only a few months before she had been a lady of refinement, protected from the coarser aspects of life. And yet, she had been unhappy. Now she was out digging graves and burying the bodies of the men she had killed.

Even so, she would not want her old life back.

She had found more than contentment in the arms of this man her father had labeled a savage. In his arms, she had found love.

She sighed deeply, nestling her head in the curve of his good shoulder. Then her body slowly relaxed, and she succumbed to sleep.

*   *   *

The next few days were the happiest she had ever known. She loved and knew she was loved in return. Although she knew they would have to leave their haven of safety soon, she intended to savor every moment of happiness she found there.

Swift Arrow was fast recovering his strength, and although she was glad, she could see he was growing restive. She knew it wouldn't be long before he would speak of leaving.

If only they could hold this moment in time forever. If only they had some means of shutting out the rest of the world. But they couldn't. The world always had a way of intruding. Sooner or later her father's men would come here looking for them. She knew he would leave no stone unturned until he found her. Their only hope for escape was to get as far away from him as possible.

Sighing, she moved across the outer courtyard to the ledge. She stared down into the valley, wondering just how much time they had left.

"Why do you sigh?"

She turned. He had come up on her silently. His gaze probed hers, searching her face as though he would find the answer there.

"I was just wishing we could stay here forever," she said, placing a palm on each side of his face. Her smile was wistful.

"I have the same wish," he said. "But we cannot. Your father would find us, and he would try to take you from me. Then I would have to kill him. For I will never be parted from you."

"Nor I from you," she whispered.

"Come with me, my love," he said. "We will bathe together."

Taking her hand, he led her down the trail until they reached the waterfall. When she started to unfasten her dress, he lifted his hand and caught hers in it.

"Let me," he said.

She allowed her hands to fall limply to her sides. Then she stood silently as he began to unfasten her clothing. Lifting her arms, she allowed him to slip the garment over her head. She waited until he had shed his clothing and then they stepped together into the waterfall.

She gave a startled gasp as the cold water struck her body. "It's cold," she said.

He laughed and clasped her tightly against his warm skin. They stood together for a while, naked flesh against naked flesh. And then he began to rub her softly with his hands. He made small circular motions with his palms, then larger ones, until she began to feel a need rising in her loins. She pushed herself against him, feeling the heat emanating from him as his hard maleness pressed against her lower stomach. His mouth left a trail of golden fire as he followed the curve of her jaw, moving on down to the smooth column of her neck. She tilted her head back to allow him greater access, while she trembled with desire.

She found his warmth enervating. He was creating a hot, languorous passion deep within her, an ever changing array of sensations that swept over her like a slowly turning kaleidoscope. Her skin tingled beneath his caresses, and she felt completely intoxicated with the heady male scent of him.

She shaped her hips to fit his, pushing against him, trying to ease the throbbing ache within her. He made a soft sound in his throat. His lips closed over hers and he drew her tongue into his mouth.

His hands spread wide over her rounded bottom, holding her still. And then, to her utter astonishment, he entered her. Her gray eyes widened in shock, and she stared up at him. His dark, slumbrous gaze held hers as he plunged deep within her body. And then he began a slow, rocking motion, designed to drive her out of her mind.

She could hardly believe what was happening. He continued the rocking movements, bringing her senses to a vibrant pitch with mind-stopping deliberation. Spirals of sensation began to build deep within her body, flooding through her in never-ending waves.

He grinned down at her, his eyes glazed with intense satisfaction. His hands clutched her hips more firmly. Then, he lifted her against him and began to move harder . . . faster . . . penetrating her deeper than he ever had before.

She threw her head back, her breath coming in short pants. God! she couldn't take much more. Wrapping her arms around his neck, she moved with him until they were spinning together in a vortex of ever increasing pleasure that exploded into a million fragments of rapture.

He held her against him until her breathing became normal, and then his hands began to move slowly as he washed her body with the cold spray that was still flowing over them.

Katherine felt exhilarated as they left the waterfall. He picked up a blanket he had left on a nearby rock and dried her body.

After they had dressed, he took her into his arms for a long kiss before they went back up the trail to the cliff dwellings.

As soon as they rounded the bend, Katherine saw him.

She stopped abruptly, staring in amazement.

"Blackie?" she asked, her gray eyes widening with delight as she recognized the gray and black fur curled up on the courtyard wall.

Swift Arrow frowned and pushed her behind him. "Stay there," he commanded.

"What's wrong?" she whispered, her gaze sweeping the area for some hidden danger.

"When did you last see the raccoon?"

Fear flickered in her eyes. "At the fort," she said, keeping her voice low. "You don't think my father had anything to do with him being here, do you?"

"He couldn't find his way back alone," Swift Arrow said. "Someone brought him."

"Dang right they did," growled a voice from behind them.

They both jerked around in time to see Buck step from one of the rooms. "An' if'n I was one of them army gents, I coulda blowed both yore ears off."

"Buck!" Katherine squealed, throwing herself at

378

him. She wound her arms around his neck and kissed him soundly on the cheek.

To her surprise and delight, his face turned bright red.

He squeezed her shoulders gently and set her aside. After spitting out a wad of tobacco, he frowned at her. "Darn near caused me to swallow thet tobacco, youngun. You oughta give a body a warnin' when yore aimin' to throw yourself at 'im."

"How did you find us?" she asked.

"Jist used my head fer somethin' besides holdin' my hat up," he said. "Knew there warn't no other place fer you to go, 'ceptin' here."

"Did you reach the village in time to warn them?" she asked.

"Yep. They was long gone a-fore the major's men ever got there." His eyes grew wistful. "Hated to see 'em go, but I knew it was best." He grinned. "When I got back the whole fort was in an uproar." He chuckled. "Did my heart good to find thet major so undone. Hear tell he locked hisself in his office fer near a whole day whilst a messenger went to one of them ranches to round up some more hosses. Didn't come out'n there until them hosses was brought back. Then they all rode out hell bent fer leather."

Katherine shivered with fear. She had known her father would waste no time in coming after them. "Do you know where they went?"

"Headed north. I'm a-thinkin' he figgered you'd head fer Chief Tall Feathers's village. Sure is a good

379

thing I was there first, 'cause I figger he was mad enough he'd a-killed 'em all."

Katherine knew he could be right.

"Do you know where Chief Tall Feathers was going?" Swift Arrow asked.

"Reckon they was a-headed up Colorado way. I come lookin' fer you to tell you. Thought maybe you two would maybe like to mosey on along up there. After seein' the dead man you two left behind, not countin' the one what was all beat up, I thought you might just need some help." His lips lifted into a smile. "I reckon as how I mighta been wrong, though."

"No," Katherine said. "You were right. I did need some help. Swift Arrow is just now recovering from his wound. But what took you so long?"

"I had to be mighty careful. I ran into Running Horse on the way here and had to lead 'im off in the other direction."

"Running Horse!" Swift Arrow said. "If he is near, then the blue-coats are not far behind." He turned to Katherine. "I'm afraid we must leave this place," he said. "I knew we could not remain here forever."

Buck reached into his pouch and pulled out his plug of tobacco. Cutting off a chunk, he popped it into his mouth. "No need to hurry," he said.

"Why not?" Swift Arrow asked sharply.

"I didn't have no luck leadin' 'im off."

Katherine looked around fearfully, as though she was convinced the Apache scout was about to materialize.

"Where is he?" she asked.

380

Swift Arrow's gaze was intense, his body stiff as he waited for Buck to finish his explanation.

"No need to worry 'bout 'im fer a while," the old mountain man said.

"Why?"

"He got off his horse, a-lookin' fer tracks. An' I stole it."

Chapter Thirty-Five

"You stole his horse?" Swift Arrow's voice held a mixture of surprise and disbelief.

"Sure 'nuff did," the old-timer said.

Swift Arrow frowned, his face reflecting puzzlement. "It would not be easy to take Running Horse's mount from him. Unless he wished it so."

Buck threw him a quick look. "You reckon not? I thought it seemed a might too easy." He scratched his grizzled head. "Now you got me a-wonderin' why he'd let me steal his horse. If'n he let me."

"Do you really think he let Buck take it deliberately?" Katherine asked.

"It is possible," Swift Arrow replied.

"Why would he do that?"

"Maybe he figgers he owes the boy," Buck commented.

Katherine flicked a questioning glance at Swift Arrow. "Does he owe you?"

"Yes. But I did not think he would care."

"I think he does," she said softly. "He told me he didn't know you were with the Apaches when he led them to us before."

Swift Arrow's expression hardened. "That does not make him less of a traitor to his people."

"He don't think he's a traitor," Buck growled. "He's been on the reservation fer a long spell now. He's used to the white man's ways. Maybe even thinks they're right."

Swift Arrow remained silent.

At that moment the raccoon woke from his nap and arched his body upward. Katherine was vaguely aware of Swift Arrow crossing the courtyard to the ledge. But her attention was on Blackie, who had seen her. The raccoon leapt off the wall, landing lightly at her feet. Then he stood on his hind legs and held up his tiny handlike paws to her.

Leaning over, she picked him up and cuddled him against her. "I'm glad to see you," she whispered. "Did you miss me?"

"He sure did," Buck said, sitting down where the coon had been. "When I got back to the fort, thet housekeeper of yore'n said he hadn't et a thin' since you left."

"Oh, Blackie." She stroked the animal's soft gray fur. "You can't be that way. If you don't eat, you'll starve to death. And I can't take you with me when we leave here."

384

Her gaze flicked to Swift Arrow who was staring down across the valley.

Was something wrong?

"Shouldn't orta have made a pet out'n a wild animal thet-a-way," Buck growled. "But they ain't no need to worry 'bout 'im none when you leave here. He'll survive like he done afore you came."

"Are you certain? You said he wasn't eating after I left the fort."

"Thet's a mite different," the old-timer said. "He warn't among 'is own kind back at the fort. Yore all he had. But that ain't true here. When yore gone, he'll find hisself a mate." Buck's gaze slid to Swift Arrow, who had not moved from his position. "Everybody needs someone to call their own," he added. "Even wild animals."

"What about you?" she asked softly, remembering what she'd been told about his ill-fated love. "Do you need someone?"

"Reckon I do," he growled. Seeming to sense the direction her thoughts had taken, he added, "I know what yore thinkin', but I didn't spend all my years a-grievin' fer Rachel. I looked fer her nigh on to five years afore they told me she was dead, killed whilst tryin' to escape." His faded gaze became pained. "Lied to me is what they did. Onliest time I ever knowed the 'Paches to lie. It's against everythin' they do . . . but thet whole damn village lied to me and told me she was dead."

"Perhaps they thought it was kinder to make you think so," Katherine said softly.

"Rachel told 'em to tell me that."

"Why?"

"Said she knowed I'd never stop searchin' fer 'er long as I thought she was alive. She was right, too." His gaze turned inward. "Never knew a man could feel as much pain as I did when they told me she was gone. I wanted to kill ever last one of 'em, right then and there."

"What did you do?"

"Nothin'. I jist walked outta thet village and left 'em all there. Figgered nothin' I could do was a-gonna bring 'er back." He sighed heavily.

"Do you think she was there at the time?"

"No. Panther, thet's 'er man, had took 'er away. He was a-feared I'd find 'em, an' he'd promised 'er he wouldn't do me no harm."

"How long was it before you saw her again?"

"Nigh on to forty-five years."

"How terrible for you," she cried, hugging the raccoon closer against her.

"No," he disagreed. "It warn't neither."

"It wasn't?"

"No. I was jist glad she was still alive. She was only a youngster when she was took. She deserved more outta life than to live all those years with the Injuns. But I could see she was happy with thet man of her'n." He chuckled softly. "Done tole Panther if he ever dies, I'm a-takin' over. Reckon as how thet'll make 'im outlive me jist to make sure I cain't have 'er."

"So you never married."

"Didn't say thet. Fact is, I did. Married me a 'Pache woman, 'bout ten years ago." He grew still. "She was

386

quite a woman, too. Treated me right, she did."

"What happened?"

"She died," he said gruffly.

Katherine put a comforting hand on his arm. "I'm sorry," she whispered.

He nodded and rose to his feet. "Guess I'll go see what thet man o' yore'n is doin'."

Swift Arrow was aware that the low hum of voices behind him had ceased. And, although he knew the moment Buck joined him, he didn't turn around. His gaze never faltered as it searched the valley below before moving farther, scanning the forest and then the desert in the distance.

"Reckon the major might be lookin' this-a-way fer the two of you?"

"Yes. He will look here. And we must be prepared," Swift Arrow replied, his voice filled with certainty.

"You could be right. The major didn't strike me as a man who'd let what you did go without at least tryin' to get revenge."

Swift Arrow nodded. "This place will not be safe much longer," he said.

"I 'spect yore right." Buck was silent for a moment. "One other thin'."

Swift Arrow turned to look at him. "Thet young lieutenant's all right, but thet captain you had yore fight with is another thin'. If you two get caught, it'd best be somebody else what took you."

Swift Arrow felt a surge of hate for the man who had

387

thought to abuse Katherine. But nothing showed on his face. "Why?" he asked.

"'Cause last time I saw 'im, he was runnin' off at the mouth, lettin' it be known he's out for yore blood. If'n he was to ketch you, it's likely neither one of you would reach the fort alive."

"You think he would take Katherine's life?"

"Not until he finished with 'er," Buck said. "You know what he means to do."

Swift Arrow nodded. "It is as I thought."

"When I stole Running Horse's mount, I left a trail a mile wide fer the cavalry to follow," Buck said gruffly. "Figgered I'd buy you an' the girl a little time. But to my way of thinkin', you'd best be leavin' here mighty soon."

Swift Arrow nodded. "You are right," he said. "How long do we have?"

Buck thought for a moment. "You should have maybe two days a-fore they find out what I done. If Running Horse is tryin' to help, might be a little more. Then they gotta decide which way to look. If'n this'n comes to 'em first, then you ain't got more'n three days a-fore they'll come a-lookin'." His shrewd gray eyes held the warrior's. "You cain't be leavin' too soon, neither, son. Thet could mean you'd run slap-dab into 'em. Be safer to wait here a spell, an' see which way the wind is a-blowin'."

Swift Arrow nodded. "We will watch . . . and wait." He turned to the old man. "We will not speak of the danger to Katherine. The time will come soon enough."

Buck nodded his grizzled head in understanding.

"Where'd you leave yore hosses," he asked. "Couldn't find 'em no place."

"They roam free."

"What'd you turn 'em loose for? Supposin' you needed 'em fast?"

"The stallion will come when he is needed," Swift Arrow said. "And it is my way of thinking the other horse will stay with him."

"You put a lot of faith in thet horse," Buck commented. "He looks a tad familiar. Mind tellin' me where you got 'im?"

"No. He was a gift." Swift Arrow's eyes glinted. "From Robert Shaw."

"Robert Shaw?"

Both men turned to look at Katherine, who had come to stand behind them.

"What about Robert Shaw?" she asked the warrior.

"Robert gave 'im the stallion," Buck explained.

"He did?" She looked at Swift Arrow. "I forgot to tell you that Robert went to Washington to try to gain your release."

"It will do no good," he said. "Washington will not listen."

"That's what I feared," she said. "It's the reason I decided not to wait for them."

"You were wise," he said.

She wondered what Robert and Heather would say when they returned to find her gone. A feeling of sadness flooded through her as she realized she would probably never see her friends again.

"When did Robert give you the stallion?" she asked

Swift Arrow.

"The day they were married with the white man's ceremony."

"You were there?" she asked, her eyes widening in surprise. "I was at their wedding, too, but I didn't see you."

"Perhaps I left before you came."

"You should have stayed," she said.

Swift Arrow wondered what would have happened if he had stayed at the ranch. He would have met Katherine. But how would she have reacted to him?

He thought perhaps it was best that he had left when he did. If he had not joined Geronimo and his renegade band in their flight to the Sierra Madres, he would have gone back to his tribe in the mountains. Then, when Katherine needed him, he would not have been there.

The wind blew a lock of pale hair across her cheek, and he brushed it away with the tip of one finger. "It is good we met when we did," he said softly.

Buck cleared his throat, startling them both.

"It is time for us to think about food," Swift Arrow said. "I am hungry."

She laughed. "I suppose you want me to cook."

"I didn't hear him volunteerin' to do it," Buck said. "An' I ain't, neither. I get tired of my cookin'."

"I'm not surprised," she said. "I'll start a pot of soup."

"Soup." Buck snorted with disgust. "Didn't have soup in mind. I was a-thinkin' more of a chunk of rabbit meat. Or maybe a big hunk of venison."

"Sounds good," she laughed. "But we don't have

fresh meat. We've been using the dried meat and vegetables Swift Arrow's friend left here."

"Lone Wolf?"

"Yes," Swift Arrow said.

"They sure lasted a long time," Buck said. "Far as I know, it's been better'n six years since he brought Miss Rebecca here."

"Rebecca?" Katherine frowned. "Is that the girl's name?"

"Yeah," Buck said. "You pro'ly know 'er. Miss Rebecca is Robert Shaw's sister."

Katherine's eyes widened. "I met her at Heather's wedding." She looked at Swift Arrow. "You told me she was Lone Wolf's captive."

"She was."

Her expression became confused. "But . . . it was my understanding that Rebecca was very happy with her marriage."

"She is," Swift Arrow replied. "She is married to Lone Wolf."

Lone Wolf was Rebecca's husband. He was also the Apache warrior who had kept his bride at the cliff dwellings so she could not run away from him. But that was no longer her wish.

"Why didn't you tell me?"

"Did it matter?"

Did it matter?

Exasperation filled her. Of course, it mattered. It was part of the reason she had left him. She had thought him unfeeling toward his friend's white captive, believed the girl was still suffering after all

391

these years.

"Yes," she said peevishly. "It mattered. I thought he had held her captive for all those years. It made me worry about our future together."

Something flickered in his dark eyes. He tilted her chin and spoke softly. "Is that the reason you left?"

She swallowed. "Part of it." She lowered her eyes. "The other part was your hatred of my father. I thought you were only using me to punish him."

Buck cleared his throat. "Reckon I'll just mosey on down into thet valley and get us a chunk of fresh meat," he said gruffly. "I ain't a-hankerin' to eat no meat what's been a-layin' 'round fer so many years."

She laughed self-consciously. "There's nothing wrong with it, Buck."

He grinned. "I'll go huntin' just the same," he said.

Swift Arrow's eyes were amused as they met the old-timer's. "That would please me," he said.

He watched the old man leave, then cupped Katherine's face in his palms. "He is a wise man," he said. "He knew I wanted to be alone with you."

"Why?"

"For this."

Gathering her into his arms, he lowered his head until their lips met. Then, slowly, his mouth moved against hers, his lips lingering as they caressed and tasted hers, deliberately tantalizing her desire.

Katherine felt his lower body move against her, and she couldn't suppress the moan of arousal that escaped her throat. She didn't want the kiss to end and felt bereft when he lifted his head.

392

Her face was flushed with passion as she looked up at him. He was so dear to her. He had become the most important thing in her life. If only they could find a way to live in peace. Why did her father see the Apaches as different from himself? Why couldn't he be more like Robert Shaw?

Suddenly, an idea came to her. Suppose they went to Robert and asked him for work? Surely her father wouldn't be able to touch them at the Shaw Ranch.

"Swift Arrow," she said hesitantly. At his inquiring look, she went on. "Robert gave you the stallion because he felt indebted to you, didn't he?"

"Yes," he agreed.

"Perhaps he could help us."

"He cannot help," Swift Arrow said. "It is not in his power to call back the blue-coats. Your father commands the cavalry. They obey his orders."

"I know. But suppose there was another way. Perhaps if we went to him . . . well, maybe he could find you some work or—"

"No," he said. "I could not live as the white men do. I was born to roam the land, to be free to hunt and go where I please. Life would not be worth living if I had to live as the white man decrees."

Tears filled her eyes. She looked away from him. "But as long as we were together, we could be happy." Her voice was husky. "Couldn't we?"

He tilted her chin, forcing her to look at him again. "Do you wish me to tell an untruth?"

"No," she whispered.

"Then surely you know I could not live in such a

393

way. I must be free. Is it so much to ask for you to join me?"

"No," she said quickly. "It's not asking too much."

"Do you long for the life of the white men? Is it your wish to return?"

"No," Katherine said. "The time I've spent with you has been the happiest time of my life. I love the mountain air. And the freedom to move about as I please and do what I want without worrying about what everyone else thinks about it."

He laughed. "Did you ever care what anyone else thought?"

"I didn't," she admitted. "But my father does, and he had a tendency to express his displeasure in ways I wouldn't forget."

"Let us not speak of your father," he said. "We will have to think about him soon enough."

She agreed with him.

He looked toward the ledge. "How long do you think it will take Buck to find some fresh meat?"

"I don't know," she said. "Why?"

"I would not wish him to return very soon."

"If you have something in mind, perhaps we'd better get to it."

Without another word, he scooped her up into his arms and carried her into their sleeping room.

That night Katherine had a dream. She saw an Indian chief sitting on an Appaloosa, high on a mountaintop. Across his shoulders was a coat blazing with many different colors. He was beckoning to her.

When she woke she puzzled over the dream. She thought it meant something, but wasn't sure what it could be. The Indian was no one she knew, and yet. . . .

She worried over the dream all morning, searching her memory for the answer, but it remained elusive.

As she began preparations for the noon meal, Swift Arrow approached her. "You are very quiet," he said.

She started. She had thought she was alone.

"Is something wrong?"

"I had a dream last night," she told him.

He looked at her. "Tell me about it," he said.

She told him about the Indian chief sitting on the mountaintop, beckoning to her.

"Did you know this man?"

"No. I'm sure I've never seen him before. But for some reason, the dream was unsettling." Her brow wrinkled. "He was riding an Appaloosa," she said slowly. "And the strangest thing was, he was wearing a coat, blazing with colors."

"I do not know what it could mean," he said.

Neither did she, but she couldn't get it out of her mind. Katherine hardly ever dreamed, and she felt the dream had to mean something. Could it perhaps contain the answer they sought?

Chapter Thirty-Six

Swift Arrow and Buck sat beside the fire talking quietly while Katherine cleared away the remains of their meal. She was banking the fire when she heard Buck telling Swift Arrow he would be taking his leave of them.

Katherine looked around at him. "You're going?" she asked.

"I reckon so," he said. "I'll be thankin' you for the hospitality."

"But where will you go?"

"Don't know where I'm bound from here," he said. "But I figger I might wind up in Silver City."

"I thought you'd be traveling with us."

"Reckon I would if you needed me," he said. "But I cain't see thet you do. An' could be I might be able to lead thet cavalry away from here. Anyways, thought it

397

might be worth a try."

She could see his reasoning, but she knew if her father was with the men who searched for them, there was no way Buck, or anyone else, could convince him to leave one stone unturned to find his daughter and the man she had escaped with. To his way of thinking, he had been betrayed by her. And he wasn't going to forget it.

Buck turned to Swift Arrow. "If'n you spot thet bunch of troopers a-comin' this-a-way, get out as fast as you can. A good thin' to remember is they've already searched the area aroun' Chief Tall Feathers's village. So it'd make damn good sense to travel thet-a-way. Might be you could even ketch up to 'em, since you both got horses and the chief's got a whole bunch of 'em a-travelin' by foot."

Swift Arrow nodded and gravely thanked the old man.

Buck gathered up his belongings, shouldered his rifle, and turned to go.

Swift Arrow stopped him with a hand on the old man's shoulder. "May the Great Spirit lead you," he said.

"Same here," the old man said gruffly. "You take care of thet youngun there. Wouldn't want nothin' to happen to 'er."

Swift Arrow nodded.

A feeling of sadness washed over Katherine. Her eyes filled with tears. Putting her arms around the old man, she gave him a hug. "Thank you for all you've done," she said huskily. "I hope we'll meet again."

"Like as not we will," he said, patting her on the arm.

Katherine released the old man and stepped back. He had come to mean a lot to her in the time she had known him. She was going to miss him.

Without a backward glance, Buck strode across the courtyard and started down the ladder.

Tears blurred Katherine's vision as he disappeared over the ledge.

Swift Arrow put an arm around her shoulder, squeezing lightly.

"Do not feel sad," he consoled. "We will see him again."

Buck's departure had cast a feeling of gloom over the day for Katherine. Although she had known he would go, his leaving seemed to say their idyllic days had finally come to an end.

Her heart was heavy as she busied herself with the mending of Swift Arrow's buckskin shirt. She knew there would be no time once they began their traveling. As though sensing her mood, Swift Arrow sat sharpening his knife and cleaning the rifles they had taken from the dead men.

Blackie chittered loudly, rolling a rawhide ball that she had made him around the courtyard. He slapped it and the ball lifted a few feet into the air and landed on her foot. He looked at her expectantly.

She shook her head. "I don't have time to play right now," she chided. "I have too much to do." At times the raccoon was more like a mischievous child than a wild animal. She knew she was going to miss him when they left. She sighed.

"What is wrong, my love?" Swift Arrow asked, looking up from his work.

"I hate to leave Blackie," she said.

His look was probing. "I think that is not all," he commented. "But you must not worry about the raccoon. He can take care of himself."

"I know."

She sighed again, then got up to replenish the fire. When she passed him, Swift Arrow laid aside his knife and pulled her down into his lap.

"What are you doing?" she laughed.

"Stealing a kiss," he said, and proceeded to do so with one which took her breath away.

"You didn't have to steal it," she murmured when he lifted his head and studied her flushed face with a look of satisfaction. "All you had to do was ask and I would have given it gladly."

His arms tightened around her and his eyes darkened. "If you continue to look at me in such a way," he muttered, "I will take more than a kiss from you."

She lowered her eyes and peeped at him through a fringe of thick lashes. "I think I have a man who is all promises and no action," she teased.

The words had no more than left her lips when he shifted her in his arms and rose to his feet with her cradled against him. He started toward their sleeping room.

"No. Wait a minute," she laughed, struggling against his embrace. "I was only teasing. We've got too much to do. If we go back to bed, we'll stay there all day."

He groaned loudly and swung her lightly to her feet. "You are right," he said. "I must go hunting, and we have to make ready for the journey that lies ahead of us."

Katherine knew he was right, but she didn't want to be left alone. "Let me go hunting with you today," she coaxed.

He hesitated for a moment, then shook his head. "No," he said. "It is better that you remain here. We do not know how safe it is down in the valley. If you remain here, I will be able to empty my mind of all but the hunt."

She frowned at him. "You needn't worry about me," she muttered. "I can take care of myself. Haven't I already proved that?"

"Perhaps you can," he said. "But nevertheless, I would rather you stayed here. The blackberries are ripe. If you pick them we can carry some along with us."

Knowing he was right, she stopped arguing with him and watched quietly as he slung the quiver of arrows across his shoulders and picked up his bow. When he was ready to leave, he gathered her into his arms.

"Be careful," she whispered, lifting her face for his kiss.

"Do not worry," he said. "For there is no need. I will return safely."

But she did worry.

She worried while she finished mending his shirt.

She worried while she picked berries.

She worried while she carried water, and she was still

worried when she returned to the city of rocks.

She went straight to the ledge and looked down into the valley hoping to catch a glimpse of Swift Arrow. But he was nowhere in sight.

Instead . . . off in the distance, she saw a long black line that seemed to be moving in their direction. Her heart gave a leap of fear and she lifted her hand to shade her eyes from the sun, praying she had been mistaken.

There had been no mistake.

It was the cavalry.

The forest was still between them and the canyon where the cliff dwellings lay—but she had seen such a column too many times not to know what it was.

Would they find the box canyon?

Fearing she would be seen, she took refuge behind the spruce tree growing in front of the ancient city. From there she could watch, and her form would blend with the tree. She knew the cliff dwellings could not be recognized for what they were at such a distance, but nevertheless, she still felt exposed.

It seemed that she stood and watched for hours, her body stiff with tension. Questions tormented her. Was Swift Arrow safe from them? Had he been seen? She could only wait and see. She nearly fainted with relief when she realized the troopers were going to bypass the entrance to the canyon.

The cavalry was traveling in a northerly direction a few miles west of the canyon's entrance. Was Running Horse with them? Did he know of the existence of the cliff dwellings? Katherine felt sure he must. Even if he kept the secret, the searchers would eventually find it and make their way into the box canyon.

Katherine knew the time had come for them to leave.

She was sitting on the courtyard wall hugging Blackie to her breast when Swift Arrow returned.

She was so deep in thought, she was unaware of his return until he touched her gently on the shoulder.

"You saw them," he said.

"Yes." She looked up at him with sorrow and fear. "I feel certain my father was with them. And he won't give up until he finds us. I just know he won't."

Swift Arrow pulled her up into his arms and held her tightly against him. "Do not worry so," he said. "He will not take you from me. I will not allow it." He pressed his face against her silky hair. "When the sun rises tomorrow, we will go from this place. For even though the blue-coats have gone north, the white eyes' numbers are many. It will not be long before they find the box canyon. And then they will come to the city of my ancestors." His eyes darkened. "We no longer have a choice. We must go."

"Where?" she asked.

"Buck told us my people have gone to Colorado," he said. "We will go there. And we will find the new village of Chief Tall Feathers."

That night he held her close against him, and they made love for the last time in the place where they had found such happiness together.

The next morning they packed what they needed for the trip and left the cliff dwellings.

They traveled for days, going deeper and higher into

the mountains. Each night they found shelter and lay with their arms wrapped around each other.

Although Katherine worried constantly, she tried to keep Swift Arrow from knowing. He had enough on his mind without worrying about her.

After five days of travel they came across an abandoned campsite.

"Do you think it belonged to your people?" she asked.

"Yes," he said. "I believe it to be so. We will rest for the night. And we will decide what to do."

Knowing she was tired, both in mind and spirit, he prepared the meal and brought it to her. She shook her head, refusing the food.

"Eat," he commanded.

She looked up at him. "What are we going to do?" she asked.

"We will decide later," he said firmly. "Now we must eat and sleep."

She took the bowl and ate the food he had prepared. Then they lay down, and he gathered her close against him. Although she was weary, Katherine found it hard to fall asleep. She couldn't help but worry about their plight. She wondered if she should appeal to her aunt and uncle for help, then dismissed the idea. They couldn't give Swift Arrow back his land, and he couldn't live in the way of the white man. Finally, her weariness overcame her and she fell asleep.

While she slept, Katherine dreamed again. She dreamed of the Indian on the Appaloosa horse. As before, he was high on a mountaintop, beckoning to her . . . and, as before, he was wearing a coat blazing with many different colors.

When she woke, she told Swift Arrow of her dream.

"I know it means something," she said. "Why should I have the same dream twice?"

He agreed with her that the dream had to mean something. "But I do not know what it means," he said. "The Nez Perce rode Appaloosas. But, like Sitting Bull, they now live on a reservation. I think it would help if we knew who the Indian was who wore the coat of many colors.

The Nez Perce rode Appaloosas.

Something about what he'd said struck a chord in her memory. What was it about an Indian who wore a coat of . . .

Coat of many colors.

Not an Indian! It was from the Bible! Joseph wore a coat of many colors.

As though a door had been opened in her memory, it all came flooding back to her.

Several years before, in 1877, every newspaper in the country had followed the flight of Joseph, chief of the Nez Perce Indians. Throughout the whole summer, Americans from coast to coast had followed the newspaper coverage of the courage and endurance of five bands of Nez Perce Indians. Men, women, and children alike, about seven hundred in number, had fled their homeland in the Pacific Northwest and were trying to find refuge from the U.S. Army. Although the Nez Perces were constantly pursued and attacked by vastly superior forces, they repeatedly defeated, fought off, or managed to outwit them.

Katherine, along with countless others, had read of the desperate flight. As many others had, she had come to agree with her aunt and uncle that the refugees had a great deal of right on their side. They found themselves rooting for the Indians and their heroic leader. But freedom was not to be theirs. The Nez Perce were stopped only forty miles from the refuge they were seeking in the land called Canada.

"Swift Arrow," she said. "Have you ever heard of Chief Joseph of the Nez Perce tribe?"

"Yes," he said. "I have heard of him. Why?"

"When the government tried to put his people on a reservation, they took flight and sought to reach another land where they would be given refuge. The land is called Canada."

"Yes." His eyes were dark, brooding. "I have heard of this land. Sitting Bull fled there after the battle at the greasy grass. Could this be the answer we have sought? Is there really such a place?"

"Yes," she said. She gazed earnestly into his dark eyes. "There really is such a place. And I think it's our answer. I have heard in Canada there are many forests where no white man ever travels." Her eyes were shining with hope. "If we could reach there, my father could never touch us."

"How far is this place?"

Her voice was wry as she answered. "A long way, I'm afraid. Chief Joseph didn't make it. He was stopped only a day's journey from his destination."

"And you would be willing to travel there with me?"

"Yes," she said. "I would go anywhere you wanted. It doesn't matter where we are, as long as we're together."

"Then we will go there," he said. "For I fear that it is the only way left to us." His eyes held a world of sadness. "The white eyes have won, after all, Katherine. In my heart I have always known they would. There are too many of them for us to fight. The sun has set on the Apache way of life. We will never be free a long as we remain where the horse soldiers can reach us."

"Canada is a long way from here," she said. "I'm not sure we can make it."

"We will make it," he said, and she heard the steel running through his voice. "We have no other choice, Katherine."

She knew he was right. There was nothing else to do. Her father would never allow them to live in peace.

"Do you know the way to this place you speak of?" he asked.

"It lies North," she said. "But there are high mountains that must be crossed, and miles upon miles to travel."

He nodded, his dark eyes somber. "We will travel the land and we will cross the mountains," he said. "We cannot do otherwise. I will not live on a reservation, and I will not allow you to be taken from me."

His voice was confident and she took heart from that.

She lay in his arms taking comfort from his embrace. It would be a simple matter to reach Canada if they were able to travel in the white man's way. Not so easy to cross the mountains. At least a thousand miles separated them from the border, and yet, they would have to make the journey if they intended to have a life together.

"Do not worry," he whispered against her ear. "We will face whatever comes together. Have no fear. I will take care of you."

She sighed, snuggling against him. "I know," she said. "I am not afraid."

Chapter Thirty-Seven

The next few weeks were hard on Katherine. They traveled endlessly. She figured they must be in northwestern Colorado now.

Wary of being seen by outlaws or Major Carpenter's men, they traveled by night and slept during the day in whatever shelter they could find. Although they were living like hunted animals, Katherine found a measure of contentment in the fact that they were together. As long as she could remain by his side, she would find the strength and courage to endure whatever came.

During their weeks of travel they had had fair weather, but on this day, by the time they had stopped for the day in the shelter of a ravine, the air had turned sultry and the sky had darkened as heavy clouds rolled in. The slight breeze had turned into a brisk wind that whipped Katherine's pale hair around her face.

Although Swift Arrow knew they would more than likely be caught out in the storm, he decided they could not afford to delay their departure. He loaded the supplies on their horses, fastened one of the hides around her shoulders to keep her warm, then helped her to mount.

As they rode away from their camp, thunder rumbled in the distance. Streaks of lightning could be seen reaching for the ground, and they knew that rain could not be far behind. Katherine flinched as the sound of thunder came closer. It seemed almost to split the heavens. Another streak of lightning flashed. Then the clouds opened up and the storm broke in full force around them.

She shivered, clutching the deerhide closer about her shoulders as the elements raged around her. She could hardly see through the sheets of rain that pelted them, and she left it up to her mount to follow Swift Arrow's.

Moisture seeped beneath the hide covering, wetting her clothing and chilling her body. The rain kept pouring down, and Katherine tried not to dwell on her discomfort. She wondered, not for the first time, if their flight would be in vain. Canada was still such a long way from them. Could it really be possible that they might reach there?

Finally, after what seemed like hours, the rain slacked off. But the clouds were still heavy, the moon hidden from view. And it was so dark that she almost welcomed the bright flashes of lightning when they came. There would be a brief period of silence, then a loud crack of thunder followed once more by another flash of lightning.

Slumping with weariness, Katherine rode with her head bowed. As thunder crashed again, followed by another flash of lightning, she looked up. Her eyes widened in alarm, her pulse leapt wildly, for the clouds had turned silver and red, palely illuminating a horse and rider on the hill.

As if at a signal, her mount stopped. The horseman remained on the hill, staring down at them.

"Stay here," Swift Arrow said. Not waiting for a reply, he urged his mount up the hill.

Katherine's heart pounded loudly in her ears as she watched the two men face each other. Lightning flashed again, and in that moment of brightness she could see the rider was an Indian.

What could it mean?

Turning in the saddle, Swift Arrow motioned for her to follow them. If the situation hadn't been so tense she would have smiled, for she could do little else. Her horse had become spooked by the fury of the storm and refused to do anything except follow Swift Arrow's mount.

Together with the horseman, they rode toward the dubious shelter of a sparse cluster of tall trees. But looks could be deceiving, she discovered. As they neared the thicket, she could see the growth was thicker than she had suspected. The shadows beneath the trees seemed black as dungeons. She could barely make out the trunks of trees, the black of bushes.

As they rode the path turned downhill, winding its way beneath a canopy of branches. Then they entered a grove, and she was surprised to find the small forest hid a deep, wide gully.

Katherine held on tightly as their mounts stumbled and slid down the slick sides until they reached the bottom of the gully. It was then that she discovered that a wide rock ledge, hidden from view up above, was being used to shelter a band of Indians.

A handful of warriors sat around a blazing fire, while the other Indians had bedded down farther back into the cavern.

Swift Arrow dismounted and came to help her down. Then they moved to join the others around the fire.

"How are you my friend," said an old man in the language of the Apache.

"I am well, my chief," Swift Arrow replied.

My chief. Could the man be Chief Tall Feathers? Katherine suspected he must be. It was apparent that Swift Arrow knew him.

"We were lucky to find you," Swift Arrow said. "We have only traveled at night since we left the mountains."

"Yes. It is dangerous to travel during the day," the old man said. His dark eyes were piercing as they fell on Katherine. His face was without expression as he returned his gaze to Swift Arrow.

"She is my woman," Swift Arrow explained.

"Then she is welcome to share our fire," the old man said.

After the two had talked a while, Swift Arrow turned to Katherine. "It would be best if you get some sleep," he said. "We will have to travel hard after the storm lets up."

She nodded, seeing the sense of what he said. Wrapping the hide tighter around her, she moved back into the shadows and lay down on the ground. It wasn't long before she fell asleep.

Katherine heard the soft murmur of voices mingled with birdsong and the laughter of children. Her nostrils twitched as she smelled the rain-washed earth and the aroma of fresh-cooked meat. She opened her eyes on a new day. Turning her head, she saw a young boy about five or six years old sitting beside her. His dark eyes were inquisitive as they studied her.

"Hello," she said softly. "Who are you?"

"I am Little Crow," he said formally. "Son of Brave Eagle." Suddenly, as in the way of all children, he smiled impishly. "I have been waiting a very long time for you to wake up."

"You have?"

"Yes," he said.

"Was there some reason you were waiting?"

"Yes. No one knows who you are. Only that you are Swift Arrow's woman."

She laughed. "And you wish to be the first to know?"

"Yes," he agreed.

"Well, after all the waiting you've done, I think it's only right, don't you?"

He nodded his head.

"My name is Katherine."

"Where did you come from?"

She hesitated. She didn't know if Swift Arrow wanted them to know she was Major Carpenter's daughter or not. "You'll have to get that information from Swift Arrow," she said.

His eyes widened. "Do you not remember?"

"I . . . uh, no."

He studied her curiously. "Are you going to travel with us?"

"I don't know," she said. "That's another question you'll have to ask Swift Arrow. I'm traveling with him."

He nodded. "Then you're going with us," he said.

"How do you know? Did Swift Arrow tell you?"

"No. But I heard him speak with the old ones. He told them that—"

"Little Crow," chided a voice beside them. "You must not disturb our guest."

Katherine looked up to see a small woman with dark hair and eyes standing over them.

"I am sorry," the woman said. "It was our intention to let you sleep."

"He wasn't disturbing me," Katherine said.

"He loves to ask questions," the woman said. Her dark eyes were curious as she studied Katherine. "I am Little Turtle, the mother of this young rascal."

Katherine felt awkward as she raised up on her elbows and introduced herself, giving only her first name. She pushed a strand of pale hair away from her face, looping it behind her ear.

"I didn't mean to sleep so long," she said. "You should have called me to help with the meal." She looked around the camp. "Have you seen Swift Arrow?"

"He rode out earlier with my husband, Brave Eagle. They should return soon."

Katherine felt disappointed.

"There is a creek nearby, if you would like to bathe," Little Turtle said.

Katherine's face lit up. At the moment, she could think of nothing she would have rather done.

Little Crow took her down a path that led to a pool that was surrrounded by a lush growth of fern. The water was so clear that she could see the bottom, covered with velvety green moss. Fish swam lazily by as she watched, and she felt almost reluctant to disturb them. But her need for a bath quickly overcame her reluctance.

When the boy left her, Katherine stripped off her clothing and waded out into the cool water until she was hip deep. Then she sank down into the water, luxuriating in the feel of it against her skin.

Little Turtle had said they didn't need her help, so she had every intention of enjoying her bath. For the moment she could forget the problems that faced them, the uncertainties of tomorrow. There would be time enough to face them . . . as she must. At the moment she would listen to the jay scolding in the forest, to the wind sighing through the trees. She closed her eyes and let her mind drift away.

Chapter Thirty-Eight

Swift Arrow lay flat against the top of the rock watching two army scouts, who rode nearer, unaware of the danger that awaited them. The warrior's dark eyes flickered as he recognized the scout in the lead.

It was Running Horse, the man who had been responsible for his capture. Disgust raced through Swift Arrow's body. He should have expected the scout. Should have tracked him down as soon as he escaped the fort, for he knew of the man's uncanny tracking ability—he could hold a trail like a wolf on the scent.

Swift Arrow had let the fact that they had once been friends sway him. But that couldn't matter anymore. There was more than his own safety involved.

With the barest nod of his head, Swift Arrow signaled to Brave Eagle that the traitor was his. He saw that Brave Eagle understood, and from that moment on Swift Arrow had eyes for no one else.

He waited until the scout drew abreast of the rock. Then he drew his knife and leapt downward.

Something must have warned the man, for he looked up at that moment, he twisted, and Swift Arrow's blade missed a vital spot and sliced into his upper arm instead.

The force of Swift Arrow's body slamming into the other man's caused them to fall together on the ground with a bone-jarring jolt.

As he hit the ground, Swift Arrow rolled quickly to his feet. Running Horse's rifle had been sent spinning wildly into the brush, but he had already pulled his knife out of its sheath.

Swift Arrow's foot came out, hit the other man's wrist, and sent the knife spinning out of his reach. Then he doubled up his fist and sent it slamming into the other man's face with all the pent-up fury of years of hate for all the traitors who helped the white eyes.

Running Horse's arms flailed wildly as he fought for balance . . . and lost, landing on the ground with a grunt. The scout shook his head to clear it. His eyes narrowed on the knife lying near him at the same time Swift Arrow saw it.

Launching himself at the weapon, Running Horse's hand closed over it and came up with six wicked inches of broad-bladed hunting knife. His eyes glittered as he leapt to his feet.

"I do not wish to fight," he said.

Swift Arrow circled just out of the other man's reach.

"Then lay down the knife."

"I am not a fool," Running Horse snarled. "You would kill me."

"As you would me," Swift Arrow agreed.

He shifted slightly to the side, seeming intent on retreat. In reality, each noiseless shift of his body carried him nearer to Running Horse, like a big stalking cat.

Forced to a constant clumsy turning to face Swift Arrow's circling, Running Horse was becoming confused. Swift Arrow lunged at him, and he leaped aside, but not fast enough.

Swift Arrow came in low and fast. His knotted fist met Running Horse's belly beneath the right ribs. It was like connecting with a brick wall.

Running Horse gave a coughing grunt and fell back a step, then brought up his blade in front of him. Swift Arrow twisted fluidly, and the knife grazed past his shoulder.

Still at close quarters, he smashed his lifted forearm across Running Horse's neck muscles. Swift Arrow followed the blow with another to the scout's solar plexis. It stopped the man cold.

Running Horse's hands dropped to his belly, and the knife clattered to the ground. His legs crumpled beneath him, and he collapsed.

Swift Arrow stepped smoothly forward and picked up the knife. He pivoted on his heel and knelt over the scout. He knew one swing would end the traitor's life.

Running Horse stared up at him, "Kill me, if you must," he said. "But I have not betrayed you."

Swift Arrow stayed his hand. "Then why are you here?"

"I wish to join you," Running Horse said.

Swift Arrow lowered his knife hand. "Do you speak the truth?"

"I have never lied to you."

"What about the other scout?"

"He is not with me."

A movement near them brought their heads around. Brave Eagle stood close by. Swift Arrow's eyes flicked to the other scout, who lay dead several feet away. From the looks of the arrow protruding from the other man's chest, Brave Eagle had dispatched him with more efficiency than Swift Arrow had used. But that was lucky. Otherwise, Running Horse would be dead.

"Why have you let him live?" Brave Eagle asked.

"He wishes to join us."

"Do you trust him?"

"Yes," Swift Arrow said gravely. He looked at Running Horse. "But if you betray us, I will kill you."

"I have not forgotten how you saved me from drowning when we were children," Running Horse said. "I have lived the way of the white eyes since they sent us to the reservation. I knew we could not be free in this land. But now you go to another place. A place where we can be free. If you do not wish me to come, I will stay. Although the blue-coats are near, you need not fear I will betray you."

"You are welcome, my friend," Swift Arrow said. "But how did you know where we were headed?"

"The major said you were trying to reach Canada. I

420

think he does not know for sure. But he is not far behind."

"Perhaps you would have done better to stay with him," Swift Arrow said. "It might have been safer for you."

"I am not concerned with safety now," Running Horse said. "I have been long without friends. I will fight for them, if necessary."

Katherine was on her way back to camp when she heard the sound of approaching horses. She had expected the men to be gone longer. Wondering if something was wrong, she hurried up the path.

Her eyes widened when she saw Running Horse with the other two men. Where had he come from? Her heart gave a sudden lurch of fear. Was he leading a cavalry troop? Had their time already run out?

As she drew nearer, she heard voices raised in anger.

"He is a traitor."

"I am not a traitor," Running Horse denied. "It is true I have lived with the white eyes. Now I wish to leave—"

"Why should we believe anything he says?" asked one of the braves.

"I do not lie!" Running Horse growled.

Swift Arrow put a hand on the scout's shoulder. He faced the other Apaches. "Running Horse is my friend," he said. "I believe he speaks the truth. If you wish us to leave, then we will do so."

"Where are the blue-coats?" Chief Tall Feathers asked.

"They are not far behind," the scout answered.

"Is that not proof he still leads them?" an angry voice called.

"How could they have known where we were if he did not lead them?" asked another.

"Because they are following me," Katherine said, stepping forward.

The crowd fell silent. They focused their attention on Katherine.

She flicked a quick glance at Swift Arrow, found him looking at her. What was he thinking, she wondered. Should she have held her silence?

Chief Tall Feathers studied her for a moment, then spoke. "Why do the horse soldiers follow you?"

"I am Katherine Carpenter."

Silence met her pronouncement. She looked around the crowd and realized they didn't understand. They didn't know yet.

She swallowed hard. "My father—my father is commander of Fort Bayard."

Instantly, she felt their hostility. It vibrated out toward her in waves.

She searched the crowd, found Little Turtle's face, and took heart. There was no condemnation there. Instead, she found compassion.

Katherine turned her attention back to Chief Tall Feathers. "You have a right to know what to expect if we stay with you," she said. "My father knows I'm with Swift Arrow. He wants me back. We have been trying to reach Canada. We hoped we had left him behind in New Mexico." She swallowed again. "Perhaps if we leave you—go on ahead—he won't suspect you're here."

Swift Arrow came to stand beside her. "Perhaps she is right," he said. "If we leave you here, then you would stand a better chance of escaping the blue-coats."

Chief Tall Feathers was silent for a moment. Finally, he spoke. "If the blue-coats are following us, the woman's departure will not help us. But I think her father would not wish to see her harmed. Our only hope may be for her to remain. That is something the council will have to decide."

There were murmurs of agreement, then several of the men left the others and moved a little distance away from the others.

"Come," Swift Arrow told her. "We must speak together while we wait for their decision."

She nodded, following him to the privacy of the forest.

"It is a brave thing you did," he said when they stopped.

She shook her head. "No," she denied. "They had to know about my father. Why is Running Horse with you?"

"He was sent ahead of the blue-coats to scout," Swift Arrow said. He explained what had happened. "He does not wish to remain with them. He wants to come with us."

"Will your people allow it?"

"The council will decide."

"My father isn't far behind us, is he?" she asked, her voice reflecting her fear.

"No. But Running Horse and the scout we killed led them. With both of them gone, there is hope we may elude them. We have covered all our tracks."

"Perhaps we should stay where we are. There are not enough horses for the women and children. It won't take them long to catch us." She squeezed her eyes tightly shut. Her hands clenched into fists. "Why can't he leave us alone?" she cried. "Why is he so bent on ruining my life?"

"It is not only your life, Katherine," he reminded her. "Your father has many lives to answer for."

"I know," she whispered, feeling suddenly ashamed. "Of course, he does." She pressed her face against his chest. "I feel so helpless," she said. "There are old people and women and children here."

Raising her head, she looked up at him. "Perhaps it would be best if I leave you. I can go back alone. I'll tell him that you left me weeks ago. That I've been traveling alone. He might believe me."

"No," he said. "Whatever the council decides, you and I will remain together."

When they returned to camp, the council had reached their decision. They would go on. And Katherine and Running Horse would remain with them.

They saw the troopers coming from far off. And they knew there was no way they could outrun the cavalry. The women and children were on foot. Their only hope was to hide, to try to escape detection.

The Apache scouts found a shallow gully with brushy slopes. The women and children and old people hurried into the gully and began to cover themselves with weeds, brush and soil, whatever they

424

could find. The warriors were busy making the horses lie down.

Swift Arrow's eyes were drawn to Katherine's hair, gleaming silver beneath the bright sunlight.

"Cover your hair with this," he said, removing his shirt and flinging it toward her. "Then cover yourself with weeds and dirt."

Her heart was pounding with dread as she followed his instructions. Her nostrils twitched at the pungent smell of broomweed she pulled from the ground. She curbed the impulse to sneeze as she continued covering herself.

The waiting seemed endless to Katherine as she lay hidden beneath the broomweed. She wanted Swift Arrow beside her, but knew he must stay with her mount to keep the animal calm.

Above the pounding of her heart, she could hear the clip clop of hooves, coming ever closer to their hiding place.

God! she thought. What if the cavalry came into the gully? All of them would be crushed beneath the deadly hooves.

The waiting was agonizing.

The clip clop of the horses' hooves became louder, almost overpowering, drowning out even the sound of her heartbeat drumming in her ears.

When she thought she would surely break, would stand up screaming with the fear of being crushed beneath the horses' hooves, she suddenly realized the sound was diminishing.

The horses were passing them by.

Elation filled her being. They had done it. They had

425

fooled the cavalry! Just a little while longer and they could get up.

It might have been true if a young trooper with alert eyes had not spotted one of the horses.

An alert warrior sent a knife sailing through the air. It struck the trooper in the chest and he fell to the ground with a muffled thud. The fellow in front of him looked back at that moment.

"Injuns!" he shouted.

And then all hell broke loose.

Chapter Thirty-Nine

The cavalry spread out over the plains, their numbers nearing the hundred mark, almost double that of the Apaches.

Fear closed Katherine's throat as Swift Arrow rose amid the sound of war cries and gunshots. She was barely conscious of the smell of the earth as she lay there on the ground.

The soldiers fired on the Indians, unmindful and uncaring of who their victims were.

She pushed herself slowly to her knees, knowing the time for running was past. The time had come to confront her father—and whatever fate awaited her.

"Don't let them see you," Swift Arrow ordered, pushing her down again.

Why? she wondered. They know I'm here. They have to know. She looked up at Swift Arrow who was reloading his rifle. She couldn't stay here in the dirt while he was fighting off the enemy.

Her gaze fell on Chief Tall Feathers. He was deep in conversation with an elderly woman. She nodded her head, then began to move among the women and children.

As Katherine watched, they scattered, bending low to escape the bullets as they ran up the sandy gulley. The warriors fired more rapidly at the soldiers. When their rifles were empty, they sent a barrage of arrows winging toward the horse soldiers, covering the retreat of their families.

Katherine stayed where she was, knowing the high banks of the gulley offered some protection from the soldiers' bullets. And she had no intention leaving Swift Arrow alone.

She crept closer to Swift Arrow, intent on reloading his weapons for him, feeling she must help in some way. He noticed her movement and shoved her back.

"Stay down!" he ordered.

"I want to help!"

"Then dig a hole."

For a moment she thought he was being sarcastic, and she stared at him, her mouth open. Then she became aware that several of the warriors were digging. As soon as a hole was dug a warrior would fall into it and commence firing at the soldiers.

She realized suddenly that they were digging firing pits. She had heard of them, but had never had occasion to see them before.

She began clawing at the dirt with her fingers.

Soon, many firing pits had been dug in the soft sand. Although gravely outnumbered, the warriors continued fighting, intent on giving their families as big a head start as possible before they joined the movement up the gulley.

The battle seemed to go on forever. Katherine didn't know how many lives had been lost, couldn't even estimate the number.

She watched another warrior pitch forward from a bullet wound, then one of the soldiers.

Suddenly, she could stand it no longer.

She had to stop this endless slaughter.

Katherine swallowed around the lump in her throat. To give up would mean the end of her life with Swift Arrow. And she would rather die than lose him.

But she wasn't the one who was dying.

Determination flared in her gray eyes. She pulled the buckskin shirt away from her fair hair, pushed herself to her knees, then stood up, knowing she could be brought down by a bullet any moment if she wasn't immediately recognized.

The air stirred around her as a bullet whizzed by. Although Katherine trembled inwardly, she gave no outward sign as she faced the guns of the cavalry. The breeze blew warm against her face, lifting the pale hair that gleamed with silver lights beneath the noonday sun.

Suddenly she realized the firing had ceased. She lifted her chin at a defiant angle, waiting for whatever came.

A movement in the center of the column caught her

attention. Several men dismounted, but they were too far away for her to recognize them.

The men seemed to be having a debate. There was a flurry of movement and a horse and rider moved forward. The white flag he carried was clearly visible.

"Get behind me," Swift Arrow ordered, stepping in front of her.

Brave Eagle and Running Horse and several of the other warriors moved forward, forming a barrier in front of Katherine. All she could see were their backs. She knew she must be completely hidden from the horse and rider.

"Wait," she said. "They want to talk. Listen to what they say."

"I will talk with them," Brave Eagle said, stepping in front of the others.

The silence seemed to go on forever as Katherine waited, unable to see what was taking place. A moment later she heard a voice.

"Major Carpenter wants his daughter," the man called. "He said you're all breaking the law by keeping her against her will. If you send her out now, you won't be punished."

Katherine felt outrage flow through her body. Her father knew she wasn't being held against her will. He was only trying to intimidate the Apaches.

The knowledge brought her a small measure of relief. If he was willing to try to bargain with the Indians, then perhaps he was ready to listen to reason. She remembered the way he had looked when she was brought back to the fort. He had thought her dead and had been glad to see her. At that moment, she had felt he loved her.

Perhaps he had had time to regret his actions. If she went to him and tried to explain her feelings for Swift Arrow, perhaps he would even let them go.

"Swift Arrow," she said. "Let me talk to him. Perhaps I can make him see reason. Perhaps—"

His gaze darkened with anger. "You will accomplish nothing by going to him. If you leave he will have no reason not to kill us all."

She considered his words for a moment. "I think you're wrong," she said. "My father wants me back. But he wants me to stay willingly. Despite everything that's happened, I believe he loves me as much as he's capable of loving anyone. He just doesn't know how much I love you. If I can make him understand, then he may listen to reason."

She could see he remained unconvinced.

"The major is waiting for your answer," the trooper called.

She stepped from behind Swift Arrow so she could be seen. "I want his promise that he won't fire on the Apaches," she said.

The trooper wheeled his horse and rode back to the group of men. After a brief discussion, he came forward again.

"You have the major's word," the man told her. "He said all he wanted to do was talk to you."

She looked up at Swift Arrow. "I will have to go," she said. "There really is no choice. We're trapped here. There's no way we can outrun them."

"Go if you must," he said. "At least you will come to no harm from your father."

She laid a hand on his arm. "I won't go with him. And somehow, I'll convince him to let your people go."

His eyes were dark and turbulent as he studied her features. He seemed to feel it was the last time he would see her. He laid a hand against her cheek.

"Go to him," he said. "And remember that I love you."

She swallowed hard. "Don't say it like that," she whispered.

"Like what?"

"Like you'll never see me again. I won't allow him to part us." Tears blurred her vision as she turned away from him.

"Wait," he said, reaching for her. He pulled her into his arms and his lips closed over hers in a passionate kiss that took her breath away. His eyes were sad as he released her.

"Go," he said harshly.

Her feet felt leaden as she walked the distance that separated her from her father. For some reason she felt an urgency to retreat, to throw herself into the arms of her beloved. But she made herself go on. After all, the man was her father. Despite his many faults, he did love her. Of that she was sure.

As she passed the nearest troopers they closed ranks around her, blocking her from the Apaches. Finally she stood before her father.

"All right," she said, forcing herself to a calm she did not feel. "You wanted to talk. Let's get it over with."

His eyes swept her body as though inspecting her for damage. She had expected him to be livid with rage, but instead she encountered a coldness that was more intense than she had ever seen in him. It was as though his emotions had become frozen.

His eyes left her, flickered to a trooper standing nearby. "Take her," he said calmly. "And don't let her get away. I want the rest of you to open fire on those damned savages. Kill every last one of them!"

"No!" she screamed, struggling against the arms that tried to hold her. "You can't do that! You promised!"

She kicked out hard, landing against a shinbone, and her arms were released. She leapt around the soldier, who was trying to grab her again.

"Grab her, dammit!" shouted her father. "Don't let her get away!"

Several hands reached for her. But she had a slight advantage over them. She was the major's daughter, and even though he had said to grab her, they were still trying to be careful where they did it. She used it to her advantage and sprinted toward the Apaches who stood watching.

"What're you waiting for," her father shouted. "Open fire before she can reach them!"

As she continued to evade the troopers' clutches, she ran toward the small knot of Indians. Her eyes widened in fear. Swift Arrow had left the group. Thinking that she was in danger, he was running to help her.

She had to reach him!

She must!

Her arms were caught again, but she kicked out

wildly at her captors, connecting viciously with their flesh.

She could hear the sound of gunfire, but she paid it no mind as she ran toward her love. Everything seemed to be moving in slow motion as she moved toward him amid a hail of bullets.

Then she was there . . . looking up into his dear face. She threw herself into his arms, pressing her face against his chest as they fell together.

"Kathy!"

The anguished cry filled the air. She was vaguely aware that the cry came from her father, torn from his throat when he saw his only child fall beneath the hail of bullets that had been released on his order.

Suddenly there was silence.

Her eyes opened wide and she stared up at the face of her beloved. His body was lying protectively on top of hers.

Slowly he lifted his head and looked anxiously down at her.

"Are you hurt?" he asked.

She shook her head slowly. It was unbelievable. But it was true. She had come out unscathed.

"And you?"

He shook his head, then turned it to study the men who remained unmoving, staring in horror at their fallen bodies. Slowly, he rose to his feet, expecting any moment to feel a bullet strike his body.

Nothing happened.

Leaning down, he caught her hand and pulled her to her feet. Keeping a cautious eye on the major, he

434

whistled for his stallion. The warriors still stationed beside the gulley eased backwards. As Swift Arrow's stallion left the gully and came forward at a gallop, she could see the other horses were being mounted.

The stallion whinnied as it stopped beside Swift Arrow.

The warrior lifted Katherine onto the stallion's back, then leapt up behind her. His face was expressionless as he turned to look at the soldiers who had their rifles lifted and aimed, waiting for the order to fire.

The order was not given.

Touching his heel to the stallion, he urged him forward, away from the major and the troopers.

"Kathy!" The cry rang out, an anguished sound, seeming to be pulled from the very soul of the man who was her father.

She looked at Swift Arrow. "Let me speak to him," she said.

Without a word, he reined the stallion around, urging him forward at a walk until they stood in front of the major.

The proud man was no more.

Only an anguished father remained.

"Kathy," he begged. "Please don't leave me. You're all I have left in this world."

"Your daughter is no more, major," she said coldly. "She is dead. I am Swift Arrow's woman."

"No," he cried. "I didn't intend for this to happen. Come home with me. I'll let the Apaches go. I promise. I'll do anything you want. Just don't leave me alone."

She looked down at him. Somehow, she didn't fear

him anymore. She felt nothing but contempt for him now. She found she had nothing else to say to him, so she turned her head away. She had no pity for the man who had tried to take the life of her love.

Looking to the north, she saw the endless prairie stretching out before her. A prairie that would give way to mountains, then again to prairies, time and time again, until at last they came to a place where they could live together in freedom.

Swift Arrow sensed her restlessness. He urged the stallion into a gallop, and they rode back to join his people who were waiting for them.

A moment later they heard the bugle blow retreat, and the troopers began their journey back to the fort.

436

Chapter Forty

The sky was a cloudless blue, the sun warm against her skin as Katherine and the Apaches reached the top of the mountain. Swift Arrow, who had been leading the stallion, came to stand beside Katherine. Together, they looked upon the place that would be their new home.

"So this is Canada," she breathed, hardly able to believe what lay before her.

Rocky cliffs sheltered a valley that was lush with a verdant growth of trees and bushes. Sunlight sparkled on the small river that lay like a silver band in the middle of the valley.

"Yes," Swift Arrow said, taking her hand and gripping it tightly. "This is Canada. Our new home. And it is exactly as I saw in my dream."

Katherine looked up at him. "Mine too," she

437

murmured. "It's worth every mile we traveled. And then some. In this land we can surely live in peace."

Swift Arrow nodded gravely.

When Chief Tall Feathers gave the word, the warriors moved forward, and Katherine and the other women followed as they began the descent down into the valley.

Several hours later they reached the bottom. After a short consultation, the council decided they would build their village beside the river.

The work began.

The women talked happily among themselves as they erected huts, while the men hunted for game. There was an air of festivity when the men returned with an elk big enough to feed everyone.

The children scampered through the village, laughing and playing games as the feast to celebrate their new home was prepared.

By the time darkness had fallen, all was ready.

Katherine sat beside Swift Arrow as the beat of drums filled the air. Several unattached women began to dance.

One young woman peeked from beneath her lush dark lashes at Swift Arrow. Katherine had had occasion to notice her before. The girl had made her admiration for Swift Arrow obvious on more than one occasion.

The girl moved closer to him, her hips swaying to the rhythm of the drums. Her teeth gleamed whitely as she smiled widely at the warrior.

Katherine's glance slid to Swift Arrow. She frowned

as she noticed his dark eyes gleaming with frank admiration for the girl.

The girl lifted her arms and tossed her dark hair back in a sensual movement. Then she held her hand out to Swift Arrow.

He laughed aloud at the girl's blatant flirtation.

"Who is she?" Katherine asked. Although her voice was calm, indignation raged through her. He seemed to be inviting the girl's attention by his admiration of her.

He spared a quick look at her before returning his attention to the girl. "Her name is Little Flower," he said. "Is the name not appropriate?"

"Certainly," she said waspishly. "I know a lot of flowers just like her. The Venus fly trap, for instance."

Swift Arrow didn't answer. He seemed completely taken over by the girl's undulating hips.

Katherine's emotions warred between anger and hurt. She was angry at the attention the girl was bestowing on Swift Arrow and hurt because he was obviously enjoying it so much.

She told herself she had no right to object. After all, Swift Arrow had made no promises to her. He had no wife and he was free to do as he pleased.

But what about me? her heart cried. *I left my people to follow him to a strange land. If he doesn't want me, then what will become of me?*

Tears welled into her eyes. Unwilling for others to see, especially the girl who danced in front of them, she scrambled to her feet. Even as she did, she expected Swift Arrow to inquire her reason for leaving, but he didn't even seem to notice.

439

The tears overflowed as Katherine slipped out of the village and made her way through the silent forest. She brushed a hand across her face, willing the tears to stop as she tried to come to terms with her emotions. In her anguish she didn't notice how far her feet were carrying her from the village.

Swift Arrow's searching gaze swept the village. He hadn't noticed Katherine had left until the dancing had stopped. Where could she be?

He wound his way through the village asking questions of the others. No one had noticed her missing. When he realized that she was nowhere to be found, he began to grow anxious. It wasn't like Katherine to disappear in such a way.

Perhaps she had gone down to the river. Yes, he decided. That's what she had done. She must have gone to the river.

It didn't take him long to reach the river. He stood on the riverbank, staring up and down the stream. He felt no surprise to find she was nowhere in sight. He had only been grasping at straws.

Fear surged through him.

Some danger had befallen her.

He hurried to the forest. He would look a little farther. If he didn't find her, then he would return to the village and call the warriors together. They must find her. They must.

He was almost on her by the time he saw her.

She was huddled beneath a pine tree. Her legs were

bent, her elbows resting on her knees. Her face was covered by her palms.

His heart beat loudly with fear as he knelt beside her and pulled her hands away.

She looked up at him with a tear-streaked face.

"What is wrong?" he asked harshly. "Where are you hurt?"

She looked away, scrubbing at her tears with the back of her hand. "Go away," she muttered. "Leave me alone."

"Leave you alone?" He stared at her. "Why? What has happened?"

"Nothing!" she snapped. Then her face crumpled and she broke into sobs.

She tried to push him away when he ran his hands over her limbs, searching for broken bones.

"S-stop it," she sobbed. "G-get away from me."

He looked at her in consternation. Where was she hurt? Was it her back? "Can you stand?" he asked, trying to tilt her forward slightly so he could run his hands down her back. Her resistance at his efforts was enough to convince him there was nothing wrong with her back. He sat back on his heels and stared at her. "What is wrong, Katherine? I cannot find your injury."

Indignation flared in her eyes, drying her tears. "No, you can't!" she snapped. "You can't see a heartache!"

"Heartache?"

"Yes, dammit! A heartache! I've had to sit all night and watch Little Flower make eyes at you."

His mouth dropped open. Comprehension dawned in his eyes. It was quickly replaced by concern.

"And you enjoyed it!" she snapped. "And don't you try to say otherwise. I know damn well you did!"

"Of course, I enjoyed her dancing," he said calmly. "So did everyone else. She does it very well, don't you think?"

She looked away, refusing to answer. What could she say? She would be lying if she said the girl was a lousy dancer.

Reaching down, he pulled her against him. "Is Little Flower the reason you have been crying?" he asked.

She struggled for a moment before she became still.

"Is she?"

She refused to answer.

"Listen to me, love," he said. "Little Flower is the daughter of my mother's sister. She lost her mother and father at an early age and was raised by Chief Tall Feathers and his wife." He tilted her chin up, forcing her to meet his gaze. "But she is my cousin. And you are my love."

"I am?" she whispered. "You told me you didn't love me."

"I was a very foolish man," he admitted. "I did not want to give my heart away."

"And now you do?"

"No. But you did not ask for it. You stole it from me."

"I'm sorry," she murmured, her arms going up around his neck. "That was very bad of me."

"Yes," he said against her lips. "Very bad. And as punishment I will take you for my wife."

His wife! Had he really said that?

She stared up at him, her mouth open. He took advantage of it and lowered his mouth over hers. When his lips found hers, it was as though it was for the very first time.

The kiss, soft and tantalizing at first, was a promise of the sweet ecstasy to come. Her fingers laced through his dark hair and she pulled him harder against her, feeling her nipple grow taut as her breasts pressed tighter against his chest.

His kiss seemed to go on to eternity, his tongue probing intimately in her mouth. He shifted her slightly so his hand could slide between them. His palm covered her breast, then the tip of one finger rubbed at the hardened peak, increasing her feelings of desire for him.

She whimpered in protest when he released her. But he was only removing his clothing. Then he slipped hers from her and pulled her with him to the grass. He kissed her passionately until she thought she could stand no more. And then he kissed her eyelids, her nose, her ear, her throat, before returning his assault to her lips again.

When his hand found her breast, she arched against him, wanting his tormenting fingers on it. His callused fingers teased the nipple and then his head bent to her body, his lips closing over the hardened peak.

She clutched his dark head to her, inciting him, begging him to continue. She moaned low in her throat as he worked his way from one breast to another. She felt almost dazed, shuddering with the sensation he was causing.

Then he moved, kissing his way down her breast, leaving a wet trail down her midriff, her waist, stopping momentarily at her navel. She gasped as he dipped his tongue in and out for a moment, then began his downward path again. He nipped her on the inside of her thigh, and while she was recovering from the jolt it had given her, his mouth closed over the center of her desire.

Shock coursed through Katherine. Her eyes opened wide. What was he doing? She opened her mouth to protest, but the words didn't come. Suddenly it took all her effort just to breath.

As though aware of her feelings, Swift Arrow looked up at her. Her face was flushed with passion, her gray eyes dark and slumbrous.

Gripping her hips tightly, he lowered his mouth again. Sensation after sensation rippled through her as his tongue worked its magic. She began to thrash and moan beneath him like a wounded animal. Tears rained down her face with the intensity of her emotions.

She erupted in a wave of ecstasy, and a high keening note escaped her lips. A note that went on . . . and on . . . and on . . . until she finally fell limp beneath him.

She was vaguely aware of Swift Arrow leaving her, and then he was above her, and in her, plunging deep within her body.

At first, he moved alone, for Katherine felt completely drained, but soon his movements began to light a fire deep within her body. It burned brighter and brighter, until she could stand it no more. She began to move with him, picking up his rhythm. Their bodies were slick with perspiration as they moved faster, plunging wildly together as they climbed higher and higher until they reached the precipice and plunged over together . . . into eternity.

Swift Arrow lay limp where he had collapsed against her. And Katherine was so relaxed that she couldn't move. Opening her eyes, she stared up at him. And smiled.

"Did you mean it when you said you loved me?" she asked.

"Yes."

"And you really want me to be your wife? Your *only* wife?"

"I would have no one else as the mother of my children."

She arched her brow. "Oh? Will you be having many children?"

"Yes," he said. "We will have a village full."

"In that case, perhaps we had better make a start."

"Perhaps we should," he said just before his lips closed over hers.

Now you can get more of HEARTFIRE right at home and $ave.

Preview
Four Brand New
ZEBRA

Heartfire

Romance Novels...

FREE for 10 days.

No Obligation and No Strings Attached!

♥

Enjoy all of the passion and fiery romance as you soar back through history, right in the comfort of your own home.

Now that you have read a Zebra HEARTFIRE Romance novel, we're sure you'll agree that HEARTFIRE sets new standards of excellence for historical romantic fiction. Each Zebra HEARTFIRE novel is the ultimate blend of intimate romance and grand adventure and each takes place in the kinds of historical settings you want most...the American Revolution, the Old West, Civil War and more.

<u>FREE</u> Preview Each Month and $ave

Zebra has made arrangements for you to preview 4 brand new HEARTFIRE novels each month...FREE for 10 days. You'll get them as soon as they are published. If you are not delighted with any of them, just return them with no questions asked. But if you decide these are everything we said they are, you'll pay just $3.25 each— a total of $13.00 (a $15.00 value). **That's a $2.00 saving each month off the regular price.** Plus there is NO shipping or handling charge. These are delivered right to your door absolutely free! There is no obligation and there is no minimum number of books to buy.

TO GET YOUR FIRST MONTH'S PREVIEW... Mail the Coupon Below!